HE WHO FIGHTS

MIKE MORRIS

HE WHO FIGHTS

A Nathaniel Rane Novel

by Mike Morris

He who fights with monsters should look to it that
he himself does not become a monster.
Friedrich Nietzsche

PROLOGUE

"Don't take my son!" the woman pleaded, holding on to her boy with all her might. "He's too young."

"He's old enough," snapped the soldier as he tried to pull the lad free. The soldier wore a blood-stained tunic and the battered chest plate of the city guard; the child looked no more than twelve. "Be grateful we're not taking you, too."

The woman lunged, sacrificing her grip on her son to dig her nails into the soldier's face. She was fast, gouging a bloody streak across the soldier's cheek before his fist caught her in the jaw, knocking teeth and most of the fight out of her. He wiped the blood off his face with the back of his hand and spat on the woman.

She had some spark left, and anchored herself around her son's feet. It made no difference — she was dragged screaming down the street along with the boy. Another soldier planted a solid kick to her ribs. The crack of bone was enough to silence her cries. A second boot, harder than the first, sent her rolling into the gutter.

"Please," she sobbed. "He's all I have left. The Rastaks have taken everything else. We came here for protection, not to fight."

The soldiers ignored her and marched the boy down the street, holding on to an arm each. The boy, petrified and crying, had the body of someone more used to starving than to warfare.

"Someone stop them!" cried his mother as she stumbled after them, but the other refugees averted their eyes. No one wanted a visit from the soldiers next.

Nathaniel Rane watched from the end of the street, aware that he should feel something for the woman's plight, but didn't. The soldiers nodded at him as they passed, hard men equally numb to the task given them.

The woman reached Rane and, on seeing his shaved head and black uniform under his leather longcoat, threw herself at his feet. "You're a Legionnaire. Do something! Please!"

"There's nothing I can do," said Rane. Up close, she looked more like the boy's grandmother than his mother, but war did that to a person. Aged you so fast that if death didn't come calling in the shape of a sword or an axe, it would just steal away the years until a cold night was enough to finish you off.

"But your oath. You swore an oath," said the woman, groveling at his feet. "You're supposed to protect people like us."

Rane sighed. "Guards," he called.

The two men stopped and looked back, weary at yet another hold-up in their duties. "Yes, sir?" asked one.

"Let the boy go. He's too young and too weak to be of any use to us," replied Rane.

"But our orders..."

"If you want to complain, tell your commanding officer that Captain Nathaniel Rane of the Legion of Swords ordered you to let him go."

"Yes, sir." They released the boy and he ran back to his mother's arms. Shaking their heads, the guards headed off down the next street to look for more recruits to press-gang. They probably thought Rane a fool, but chances were they'd all be dead in the next twenty-four hours anyway. Whether the boy stood on the wall or not wasn't going to change that. At least now he and his mother could be together for a few hours more.

Rane continued on his way to the West Tower of the city walls. The woman had been right about his oath. Everyone in the Legion of Swords had sworn to protect and serve those weaker than themselves. If they didn't honor that, they were nothing.

The Legion was made up of soldiers from the allied southern nations — Ascalonia, Fascaly, Nortlund, Naijin and the Souska Islands. Every man and woman was a master with the sword, dedicated to a frugal life, loyal to each other and bound to that oath. Rane was proud to be one of their number. He'd grown up a street urchin only a few miles from where he now stood, but the Legion had given his life meaning and he considered his fellow soldiers his family. Yes, Rane had sworn an oath to protect people like the woman in the street, and his failure to do more for them wore heavily on his soul. But that was the time they found themselves in. It was the end of days for all.

Two streets down, he passed a funeral detail placing bodies on a pyre already stacked high: refugees succumbed to injuries, disease or hunger; soldiers from every nation killed on the walls that day. Yet more deaths to lay at the feet of the Rastaks and their king, Mogai.

Two soldiers stood nearby with burning torches in their hands, ready to set the pyre alight. It probably wasn't the first they'd lit that night and it certainly wouldn't be the last. A priest said prayers, but his words were directed to Odason, the God of Life, instead of to Heras, Goddess of Death. Something else the war had changed.

The people of the five nations had worshipped both equally, for that was the duality of existence, but Mogai and the Rastaks had changed all that. Mogai claimed Heras was the one true Goddess, and waged war in Her name and honor. His troops slaughtered innocents as sacrifices to Her. His strength came from Her gifts. His army was bolstered by Her demons, gathered from the underworld to massacre all in their way.

No one understood why, after all this time, Heras had started playing a greater role in mankind's lives — after all, no one was spared Death's touch in the end. But Mogai had found a Goddess grateful for his sacrifices.

Abandoned by Heras, the people of the five nations had called on Odason for His help and protection, but He seemed less willing to meddle in human affairs.

A group of refugees stood near the fire, weeping and wailing. Rane wished there was a way to offer them some sort of comfort, but there was none to be had. At least they were still alive. For now. Without thinking, he ran his eye over them, noting any who might be fit enough to fight. He didn't stop, though — the soldiers would call and make their selection soon enough.

He crossed the courtyard and headed into the West Tower, nodding greetings to anyone he passed and trying to look as positive as he could. Too many faces had an air of resignation about them, worn down by death's constant presence. If he could bolster their morale even just a little, it was worth faking a smile or two.

Inside, he took the stairs to the parapets. Rane climbed slowly, trying to use as little energy as possible. The last few days' heavy fighting had allowed for no more than the odd hour of sleep, snatched here and there as they repelled wave after wave of attackers. He'd lost count of the times that day alone they had faced the Rastaks and their pet demons, brandishing sword and club, tooth and claw, with the sole intent of wiping everything in the city from existence. Now all Rane wanted to do was find a dark corner, curl up in a ball and close his tired eyes for just a few minutes.

But he knew that wasn't going to be possible. There was still too much to do. Sentries to check, ammunition to resupply, soldiers to reposition — a long night lay ahead, and still the morning would come too quickly.

He paused in the stairwell a few steps away from the top and blinked some life back into his eyes. He couldn't let the troops see how exhausted he was. He had to give them hope and strength, even if he had none.

As he stepped out onto the parapet, he was grateful for the bitter wind that slapped him across the face, waking him some more. It wouldn't be long before the weather turned against them as well. If they lived that long.

As he always did when he reached the top of the wall, Rane first looked to his right.

The capital lay spread out before him. For centuries, Candra had been the heart of government, of trade, of learning. A city to boast of; a place to be envied. It was where he'd been born, and no doubt where he'd die.

Sitting on the southern bank of the River Tryste, the Royal Castle loomed above all. Spread over twelve acres, its walls sheltered Queen Ryanna and what was left of her government. Three ships were harbored nearby; the queen and her council could flee at any time, down the Tryste and out to the Pacini Sea to sanctuary in the Souskan Islands. Rane wouldn't have that luxury.

To the west of the castle was Temple Square, where temples to Odason and Heras sat facing each other. The square itself had become a shanty town of refugees, camped out under whatever could protect them from the elements. They filled the air with prayers begging protection. One day soon, they'd find out if their words carried any worth.

It had been five years since Mogai united all the tribes of the Rastaks under what he called the 'one true faith' and launched his invasion south over the mountains. They'd swarmed through the five nations, putting all non-believers to the sword; bloody years during which Rane had seen far too many lives lost, the brightest and the best of mankind snuffed out long before their time. And still more would follow. Perhaps by the morrow, Candra — the capital of Ascalonia and the allies' last bastion — would fall beneath the Rastaks' blades.

Rane gazed out over the rooftops of the city sheltering the last of the free world, and wondered what would happen to them all when the walls fell. Would they all be sacrificed to Heras' glory? Or would the Rastaks keep some alive to use as slaves? Rane's oath wore heavily on him. They were the ones he'd sworn to protect, but his sword wasn't enough to save them. The Legion of Swords wasn't enough. All he could do was die trying.

When he couldn't put off the moment any longer, he looked to his left.

The enemy spread out as far as the eye could see, camped just out of cannon range. Warming themselves around fires of their own were the death-loving Rastak soldiers and all their pet demons: the ten-foot Jotnar, the vicious dog-like Bracke, the mountainous Grenduns and the winged Valkryn.

Rane had long since given up guessing at the enemy's number. What did it matter if there were forty or fifty thousand of them? The only thing in their way was the thirty-foot wall on which Rane stood, and nine thousand men and women — all that was left of the army — from the allied nations. Nortlunders, with their blond hair, crazy beards and elaborate tattoos, battled alongside dark-skinned Souskans, while Naijins stood side by side with Ascalonians. Only Balrus in the west had refused the call, claiming neutrality, though no one believed them. Everyone knew the horse-eaters were negotiating with Mogai, intent on saving themselves at the rest of the world's expense.

Different languages carried on the wind as men and women huddled around fires, pretending death wasn't waiting for them with the dawn. A few of the more seasoned fighters slept, taking advantage of the respite in a way that seemed impossible to the newer recruits. Dotted along the line were the soldiers from the Legion of Swords — the only professionals amongst the lot of them. Like Rane, their shaved heads, leather greatcoats, and curved, single-edged swords made them easy to spot as they lent their experience to those around them, adding steel to frayed nerves.

Rane's first call was with one of the gun crews. Thomaz, a young Nortlunder still struggling to grow a wisp of a beard on a face far older than his years, stood by the front of the cannon while the other four men and women of his crew sat around a small brazier, keeping themselves warm. Their skin was stained with soot and gunpowder and streaked by sweat and blood. They struggled to rise as he approached, but he waved them down. The days of demanding a soldier stand when an officer was present were long gone.

"How are you, Thomaz?" he asked. The boy seemed shocked that Rane knew his name, but Rane always made a point of remembering who was under his command. It made a huge difference to fighting men. Not everyone in the Legion felt the same, though. Many thought of the new recruits as nothing but fodder for the Rastaks; why bother putting names to the dead?

"Been better, sir," said Thomaz.

Rane smiled. "Haven't we all."

Thomaz nodded in the direction of the enemy. There was no hiding the boy's fear. "There's a lot of them out there to keep us busy."

Rane followed his eye. "True."

"Can I ask you a question, sir?"

"Certainly."

"Are we going to die in the morning?" The boy's voice almost broke with the words.

"How old are you, Thomaz?"

"Nineteen."

"Do you have a Legionnaire assigned to you?"

Thomaz nodded. "Her name's Myri Anns."

Rane looked past Thomaz and saw Myri talking with another group, demonstrating a basic sword movement. A tall, lean Souskan as ruthless as they came, she caught his eye and nodded back.

"She'll certainly look after you," Rane told the boy. "Tomorrow, when the Rastaks come, listen to her. Do what she says. And don't be too scared. We've got good soldiers here with flintlocks, cannon and good old-fashioned steel on top of high walls. Stand strong and you'll survive."

"If you say so, sir," replied Thomaz, sounding far from convinced. He looked over the massed hordes again. "Why do the Rastaks hate us so much? They're human too, aren't they?"

"Aye, they're human." Rane scratched his head. "They just believe in different things to us. The Rastaks only worship Heras, and they think the more lives they sacrifice to Her in this world, the greater their reward will be in the afterlife."

"Is that true?"

"Our priests say no. Theirs say yes. Who knows who's right or wrong? All I know is that this is my home they threaten, and I'm sworn to do everything in my power to stop them."

"But no one has ever won in battle against them. Not with those demons on their side, too."

"We will." Rane squeezed the boy's shoulder. "Tomorrow will be different. You'll see. Now get some rest — you'll be busy enough in the morning."

"Thank you, sir."

He left the crew and walked over to Myri, who'd finished her lesson. Her troops were lucky — if there was anyone better with a sword, Rane hadn't met them yet.

"Nathaniel." Myri's voice carried the lilt of the Southern nations, and immediately made Rane think of warmer climes and happier times. Many a Legionnaire had fallen for her dark-skinned beauty, and others wanted her because she was one of the deadliest fighters alive. She'd laughed most of their attentions away. Myri was too busy keeping everyone alive. Rane had had a fling with her when they had both been raw recruits, but that seemed a lifetime ago. He'd be surprised if she even remembered it happening. He was surprised that he remembered it so well.

"Myri."

She nodded back towards Thomaz. "Still trying to inspire the troops?"

"Someone's got to give them some encouragement."

"Any news from the rest of the world?" At least Myri had the decency not to tell him how foolhardy he was.

Rane leaned over the wall, gazing down at the drop to the ground below and the spikes embedded there. "Just that it's all fucked up. You should have stayed in Souska. At least the sea should stop the Rastak advance."

"Do you really think that?" laughed Myri. "Some death worshipper will give them ships soon enough. Maybe not this year, but not long after. A bit of water won't be a deterrent for Mogai."

"We're not beaten yet."

Myri laughed again. "Always the optimist."

Rane wished he were; wished he could believe there was some miracle coming to save them. But hope, as with everything else, was in short supply. "I'd best be getting on," he said eventually.

Myri held his arm before he could move off. "If you've got any sway downstairs, it might be a good idea to get some food up here for everyone if we're to stand a chance. Dried biscuits aren't exactly filling."

Rane nodded. "Must admit I could do with something myself."

Myri gave him a look that said how likely she thought that was going to be.

Rane didn't blame her for thinking that way. "I'll talk to the Lord General, see if I can get anything extra sent out to everyone. It's going to be a long day tomorrow."

Myri stiffened, looked over his shoulder. "No time like the present."

Rane turned. The Lord General of the Legion, Sir Henry Jefferson, was on the wall and walking towards them. His uniform was perfect as ever, his white beard neatly trimmed. Seeing him galvanized all the troops into action. They jumped to their feet and saluted as Jefferson walked past, the slouch of defeat disappearing as military pride came back. No one wanted to look bad in front of the Lord General — they all owed him too much.

Jefferson stopped and talked to the odd one here and there, leaving them with smiles — genuine smiles — on their faces as he moved on. The old man always had that effect on people.

Myri and Rane snapped to attention when he reached them. "At ease, soldiers," said Jefferson. "How goes the watch?"

"Quiet, sir," said Myri. "The Rastaks seem happy to wait till morning."

"No sign of any riders?" asked the old man.

Myri shook her head. "None. Are we expecting any?"

The Lord General leaned against the parapet as he scrutinized the Rastaks' camp. He wasn't a young man, but the last few days seemed to have aged him by decades. There was still some fire in his eyes, but it pained Rane to see how frail he'd become. But then, the war had affected them all.

Jefferson rubbed the white fuzz of hair on his head and sighed. "They've made some assault platforms, I see." Four wooden towers stood outside of cannon range, illuminated by dozens of campfires.

"We've managed to stop them each time they've scaled the walls with ladders, sir. The towers will be just as unsuccessful," said Myri. "Once they're in range of the cannon, they'll make good target practice for my crews."

"We're lucky the Rastaks don't believe in using guns or cannon. Apparently, they think it cheapens the kill. They like to look into the eyes of whoever they send to Heras. Bloody savages." Jefferson sniffed the air and grimaced. Burning flesh from the pyres tainted the night. "And how are you, Nathaniel?"

"Tired. Hungry. The same as everyone else," replied Rane. "But always ready, sir."

"Such is a Legionnaire's lot."

"It is, sir."

"Do you remember when I first met you, Nathaniel?" asked Jefferson.

"Like yesterday. I'd just finished my training at the camp outside of Napolin. You told me I could change the world."

"You probably should've told me I was a fool and walked away," said Jefferson.

"And missed all the fun we've had over the years, sir? Never." Rane laughed. "You made me the man I am, more so than my own father. I'd follow you to the heart of Mogai's kingdom if you asked." And he knew he'd do it without a moment's hesitation.

"I may do that, Nathaniel. I may well do that. Only the Gods know what we'd find on the other side of that mountain range of theirs, though. I can't imagine they have too much in the way of art and architecture. Probably just mud huts and human sacrifices." Jefferson looked him in the eye, all humor gone. "We must stop them here. If we can do that, we can start forcing them off our lands and away from our homes."

"Do you think we can?" asked Myri.

Jefferson smiled grimly. "These are dark days we find ourselves in. If the Rastaks take Candra, then what's left of the continent will follow soon after. Life as we know it will be gone forever. Hundreds of thousands of people will die. This is our last stand, and even though common sense tells us to give up and run away, we must fight on. Discover the way through obstacles that would make others curl up and die. Mankind stands on the precipice, and only the Legion can stop its fall."

"You have our swords, Lord General," said Rane, bowing. "And our lives."

"There is nothing I value more," replied Jefferson. "Know that as we face the days ahead."

"Captain!" Thomaz cried out, pointing to the east. "Riders!"

Rane and Myri rushed over and looked out across the expanse. Riders were coming in hard from the northeast, heading for the main gate. They'd not gone unnoticed by the enemy, and the Rastaks were in pursuit.

Rane removed his telescope from a pouch on his belt and extended it for a better view. Magnified through the lens, he could see the riders clearly. The lead rider was Marcus Shaw, his oldest friend, and the fear on his face reflected how dire his situation was.

"Four riders," he told the others. "Three of ours. Don't recognize the fourth man."

"Get ready to give covering fire," screamed Myri, and the men and women along the wall scrambled to life. "And get some more archers up here. I want hell raining down on anything that isn't ours."

"I'm going down to the gate," said Rane. "They're not going to make it without help."

"May the Gods look after you, Nathaniel," said Jefferson, but Rane was already moving, trying not to think of what he actually had to do, trying not to let the fear take hold. He took the stairs two at a time, nearly knocking another soldier flying on the way down. Once in the courtyard, he looked for anyone to help.

"Hedin!" A giant of a Legionnaire looked up. Rane was tall, but

Hedin of the Axe had a good five inches on him. Hedin was famed for the double-edged blade that never left his side, and always happy for a fight. "Some of our lads are coming in with the whole Rastak army on their tail," shouted Rane without breaking stride.

"Shit." Hedin looked to the gates, as if he could see the danger on the other side. Gods bless the man, because he stood up anyway, weapon in hand. "We're with you, Nathaniel." Five others followed, each one calling out to others to join the group.

Overhead, the first cannon boomed into life, shaking the air and ringing their ears. Despite their tiredness, Myri would have her gunners working hard to help.

By the time Rane reached the gate, he had a fighting force of twenty soldiers, all willing to sacrifice their lives for their brothers in danger. If there were better men and women in the world, Rane had yet to meet them. He drew his sword and found his voice. "We have four riders approaching the gate. They're pursued by Rastaks on horse and foot. Our only objective is to get them inside quickly, so do what you need to do to make that happen. No more, no less. No unnecessary heroics. If a demon comes at you, shoot the bastard. If you can't, just get out of their way so someone else can. Don't try and fight them one on one. Stick close together; don't get separated. I don't want to lead another rescue party to get you. Got it?"

The others grunted their acknowledgement, all wide-eyed, working themselves up for the fight. Rane's mouth was dry as the blood roared through him. By the Gods, he could've done with a drink of water and a piss. He could've done with being a million miles away from where he was right then, as scared as a man could be, and most likely dead in five minutes time. He wished he'd time to get his armor, his helmet, or even just his bloody shield.

Boom. Boom. Boom. Boom. The cannons roared, a steady beat, drowning out their racing hearts and smothering the war cries of their enemies. The zip of arrows filled the space in between shots, each one a raindrop trying to hold back the tsunami of Rastaks racing towards the city.

"Open the gates!" came the call from above.

Fear gripped Rane, but he pushed the feeling down as best he could, and concentrated on the weapon in his hand. He would survive this. It wasn't his day to die. Not yet. "Come on — let's go hurt the bastards!"

Swords and axes, knives and guns were readied as the portcullis groaned into motion. The wooden beam that held the gates in place was manhandled out of the way and the doors pushed open. Rane could see Marcus, two other Legionnaires and a bearded man riding for their lives with what looked like the whole Rastak army in pursuit. By the Gods, they'd no hope. Not knowing what else to do, Rane screamed and charged out to meet them. His men followed.

His feet pounded the ground as his heart hammered in his chest. Time slowed as they closed on the enemy. A cannon ball blasted a cluster of Rastaks into the air and blood and guts rained down on them all, mixed with rock and rubble. Another wave of arrows fell, brushing a dozen soldiers off their feet — but there were so many of the bastards still coming at them.

A Rastak dressed in mismatched leather armor and a demon-skull helmet ran alongside Marcus's horse, trying to snatch him from the saddle. The Legionnaire hacked down with his sword, slicing the man through the jaw. The Rastak went down, but another took his place. Rane crashed into him, allowing Marcus to ride past.

The Rastak rolled back onto his feet, a short sword in one hand and an axe in the other. Rane didn't wait for the bastard to try anything with either of them, and shot him in the head.

He spotted movement out of the corner of his eye and ducked just as another axe flew past. He slashed out with his sword, catching a Rastak in the guts. His arm shook with the impact, but he still managed to twist the blade as he pulled it free, doing his best to open the man up. The Rastak screamed in pain and rage, face contorted, spitting, swearing. Rane thrust his sword up into the man's heart and silenced him for good.

Another Rastak soldier came at him, swinging a badly notched sword at his head. He stepped aside, felt the blade brush past his shoulder, and slashed the Rastak's throat open. A red mist blew past

Rane's face as he looked around, breath ragged. It was chaos as his small force battled with the oncoming wave of Rastaks. The cannons fired and the arrows fell, keeping the worst of the enemy away, but even so, his troops were on the verge of being overwhelmed.

Hedin was nearby, swinging his axe from one foe to another. He was mowing them down as soon as they came near him, bodies piling high, until a spear nicked him in the thigh and he stumbled. Rane lunged in and skewered another Rastak before the bastard could bring a sword down on Hedin's neck.

Suddenly, a shadow fell over Rane. A Jotnar, ten feet tall, towered over him. The demon roared, filling Rane's vision with its razor-sharp teeth as spit flew over his face. Fear gripped him; he felt so small before the monstrosity. Shell covered most of its body like armor, leaving few vulnerable parts to attack. Spurs jutted out from its elbows, forearms and knees, sharp enough to gut any man foolish enough to get close. And Rane was far too close.

The survival rate for one-on-one combat with a Jotnar was zero. Rane had lost count of the good men and women whom he'd person- ally seen fall before them, some ripped apart, others pulped under giant fists or hacked in two with massive weapons.

Rane barely saw the creature move before its fist battered his head. White light exploded in his vision as he hit the ground hard, somehow finding the sense to roll out of the way of a foot stomp that would have crushed his chest.

Before the Jotnar could attack again, another Legionnaire — Simone — joined the fight. Her sword bit into the creature's arm, cracking its shell, but no more than that. The Jotnar sent her flying as it shook the weapon free.

Others rushed to their aid — Hedin, axe swinging, along with two conscripts armed with pole and pike. With a roar, the Jotnar turned to deal with the Nortlunder, offering Rane its back.

Rane forced himself to move. He staggered to his feet and attacked once more. He hacked at the back of the creature's legs. Black blood traced the blade's path as it bit deep, slicing hamstrings. The demon crashed to its knees, no longer able to stand. Rane darted back as a conscript thrust his pike into the demon's heart. The Jotnar's death squeal was cut short as Simone, mouth bleeding and one eye swollen shut, separated its head from its shoulders.

"Pull back!" Rane ordered at the top of his voice. "Pull back! Pull back!"

His words reached his men's ears over the roar of blood and the clash of steel. More arrows struck the enemy around them, forcing the Rastaks back, buying the defenders space and time.

Rane and his men only had a hundred yards to run, but Hedin went down when a Rastak tackled him around the knees. Three more soldiers from the gate rushed out to help. Blades flashed left and right as Hedin was hauled to his feet. Rane took him under the arm and they ran the last few yards through the gates and into the darkness of the castle.

The doors slammed shut and the portcullis dropped back into place. Rane fell to his knees, sucking in air, hands shaking. He thanked all the Gods for keeping him alive yet again, not quite believing he'd actually survived. His stomach lurched and he vomited over the ground. The bile burned his throat, but Rane didn't care. He was alive.

Marcus and the others were helped from their horses. One of the Legionnaires didn't have long left — both he and his horse were covered in far too much blood — but Marcus looked relatively unscathed.

The fourth man stood to one side, watching the commotion with a look of amusement on his face, as if he'd just had a leisurely ride through the countryside. Tall and thin, his bald head accentuated his deathly-white skin. A hint of teeth sneaked through a closely cropped beard. He carried no weapon that Rane could see, and his robes resembled a priest's — though of what religion, Rane knew not. But it was his eyes that made him stand out. A darkness fell over them, as if they were in permanent shadow. Rane could feel the intensity emanating from them. The danger. Whoever he was, Rane didn't like him. There was something wrong with the man.

"Nathaniel! Thank the Gods you came to help," said Marcus, offering a hand to help him up from the ground.

Rane accepted the assistance, noting his friend's lined and worn face. "You look like you've been through the gates of hell, brother."

"Nothing a month of good food and sleep can't fix," replied Marcus.

Rane indicated the stranger with a tilt of his head. "Who were you escorting?"

Before Marcus could answer, four members of the Lord General's personal guard rushed over from the great hall. "Mr Shaw. You're required to come with me," said the lead guard.

Marcus nodded. "I'll see you on the wall, Nathaniel. May the Gods keep you safe."

"And you, my friend." Rane watched him go, the stranger with him.

"Nice," said Hedin, standing next to Rane. "Not even a 'thanks for nearly getting yourselves killed'."

Rane smiled. "You have my gratitude, at least. Did we lose anyone out there?"

Hedin shrugged. "One of the kids. Brave lad, but when it's your time, what can you do? Other than that, a few scratches here and there, but nothing serious. Well... apart from Diavan. He won't fight again."

Rane looked down at Hedin's leg; a nasty gash ran from one end of his thigh to the other. "You better get that seen to."

"It's nothing." Hedin laughed and beat his chest with his fist. "I'm a Nortlunder, and proud of it. A few stitches and this thing will be forgotten. It won't stop me from killing more of those Rastak scum in the morning."

"Well, there's more than enough to keep you busy." Rane wiped black blood off his sword before he slipped it back into his scabbard.

"Aye. It'll be wet work tomorrow."

"Then it'll be the same as every other day," replied Rane.

More of the Lord General's personal guard appeared and quickly dispersed out into the streets. One came over to speak to Hedin and

Rane. "The Lord General wants all the Legion gathered in the barracks."

"Now?" asked Rane.

"Now."

"But what about my men? If the Rastaks attack—"

"Then the alarms will ring and you'll run like hell to get back to your posts. I'm sure he has a good reason for calling you in. No doubt he'll tell you when we get there."

Rane looked to Hedin, who shrugged once more. "I do as I'm told."

"Then let's go to the barracks."

The Sword Tower was only a short walk from the gates, but for Rane's tired body, it might as well have been a million miles away. Each step hurt, and he wondered why they had been summoned. The barracks, home to the men and women of the Legion, stabbed the skyline ahead, a curved column of stone with no concession for aesthetics; just brutal function. It reflected the Legionnaires' way of life perfectly.

More Legionnaires joined Rane and Hedin as they got closer. Apart from the odd nod of recognition from those happy to see old friends and comrades still alive, no one spoke. Talking took energy, and no one had that to spare. Judging by the haunted eyes around Rane, hope was in short supply too. They trudged along together, each lost in their own thoughts and fears, wondering why the Lord General had summoned them for what would surely be the last time.

Stepping through the doors of the barracks brought some relief. It was cooler inside the building, and almost tranquil. It was good to leave the war outside, even if it was for a short while. Rane nearly laughed at the thought that perhaps a good meal and a comfortable bed waited for them — he knew they'd not be that lucky.

Rane and Hedin marched down a long corridor and joined the other Legionnaires already gathered in the great hall. Four hundred and fifty men and women, all with the same battle-weary look about them. Rane felt immense pride standing alongside them — they were the best of the best. It was no idle boast to say that mankind's forces would have fallen long ago if not for the Legion.

Jefferson watched them intently from the dais. Next to him was the stranger whom Marcus had brought; he looked very comfortable, but Rane's unease about the man grew. Even though he stood still, the man seemed to slip in and out of the room's shadows, making it hard to focus on him. All Rane's instincts told him this was a dangerous man, someone not to be trusted, but he had no real reason to think that. He was just tired, Rane told himself. The lack of sleep was making him paranoid. If the Lord General was happy to have the man with him, that should be enough for Rane.

Satisfied all the Legion were present, Jefferson raised his hand, and the doors to the great hall were closed. The *thunk* of the locks sliding into place echoed across the room. Thick beams secured the doors. Everyone — all four hundred and fifty men and women of the Legion of Swords — was focused on what the Lord General had to say. The only sounds were the shuffling of feet and the occasional cough.

Jefferson bowed his head in greeting. "Brothers and sisters, thank you for answering my summons. I wish it was under better circumstances, but these are desperate times." He paused to look over the sea of faces before him. "And, if mankind is to survive the morrow, we must risk all that we have in one last, desperate gamble."

PART I

1

Rane sat cross-legged in the glade, concentrating on his breathing. He counted to five as he inhaled, and then to five again as he exhaled, trying to clear the noise from his mind.

Sunlight sneaked through the trees, warming his body. Somewhere, a bird sang, and other creatures sniffled and scratched around, but he was the only human for miles in either direction. Just the way he liked it. He breathed in, filling his lungs with air that was free of city stink. A gentle breeze rustled its way from the south-east, bringing with it a hint of the ocean a few miles away.

Even so, the voice whispered at the edges of his mind. It promised to take away the guilt that haunted him, the memories that shattered his sleep. It offered strength and power, a way forward — if only he were willing to pay the price. All it wanted was blood, violence and death. A small price. A good price. A price he'd once been so happy to pay.

But he'd not killed anyone for six hundred and forty-two days, and Rane didn't want that to change. He was better than that. A man, not a monster.

One, two, three, four, five, he counted as he breathed in, and he almost couldn't hear the screams of the dying. *One, two, three, four, five,* he counted and exhaled, but it wasn't enough to remove the sweet music of steel against steel that filled his mind, or the smell of blood that tainted his thoughts.

He opened his eyes and saw his sword leaning against a tree. The red scabbard was dented and scratched from all it had been through, the handle worn by years of use. But he knew the blade inside was as perfect as the day it was forged by the Naijin swordsmith, Edo. Two years had passed since he'd last shown its steel to the world, but he could remember it like yesterday: the joy as he cut the man down, the ease with which the sword sliced through flesh. The rush that filled his veins. The power death gave him. How he'd reveled in it. How it'd disgusted him. The Legion might've saved the world, but Rane had lost himself in the process. Sometimes he didn't know if he'd ever find himself again.

He wanted to look at the blade; peek at a sliver of its steel. He told himself that it didn't matter, that there was no harm in looking, but he knew where that path would lead. Better it stayed hidden. Better he stayed safe. He'd had enough of death. If only death had had enough of him.

Rane abandoned his attempts at meditation, knowing when he was past such passive attempts to quell the temptations within him. He cracked his neck, stretched his arms, and flexed his hands. The scar on his right palm shone as bright as it ever did against his suntanned skin.

After placing a log on the chopping block, he picked up his axe. The handle was worn smooth with hard use, but the head gleamed, and its edge was sharp enough to cut the very air. The axe felt good in his hands, heavy but comfortable.

He swung. A perfect arc. Overhead and down. The axe bit into the log with a satisfying thunk, splitting it neatly down the center. He flicked the pieces to one side of the block and picked up the next log.

A crow perched on a nearby tree stump and watched as Rane continued for hour after hour. The relentless action burned away the voices, took away the desire. His muscles complained, but he ignored them, too. He vented his fury on the wood, enjoying the violence of the axe, seeking exhaustion and the silence it guaranteed.

By the time he stopped, he'd more than enough wood to last a long winter and barely enough strength left to hold the axe. He filled a basket and sat down on the block to cool off. The late summer sun had enough heat left in it to leave a tingle on his skin, and for the first time that day, he enjoyed the view of his surroundings.

He pulled his hair back from his face. He thought about tying it up out of the way, but dismissed the idea. He liked it long. Loose. Even all sweaty and sticking to his face. It told him he wasn't a Legionnaire anymore; that the war was over, and he'd survived. He wasn't what the sword had made him; he wasn't a warrior. He was a man of peace.

He used his shirt to wipe the sweat from his heavily scarred chest, grateful there was no one around to gawp at all the old injuries or ask questions he didn't want to answer about how he got them.

His little spot of land was tucked away near the south coast, a part of Ascalonia the Rastaks had never reached. As a result, some of his neighbors hadn't fought in the war. Some had managed to hide away until it was all over.

He was a curiosity to them, someone they imagined to be full of exciting stories of bravery and heroism. In their minds, the war they'd avoided had been glamorous and exciting. They didn't want to hear about the shit and the horror, the death and despair, the starvation and the madness; how he could still hear the screams of the dying and the drums of the Rastaks promising more pain. They didn't know what was done to win the war, and they didn't want to hear how he woke up screaming, the blood of his friends still on his skin. Some days Rane wanted to take those cowards for a ride north, to show them the reality. Show how close the horrors had come, and let them see the mass graves of the thousands butchered by the Rastaks. They'd not have to ride for more than a day or two to find something to see that they'd never forget.

Worse were the ones who wanted to tell him how they would've fought 'if only I wasn't too old' or 'too young' or 'had a bad knee'.

Whatever their excuse for not fighting, they always imagined them-selves to be able to win the war single-handedly if only things were different. It took all Rane had not to kill them where they stood.

There were many reasons why he lived in the middle of nowhere. 'People' ranked high up on that list.

He pulled on his shirt, looking forward to getting home and seeing Kara. She was the exception. She was the one who'd brought a little bit of Rane back from the hell he'd found himself in. Even so, he'd left home early that day, without speaking to his wife, not trusting himself around her — not when the voice was so loud in his skull. He knew she'd understand. She of all people knew the dark-ness that had stayed with him after the war, and accepted his constant need for solitude. She'd enough scars of her own still to heal.

He picked up his sword. Despite his tired muscles, he barely noticed the weight of the weapon. He paused again, thinking about how he'd like to see the blade once more, but other thoughts quickly followed: of blood and battlefields, and the dead he'd left behind. His heart raced, but he forced himself to breathe deeply once more until the memories fell away. He wasn't a killer anymore.

Rane slung the weapon over his shoulder, placed his axe on top of the basket, picked it up, and began the walk back home. The dirt track took him up a short hill, just steep enough to make Rane wish he'd packed fewer logs into his basket. He smiled at the thought. Compared to some of the weights he'd had to march with, the basket was nothing. He was getting soft in his retirement, past it at twenty-eight. He couldn't help but think that was a good thing. He might even get fat next.

Something caught his eye up ahead, off the track, in the woods. It looked like a large fox eating some prey. Rane stopped, reminded of an animal the Rastaks had used against the allied nations in the war. One of Heras' pets.

But that was impossible. He'd not seen one of those since the war ended, and they'd never come that far south.

His hand drifted to his sword's hilt without thinking, but he paused. He was jumpy. He knew that. The growing unease was nothing but a hangover from the urges he'd felt earlier. There was no need to draw his sword. He wasn't going to be spooked by a memory. He'd resisted the temptation to use his sword for six hundred and forty-two days. He could last another day without giving in.

Rane walked on, slower than before, watching the creature tear into its catch. It was only a fox. Nothing to worry about. Nothing at all. But Rane's mouth was dry all the same and his heart raced.

He was ten feet away when the animal froze, aware of Rane's approach. It whipped its head around in his direction, snarling, revealing blood-stained teeth. It was no fox. With a clear view of its head, Rane knew exactly what the animal was.

A devil dog. A Bracke. He blinked, still not believing it, but there it was. A ghost from his past, alive once more. The impossible in the flesh, returned from Heras' kingdom.

The first time Rane encountered the Bracke, the Legion was retreating after the battle of Mislan, in the north of Fascaly. They slogged back over hard, cold ground, stretched out in a straggly line. They'd taken a kicking from the Rastaks that left them with more walking wounded than fighting fit. They were all desperate to get home, back to safety, but it seemed every few yards another body was left for the crows.

The main camp was two days' march away when the first Bracke struck. It charged in from the side, keeping low to the ground until the last minute. It dug its claws into some poor sod's belly, eviscerating him. By the time two other soldiers shot it dead, more dogs had attacked from the other flanks.

The Legion formed squares, huddling together with swords, spears and muskets facing outwards, but already the creatures had claimed the lives of over a dozen more Legionnaires. They were so fast. So deadly.

The Legion stayed like that for the rest of the day and the night, too scared to move, as the Bracke kept throwing themselves at the squares time and time again. They didn't care that they faced certain death by doing so. All they cared about was killing, and they weren't going to stop while there was one man alive. In the end, the Legion killed less than a dozen of the creatures, while the Bracke had slaughtered twenty soldiers and left probably twice that number injured.

And now Rane was staring at one again in the flesh.

The voice in his head screamed at him to draw his sword, to kill the demon before it killed him. He knew only too well the pain of a Bracke's claws ripping through flesh, how lethal its teeth were, what damage it could do. Fear surged through him. Suddenly, the war didn't seem so far away.

It stepped forward, still holding a piece of flesh in its front paws. The only thing it had in common with a fox was its short brown fur, but there the similarities ended. Its hind legs were larger than its forelegs so that it could rise up in front of its prey before falling on it with all its weight, pinning it down and slashing with the large sickle-shaped claws protruding from its middle toes. Its jaw jutted from a small head filled with teeth, and its tail was as long as the rest of its body.

Without taking his eyes off the Bracke, Rane slowly bent down and placed the basket on the ground. The Bracke's nostrils twitched; it cocked its head from one side to the other as it weighed up what was in front of it. Rane took the axe off the basket. He could deal with the Bracke without using his sword. The voice told him he was a fool, but he ignored it. The axe would do.

When he straightened back up again, the Bracke attacked.

He'd faced them many times in the war, but even so he'd forgotten how fast they moved. In the space of an eye blink, the Bracke closed the gap on Rane and leaped, curling up to hook its claws into him. Rane brought the axe up to block and the Bracke clamped its teeth on the shaft as it crashed into him.

They wrestled, the Bracke thrashing away as it tried to hook its claws into Rane. It sliced his arms to ribbons, and a foot caught his stomach. Pain flared across his gut as the creature's claws cut deep.

Rane ignored the pain. He'd been hurt before and survived. He twisted and threw the Bracke — still gripping the axe — into the bushes before it could hurt him more. The demonic dog rolled until it hit a tree, but was back on its feet in a second and racing once more towards Rane.

As it leaped a second time, Rane's sword swept down to meet it. There was no thought, no decision. He'd not drawn the weapon in two years, but it was as if no time had passed; the movement came as natural as breathing, and he carved the creature in two.

A rush of energy hit him as the sword did its work. His tiredness was gone, and the pain with it.

He stood with his sword held at eye level, parallel to the ground, shining bright in the twilight. Bracke never travelled alone. If there was one, there were more. No matter. He'd kill them all. By the Gods, he hoped there were more of them. He'd show them the error of their ways. He scanned his surroundings, listening for movement, finding none. His fury was building. The war had found him once more.

Rane stood there unmoving, muscles tensed. Blood from his gut ran down his legs but he ignored the injuries, knew they didn't matter. Only when he was sure he was alone did he lower the blade. The voice warned him to be careful, to keep his sword free and ready. Its urgings were no longer a whisper, nagging away at the back of his mind. It commanded him, demanding more blood. It scared and thrilled him. It was the killer in him, the darkness, and it was free once more.

Rane moved off through the undergrowth, searching for other Bracke tracks. His home, where his wife waited, was only a few hundred yards away. He didn't want to think about what one Bracke could do to her.

Rane searched until the light started to fade. He found nothing. Perhaps the creature had been alone after all.

He looked down at his sword; it was his life and his soul, and he loved it. Loved it more than anything in the world. What else did he need when he had that?

His skin tingled as he tried to calm himself. He'd forgotten what it felt like to kill. The charge that rushed through him, setting his nerves on fire. Every sensation so beautiful. Delicious. Power surged through him, changing him. He was stronger, faster, a god of death.

He wanted to kill again, kill more, kill anything — anything to keep the feeling alive.

No.

Rane had to put his sword away. That was the choice he'd made before. The only choice to make now. One he meant to live by. He wasn't that man anymore. The monster was gone.

He kept that thought lodged in his mind as he forced the sword back into its sheath. Hiding its beauty once more hurt, but he did it all the same. He slung it back over his shoulder, but it felt different. The weight of the sword pressed down on him, reminding him it was there, waiting, patient as death. If only he could leave it behind somewhere, he'd have a better chance of forgetting his past, ignoring the temptation, but he knew he could never do that. The sword was a part of him forever.

With the basket in his shaking arms once more, he walked the rest of the way to his cottage. As he entered the clearing at the front of his house, his mind was a mess of thoughts and emotions. The Bracke had changed his whole world once more. Back to what it had been. Back to something he'd tried so hard to leave behind.

As he approached the cottage, he didn't see his home, his refuge from the world, built by his own hands. He saw a building that was defensively unsound, with too many windows, doors without locks and not one place he could defend without being exposed and vulnerable elsewhere. How could he've been so stupid to build it in such a way?

Because it was built for love and hope, not death and despair.

It was a simple cottage, with a living room just large enough for Rane and Kara. A smaller bedroom at the back had a window overlooking the brook that provided them with supper most nights. A small garden to grow vegetables. Plenty of game nearby. It was all they needed — and wanted. Now Rane wanted to build walls and fences around it all, traps and deterrents to protect it from the world. To kill anything that came against it. Kill anything that came for him.

He stopped by the door, trying to clear his mind. Guilt and excitement battled inside him. He hated that using his sword made him feel so good. Hated how much he wanted to use it to fight and kill again.

But he knew where that path led, and the end of the journey wasn't pretty. He'd managed to walk away from it before, and he wasn't going to risk losing everything he had worked so hard for over the last two years. He was stronger than that. Better.

Kara was by the stove when he came in through the front door, a welcome reminder of who he was now. A husband.

And soon to be a father. The bump showed even more. It was still hard to believe Kara was four months pregnant. He would've laughed two years earlier if someone had told him he'd have a child. Such things didn't belong in a world of blood and fire. But meeting Kara had changed that, shown him another way. That death wasn't always the answer.

After the war, he'd gone with Marcus to Rooktown to make sure his friend's family was safe and alive. They'd not expected to find his baby sister leading the local resistance. Kara was as tough and as resilient as her brother, and had been through just as much as they had. Even so, it had surprised both Rane and Kara when they had fallen in love.

She looked up and took in the blood on his arms, his ripped-up shirt. "What's happened? Are you all right?" She rushed over.

Rane placed the basket of wood on the floor and leaned his sword next to it, taking his time, not meeting her eyes, avoiding her touch for a moment. The blood still roared in his ears, and his arms trembled with the thrill of the kill. He didn't want her to see him like that.

"Nathaniel?" she asked again, lifting his shirt to see what wounds he had and finding none. "Where's the blood from? What happened?"

"I need to wash." He left her standing there and headed into the bedroom. He knew he wasn't being fair, but he needed to compose himself. He poured water into a bowl with shaking hands and wiped the blood from his skin, his wounds now no more than scratches. Clean, he changed his clothes and felt calmer. He was a husband; a farmer. He was building a home, a life, a family. He wasn't a soldier, a killer, a destroyer. He took deep breaths, clearing his mind as he watched his hands settle. He had to remember who he was. *Not a monster.*

He returned to the other room and joined Kara by the window. The sun had slipped down behind the trees, washing the world in black and red. To Rane's eyes, every growing shadow housed a demon, every bush hid a monster. He shook the thoughts from his head. It wasn't healthy to think that way. There had been no signs of any other Bracke. They were safe. His stomach churned at the thought. Disappointment.

"Are you going to tell me what's going on?" asked Kara, her voice edged with annoyance. She fiddled with the locket that hung around her neck between finger and thumb, trying to stay calm. Her hair, as black as Rane's, curled down, framing her face and falling over her shoulders. The setting sun cast a golden sheen over her skin, highlighting the single scar that ran from her hairline to her jaw. The war had left its mark on so many.

Rane sat in one of the chairs by the window. "I was attacked by a Bracke half a mile down the hill. I... killed it. I looked for others, but there was no sign."

"A Bracke? Just one?" Kara lowered herself into the chair opposite. She knew the demon dogs and what they could do. "You were lucky."

"I... had my sword."

"They've never been this far south."

"That's what we all thought, and yet I found one today."

Kara looked out the window, searching the shadows as he was, but not with the same enthusiasm. "The Rastaks had packs of them when they occupied Rooktown. They'd tie troublemakers to stakes and let the devil dogs loose. Laughed as they watched them go to work." She rubbed her face. "Are you sure there aren't any others?"

"As sure as I can be. How did it even get here? It would've left a trail of bodies all the way from wherever it came from. There's no way it'd be able to stay hidden."

"Maybe everyone does know? We haven't been into town for a while."

"Someone would've warned us."

"We need to head over there, see the sheriff. Find out one way or the other. Maybe they've already heard stories of other Bracke out there," said Kara, all tensed up. She couldn't take her eyes off the yard, looking for the creatures. "If they haven't, we have to let them know. Warn them."

"It'll mean search parties coming up here, walking over our land," said Rane.

"So? Better than us being attacked by another one of those things."

"It's just..." How could he tell her that a part of him didn't want peace? That he enjoyed killing the Bracke? That there was a monster beside her just as terrible as what could be lurking outside their window? No, the time for confession was long gone. His secrets had to stay buried. He couldn't listen to that voice that knew him too well. He'd spare her the truth.

Kara looked at Rane as if she was gazing right through him, taking in all that was unsaid, all of what his heart wanted. It took all his courage not to look away. He'd rather have an army to fight than stand under scrutiny from his wife. She deserved better than him.

"It's the right thing to do," she said.

Rane nodded. He knew she was right. Kara was normally right about everything. He glanced over, smiled at her strength. She made him want to be a better man than he knew he was.

They watched the night draw in, lost in their thoughts.

"I was thinking we should go and see Marcus before I get too big to move," said Kara eventually.

" Rooktown is a long way."

"It's been nearly two years. He's my brother. And your oldest friend."

"It didn't seem like that when we parted. He threatened to kill me if I married you."

She laughed, a beautiful sound that filled Rane's heart, chasing the darkness away. "What did you expect? I'm still his baby sister. That'll never change, no matter how many demons I've killed or lives I've saved. He just didn't want you running off with me."

Rane grinned, welcoming the memories. "I don't think I ran off with you. I think there was courting. Romance. I even asked Marcus for his permission."

"Was that when he knocked you out?"

Rane pretended to get indignant at the thought. "It was a sucker punch. Knocked me straight onto my backside."

"I thought the pair of you were going to draw blades at one point."

"You put a stop to it before it got out of hand." Rane looked at Kara, so beautiful, so clever, so strong. He'd be lost without her. "You were worth getting beaten up for."

"It was Marcus' fault for bringing a good-looking man like you back from the war. What did he expect was going to happen?"

"From the way he talked about his little sister, I'd thought you were going to be all of ten years old. I think he did, too. Wasn't expecting to see you so grown up when we arrived."

"You were gone a long time. And I had to grow up fast. We all did. The Rastaks saw to that."

"But things are different now. You've got the baby to think of."

"We've got the baby to think off," corrected Kara. The humor fell from her face for a moment. "It'll be good to see Marcus. Mend things. He should know he's going to be an uncle. Remind him he has family. I miss him."

"You don't regret marrying me, do you?" Rane kept the question quiet, as if it and the answer didn't matter as much as they did.

"Not for one minute. You're the best thing that's ever happened to me, Nathaniel Rane. Don't ever forget that." She kissed him, her lips soft against his skin.

"I'll try not to," he said, returning the kiss.

Kara stood up and stretched her back. "Everyone may think it's a new golden age of peace, but it's going to be generations before the world's recovered from what Mogai did. We need to do our best to help." She kissed him again. "I'm tired. I'm going to bed. Come with me."

"I'll be along shortly," he replied. He watched her head into the small bedroom, and then picked up his sword. With it in his lap, he watched the world outside. He ran his hand along the length of the scabbard, fighting the urge to free the blade once more. But there were no more monsters for him to fight, no excuse he could find in the darkness. He told himself that was a good thing. He wasn't a killer anymore.

Sword in hand, he followed Kara to the bedroom as the voice called him a liar.

2

They took the wagon into town early the next morning, each lost in their own thoughts. Rane was edgy after a troubled night's sleep. He'd not shaken off the effects of the day before, and the thought of being amongst people again wasn't helping things.

Eshtery had never been much of a town: a central marketplace where you could trade goods and maybe make a bit of money; an inn to wet your thirst after a long day's work; a general store that sold most of anything you could think of; churches to Odason and to Heras, and a sheriff's office with a small jail — used more for people to sleep off their drunken mistakes than for any serious crime.

The war had changed that, though. People had fled south, trying to stay ahead of the Rastak armies as they'd swept across Ascalonia, looking for somewhere safe. Eshtery had given them that. More had followed, looking for food and work, and the town had both of those, too. One of Ascalonia's biggest stone quarries was only a few miles away, and as the country started to rebuild, the demand on the quarry was far greater than what could be produced, even with the extra manpower.

Growing out from the main square was a motley collection of

buildings, thrown up in a hurry without much planning or fore-thought. Cheap housing for the new workers to sleep in, cheap bars for them to get drunk in, and cheap brothels for them to screw in. There was even talk of a school being built for all the children that had arrived with their parents or suddenly sprung up since.

The church to Heras had been demolished as per the law, and Odason's temple was twice the size it had once been. Eshtery was far enough away from the capital that they'd not had the Inquisition come calling, but most attended the services nonetheless. Rane and Kara were among the few that didn't. He knew that was a topic for the town gossips, but no one had reported them for it — yet.

As his old cart trundled up the main road, shaking his bones as it bounced and rattled over rocks and into potholes, Rane wanted to be back at his cottage more than anything. If Bracke were roaming the woods, his time would be better spent hunting them down. He told himself it was because he wanted Kara to be safe, but he knew that wasn't the only reason. His sword lay next to him in the wagon. Always close, always to hand. Ready to use. It was hard to believe he'd gone two years without drawing it. Now all he could think of was using it once again. And nothing deserved killing more than Heras' demon spawn.

But Kara had been right, as she normally was. As much as he wanted to hide away, they had to warn the others about the Bracke and see what else was happening in the world.

Kara sat beside him, running her thumb over her locket, her eyes roving across the road ahead to the verges, the bushes, the trees, looking for any sort of threat. It wasn't just the news about the Bracke that made her vigilant. Three years living under a Rastak occupation had taught her to always be alert. Decades of peace wouldn't break that habit.

The sun framed her, covering her in golden hues and finding highlights in her hair, sparkling off the locket in her fingers. He reached over and squeezed her other hand, and she smiled in return. She deserved better than him.

The landscape changed as they drew nearer to Eshtery. Gaps

appeared in the woods where trees had been hacked down for building materials or firewood. Detritus littered the side of the road — a cast-off boot with its sole missing, a child's toy buried in mud, the skeleton of a wagon left to be forgotten. All signs that Rane had left their little sanctuary and was back in the world.

The town itself had grown even more since their last visit. A row of rickety houses, knocked together with more hope than nails, had sprouted out from the original borders. More workers for the quarry, no doubt. More strangers.

The wagon rattled along the rutted road as Rane and Kara headed to the center of town. Samuel, the miller, walked towards them with a couple of sacks of grain filling his wheelbarrow. He was a brute of a man, happy to bully anyone foolish enough to get in his way, always eager to challenge anyone he felt was weak. Normally, he'd at least try a bit of posturing in front of Rane, trying to prove only the Gods knew what. But this time, when he spotted Rane and Kara driving towards him, his cheeks flushed and he scuttled off down a side road, almost spilling his load in his haste.

"That's odd," said Rane, watching the miller.

"What is?" replied Kara.

Rane pointed behind them with his thumb at Samuel's rapidly departing figure. "Never seen him run like that before."

"Be grateful. The man's a fool."

Rane couldn't argue with Kara's assessment of the man, but still his behavior didn't sit well.

Up ahead, a crowd had gathered around Jahn Mathew'son, the sheriff. A few locals stood having a heated debate with half a dozen strangers.

The new faces weren't quarry workers, though — that much was obvious. They were veterans; their battered and scarred faces promised trouble, and they carried enough weapons to start a war on their own. Rane spotted a mace on one. A crossbow was slung over the back of another with a full quiver of bolts on his hip, and swords and knives were spread amongst the others.

A primal urge to confront the men rushed through Rane. He had to force himself to keep the cart trundling along, but his hand twitched towards his sword. They were men worth fighting. Worth killing.

The argument stopped as Rane and Kara drove past. One man — missing an ear, and with a nose that had been broken far too many times — stepped forward as if he wanted words with Rane, but Jahn put a hand on his arm. Violence polluted the air, filling Rane's nostrils with the tang of blood. He wanted to stop, wanted to jump down and cut them apart, but Kara squeezed his hand and somehow Rane kept driving the wagon down the road.

"What's going on there?" asked Kara once they had passed. "Who were those people?"

"I don't know," said Rane. But he did. They were men like him. Killers. "Let's just go to the hardware store and get what we need. We can talk to Edward about what's going on. He knows everything anyway, and will be more than happy to spread the word about the Bracke if we tell him."

"Okay," replied Kara, her voice no more than a whisper as she looked back over her shoulder at the men. "Sure."

They stopped their wagon in the square by the general store, climbed down and tied up the horses. Rane caught Kara watching him as he slung his sword over his back. For once, she didn't object to him wearing it. Better to have a sword and not need it than need one and not have it. Not that he'd ever leave his sword behind.

Edward Marster was behind the counter, beaming that grin of his at the sight of money walking through his door. He smeared his thin white hair back down over the top of his head. "Morning, Mr and Mrs Rane. What can I do for you today?"

Kara stepped forward, smiling in greeting. "Strange group of men gathered at the sheriff's. There been some trouble that you know of?" Rane stood to the side, happy to let his wife do the talking.

Edward leaned forward to peer out the window, unable to hide his annoyance at not noticing for himself what was going on. "I couldn't possibly say. Best to mind one's own business and leave others to mind theirs. That's my motto, and it works well enough for me."

Kara caught Rane's eye. They both knew Edward's words couldn't be further from the truth. The man's knowledge of local gossip spanned generations.

"We're just here for supplies, Mr Marster. Nothing else," said Kara. "We need some door locks if you have them, plus some metal bolts for the windows, to start."

"Well, now, that I can help you with. Got some good ones just arrived the other day from up in Candra." Edward put a box on the counter. "The queen herself has these in her palace. They're what stopped the Rastaks from eating her up back in the war days."

"Now, Mr Marster, you wouldn't be exaggerating just a little bit?" said Kara, laughing.

"You doubting my word?" Edward sniffed at the suggestion. "It says so on the box. 'By Royal Appointment' — what else do you think it means?"

"Even so," replied Kara, "I hardly think..."

The doorbell above the door rang as someone entered the store.

"Morning all," said Jahn Mathew'son. Jahn had been too old to fight in the war, but he still had the build of a man who could handle himself, even if age had softened the edges. His long white hair was tied up in a ponytail and a beard covered half his face, giving him the look of a kind grandfather, but no one was fooled. You didn't mess with Jahn if you had any sense, as many a miner had found to their cost. "Hope I'm not interrupting anything."

"I was just telling Mrs Rane about this here window bolt," said Edward, "and how the queen herself—"

"Then you won't mind if I steal Mr Rane off you for a bit," said Jahn. "He and I need to have a chat about a couple of things."

"Is everything all right?" asked Kara.

"Nothing for you to worry about. Just some questions I need answering." He turned to Rane. "Would you mind stepping outside?"

"Sure," replied Rane. "But whatever you've got to say to me, you can say it in front of my wife."

Jahn tilted his head in agreement. "As you wish." He waited while Rane and Kara stepped back out into the street before following.

"What's this about, Jahn?" asked Kara.

The sheriff glanced at the sword on Rane's back before answering. "You might've noticed some men at my office as you passed."

"I did," replied Rane.

"They're bounty hunters." Jahn shrugged. "Not how I'd earn my living, but these days I suppose you do what you have to do."

"What have they got to do with my husband?" asked Kara.

Jahn glanced her way then turned his attention back to Rane. He produced a folded piece of paper from his waistcoat. "Have a look at this."

Rane opened up the crumpled paper, torn at the edges where it had been ripped from a wall. The queen's standard stood next to the imperial seal of Fascaly and the sigils of the other allies from the war — Souska, Nortlund and Naijin.

The words were smudged but clear enough to make out. 'Reward: ten thousand gold pieces for any member of the Legion of Swords, dead or alive. Known by the scar on their right hand and by the sword they carry, they are wanted for the crimes of murder, collaboration and treason.' Both the scar and the sword were illustrated. Rane had to read the poster several times as his mind struggled to take in the words, his anger building. Why would the rulers of the five nations put out an arrest warrant on the Legion? For those crimes? "What's this mean?"

"Just what it says there, Mr Rane. Someone's offering a lot of money for Legionnaires, and they're not fussed what state they get them in."

Rane glanced at the reward note one more time. There was no mistake; he was a wanted man with a price on his head. "This doesn't make any sense."

Jahn shifted his feet and chewed his lip, looking as uncomfortable with the situation as he could be. "It is what it is. I'm just a small-town sheriff, so I'm not privy to the thinking of governments. But it leaves me with a bit of a problem, not least of which is I've got six men looking to collect a share in that reward."

Rane swallowed the urge to draw his sword there and then. "Go on."

"They seem to think you're one of them. A Legionnaire." Jahn glanced at Kara. "Now, I know you were a soldier, and did your duty in the war." He looked back at Rane. "But I told them boys they're mistaken when it comes to you. However, there's no denying that's a Legionnaire's sword on your back, now, is there?"

"No. No, there's not." Rane's jaw tightened.

Jahn's moustache twitched as he tried to smile, as if he knew how close to dying he really was. "Of course, I told them that it was just a souvenir someone gave you, and that owning a sword isn't proof in itself. So, I've come down to see if you have a matching scar, too. Because if you do, that'll change things."

Rane knew what he wanted to see. The scar. Still violently white against his sunburned skin, as if it were only a few weeks old. The permanent reminder of a night long ago; the mark only he and his fellow comrades bore. The proof of who he really was and what he'd done.

The voice inside told him to draw the sword; to kill Jahn, kill Edward and anyone else foolish enough to get in his way, then take Kara and get out of there. He all but shook with the force of the emotions clashing inside him. But no; these people were his neighbors, not his enemy. They were good people.

"Nathaniel?" asked Kara.

Rane kept his eyes on Jahn, aware of the sword on the sheriff's hip; a short doubled-edged weapon so different from Rane's own. He uncurled his right hand and presented his marked palm, ready for whatever happened next.

They both stared at the scar there.

Jahn sighed. "Thought as much." He looked back up at Rane, searching his eyes for something, but only the Gods knew what.

Strike now, urged the voice. *Kill the fool.*

Jahn moved his hand. Rane almost drew then, almost cut the man down, but the sheriff only offered him a hand to shake. "Glad to see there's no scar. I told them you weren't one of the Legion. I'm not sure what they've done to get the world out hunting for them, but that's not your problem."

"Thank you," said Rane, taking Jahn's hand.

"I like the pair of you and I consider myself a good judge of character, so I hope this nonsense blows over without affecting you none. In the meantime, I'd maybe get rid of that sword. Wouldn't want a souvenir getting you into trouble. And maybe stay out of town for a while." Jahn nodded at Kara. "Mrs Rane. Nice seeing you both. I'll let you get back on with your business now. You can keep that." He tilted his head towards the poster in Rane's hand, smiled, and walked back down the street.

"Nathaniel?" said Kara.

Rane showed his wife the poster. "I think we'd best head home. The others might not be as reasonable as Jahn."

"You in trouble, Mr Rane?" asked Edward, watching from the doorway.

Rane shook his head. "No. Just some folks mistaking me for someone else. I'll be seeing you soon."

"What about these?" said the shopkeeper, holding up the bolts. "You won't find any finer."

"I'll be back to pick them up in a day or two," said Kara as they unhitched their horses and climbed back into the wagon. "See you soon."

Edward watched them, looking none too happy at losing their business.

"Maybe we should've bought those bolts," said Kara as they headed in the opposite direction to the sheriff's office. "Might stop him from telling the world what just happened."

"What's there to say?" replied Rane. "He couldn't have seen what was on the poster."

"That's never stopped him before. The man can sniff out gossip from a hundred miles away."

"It'll be fine," said Rane, not believing it.

"This is a bounty on the whole Legion, signed by the five nations," said Kara, clutching the poster and rereading it as if that could change the meaning of the words on it. "Ten thousand gold pieces. That's a fortune. I can't even imagine that much money."

"That's per head. There were four hundred and fifty of us at war's end."

"Is there that much money left in the world?"

"I don't know. I don't understand any of this," said Rane. "It makes no sense."

"I thought the scar on your hand was just an old wound. The Gods know you have enough all over your body — but this says you all have the same mark."

"We do." There was a tightness in Rane's chest as he forced the words out, his eyes fixed on the road but seeing nothing but the past. He couldn't look at Kara now. "We all made a blood oath. It was towards the end of the war. We all thought we were about to die."

"What were you doing? Swearing allegiance to each other or something?"

"Something like that." The lie was like ash in his mouth. It was that, and far more. Far worse.

Kara folded the poster. "Well, you've got to get rid of that sword now. Destroy it or hide it until this whole mess is cleared up."

"I can't get rid of the sword."

"Why not? I know it's important to you, but it's not worth keeping — not if it's going to get you killed."

"It's not that simple."

"Are you worried about that beast you killed yesterday? You've still got your pistols — you don't need the sword as well." Kara sighed. "You heard Jahn — people will see it and see ten thousand gold pieces waiting to be claimed. We'll have bounty hunters and the Gods know what else coming after us. We'll never know a moment's peace. We've got a baby on the way. We need to think about what's best for it."

"Getting rid of the sword isn't an option." There was an edge to his voice that was uncalled for, but he couldn't help it. He just wanted the conversation over.

"Not an option? Haven't you been paying attention? I know you love that bloody sword, sometimes more than you love me, but people are going to try and kill you because of it. Surely that outweighs some stupid sentimentality you have for an old war relic."

"I'm asking you to accept it, Kara. It's just the way it is." Rane steered the wagon through the narrow streets, taking a circular route out of town. He didn't want anyone following them home.

"By the Gods, you can be a stubborn fool," hissed Kara. "Burying your head in the dirt isn't going to make this go away."

"I'm not suggesting that. My brothers and sisters are being hunted. I can't just leave them. I need to find out what's behind all this. Try and help if I can."

That got her attention. "What are you going to do?"

He looked at her, then; knew she wasn't going to like his answer. He wasn't sure he liked it himself, but he had no choice. "Once the bounty hunters have gone, I'll head up to Candra. Try and find the Lord General, get some answers. See if I can help fix things."

"You've got to be joking. Tell me you're not serious."

"I took an oath. Leaving the Legion doesn't change that. I can't just turn my back on my brothers and sisters. Not if they need my help."

"What about me? What about the oath you swore to me?"

"I haven't forgotten that, but those bounty hunters aren't going to be the last ones to come calling. If they found me, others will. Maybe Jahn won't be able to put off the next ones. If we're going to have a future, if I'm going to look after you and our child, I need to find out what's happening and deal with it. Otherwise we'll never be safe."

Kara shook her head, angry as he'd ever seen her. "Fine," she said through clenched teeth. "We'll leave in the morning."

"We? You're not going anywhere. You're staying here where it's safe."

"It doesn't work like that, Nathaniel. We're a team. If you're going, I'm going. I'm certainly not going to sit at home, knitting by the window, wondering if you're ever going to come back. I'm not that kind of woman. You'd never have married me if I was. No, if you're going, I'm coming with you. You'll be less conspicuous if we travel together. And afterwards we'll head to Rooktown and find Marcus. Make sure he's okay."

"It'll be dangerous. Too dangerous."

"I'm not some bloody kid. I've ambushed Rastak troops. I've killed collaborators. Don't tell me what's too dangerous."

Rane held up his hands in surrender. "Okay. We'll leave in the morning."

"And you'll leave the sword behind."

"No."

"No?"

"No."

Kara's face reddened. "By all the Gods in the Heavens, if you keep the sword, you might as well just hand yourself in to Jahn right now. You can give the reward money to me if you're so keen to get caught. At least then I'll get some compensation for your stupidity."

The wagon rolled over the last hill before their home. "I'm not getting rid of the sword. End of discussion."

Kara glared at him for the last few hundred yards. When he drew the wagon to a stop outside the house, she jumped down, giving him one last look that said he was a fool and he hadn't heard the last of the matter before marching inside. Still sitting on the wagon, Rane rubbed his face as he took a deep breath. He should tell her everything. She'd understand. It was the right thing to do; he knew that. But some secrets needed to stay buried no matter what. Even though he'd no doubt Kara loved him, he wasn't sure she'd forgive him for what he'd done. For what the Legion had done.

He picked up his sword and pulled just a fraction of the blade free from its sheath. His eyes looked trapped in the pristine steel.

Some things just couldn't be undone.

3

Rane woke screaming.

His body was on fire. A thousand injuries roared in pain. He opened his eyes, snapped out of his dreams of the war. It took a moment to register he was at home, alone in his bedroom at the back of the cottage. The brook bubbled away outside his window as early morning light chased away any lingering shadows. Just another day. And yet...

He shuddered as another stab of pain struck in his stomach. His hand went to the spot where he'd taken a spear fighting outside Hallington, felt an open wound. His hand came away stained with blood, but already the pain was spreading across his body, the memories of a thousand knives and a thousand swords attacking him anew. They cut and sliced across his body from head to foot, shallow and deep, fast and slow. Killing him.

He pushed himself up, reached for his sword. But his hand flailed in empty space. The sword was gone.

"Kara!" he screamed.

He stood up, desperate for his sword, hoping that it had simply fallen down, or rolled under the bed. Wanting to believe it was anywhere but gone. Another wave of agony punched him in the gut, knocking him to the ground, spitting blood.

"Kara!" A sob this time.

The pain intensified, driving all thought from his brain and making it hard to breathe. Blood poured from all his old wounds, leaking down his torso, his arms, his legs. He was bleeding everywhere.

Panic flared as he tried to get out of the bedroom, half-stumbling, half-falling as he did so.

His sword. He needed his sword. He groped along the floor but found only empty space.

He screamed as the agony reached new heights, forcing him into a ball on the ground. Blood — his blood — blossomed out from under him, staining the floorboards.

Somewhere, far away, he heard a door open. He looked up and saw Kara, hands covered in dirt, dress filthy.

"Nathaniel!" Kara rushed to his side. "By the Gods! What's happening?"

"Sword." The word was but a whisper, forced out through shallow breaths. It was all he could manage. He prayed she understood. "Where?"

Kara stared at him, horrified. "I buried it. I hid it."

"No." Rane closed his eyes. The pain began to fade. He began to fade. He knew he was dying, but he hadn't the strength to fight it. It was long overdue. He'd been living on borrowed time. Heras came for everyone in the end. Faces drifted through his mind of comrades long since gone, people he'd not thought about for years. The fallen. He was going to join them, united again.

Kara. By the Gods, he'd miss her. Miss their child.

The darkness grew, embracing his thoughts, cushioning his fall, snuffing the fire. Even the voice was quiet at long last, no longer interested in him now his sword was gone.

The world went black. Rane died.

A JOLT of energy hit him, as powerful as the pain, pulling him back. His eyes snapped open as air rushed into his lungs. His sword lay in his hands and Kara stood over him. She was shouting at him, but he couldn't take in the words. Didn't care what she was saying. He gripped the sword as its energy flowed through him, as life pulsated back into him. Let it do its work. Close the wounds. Heal all the damage done.

He had no idea how long he lay there, waiting for the pain to fade, his injuries disappearing once more into the past.

Cold touched his face.

He became aware of Kara wiping the blood from his skin with a wet cloth.

"Kara."

"Odason's blessings, you're alive." She hugged him, tears running down her face.

"What happened?"

"Nathaniel, I'm so sorry. I took your sword. You wouldn't get rid of it, so I did." He saw his pain reflected in her eyes; her fear of what had happened, and of him. "I thought if I buried it, you'd see that you didn't need it. That we'd be safe from anyone looking for you. They'd not think you were a Legionnaire."

He groaned, his body sore, tingling with residual pain. "Don't... don't do that again."

"Why were you bleeding? By Odason, what's going on? Please tell me."

He pushed himself up with one shaking hand so that he could lean against the bed and catch his breath. "It's the sword. It's why I have to keep it near."

"Why? I don't understand."

Rane reached for a cup of water near the bed, took a sip, then another. Everything ached. He gazed at Kara sitting next to him, covered in his blood, wondering if she'd still love him after he confessed. Knew he wouldn't blame her if she didn't.

"Did you know my sword has a name? It's called *Kibon*; in Naijin, it means "hope". Before I tell you what we did, it's important to know that, because at one point we didn't have any hope of any kind. Candra was about to fall, and Ascalonia with it. Things were as desperate as they could get." Rane took a deep breath, felt more of his strength returning. "I was on the wall, preparing our defense for the Rastaks' final attack when Marcus returned from a mission with a man called Babayon. The whole Legion was summoned to the great hall in our barracks, and we were told we had a chance to change the war, change everything — if we were prepared to make a sacrifice."

He paused as the memories dragged him back to that night and the despair they all felt. "When you think you're going to die in the morning, it's easy to agree to anything. What did it matter? We were dead anyway. Some hope was better than none."

"What did you do?"

"The man Marcus had brought — Babayon — was a mage."

Kara sat back. Even after everything she'd seen, some things could still shock her. Mage, magician, wizard, witch — it didn't matter what name they practiced the dark arts under. They were all outlawed, feared, declared evil. To practice magic was to sin against Odason. Magic carried an automatic death sentence, and guaranteed you a visit from the Inquisition. "What? Why would Marcus bring such a man to you?"

"Jefferson knew him from somewhere. Knew what he could do. Babayon promised to make us stronger, faster, and almost impossible to kill; to make us even more powerful than the Rastaks. But the price was terrible. We were led deep into the bowels of the castle. The dark covered everything, eating our torchlight. I remember wanting to turn back, questioning everything, being so scared, but I just marched down with the others, following like sheep."

Kara stared at him, silent.

"I don't remember much after that. Just images. Flashes. There was a ceremony. Babayon ordered us to cut our hands with our swords. Used our blood..." Rane paused, sifting through his memories. "Even telling you now, I almost don't believe it, and I was there. Most of the time, it feels like a dream I once had instead of something

I did. Sometimes, the only way I know it happened is when I look at the scar on my hand."

"Why?" asked Kara. "Why did this Babayon need your blood?"

"Powerful magic needs blood to fuel it. And this was magic on a scale unheard of." Rane's mouth went dry. He feared how Kara would react to the truth, but there was no hiding it now. "Babayon took part of our souls and merged it with our swords."

"What?" Kara's eyes darted from the sword to Rane and back again. She edged slowly back from him, as if really seeing him for the first time and not liking what she saw. "He did what?"

Rane held up his sword. "Part of my soul is trapped within this blade. Every time I use it, it makes me stronger than a normal man. Faster. It's all but impossible to kill me when it's in my hand. Almost any injury will heal in seconds. But if I'm separated from it — if it's taken away from me, or destroyed — I'll die. All its magic is undone, and my soul is lost."

"So all the cuts that were bleeding on your body..."

Rane nodded. "They were all injuries from past battles, healed by the sword, reopened once more."

"Is that why you take the sword with you everywhere? Why you won't get rid of it?"

"Yes. Its magic stops working if it's more than a few feet away from me. Without it, I'll die."

There was no hiding the disgust on Kara's face. Her reaction hurt more than anything he'd just endured. "Why didn't you tell me about this?"

"I wanted to forget about it. Pretend it'd never happened. I didn't like who I'd become by the end of the war." He looked away. "At first, we were all excited. We defeated the Rastaks outside Candra. Killing them was so easy — even the demons — and each death fed the sword. There's a jolt of energy, a rush. It feels... amazing. Addictive. It heals any wounds, makes you stronger still. I liked it too much. Needed it too much. We all did.

"When the war ended, I wanted to feel it again and again. I killed anything or anyone who crossed my path. It was driving me insane.

I'd sworn an oath to protect and serve those weaker than myself, but suddenly I was a danger to everyone. I became a monster. Better to leave the Legion, get away from anyone I could hurt."

"But it was all right to be with me? To put me in danger?"

Rane shook his head. "You make me a better person; make me feel like the person I used to be. The urges have all but disappeared since I met you. I'd never hurt you."

Kara was about to reply when another thought struck her. "By the Gods. Marcus, too? My brother did this as well?"

"The whole Legion did." He reached out to touch her, to reassure her everything was going to be okay, but she pulled away.

"Is this why they want to arrest you all? Because they found out what you did? No wonder."

"I don't think so. Why would they? We were told we had the queen's blessing, the Council's agreement. Why would they turn on us now when we gave everything for them?"

"I don't know. Maybe because magic is against the law? Against Odason's will?"

"It's not like that," whispered Rane. But he knew it was.

"You stupid fool. You stupid, stupid fool. Why'd you do it?"

"Because we had no other choice."

"And you didn't tell me?" Kara shook her head. "Didn't you think I had a right to know? That my husband had taken half his soul and put it in a bloody sword? Using some devil-magic?" Kara drew her knees up and wrapped her arms around them as the tears fell freely. "What about the baby? Will this... magic... affect the baby?"

There it was — the question he'd never dared ask. The question he didn't know the answer to. Kara saw the truth in his eyes and shook her head in dismay.

"I'm so sorry." Rane tried to put his arms around her. Kara flinched from him, but then her shoulders sagged and she sank into his embrace. He held her while she sobbed, hating himself for hurting her.

Eventually, she stopped and wiped her eyes. She looked up at him, red-faced and bleary-eyed, but already he could see her pulling herself together, her vulnerability fading. "I swear by Odason himself, if there's something wrong with my baby because of what you did, I'll kill you. Do you understand? I love you, Nathaniel, but I had a right to know about this. Having a child while you're riddled with magic was a choice we should've made together."

"I know. I'm sorry."

She stood up, scrubbing the last of her tears away with the back of her hand. "We can't stay here. We need to stick to the plan. Go to Candra, find Marcus, warn him too. Hopefully no one's gone after him yet. Find some way to reverse the magic."

"I don't know if the magic can be reversed."

"What about this Babayon? Where's he? If he did this to you, he can undo it."

"I've no idea where we'd find him. The last I saw of Babayon was on the Great Plains."

"At the last battle?"

Rane took a deep breath. Let everything come out. "It wasn't a battle. We didn't even fight them. Babayon used more magic, set fire to the Plains. Burned them all." Rane shook his head. "How we cheered. We'd won the war, but we'd become as bad as the enemy we fought."

"No one said you used magic."

"How could we? We're taught from the time we can talk that magic is wrong. Cursed. Odason's priests had only become more powerful since the war with the Rastaks. They would've sent the Inquisition after us without hesitation. It had to be a secret."

"The Rastaks were evil, Nathaniel. They deserved it. They'd have done worse to us if the positions had been reversed."

"That's the argument everyone used to justify it. But as we watched them burn for days and days, long after there was anything left to feed the flames, it didn't feel like the right thing any more."

"And Babayon?"

"Just disappeared one morning. No one saw him leave, or knew where he went."

"But a magician that powerful can't stay hidden. Someone must know..."

They both heard the horses. In his mind's eye, Rane saw them racing up the hill, galloping hard along the dirt road that led to their house and only their house. Kicking up dirt and dust behind them, the land dry from a long summer.

"Nathaniel..." said Kara.

"It's okay," said Rane as he got to his feet. He pulled on his trousers, laced them up quickly and found his boots. If it had been only one rider, he could perhaps have believed it was a messenger, or someone lost and looking for a way back to civilization. But only bad news required company. Only trouble travelled in a pack. Only danger travelled so fast.

"What's going on?"

He held out a hand. "Stay in the house."

Of course, there was still a chance his visitors came in peace.

He almost laughed at that. The war had taught him the folly of such wishful thinking, a fact he should've remembered earlier. Men like him didn't have their dreams come true. With one last glance back at Kara, he walked outside, bare-chested and covered in dried blood, to greet his unwelcome visitors. The sun shone down on his back, throwing his shadow along the ground ahead of him.

That voice in his head was loud, bold, excited, urging him to draw *Kibon* from its sheath and be ready for whoever came calling. It sang with joy at the thought of violence and death. It knew its time was near.

Seven horsemen appeared a heartbeat later. They slowed when they saw him and brought their horses in at a trot. Rane recognized all of them from the previous day; the bounty hunters looking to collect ten thousand gold pieces. With them was Jeriah Miller'son, Samuel's eldest. The boy was only a few years into his teens, too young to have been drafted during the war, but it was hard to call him a kid now. Trouble was, he was at that awkward age where he had the body of a man but the mind of a child still. A dangerous age, if Rane remembered rightly. The boy had obviously been the one who'd led the bounty hunters to his house. Stupid child.

They stopped their horses a few yards from him.

"What're you doing here, boys?" asked Rane, with a cold smile. "Long way to come for a visit."

"Some people are worth visiting." The leader pushed his horse to the front and leveled a loaded and cocked crossbow at Rane. He grinned back, showing the few teeth he had left, all black and ruined. He wore leather armor over stained clothes; a desperate man, indeed. "Looks like we interrupted you doing something interesting, you standing there, sword in hand, covered in blood. You've not been killing that pretty wife of yours, have you?"

"She's inside, safe," said Rane.

The leader chuckled. "That's good. I'd hate to think of her coming to harm before she's got a chance to know the boys and me."

"Why're we bothering talking? Just shoot him, and let's get paid," said the man next to him, covered in Nortlunder tattoos even though he had a Balrussian's flat face. He produced a double-edged sword from a battered scabbard. The blade had more notches in it than straight edges, but Rane had no doubt it could still do what it was designed to do.

"I recognized the sword," shouted Jeriah, sitting further back in the group, all red-faced and spitting as if trying to work himself up into a righteous fury. "It's a Legion blade. Just like I told you." He had a rusted old sword in his hand, probably stolen off his father. Rane was amazed he even knew which way to hold it.

Rane looked over the others, as calm as if he'd just met them while out for an afternoon stroll. He could see no threat amongst them. None that would stand before *Kibon*'s might. Still, he reminded himself that he'd not killed a man for two years. Better to talk them out of their foolishness and send them home. "Why don't you just get down from your horses, and we can sort out whatever's got you all so worked up."

The leader jabbed his crossbow towards him. "That old fool of a sheriff tried convincing us that you were just some old veteran like us, trying to get by after the war. But we knew better. You Legion types are always so easy to spot. Think yourselves so fucking clever. Now put your sword down and step away from it, with your hands where I can see them."

"You've got the wrong man — you really have. Allow me to offer you some water, and you can be on your way," Rane replied, watching each one to see who'd move first. He took a step closer to them as he spoke. Excitement raced through him. His sword screamed to be unleashed. "My home isn't much, but it's not completely lacking in hospitality."

"Put down your sword," snarled the man, squinting against the sun. "I won't ask again. There's a reward out for you Legionnaires. Ten thousand gold pieces, and they don't care if you're dead or alive."

"Why would anyone want to offer a reward for me?" replied Rane. He stepped closer to the leader's horse as his mind calculated the order of the bounty hunters' deaths. "You've made a mistake."

"Get off our land," shouted Kara, stepping out on to the porch, pistol in hand. "I'll not warn you again." Her voice startled the leader, her weapon even more so, and Rane watched the man swing his crossbow towards her.

There was the faintest of whispers as Rane's sword slipped free of its sheath. It was the most seductive sound in the world. *Kibon* — curved, single-edged, beautiful — sang as it cut through the air, just as the crossbow discharged. Blood followed as the hand still gripping the crossbow tumbled towards the ground. Rane flowed forward, taking the Balrussian next. He felt no resistance as he sliced the man from hip to hip. *Kibon* had been created to kill demons, after all, and there was no man nor armor that could resist it. Energy flooded into Rane as he took the man's life, a thousand times more powerful than when he'd killed the Bracke. He almost screamed in delight.

He continued past, his veins on fire, moving on to the third man and plunging his sword through the bounty hunter's horse. He was one with his sword. Rane was aware of someone somewhere shouting, of horses snorting in fear as the tang of blood filled their nostrils, but none of it mattered. The man fell, and Rane took his head from his shoulders with a flick of his blade before he hit the ground. Every move was instinctive, as if Rane had never left the battlefield.

One of the other men charged. Rane skipped to the side, watched a blade slice empty air in front of him and struck back on the turn. Rane's sword sliced through the rider; blood sprayed across his face, warm and wet, and it took one heartbeat more before the man realized he was dead.

The fifth man fared no better.

One man was left, all fight gone. He looked down at Rane in horror, facing his death. "You're a demon!" he cried before turning his mount. He spurred it into a gallop back the way the hunters had come only moments earlier. Rane knew he couldn't let him get away. He ran after the man, legs pumping, picking up speed. Energy flowed through him from the sword, powering him. He pounded along the dirt track, staring at the bounty hunter's back, willing himself to close the gap. *Kibon* screamed in his mind, demanding the bounty hunter pay the price for his folly.

But the man had too much of a lead and had picked up too much speed. Rane stopped, cursing, and watched him disappear over the crest of the hill. The kid would be back with more men — you could bet on that. Rane smiled. Let them all come. They would find death waiting for them.

He turned and walked back to his front yard, catching his breath and letting the pounding of blood slow down in his veins. He could see the bodies scarring his beautiful home. Five men dead in just under two minutes.

Jeriah lay in the dirt, cut from shoulder to hip. His dead eyes stared up at the sky as if he was watching the clouds drift past. Rane bent down and brushed his eyelids closed, unable to remember killing him. Rane had acted without thought, as he'd been trained to do. He tried to feel some regret at the boy's death, but he had none. The boy was a fool. He'd thought he'd found easy money. His choice had brought him nothing but death.

Rane glanced down at *Kibon* in his hand. Not a drop of blood remained on it. It hummed with energy, alive, beautiful. Let the world's armies come against him. It would carve a hole through them all.

Only the leader was still alive. He sat on the ground, covered in his own blood, clutching the stump that was once his right hand and crying in fear and pain. Rane crouched before him. "Why's there a bounty on my head?"

"Bastard. You evil bastard. You've killed me," spat the man. Tears ran down his face, a hard man broken by the touch of death. Already his skin had turned marble white as the blood leaked from him. He didn't have much time left.

"I didn't ask for this," replied Rane. "You came to my door. So I ask again — why?"

The man glared at him, full of anger and fear. "Fuck you. Who knows? Who cares? There's a price on your head. Nothing else matters."

"It does to me. We fought the Rastaks and their demons. We killed them all. Mankind is still alive because of us," replied Rane. "Why would anyone want us dead?"

"Fuck you," said the leader, blood spilling from his lips. "We both know you're not letting me go. So just kill me. And kill the next poor bastards who come to get you. And the next. But one day, you won't be quick enough, or you won't have that fucking sword to hand, and then you'll pay for all you've done."

"All we did was win the war," whispered Rane.

The bounty hunter crumpled at Rane's feet, more blood staining the ground. Rane lifted him up to see if he was still alive, but the thin, delicate cut from one side of his neck to the other told him there was no point. Again, he looked at his sword, unaware of even making the killing stroke. He shivered as the magic flowed through him.

Rane rose to his feet and retrieved the scabbard. It was a simple red sheath, as elegant in its own right as the blade it housed. He placed the tip of the sword into it, but stopped. The thought of slipping the blade back into darkness pained him. After being asleep for so long, it deserved to stay out in the world. He looked at his reflection in the polished metal and his own eyes pleaded for him not to do it. The blade was his. Its power was his. There'd be more men to kill. Best be ready. Best be waiting.

Only when he gazed around at the dead bodies that littered his land and saw his beautiful home stained with their blood did he find the strength to push the blade home. It sighed as it disappeared from view. He may love the sword, but the sword loved death more.

"Nathaniel?"

He spun around. "Kara?" She sat propped against the side of the cottage, barely visible in the rising gloom. A crossbow bolt jutted from her breast.

4

The bolt had struck Kara high on her breast. The fact that she was still alive was a good thing — it had missed her heart. If it had missed her lung as well, it was nothing he couldn't fix. He'd dealt with far worse in the war. As long as there was no blood on her lips, she'd be fine.

"It hurts." Kara's words were a whisper. "I think I'm dying."

"It just feels that way." Rane took her hand, and tried not to worry about how cold her skin felt. "Just breathe slowly. I'll fix everything."

"Will your sword work its magic on me?" Kara tried to laugh, but only cried out in more pain. She looked up at him with tear-filled eyes. "I'm scared, Nathaniel."

"Don't be. Everything is going to be all right. I'm going to get some bandages from inside, and then I'll come back and remove the bolt. Okay?"

Kara nodded. Rane squeezed her hand one more time and ran inside the house. He rummaged through drawers, looking for the bandages. How could his home, his sanctuary, have come to this? He had chosen the location to avoid the world, and yet death had still found him.

He returned to Kara a few moments later. She smiled when she saw him. He knelt beside her, kissed her cheek. "I told you I wouldn't be long."

"Do you think the baby's safe?" asked Kara.

"If it's anything like you, it'll be fine. Tough as can be," replied Rane. He almost choked on the words, and tried not to think too much about the truth behind them. Instead, he concentrated on treating her wound. He used a small knife to cut her blouse away from the bolt, only to find it was much lower than he'd hoped. He stopped and checked Kara's face once more. She was pale, but there was no blood on her lips. A good sign that the bolt had missed her lung.

Kara groaned as she tried to shift position.

"Try and stay still," said Rane, helping her.

She squeezed his hand back, but there wasn't much strength left in it. Fear swept over Rane. She shouldn't be fading this quickly if the bolt hadn't hit anything vital.

"I'm going to pull the bolt out now," he said, wrapping his hand around it. "It's going to hurt, probably more than it does now, but it'll pass. I'll be able to fix the wound once I've done it. Okay?"

Her eyes fluttered. She coughed. "Do it."

Rane let go of the bolt. He stared at the blood on her lips; the blood he'd been dreading, the blood that said the bolt had punctured a lung. He couldn't pull it free — doing so would kill her instantly. He rested his head against hers.

She coughed more blood. "Have you done it yet? Have you pulled the bolt out?"

"Yes," he lied. Tears ran down his cheeks. He didn't want Kara to see him cry, but there was nothing he could do.

"Huh. Wasn't so bad after all."

"You're so brave." He kissed her cheek.

"Feeling cold. Has it got cold?"

Rane shifted her until she lay in his arms, resting against his chest. They had a view over the front yard unspoilt by the dead. The sun washed over the grass, and somewhere a couple of birds sang. "Is that better?" he asked.

"My favorite place is in your arms." Kara coughed again, and Rane held her tighter as if that could stop Heras from taking her.

"Just rest. You'll feel better soon."

"It's stopped hurting."

"That's a good sign."

"You're a terrible liar, Nathaniel Rane. One of the things I liked about you. Promise me something."

"Anything."

"Find Marcus. Make sure he's safe. Tell him I love him."

"You can tell him yourself. We'll go and find him together." His voice started to crack. After all the death he'd seen, all the friends and comrades lost, he should be able to handle this, but it felt like he was dying, too.

"Promise me, Nathaniel." More blood spilled from her mouth.

"I promise." The tears ran freely down his cheeks as his heart broke. He wiped the blood from her chin.

"I'm scared. I..."

"Shhh. I'm here." Rane stroked her face. "Save your strength."

Kara's eyes grew wide as she gripped Rane's hand for all she was worth. "I love you so much."

"I love you too," replied Rane, but the light had gone from her. He brushed his hand over her eyes, closing them. At least her suffering was over. He put his hand over his mouth, as if that would stop all the emotions within him from spilling out, but as he gazed down on her, he knew it was impossible. He held her as gut-wrenching sobs shook his body, unable to believe his beautiful wife was dead. Her life — their life — gone. Their baby...

He sat with her in his arms, looking out over their home. All of it was gone now. Whatever dreams, whatever hopes — dead and ruined. He was a husband no more, a father no more. How could it be? How could their life turn around so completely in the space of a day?

Rane picked up Kara, carried her into the house and laid her on the bed, pulling the covers over her so she looked like she was sleeping.

Rane knelt beside her. "I'm sorry, my love. I let you down. I should've protected you and kept you safe. I'm sorry." It was hard to believe he'd never see her again, laugh with her, make love with her. Never kiss her lips, or hear her say his name. Two years together hadn't been long enough. Not nearly enough. He tried to memorize every detail of her face, from the little cluster of freckles on her cheeks to the wrinkle in her brow. His emotions got the better of him, and the weight of his love threatened to crush him there and then. He had no idea how he'd survive her loss.

He ran his hand over her stomach, over the baby within; tried to imagine the life that had been growing in there, a child he was never going to be able to hold in his arms. He rested his forehead against it, and sobbed. He cried for Kara, for the baby, and for himself.

But the voice didn't let him mourn for long. It whispered that there wasn't time to grieve. The bounty hunter would be back soon, with more men. Of that there was no doubt. Men to punish for what the others had done.

With the voice came anger, pushing his grief to one side. Let them come, he thought. There was a reckoning to be had. He looked at the bodies in his yard. Those men had destroyed his home and his life, and their deaths hadn't come close to addressing the balance. He would paint the world red if he had to, for it owed him a debt that he would collect. Someone had set these killers on him, set killers on the rest of the Legion, and caused Kara to get killed. Killed his unborn child. Whoever had done that was going to pay, even if kings and queens had to fall beneath his blade.

He left Kara, went inside and cleaned all the blood from his body, hands and face. He looked at himself in the mirror as he did, and saw a long-unseen face stare back. He wasn't a man of peace. What a fool he'd been to think otherwise.

After dressing, he stuffed spare clothes into his saddlebag and then pulled out a small chest from his closet. Another relic from the war, something else Kara had wanted him to get rid of. He glanced at her still form and tried not to think of all the ways he'd let her down.

Inside were two flintlock pistols, made by the famous gunsmiths of Eldacre especially for the Legion. Beside them were two horns of powder and a pouch of lead balls. Rane took his time cleaning both pistols, and then loaded them. He poured fresh powder into the flash pan and closed the frizzen to keep it safe, then poured powder down the barrel, followed by one of the balls wrapped in a bit of wadding. He pushed the ramrod down to compact everything as tightly as possible in the barrel before plugging everything in place with another piece of cloth. He strapped the holsters to his belt, then added the powder and ammunition to the saddlebags. Armed, he pulled the last item out of the chest — his old leather greatcoat. He slipped it on and it was like he'd never taken it off. The coat hid the guns, but not his intentions.

In the main room, he built a fire in the hearth and, with a few strikes of a flint, set it alight. He watched the flames catch and dance across the wood, feeling the heat on his skin. Once it was burning well, he used the poker to knock some of the wood out of the hearth and into the room. It didn't take long for the fire to spread, finding its way along the floor to the walls.

As smoke filled the room, he returned to Kara. By the Gods, how was he going to say goodbye? She looked so beautiful lying there. Some part of him believed that, somehow, she'd open her eyes and life would go back to normal. But the fury in him knew otherwise. The voice reminded him that a different path waited. He kissed her already-cold skin. "I love you. I love you so much."

He took her necklace and locket from around her neck and tied it to his wrist. At least he could take some part of her with him.

He marched from the house, but only managed to walk a few yards. He couldn't leave her. He turned around to look at their house, wanting to go back inside, hold her hand one last time, kiss her one last time, but the flames barred the way. The heat pushed him back. The smoke hid his home as everything he ever cared about burned away.

Just like that, his life was over. He was a man at peace with the world no longer.

Still he watched, unable to move. The rage inside him grew with the flames. He'd stick with the plan; head to Candra first and then north to find Marcus, make sure he was safe. And then, either with Marcus's help or without it, he would find everyone responsible for sending the bounty hunters to his home and kill them all, be they queen or president, lawmaker or lawbreaker. He wouldn't stop until all had paid the blood debt.

He secured his sword in place on his back. Rane the warrior had returned. The killer was free.

5

Rane urged his horse on down the dirt track, needing to get away from the cottage and the darkness within him. He rode hard, losing himself in the power of his horse, letting the thunder of hooves match the fury in his heart. The forest was a blur as he fought the temptation to head into town and look for the last bounty hunter and anyone else who might've helped him. The urge sat in his chest, pushing down on him, making it hard to breathe. The voice called out for blood. But no, he told himself, a promise had been made. An oath given. There would be blood enough later.

A mile on, he guided the horse off the track and headed north. He hated that the horse had to slow down to traverse the uneven ground, but it was a safer route to take. He wasn't going to make it too easy for anyone in pursuit.

The sun disappeared behind the canopy of leaves, throwing deep shadows around him and taking the warmth out of the day. Rane lost track of time as he allowed the horse to wander northwards, and then up — a sign that he was nearing the Eshtery quarry. If he stuck to the eastern flanks, he'd avoid the workers' huts that he knew were dotted around.

Slowing down also meant Rane had no distractions from his thoughts. Rage fought with grief, guilt tangled with sorrow. Thoughts of Kara and their child-to-be, so real only a day before, became like wisps of smoke in his mind. The pain burned inside worse than any wound he'd ever suffered. Why had those men come for him? Why couldn't the world have just left him in peace?

But he knew he'd wanted the fight, needed it. There was a part of him that rejoiced in the path of blood he now followed, free to kill. It was a madness that threatened to overcome everything else. There would be no holding back, no restraint. The guilty would die.

Rane rode on, chased by deepening shadows until he found a small stream. His horse needed water and a rest, so he dismounted, hobbled the horse, and left it to chew on some grass. He slumped down against a tree, giving in to his exhaustion. As he closed his eyes, his thoughts drifted from Kara to the men he'd killed.

Why did the five nations want the Legion dead? Their reward for saving mankind shouldn't be to be hunted and killed. It didn't make any sense.

He flexed his right hand, looking at his scar. When they'd started winning against the Rastaks, Rane had been proud of the mark. They all had. It was the sign of victory, that they'd done the right thing. Now, it could well be his death mark.

He must've drifted off at some point because when he next opened his eyes, it was dark. For a moment, he half-thought he was at home by the riverbank. He groaned when he remembered the reality. The horse was skittish, spooked by something, so he clambered to his feet to calm her down. His back complained as he did so, stiff and sore like an old man's on a cold day. He was too used to sleeping in comfortable beds in the warm. He cursed his weakness as he tried to soothe the horse.

The horse dug her hooves into the ground and neighed her discomfort once more. A second later, Rane heard what was bothering her.

Dogs. Hunting dogs. They were coming after him. The voice sighed with joy and his hand twitched to unleash *Kibon*.

The barking echoed through the woods, making it hard to judge the direction. They'd set a lot of dogs on him, too, judging by the noise.

Rane had two choices: run and hope for the best, or stay and fight, sword in hand. Hiding wasn't an option while the dogs had his scent.

The cacophony of barks grew louder, a wall of sound surrounding him as he tried to work out what to do. The horse skittered, eager to be anywhere but there.

Run or stay. Run or stay. He tossed the options around in his mind like dice. The voice told him to fight. He could feel *Kibon*'s eagerness at the thought of blood. But the dogs wouldn't be alone. Men would be with them, and only the Gods knew how many. *Good. Plenty to kill.*

But to wait in the dark for an unknown number of enemies wasn't a plan. Even with the sword's powers, to try to fight too many was suicide. Rane had no desire to do that yet.

Fighting wasn't the answer. Not yet.

The horse reared up, begging to be let loose, eyes wild with fear — and suddenly the answer was obvious. Rane removed all his ammunition and powder from the saddlebags and fixed them to his belt. He ripped an old shirt in two and tied the cloth around each of the horse's front legs.

"I'm sorry, girl," he said to the horse, then slapped her rear as hard as he could. Not that she needed the encouragement to run. Rane watched her disappear into the darkness. Let the dogs chase her. By the time they caught up with the horse and found it riderless, he'd be far away.

Picking up his waterskins, Rane climbed the nearest oak. The thick branches carried him high above the ground and mingled with other trees, allowing him to jump from one to another. He moved carefully, losing himself in the shadows and the leaves until he found a deep, dark nook to slink down into. He folded his coat around him, becoming a shadow. He waited, listening to the hounds as they got closer and closer, his mouth dry in anticipation.

He spotted them quick enough, following his trail from Eshtery. At least twenty of them — all good hunting dogs. The townsfolk must've spent the day gathering the hounds to give chase. He was a fool for falling asleep and making it easy on them. Rane had lost his edge in the two years since the end of the war. It'd been all too easy living with Kara in his cottage, being happy. He had to rediscover the soldier in him if he was going to fulfill his oath and get his revenge. He'd not make such simple mistakes again.

The dogs reached the tree he'd been sleeping under, swarming around its base and snapping at his scent, but losing it again at the water's edge. They barked and howled their frustration.

Torchlight flickered in the darkness, following quickly on the hounds' tails. Riders. One for every dog, and a lot more besides. No one was taking any chances by the looks of things, sticking together and taking care in the dark. As they got closer, he saw their weapons. Swords and knives glinted in the torchlight, and the odd pistol, too. Rane smiled. They'd no idea he was above them, watching, waiting like death. It would be so easy to just jump down and let *Kibon* loose. His heart raced at the thought.

Do it, the voice urged. *Take their strength.*

"He's crossed the water, trying to lose us," shouted one man as he caught up with the dogs. Rane tried to see who it was, but without any luck. Were these his neighbors who hunted him, or more bounty hunters?

"Well, get them on the other side then, Davey. Let's not waste time," answered an older man, a voice Rane knew well. The sheriff, Jahn. So much for his easy smiles and claims of friendship. "Shouldn't have to state the obvious."

Davey and two others cajoled the dogs across the stream. Once over, the hounds were off like a shot with the scent fresh again in their nostrils.

"Whoo!" yelped Davey. "We've got him." He took off with the other two without waiting for the rest of the group.

Jahn wasn't so eager, and waited for the others to catch up so he could watch them cross over the water. Rane could see the top of his head; the perfect spot to slip a knife in. All he had to do was drop down.

More men passed beneath. Little did they know how close to dying they all were. The voice knew. It pushed Rane to act; to strike first, to be the warrior that had driven the Rastaks to their deaths and destroyed Heras' demons. Rane ground his teeth together as he held his fury back. It wasn't the right time. These weren't the ones who had to pay.

"Is he as dangerous as they say?" asked a young lad, riding near the back of the pack, almost too small for his saddle. His voice sounded like it had only just broken that summer.

"Who told you that, son? He's just a man, like your father or me," replied Jahn. "He's just got himself in a bad situation."

"But he killed his wife, didn't he?"

"We don't know that. We've just got that bounty hunter's word for what happened up at his cottage. Until we speak with the man himself, I'm not passing any judgments."

"Yes, sir," replied the boy, but he didn't sound too convinced.

Another man picked up on it and laughed. "Think we should send Johnny back to his mam? Don't want him getting scared in the dark, now."

"Worry about yourself, Simon Wayland," snapped Jahn. "The man we're hunting has already killed six men. Only a fool wouldn't be worried."

"Ah, be off with you," replied Simon. "We've got more than enough men here. He's just a crazy man with a sword. No more than that."

The older man snorted. "I've heard enough tales of what the Legion did in the war. They were deadly fighters. If they've all gone crazy, that don't make them any less dangerous, only more so. Respect who you're hunting, or they'll be adding your name to the dead."

The men rode across the stream and passed under the tree where Rane was hiding.

"I'm scared," said the young kid, still loitering at the back. "Not sure I really want to be doing this."

"Don't you worry, son," assured Jahn. "We've got enough of us here to look after you. You won't be doing any fighting."

"Can't I go home?"

"You'll be safer with us. Can't send you off on your own in the dark in case you find him. What would your ma say to me then? Skin me alive, she would." Jahn laughed. "I'd rather face the man we're hunting than your ma all riled up."

The boy did his best to join in the joke, but his face gave away his fears. He kicked his horse to join up with the others and only succeeded in spooking the beast. It reared up on its hind legs with a snort of displeasure, throwing the boy from his saddle. He hit the ground hard and lay half in the water, dazed as can be. And staring straight up at Rane.

Time stopped. Rane knew he should move — kill the child, kill Jahn, kill them all — but the boy's face held him fast. So he just stared back, wondering when the shouting would start.

It only took as long as the boy needed to get air back in his lungs. "He's up in the trees! Up in the trees!"

"What?" Jahn spun his horse around, searching the branches.

The kid was on his feet, pointing. "There! There he is." He fumbled his sword as he tried getting it out of the loop on his belt and the weapon fell into the water, but the old man wasn't so slow. He had a flintlock pistol in his hands and pulled the trigger. He still hadn't spotted Rane, but the shot would summon the hue and cry.

Rane launched himself out of the tree, straight at Jahn. He crashed into him, knocking him from the saddle. Rane landed on his feet; the old man didn't, and a knee to the head put Jahn out for the count. The kid was screaming for all he was worth, but Rane ignored him and swung up onto the old man's horse. He could hear the others racing back, shouting and whooping. He spurred the horse and took off down the riverbed.

He bent low over the horse's neck as it galloped through the water. Bushes and trees blocked off both sides, creating a tunnel to charge down. A low branch just missed his head and Rane prayed one of the other riders wouldn't be as lucky. Again, there was the urge to stand and fight, but he pushed the thought away.

He spotted a break in the shrubbery to his left and guided the horse through it. The animal seemed happier on drier ground and found another burst of speed as it weaved through the giant oaks, growing more confident in the night. Rane risked a glance back and saw the torches burning through the darkness in pursuit. They were still a good distance away, but closing far too quickly for his liking.

The ground slowly rose, making it harder for his horse keep its pace, but Rane pushed it on. He knew the animal's strength would fail soon, but he needed to cover as much ground as possible. "Come on, you can do it," he urged as the ground climbed higher.

A patch of open sky loomed ahead as he reached the edge of the forest. Bursting out into open ground filled with nothing but tall grass felt like victory. He could do this.

Without letting the horse slow, he swung down from the saddle and hit the ground at a run. The horse carried on as Rane took off up the hill on foot. Without the drumming of the horse's hooves filling his ears, he could hear the hue and cry getting closer.

Keeping low, he ran along the edge of the forest to higher ground. He knew the quarry was somewhere nearby. If he could reach that, he could find a route down and away that the horses and dogs couldn't follow.

On and on he went. The air burned in his lungs and his legs complained, but he didn't slow down. He didn't have that luxury. How had he let himself get so out of shape? He stumbled on a hidden rock, twisting his ankle, sending shards of pain shooting up his leg. He reached up to touch the hilt of his sword and felt a burst of energy run through him, masking the pain, fuelling him on.

His world consisted of the five yards in front of his face. Up and up he went. Couldn't stop. He'd rest later, and live. Slow down now and he'd die. Sweat stung his eyes. His tongue stuck to the roof of his mouth. He'd kill for a slug of water, but there wasn't time even for that.

Just as he thought he couldn't go on, something changed in the air, a sense of space looming even though he couldn't see it yet. He half-ran, half-crawled up the rocky slope. Escape was ahead.

He clawed at stone and dirt as he scrambled onwards, his feet shifting and sliding under him. And then the world disappeared as the ground dropped three hundred feet.

The quarry lay before him, hacked into the side of the mountain as if by the Gods themselves. He flopped down onto his stomach and lay there, panting, blinking the sweat from his eyes as his heart raged inside. Rane gazed down on a sea of pine trees that covered the base of the quarry, miles long. The mining areas were to the east. Little wooden sheds were dotted here and there, with chutes and flutes zigzagging between them all. It was a route out that the hunting party couldn't follow. All he had to do was climb down. Somehow.

"You're not going to die on us, are you, son?"

Rane spun around at the voice, nearly falling over the edge as he did so.

Jahn stood beside some rocks, left eye all but swollen shut. His pistol pointed straight at Rane's head. He had ten men with him, a mixture of swords and knives in their hands, all looking damn happy to use them.

Jahn smiled, as if he was meeting Rane like any other day. "An old man like me isn't up for all this running around in the dark. That's best left to the young 'uns. Me, I like to use my brain a bit more. So when I came to after you'd kindly kicked me in the face, I thought, 'if I was a desperate man on the run, what would I do?'" He wagged a finger at Rane. "Especially after tricking the hue and cry once already."

Rane glanced back down the hill. He'd not make it two yards before the men would be on him. Same if he tried making a break for the woods. Fighting didn't seem much of an option either. He could take the others in a sword fight, but Jahn's pistol changed things. He had no idea if a head shot would kill him, but Rane had no desire to find out — and besides, getting hit by a bullet could put him down long enough for them to take his sword away. The voice scoffed at his caution, told him he was fast enough, strong enough for it not to matter. The voice wanted blood.

Jahn sniffed the air with satisfaction. "So I headed up here with some of the boys and thought I'd wait to see if you turned up. It was a bit of a walk, but I've had chance to sit and rest my legs since we got here." He glanced over at his men, most of them people Rane was on nodding terms with back in Eshtery, as if he wanted confirmation about how clever he was. He got a load of grins back, buffing up his ego. "And here you are."

"Here I am," agreed Rane. His breathing was almost back to normal. He held up his hands in surrender. "Mind if I get to my feet and have a sip of water?"

"Sure, go for it, Mr Rane," said Jahn, his gun rock-steady in his hand. "We've waited long enough for you. Another minute or two won't matter."

Rane stood up and drank, soothing his dry throat. The men's eyes never left him, swords and blades wavering as they watched. For all Jahn's confidence, the men with him looked petrified. The Gods only knew what they'd been told about Rane. It was amazing how he had turned from neighbor to monster so quickly in their eyes. So easily. Then again, he'd made the change pretty quick himself — from husband to killer, from farmer to murderer.

There was no denying, though: they wanted him dead. Rane took a second slug of water. There were five yards between them. Close enough to kill them all. If he could take Jahn first before he got a shot off, the others would fall easily enough. The sword would make him fast enough. Memories flashed by — from the war, of others foolish enough to stand before him. He'd run before he had the sword, but never since. *Kibon* made him invincible.

"Surprised you're all so keen to track me down," said Rane, buying time. "Didn't take you as a reward chaser, Jahn."

The old man arched his back and cracked his neck to one side. "I'm not, but you killed a boy. I can't let that go, reward or not — even if I like you, which I do."

"Miller'son came to my house with six killers, Sheriff. I don't regret what happened to him because he made that choice. If he hadn't, both he and my wife would most probably still be alive."

At least Jahn had the decency to look away for a moment. "Kara was a good woman. She's a real loss to the world, but the rights and wrongs and the who-did-what's are not for me to decide. My job's just to bring you back to stand trial. No more, no less. Now, you ready? We've got a long walk back down that hill, and I'd rather get back to town sooner rather than later."

Rane nodded. "I am."

"I want you to put your weapons on the ground, starting with your sword. Do it real slow and maybe I won't shoot you. Try anything else and you'll find out how much a bullet hurts."

"I've been shot before," said Rane.

"In that case, you shouldn't be in a hurry to experience it again."

"What's going to happen to me when we get back?"

Jahn shrugged. "We're going to take you back to town and lock you up. The Queen's Justice will be here in a couple of days. They can sort out this mess. You killed people tonight, rightly or wrongly, but I can't pretend you're not a Legionnaire anymore, so I expect they'll be taking you to answer for that first."

"Not sure I like the sound of that," replied Rane.

"Don't see how you got much choice, son. You've got nowhere to run, unless you want to die right now."

Jahn was right. Rane reached over his shoulder for his sword.

"Go slowly, now," warned Jahn, straightening the arm that held the pistol.

Rane smiled. "I'm just doing as you asked." His hand wrapped around the hilt. Immediately, his tiredness disappeared with a jolt of energy. The world crystallized into clarity as he lifted the sword and scabbard off his back.

He could hear the dogs barking as they ran up the hill towards them. It wasn't just Jahn and his men that he'd have to deal with if he was to escape. He gripped *Kibon* with both hands, only too aware that there was a part of him excited at the prospect of shedding blood. "You're a good man, Jahn. I wish there was another way."

Something in his eyes must've warned Jahn. The sheriff raised his pistol, but he wasn't quick enough to stop Rane from jumping off the edge of the cliff.

6

Rane dropped, gripping the sword, watching the pine trees race towards him, praying *Kibon* would protect him. Time slowed long enough for him to see the madness in what he'd done; to doubt the power of his sword's magic. And then he hit the trees.

He twisted and turned, tucked his head in his arms as he smashed into the pines hard and too damn fast, bouncing from one branch to another. Pine needles whipped him, cutting him up from head to toe. Branches battered him every which way. Every blow knocked more air from his lungs and the sense from his brain.

He hooked one arm over a branch to try and stop his fall, but only managed to wrench his arm out of its socket. He didn't even have the time or the breath to scream as he tumbled on. Two of his ribs went next as he slammed into another branch. Somewhere, the sword was knocked from his hand, but he barely registered it as his jaw crashed into a branch and the bone broke with it. Breaking through each canopy of pine needles was like hitting a stone wall. Something slashed across his face, splitting his forehead from one side to the other. Blood splattered his skin as pain piled on top of pain.

And when he thought he'd never stop falling, Rane dropped through the last canopy of leaves and hit the ground.

By the Gods, he hurt. He tried to wipe the blood from his eyes but couldn't move his arm. His broken ribs complained as he rolled over and tried to get to his feet. He found enough breath to scream out, not caring if anyone heard him.

He sucked in air, trying to suppress the agony that racked his body. At least the pain told him he was alive. Hopefully Jahn would think Rane had killed himself. Let them think he was dead, and leave him well enough alone. One thing was for sure: if they came for him now, he might as well have died in the fall. There was no way he could defend himself.

Back on his feet, he staggered to a tree and slammed his shoulder into it, knocking the limb back into its socket. He nearly screamed again, but managed this time to keep it under control. He moved it around carefully, aware of the bones grating, and thanked the Gods it wasn't his sword arm.

His sword. Panic hit him hard in the gut. The memory of it flying from his hand came back to him. Where was *Kibon*? Was that why the pain was out of control? Had the sword's magic deserted him?

His head whipped from side to side as he searched for it, breathing in ragged gulps, heart racing, pulling bushes and scrub aside. He scrambled in the dirt like a madman. A dying man. He couldn't lose it, not after everything. Not now. Where was it?

His head spun as a stab of pain took him in the gut, and he fell to his knees. Vomited what little was in him. An old wound reopened somewhere. He could feel the blood seeping out. He blinked more blood from his eyes as he crawled through the pine needles, groping for his weapon.

He wrapped his arms around a tree and hauled himself back onto his feet, and only just stopped himself from pitching over again.

Rane screamed as another past injury stabbed him in the center of his spine. He pushed himself off from the tree. Reeling like a drunkard, he fumbled along in the dark, searching for *Kibon*. Where was his sword?

He gripped his thigh as the leg went from under him. A six-inch cut opened above his knee, a wound from some long-forgotten battle-field. He'd laughed at the time, drunk on *Kibon*'s power and the invincibility it gave.

What he'd give for that feeling now. Instead, he crawled on his hands and knees, feeling his way. Desperate. Dying.

The pain lost all meaning as blood ran down his chest, his arms, his legs, over his hands. How much could one man lose before...? He shook the thought from his head. He just needed his sword. He wasn't going to die today. Couldn't give up yet.

He crawled another yard, prayed that he was close. Prayed to Heras to spare him one last time, spare him until he'd gotten his revenge. Kara demanded it. Their baby deserved it.

He sucked in air as best he could, trying to force his lungs to work as he thrust his arm out one more time. Rane dug his fingers into the earth. Tiredness swept over him, pressing him into the ground, but he forced his eyes open and dragged himself forward one last time.

Just enough strength left in him for that, but no more. He closed his eyes, too exhausted to fight any longer. Almost too dead to notice the little buzz twitching inside. Almost, but not quite. It pushed and prodded at the darkness.

Kibon.

It called him. He pushed himself up, crawled another yard.

The sword was near. It had to be. He was close enough to feel its magic. Hear its voice. Feel it healing him.

The knowledge spurred him on. On his hands and knees, eyes open, he knew it was close. He cursed the night and the shadows, cursed the wood and the pine, cursed everything that hid the sword from him. But he grew stronger with each new inch of ground he covered. It was near. He was close.

A glint caught his eye; a stray steak of moonlight resting on some-thing metal, buried in a bed of pine needles. He scrambled towards it.

The moment Rane closed his hand over *Kibon*'s hilt, its power hit him in a rush. He cried out again with a pleasure that was as extreme as the pain he'd just endured.

Holding it close, he immediately felt better. The edge of his pain softened. His wounds closed before his eyes, skin stitching back together. His breathing returned to normal and he could feel his bones knitting, tendons and muscles repairing themselves. Even his bruises disappeared. Minute by minute, cut by cut, he grew stronger until it was as if he'd never jumped.

Lying back against a tree, he checked his sword. Had to make sure it wasn't damaged in the fall. He examined every inch of the steel, slowly, carefully, as he withdrew it from its scabbard. His reflection stared back at him, bloody and filthy but otherwise unmarked. He thanked the Gods for *Kibon*. How many times had it saved his life now?

With his sword naked in his hand, the urge to go back and find Jahn and the others was overwhelming. What had he done to be hunted like that? After that scum had come to his house, they deserved to die. Bastards. Rane staggered to his feet, feeling stronger, full of fury. They'd killed his wife, murdered his unborn child, and then had the nerve to hunt him down. He'd show them the monster they'd unleashed. He'd drink their fucking blood.

No. He had to calm down. Think things through. Calm the madness down. Going back and killing them wasn't going to solve anything; wasn't going to bring Kara and the baby back, or help her brother. The plan. He had to stick to the plan. Revenge could come later, and would be all the sweeter for it.

He placed the sword back in its sheath and slung it over his shoulder once more. Then he washed the aftertaste of death away with a mouthful from his waterskin. He'd head to Candra. Find Marcus. Make sure he was safe. And then Rane could go after everyone who'd caused this whole sorry mess in the first place.

Candra was north — that he knew — so he started to walk. Anything from five to ten days north, but best not to think of that. Nor his lack of food. Worrying about that wouldn't change anything. He still had his pistols and his sword. Everything else could be found.

It took two hours of hard walking to reach the edge of the quarry.

The sun was a good way up in the sky, but the warmth of the day couldn't get past the chill he felt in his heart.

Rane kept away from the main paths as much as possible, and whenever he heard horses, he dropped down into the undergrowth until he was sure they'd passed by. It made for slow going, but only foolish men and the dead knew no caution.

When the sun fell once more, Rane found a hollow with thick bushes all around where he could settle down for the night. He cut a small hole in the side of the largest bush, just big enough so he could crawl inside and lie down. He brushed fallen leaves over himself for an extra layer of insulation; then, satisfied it would be all but impossible for anyone to see him, he went to sleep.

His dreams were full of friends long dead. One battle merged with another, full of blood, dirt, chaos. He saw the Rastaks charging, their swords and clubs eager to take lives, and he alone stood in their way. The Jotnar roared in their ranks, slavering for blood. He wanted to run and hide, but the sword told him to stand his ground and fight. Kara screamed at him for being a fool, cursing him for leaving her as she tried to run from the enemy's path. A baby cried in her arms. He rushed to save her, but the Rastaks were quicker and she disappeared under their iron-clad feet. The Jotnar turned on Rane and he hacked and slashed, chopped and cut, but nothing slowed them down. The bodies piled high around him but still they came, endless, untiring. He kept on fighting, the sword demanding everything of him, ordering him not to stop while the Rastaks and their otherworld allies still lived. But with each death, the joy of battle filled him with ecstasy. He laughed with pleasure as body after body fell before *Kibon*, until a field of corpses lay beneath his feet.

But there were no demons among the fallen. Instead, there was Kara, lying among men and women and children and babies. All human. All dead. Blood covered Rane from head to foot but his sword remained spotless, shining bright. And he was screaming.

Rane woke up not knowing where he was, petrified at the vividness of his dream. The bushes smothered him, and he crawled out frantically, relieved that he wasn't on that battlefield. He wasn't that man. Yet.

But what was he? He'd lost everything he had ever wished for in a single day. Lost his love. Lost his future. Lost his hope.

Kara's death hit him harder than any army, hurt more than any weapon. He wanted the world to end. How could Kara be dead and he still alive? Had he caused her to die? He remembered the excitement he'd felt when the bounty hunters had turned up, how much he'd wanted to fight them — to kill them. Perhaps if he'd handled things differently... had he goaded them into attacking?

By the Gods, what was he becoming? He'd tried hiding in Eshtery from the monster within him, but fate had other ideas for him.

No. Kara's death wasn't his fault. The guilt lay with the bounty hunters and whoever had sent them. First he'd go to Candra, then Marcus. Then he'd find revenge and unleash the monster on them all.

7

Candra sprawled from the sea all the way along the River Tryste on both sides of its banks. From his viewpoint perched atop a hill, Rane could see the miles and miles of buildings crammed together, with Candra Castle at its heart. The Ascalonian flag fluttered above the highest tower, telling the world that Queen Ryanna, the first of her name, was in residence. He still remembered meeting her there at the end of the war; how she shone like an angel. How grateful she'd been for what the Legion had done, handing out medals, singing their praises. Now, she wanted them dead. His finger caressed *Kibon*'s hilt. Perhaps he'd call on her and let her know how he felt about her change of mind.

Pulling his coat tight around him, Rane set off down the hill towards the city.

Candra had been hit hard during the war. The city's walls had fallen the very same night the Legion had given up their souls. They'd emerged from the barracks, humming with power, to find the Rastaks swarming over the walls. It was as if they'd known what the Legion had done and decided to throw everything they had at the city in one last attempt to take it.

The Rastaks were too late. The Legionnaires met them. Four

hundred and fifty men and women against the tens of thousands of the enemy. They fought from street to street. Killed the Rastaks and their demons one by one. Reclaimed their city yard by yard.

The battle for Candra lasted eight days. After years of defeat and retreat, it was the Allied Nations' first victory. The turning point in the war.

The wounds inflicted on the city were still clearly visible, black scars running amongst the grey buildings. Rebuilding had begun, though it would clearly be a long time before it recovered fully.

Not much was left of Temple Square from what he could see, but the ugly block of the Legion's barracks still jutted up above its surroundings. Hopefully he could find some answers there.

Seven days had passed since Kara died. Physically, he was as strong as he ever had been — the sword had seen to that. His stomach was full of easy game and he had plenty of water, as well as rest. There'd been no pursuit from Eshtery. Probably Jahn had thought him dead from the fall, and for that — and that alone — Rane was grateful.

Mentally, it was a different matter. Haunted by Kara's death and consumed by his rage, he thought of nothing but the leaders of the five nations responsible for the bounty, and fantasized about how he'd make them pay. Ryanna of Ascalonia, tucked up in her castle, thinking herself safe behind its high walls, not knowing that the Legion used to play a game working out the best ways to get in. She'd wake to his knife on her throat. Old King Legus, back in Fascaly after years of exile, still fat and more concerned about the next conquest for his bed instead of the dangers lurking in the shadows. Perhaps when Rane showed him his heart, he'd realize his folly. The chief of the Nortlunders used to be Ingarra, but she'd been old before Rane had run away from the world and he had no idea whether she still controlled the cold mountains. But whoever warmed the seat of power there would find Rane whispering in their ear. Xiao Jia, Emperor of Naijin, would be harder to reach. The Naijins were fearsome fighters and Xiao's thousand bodyguards were the deadliest of all, but they'd be no match for *Kibon*.

He'd leave Souska for last. The Southern Islands were tribal. It would take time to find who held sway, but Rane was patient as death.

For now, though, Candra was within reach. Candra, and the barracks. His barracks.

He wrapped his sword up in a battered old cloak he'd found along the way and slung it under his arm. He hoped that would be enough to disguise *Kibon* while he was in the city. The scar was harder to hide, but he bandaged his hand with a strip of cloth. He could claim a recent injury if anyone asked. Not that he intended to get into too many conversations. He knew of ten thousand reasons why that would be a bad idea.

By the time he reached the main road, it was already full of traders taking livestock and produce into the city's various markets, despite the early hour of the day. He heard no mention of the Legion. No word of demons.

Others flocked to the city looking for work, driven from their homes across the country by poverty and the real threat of starvation, carrying all they owned on their backs or in their hands and what little hope they had left in their hearts. The farmers and traders looked on this traffic with suspicion, worried about what would be stolen if they weren't careful. Rane saw more than one whip lash out at a suspected thief and, more often than not, the refugees were encouraged to move on with a curse or two.

Eyes followed Rane as he weaved his way through the traffic. He didn't blame anyone for that — he knew he looked like a vagrant — but he quickened his pace all the same, eager to be swallowed up by the city. Anonymity amongst the crowds was going to be his greatest defense.

The road became more congested the closer he got to Candra as buildings sprang up on either side of the road; shacks no better than those in Eshtery — and some much worse — that looked like a good wind or some heavy rain would be the end of them. Homes for the desperate who'd fled to Candra but found its streets just as harsh as the villages they'd left behind. The threat of impending violence seemed to grow with each new dwelling as filthy lives did what they could to survive. More than a few whored themselves by the side of the road, and the price for their bodies ranged from a copper coin to a loaf of bread. So much for the supposed golden age of peace. Rane's anger rose again as he wondered what it had all been for.

The shacks and shanties ran right up against the city walls, where men had bled and died for this future. The visible parts of the walls were scarred and broken, burnt and bruised. The Rastaks had done their foul work well against them and, if an enemy were to strike again, they had little strength left to withstand another assault.

The west gate to the city was wide open and watched by a trio of guards with their minds on other things. Rane needn't have worried about being recognized, as they'd no intention of stopping anyone or checking anything. The flood of people passing through their station couldn't have been stopped even if they'd tried.

Past the gates, the sounds and smells of the city were overwhelming. Rane had been too long hidden away with Kara to deal with the hundreds of chattering voices smothering the air; haggling and bartering, laughing and joking, shouting and swearing. He winced at the stench — sweat, mud and shit mixed with coal fires, cooking aromas and the stink from the river to make something that was uniquely Candra.

The narrow streets had grown even narrower since he'd last been in the capital. At any moment, Rane felt one of the buildings could topple down on him as he made his way towards the river. Claustrophobia nagged at him, but there was little he could do about it. Wishing to be back at his cottage with Kara wouldn't change anything.

The reward posters plastered everywhere didn't help matters. Some had little gaggles of people gathered around them, while others looked long forgotten. Hate-filled slogans were daubed on other walls, cursing the Legion and all who'd fought in it, but there were no clues as to why they had become such targets. Still, it was a reminder of the danger he was in. Rane took a deep breath of putrid air and walked on, head down.

He stepped onto black soil, and sky opened up above him. The three blocks ahead of him were nothing but ashes underfoot, with only the odd chimney or corner wall standing like tombstones amid a scattering of rubble. Soon, the ground would be reclaimed, but for now the war wound was too raw for anyone to attempt a renovation. Rane could almost hear the screams of those who'd died, their ghosts too traumatized to let go of what was once their home.

The war had made so many people do desperate things to survive, to fight for just one more day; so why had the Legion become the hunted? Were their actions any worse than those of men who torched people in their homes? How many had lived because of the Legion? Ungrateful bastards. His fingers twitched at the thought, *Kibon* heavy in his hand.

Back amongst the tight streets, he pushed his way through until he reached the Tryste. The grey sky clung to the tops of the buildings as Rane headed for the Queen's Bridge a mile upriver, the main crossing point that would take him directly to the barracks.

The Queen's Bridge at least looked unchanged as it looped from one bank of the Tryste to the other. Built for Ryanna's great-grand-mother, it was a masterpiece of engineering and design, wide enough for two carriages to pass each other side by side, high enough for a warship to pass underneath unrestricted and strong enough to with-stand heavy winds and heavier traffic. Its grandeur never failed to impress, but it too was marred with tattered and faded reward posters declaring the Legion outlaw. Rane hurried over, keen to be on his way from Candra as soon as possible.

The crowds grew the nearer Rane got to the Legion's barracks, and with them came an air of excitement. Rane moved to the side of the street, wriggling his way through gaps where he could, pushing when that wasn't possible.

He stopped dead in his tracks once he entered the square in front of the barracks. There must have been a thousand people crammed into the courtyard, rammed together shoulder to shoulder like cattle. The air was filled with a cacophony of screamed curses and insults as the mob bayed for blood.

Gallows lined each side of the square. Most had corpses dangling from them, long dead and half-rotten. Rane couldn't get close enough to see any faces, but he had no doubt all had been Legionnaires.

In front of him, the barracks stood as black as death, a towering mausoleum for their lost hopes and lost honor, nothing but broken windows, shattered doors and walls covered in scrawls of hate and venom. He guessed the gallows were filled with whoever had been housed there. He could only pray that Jefferson wasn't amongst the dead.

Even so, the crowd hadn't gathered to watch old corpses swing in the wind, or to cheer in front of a ruined building. Not when there was a fresh scaffold and three empty nooses. The ropes danced in the breeze above a stage waiting for another grim performance.

Rane was jostled this way and that, and a sick feeling spread through his guts, his arms pinned to his sides by the weight of the mob. Trapped, he had no option but to watch.

It wasn't long before a hush fell over the crowd. Necks craned forward, eager to see.

A priest — a short, broad woman — stepped out of the barracks. Her dark hair was pulled back into a ponytail, revealing shaved sides and sunray tattoos that disappeared down her neck and into her heavy woolen robes. She paused, milking the moment, ensuring every eye was on her. Rane recognized her instantly — Mother Singosta of the Church of Odason, God of Life. Head of the Inquisition. Heretic hanger. Witch hunter. Mage killer.

She continued to the front of the scaffold while four city guards marched three hooded prisoners out behind her, pikes prodding anyone who slowed as they went. They had to be Legionnaires. A final guard followed behind, carrying a bundle of some sort in his arms.

Rane clawed his way closer, heart racing, fury building, his hand on *Kibon*'s hilt. The voice urged him to throw caution to the wind and carve his way to the front, telling him everyone in the square deserved to die. All the while, he watched the procession make their way to the top of the scaffold.

"Citizens!" cried Singosta from the front of the platform, eyes full of fervor. "All good people of Candra, loyal subjects to our great queen, Ryanna. I stand before you as Odason's servant so you can witness justice being done. Witness the balance put right. Witness the death of Heras' creations. Witness the execution of evil disguised as heroes."

On that signal, the guards pulled the hoods off the prisoners. The woman was Aeger, a fellow captain. The other two were familiar, but he couldn't put names to them. He hated himself for that. Whoever they were, they deserved better.

The three Legionnaires looked weak and disorientated, startled by the sunlight even on such a grey day. No doubt they'd been kept in the dungeons for far too long.

The crowd went berserk at the sight of them, delighting in their misery. Rane wanted to kill them all.

Singosta threw her arms wide above her head, and at once the crowd quieted. "The three standing before you were once heroes, celebrated from Nortlund to Naijin to here in Ascalonia. Little did we know that they had cavorted with Heras herself, taking from her terrible powers and killing in her name. Using magic."

"Bastards!" someone shouted from the crowd. "Scum!"

"Hang 'em!"

"Demon-lovers!"

The priest nodded along with the cries, as if agreeing with every-one, until again the hand signaled for silence. "I feel your fury. I understand your anger. By using magic, they betrayed us. Because of their Godsdamned bargain, they endangered us all. Now, Odason is a God of forgiveness, but I ask you: should we forgive them?"

"No!" a thousand voices chorused.

"Should we let them walk away and pretend they did no wrong?"

"No!"

Singosta knew how to play to a crowd, making the most of the mob's attention. Some priest. Rane was going to enjoy sliding *Kibon* through her heart. He squirmed and pushed, trying to force his way to the front of the crowd, but the bodies were jammed too closely together. He might as well have tried pushing through a wall.

Singosta grinned at the crowd. "Shall we make them hang?"

The roar from the square shook the very air. Rane had never heard such pleasure voiced before. Trapped, unable to move, he had no option but to watch as the Legionnaires' heads were placed in the nooses. A drum roll began from somewhere. Rane's heart raced in time with it. The voice screamed for him to attack, kill everyone, slash a path to his comrades — but then the trapdoor fell away and the three prisoners dropped. The crack of necks breaking could be heard even above the cacophony in the square. One by one, the Legionnaires twitched until finally they were still.

Tears ran down Rane's cheeks as the crowd rejoiced. But the horror had only just begun.

It was easy enough to miss at first. When Aeger gently twisted on her noose, it could have been the wind blowing, making her turn. But then her leg kicked out and her knee lifted. She was still alive. The other two jerked back to life with her, kicking frantically against the air, trying to get free as the rope stretched their necks.

The mob had noticed, too, and screams started cutting through the celebrations.

But Singosta obviously wasn't surprised. This freak show was what she'd planned. "See their demon magic at work? Even the rope can't kill them — such is Heras' gift. But we know the source of their power. Behold!"

The last soldier stepped to the front of the stage with the wrapped bundle in his arms. Singosta whipped the cloth away, revealing three curved swords.

Next to the swords were gloves, which Singosta put on with a flourish. She picked up one of the swords and held it aloft. The steel was dark grey in color, as if blemished in some way. "This is their power. Heras' magic is trapped within this blade. Because of this, these traitors can't die like you or I!"

The thousands of spectators in the square were silent.

Singosta walked over to Aeger, slashing the sword through the air as she went. She stopped in front of the Legionnaire and lifted her head so she could see the blade. "Is this what you want?"

Singosta waited, knowing that she had everyone's attention, then thrust the blade through Aeger's heart, twisting it until the Legionnaire was still once more. Singosta looked over her shoulder at her audience, eyes wide in mock horror, and then pulled the blade free. Even from where Rane was, he could see Aeger's blood being absorbed into the blade.

Seconds later, Aeger's eyes popped open and a gurgling cry forced its way out of her strangled throat. She kicked against the air, trying to find some purchase to alleviate the pressure on her neck.

The mob was silent, transfixed by what was happening on the scaffold. When Singosta next spoke, her voice was no more than a whisper, but still it managed to reach every corner of the square. "But Heras will never be victorious. Her power — their power — can be destroyed."

From the barracks, a giant of a man emerged. Naked from the waist up, he carried a blacksmith's anvil in his hands. Sunrays had been tattooed all over his muscled torso; they rippled as he moved. He marched to Singosta's side as if he were carrying something no heavier than a child, but when he placed it down on the stage, the scaffold shook.

"By the power of Odason," said Singosta, "may justice be done." She raised Aeger's sword above her head and then brought the weapon down onto the anvil with as much strength as she could muster.

The blade shattered on the anvil's edge — and Aeger stopped her dance. With the sword destroyed, the magic keeping her alive was gone. Death claimed her at last.

Rane couldn't take any more. He sucked in all his anger and then pushed out with all his might, sending those around him flying into their neighbors. A small bubble of space opened up and *Kibon* was out in an instant. He'd carve his way to the scaffold if he had to, but he'd not let the other Legionnaires suffer the same fate. He'd not let Aeger go unavenged.

"Legionnaire!"

It hung in the air for a moment before another voice snatched it up and threw it back out once more. "Legionnaire!"

All around Rane, heads turned and necks craned as others took up the cry. Scared faces peered at him, but already he could see them doing the sums, imagining what ten thousand gold pieces could do for their lives. Enough gold could make even the worst coward brave for a time. But he had *Kibon* in his hand and rage in his heart. Blood would flow.

8

"Legionnaire!" The cries spread as others took up the shout. Voices full of greed and excitement, like children eager for treats.

A man lunged at him, but *Kibon* sang out, cutting him down before he'd taken a second step, showing all of them the real reward for trying to capture a Legionnaire. Rane reversed the blade and thrust back under his arm as another tried to take him from behind. He felt the jolt with every kill, the power that flowed with the blood, igniting his fury further as he carved his way towards the gallows.

"Legionnaire! I saw him," shouted a man, knocking people out of the way to get to Rane. "Reward's mine." He had time to raise a fist before Rane opened his throat from ear to ear.

Again and again *Kibon* slashed out, cutting bodies down, filling Rane with power. The energy rushed through him, telling him he was unstoppable, indestructible. He hacked left and right, chopping down people like wheat, but more filled the gaps left by the dead and dying. Another fool fell before him, his blood painting one and all. They would see what it cost to mistreat the Legion.

It felt so good to unleash. Hack, slash, thrust. Rane fought without thinking, his fury unquenched. It would be a bloody day to remember. Let the fools fear another gallows show. Let them have night-mares the next time they thought they'd watch a Legionnaire dance.

Arms wrapped themselves around his legs. Rane raised *Kibon* to cut himself free, but stopped when he saw who held him: a girl, no more that seven or eight, all muddied face and filthy hair. Her eyes were filled with tears as she screamed at him to stop, to let her pa live.

Rane staggered back as the voice urged him to strike, to make her pay for her folly, but Rane couldn't. She was a child, and he'd not let *Kibon* claim her life.

Then he saw the corpses of those he'd already killed. The blood on his hands. By the Gods, what was happening to him? He kicked the girl off as the crowd stared at him in horror. He glanced up at the scaffold, at his comrades dangling on the ends of their nooses. Still too far away. He couldn't save them.

Could he even save himself?

Blood roared in his ears as stolen life forces pulsed through him, but he had to get his anger under control, get out of the square. Instead of enemies, he saw desperate people, scared of the monster in their midst. Using *Kibon* only to threaten, he retreated from the square. Still people came at him, but the threat of his sword kept them back.

"Someone get him!" screamed a woman, her voice shrill. "He's getting away." But Rane could feel the parting of bodies behind him without looking. He pressed on, and the pressure around him slackened.

"Legionnaire!" shouted a man next to him, but he too backed away from Rane. Others nearby were reluctant to take up the cry, but still it carried further out from the square. The crowd ebbed and flowed around him as some pushed forward, minds full of gold, while others pushed back, keen to stay alive. Rane knew at some point the spell would break when they realized he could be overwhelmed by sheer weight of numbers. He had to get out of the square. A glance told him the exit was only ten yards away, but it felt ten times further than that.

A flash of silver caught his eye as a man lunged in with a butcher's knife. Rane stepped back out of the man's path and elbowed the man in the jaw. The blade skittered across the pavement as the man went down, but the signal had been given and the mob threw itself at him once more.

Rane sheathed *Kibon* — feeling a stab of pain as he did so, but he'd not give it any more lives that day — and then wielded it like a club; hitting, poking, prodding, blocking, keeping it in constant motion to keep his attackers at bay, fighting the urge to slaughter them all.

Arms seized him around the neck, so he smashed the back of his head into the assailant's face. A woman tried to claw his face. Rane stabbed his fingers into her solar plexus, paralyzing her lungs, while sweeping the legs away from a man to his right.

Whistles sounded over the frenzy. The city guards were on their way. Guards meant swords, and maybe guns, and neither were things Rane wanted to deal with. He whirled *Kibon* in front of him, cracking skulls and breaking bones as he drove the crowd back, wasting no more time. The voice told him to draw steel and solve the matter with blood. *No, no, no*, he told himself, even as his hands went to unleash *Kibon* once more. The blade was half out when the barrier of bodies around him fell away, opening up the road back to the Queen's Bridge.

Rane didn't need a second invitation. He sprinted down the street, pursued by people and shouts alike, but his legs were powered by *Kibon*'s magic and none could match him for speed. A guard appeared from a side street, but he wasn't expecting Rane. He barely broke stride to knock the guard from his path.

He raced along, cutting this way and that through throngs of people all looking back the way he'd come, trying to see what the commotion was. Whistles and bells sounded behind him, raising the alarm.

He turned right at the next junction. He had to disappear.

He cut down an alley between a baker's and a hardware store, barely wider than his shoulders. He hoped it was a shortcut back to the bridge.

"Oi!"

The shout came from behind him. He looked back to see three guards in pursuit.

The alley was no more than two feet wide and filled with rotting food, human waste and other refuse. Rane ran faster, opening a gap between himself and the guards. He wasn't going to be captured.

He vaulted over a fence and carried on, almost bouncing off the walls in his haste. He didn't know where the alley opened out; an army could be waiting at the exit to capture him.

The wall on one side of the alley was six feet high. Rane reached up with one hand and hauled himself on to it. He sprinted along the wall until he could jump up onto a low roof opposite. From there he bounced from roof to ledge to balcony to roof till he was high above any pursuit. He jumped over the narrow streets, taking random turns till it was impossible for anyone to still be on his tail.

Satisfied he was safe, he settled down into a deep nook under a roof awning and watched the hue and cry below. Alarm bells rang, warning the whole city he was on the loose, but no one looked up. He watched the guards, no more than little red dots, flit this way and that, frantic to find him. They had no chance.

Rane buried his head in his hands. By the Gods, what had he become? He'd known he was dangerous, knew of the urges that ran through him, but he'd never have thought he could murder so many with so little thought. No; it was worse than that. He'd killed with utter pleasure. What happened to the man who'd sworn an oath to protect and serve those weaker than himself? Kara would've been horrified at his actions. What happened to the man she'd loved? Who was he, truly?

His whole body shook at the thought of those he'd just killed. Some hero he was; some Legionnaire. How could he have failed his oath like that? Yes, his friends were being tortured, but were those he killed really his enemies? He'd made orphans and widows that day. If anyone deserved to be hanged, it was him. He used to be a better man than that.

Shame quenched the fury in him and killed the urge for

vengeance that had driven him since Kara's death. Better he'd let the bounty hunters take him. The people in the square would be alive still. Kara too, his child growing within her.

He was the one who deserved to die. Not them. Not her.

He unsheathed *Kibon* an inch, enough to see his reflection in the perfect steel. Enough to barely recognize the man who stared back at him. Who had he become?

No, the voice whispered in his head. They'd watched Legionnaires murdered, cheering the priest on, baying for blood. They would've killed him too if he'd let them. He'd acted in self-defense. The world had declared war on the Legion — and every war had casualties.

He sheathed *Kibon* once more, wishing the world wasn't what it was.

One thing was clear: there was nothing for him in Candra. If Jefferson was alive, he wasn't here. As soon as night fell, Rane would leave the city and head to Rooktown. Find Marcus. Find some hope there.

PART II

9

At first, Rooktown was nothing more than a small shadow in the distance, sat amongst vast fields of brown grass, a single gravel highway leading to it. Mist hugged the ground, and slate-grey skies promised rain sooner rather than later.

A mixture of emotions played within Rane as he drew nearer to the city. The last time he'd visited, he and Marcus had been on their way home from the war. When he met Kara for the first time. He rubbed her locket between his finger and thumb. What a woman she'd been.

They'd come back looking for Marcus' family, only to find the Rastaks had all but destroyed the place. Marcus' father and mother had died in the first wave of the invasion, murdered because they were too old to be of any use to the Rastaks as slaves, and not rich enough to buy their own safety. A common enough occurrence during the war.

Kara had survived, though. Done more than that, in fact. She'd led the resistance against the Heras worshippers, fought as hard as any soldier Rane had known.

Rane could make out the city wall — or what was left of it. More a skeleton of burnt and broken timber. It had not changed since his last visit — just another reminder of the damage done.

The entrance to the city was in as bad a state as the walls. There was no gate or guard; just a larger hole in the wall to walk through. It was a surprise to see. After Rane had married Kara, Marcus had stayed in Rooktown and taken a job up with Lord Haversham— a distant relation to the queen — to help rebuild the place. It didn't look like much had been accomplished in the two years since. The city was still a shadow of what it once was.

It was hard to believe that Rooktown was the seat of government for the western counties of Ascalonia, and the last major city before the Balrussian border. Rane walked down empty, narrow streets, watched only by the odd stray dog. There was no other sign of life. Houses and businesses were boarded up, covered with wards calling on Odason to offer His protection, or just abandoned with doors and windows wide open. Garbage was piled up in the streets, and the stench of rot filled the air.

If anything, the city was in a worse state than it had been after the war. At least back then there had been a sense of hope, of starting over. There'd been survivors. Now, Rooktown was a corpse left to rot.

The only new additions to the city were the all-too-familiar "Wanted" posters — "any Legionnaire, alive or dead" — plastered on various walls. So someone had been in Rooktown recently. Rane only hoped they'd not found Marcus.

He reached the market square in the center of town. At one end had once stood one of the country's biggest temples to Odason, but the Rastaks had been quick to destroy it. Some work had begun on restoring the remains, but now it looked like it had been left to rot like the rest of the city. Dirt-strewn steps led up to doors left open, and the sky shone through the half-built roof. Even the customary statues of Odason's guardian angels lay smashed in half.

A fountain sat in the heart of the square, filled with a mix of rainwater and rubbish. A few abandoned stalls littered the edges of the square. One was still scattered with produce in the final stages of decay, but the rest hadn't seen wares in a long time.

Rane stood, listening to the silence fill a space designed to be full of life. He remembered a beautiful afternoon with Kara, watching the world walk by as the sun warmed the square.

By the Gods, what had happened to Rooktown? He could feel that niggle at the back of his mind, telling him to draw *Kibon*, but he couldn't see any threat. It was probably the silence unnerving him; still, his unease only grew.

He headed down a side street, following his memories. He passed a baker's shop — now with a broken door and shattered windows — where he and Kara shared pastries, and retraced their steps down lanes and alleyways where they'd talked and laughed and fallen in love. Each step hurt him again and again.

Suddenly, so faint he almost missed it, Rane heard the murmur of voices. Somewhere, there were people left in the city. People who had answers.

He followed the sounds, down one street and along the next, picking up his pace as the noise grew clearer. Turning a corner, he spotted light leaking out of the shuttered windows of an inn. "The Hare and Hound" was carved into a battered sign that hung above the door. Inside, people were engaged in a heavy debate. Some spoke in anger, while others were clearly scared.

Rane paused for a moment by the door, only too aware that he was a wanted man with a price on his head. The last time he'd allowed himself to be surrounded by people, blood had flowed. The desire to go in armed and ready for trouble was overwhelming, and it took everything he had not to draw *Kibon*. What was wrong with him when his first instinct was to go in, sword swinging?

He pushed the door open and found the place full to bursting. There must have been over a hundred people crammed inside. All heads turned in Rane's direction as he entered, and the conversation died.

He scanned the faces staring at him, looking for anyone he knew as whispers raced around the room. Fear-filled eyes took in his sword. The fear level in the room went up another notch, and Rane watched to see if anyone was brave or stupid enough to attack. Let them try.

A woman's voice cut across the noise of the bar. "Quiet!"

Silence fell across the room. Bodies parted to reveal an old woman standing in the middle of the inn. Rane recognized her straight away: Kaitlyn, one of the city elders. Her hair matched the steel in her eyes as she stood, full of pride and defiance. She wore a jacket, patched and mended over many a time, the right arm of which had been pinned to the breast since a Rastak had taken her limb in the war.

"Ma'am." Rane walked over and bowed his head in greeting. "It's good to see you again."

"I know you." Kaitlyn squinted at Rane before recognition flashed across her face. "You married Kara Shaw two years ago. Nathaniel Rane, isn't it?"

"That's right, ma'am."

"She not with you?"

"No, ma'am. My wife was murdered a week ago."

Kaitlyn sighed at the news. "I'm sorry for the loss of your wife. She was well-loved around these parts. Many of the people in this room owe her their lives, or the lives of their kin."

"I'm actually here looking for her brother, Marcus Shaw. He was working with Lord Haversham last I heard."

"I've not seen him since the posters went up. Disappeared that very day. I can't blame him for that."

Rane looked around the room. "Do you mind telling me what's going on? The town's looking worse than it did after the war."

The woman sighed, looking all her years. "There's a bit of a difference of opinion on the subject, but I think you'll find the general consensus is that we have a demon in Rooktown."

"A demon?" said Rane, stepping forward. "A Jotnar?"

"No. No." Kaitlyn waved at her missing arm. "We saw enough of those during the occupation to know what they're like. What we have here is... different, but just as deadly."

"Why are you telling him?" shouted a man from the crowd. "I know him. He's wanted, a traitor. A fucking Legionnaire."

"Quiet," snapped Kaitlyn, fixing a hard stare in the direction of the heckler. "I know this man, too — and what he was. And he might be what we need."

"I can assure you I'm no traitor," said Rane, speaking to the room. "Despite what the posters say." He looked each person in the eye. "I am — or rather, was — a Legionnaire. That's true. My name's Nathaniel Rane. I've no idea why a bounty has been placed on my head. My whole life has been dedicated to serving and protecting the people of the five nations. If you want my help with this... demon, you can have it."

The room seemed to settle at that, but Rane kept an eye out for anyone with gold on their mind. "When did the demon turn up?"

"Old Mrs Davis was the first one to die, a couple of months back. No one had seen her for a while, and her neighbor called to see if she was ill. Found her cut up and half-eaten. Since then, someone's gone missing nearly every night. The people in this room are all that are left of Rooktown. Everyone else is either dead, or they've run far from here."

A man stood up near the bar, broad of shoulder and wearing a smith's apron. "A group went up to see Haversham, see if he could help us, but they never returned."

"The bastard collaborator would never have lifted a finger for us anyway," said another.

"Haversham was rumored to have helped the Rastaks during the occupation in order to keep his family and his manor house safe," added Kaitlyn. "Nothing was proved."

"He bloody well consorted with enough fuckin' demons back in the war," continued the smith. "I tell you, he's got this one living up there now."

"Only place it could be hiding," shouted another. "I say we go burn the manor down before we think about running."

"And you'll end up dead like the rest of 'em," snapped a woman next to the smith.

"We hired some men who fancied themselves demon killers," continued Kaitlyn. "But the monster either got them too, or they ran off with our money, because we've not seen them since."

"Has anyone seen the demon?" asked Rane.

There was a lot of shaking of heads in the room. Only Kaitlyn spoke up. "It's too quick, too quiet, too clever. It avoids our traps and our hunting parties don't see a thing. Only the bodies are left as proof that it even exists. And it won't be long before we run out of those."

"That's what we were discussing," said the smith. "Whether to abandon Rooktown before we're all dead, or try to kill it somehow."

The room erupted in shouts and argument once more as if Rane wasn't there. He watched as Kaitlyn called for calm, but she may as well have asked for the world to stop turning. What type of demon could have inflicted such misery on them?

There was one way to find out. A true need for *Kibon*'s might. This was why he'd joined the Legion — to help people. Here was a way to prove he was still that person, and not the monster he could so easily be. He placed his hand on Kaitlyn's shoulder. "I'll find the demon and kill it — if I can."

Kaitlyn smiled. "Thank you, Nathaniel. Thank you." She paused for a moment. "You know, the smith's not wrong. You should start at the manor house."

10

He saw the crows before he saw the house. Circling overhead, cawing in excitement to each other, dipping and swooping. Rane hated the vile creatures. They'd dogged every failure, every defeat the Legion had suffered during the war. Picking scraps off the fallen. Feeding on his friends.

The smell came next, a sharpness drifting on the wind. Most people wouldn't notice, not when it was still so faint, but a veteran would know it anywhere. His lip twisted in disgust.

It had been everywhere during the war, clinging to clothes and getting stuck in the nostrils and at the back of throats, tainting everything until it seemed to be the only smell left in the world, until no one noticed it anymore. To experience it once again made Rane sick to his stomach, because he knew without doubt what waited at the mansion.

Death. Rot. Decay.

As he walked down the twisting lane, a cold light broke through the edge of the woods. The call of the crows grew louder, and the stench grew stronger. It turned Rane's stomach.

The trees fell back, revealing a five-foot wall with metal gates to protect Haversham's mansion from the rest of the world. Unlike the walls around Rooktown, these were in good repair, chained and locked to keep unwanted guests out. Rane headed straight to the gate. One kick was enough to snap the chain with a clang and he pushed them open.

The mansion's once-immaculate gardens had been left to grow wild, running riot on either side of the path. Only the Gods knew when last there had been someone to care for them. Above, the crows protested Rane's intrusion, resenting the disruption to their meal. They perched on walls and ledges, screaming at Rane as the Legionnaire made his way to the house.

Even from half a mile away, the building was impressive. Rane couldn't remember the last time he'd seen a building with so many windows. If each one had its own room behind it, there was enough space to house an army.

It wasn't long before he found the first body. White flesh poked out from the long green grass, revealing the remains of a young boy no more than seven years old. The crows had done their work, but a much larger beast had feasted on the child first. Rane bent down and inspected the corpse. The child's neck had been broken. He only hoped he'd died before the creature fed. No one deserved to die like that, especially not one so young.

Nearby was a woman, shredded as if by sharp claws, her limbs missing.

The voice at the back of his mind urged him to be ready, to draw the sword, because there would only be more dead and demons and who-knew-what devils waiting for him inside. This time, Rane listened. As he passed more mutilated corpses, choking on the stench, Rane reached over his shoulder and pulled *Kibon* free. The difference was immediate. He felt strong. Confident. Ready. He'd faced hordes of Jotnar, snapping and snarling, baying for his blood, and lived. Not just that — he'd sent all of Heras' creatures back to the underworld. Whatever waited for him inside, it would not see another dawn.

Up close, the mansion certainly looked a miserable place, well suited to its desolate location. The outside walls were stained by the elements; in numerous places, the plaster was either missing or in the process of detaching itself. Most of the windows were still shuttered, and had been for a long time by the looks of them. Haversham may be one of the country's richest men, but none of his money had gone into the upkeep of the house. However, despite the run-down nature of the house, it was still a very imposing building, especially for someone like Rane. Haversham's manor was far from the two-room cottage he'd burned in Eshtery.

By the time he reached the marble steps leading up to the main door, he'd passed more bodies. Too many to count. Some even had weapons in their hands, but it had made no difference to how they'd met their end. Men, women and children — they all lay dead, rotting away.

Rane steeled himself for what he was going to find inside. More bodies, by the stink of it. His anger rose. It would be a pleasure to kill whatever was inside, whatever thing had caused this misery. It was why he'd been given his powers. Why he'd allowed his soul to be merged with his sword. He'd damned himself for a cause, after all.

He climbed the steps to the main doors, made of ancient oak and carved with the family sigil of a rose wrapped in thorns. Marble columns flanked them on either side, once white but stained by the wind and rain. Rane tried to push the doors — locked. A good kick would open them, but Rane didn't want to alert anything inside that he was coming.

He skirted around the house, looking for another way in. All the windows were barred from the inside. Rane was about to give up and return to the front of the house when he spotted another door, half-hidden in shrubbery. The wood was old and uncared for, the lock a simple thing. Rane sheathed *Kibon* while he peered through the dirt-covered windows, making out a kitchen on the other side.

The door didn't need to be forced. A simple push popped it loose from the frame. The wood was so rotten it barely creaked as it splintered apart, not loud enough to disturb the silence of the house.

He drew *Kibon* once more, the blade singing with joy at being released. If anything waited for him inside, it would soon pay for all the deaths it had caused. His rage soared as he stepped inside, sword at the ready. How he prayed to discover one of Heras' creatures escaped out into the world.

The manor's kitchen, where once a brigade of kitchen staff would have been busy night and day, was deserted. Cold and dark instead of warm and full of life. A layer of dust covered the surfaces. No one had used the room in a long while. The servants were probably more names to add to the list of victims.

Trapped by the walls, the smell of decaying flesh was stronger than ever. It seeped through the floors and the walls, smothering the air in the house. Rane clamped his hand over his mouth and nose to stop himself retching.

He moved into the main part of the house, taking his time with each room, ensuring they were empty before moving on to the next. The war had taught him caution, and Rane wasn't going to die because he failed to check a room properly. The dark interior provided far too many hiding places as it was. He used skills learned over hard years of warfare, skills that had kept him alive long before a magic sword was put into his hands.

Rane's heart raced as his body prepared him for action. Somewhere, a demon lurked. *Kibon* led him on, shining in the darkness, filling him full of energy. He found his eyes drawn to it again and again. Killing demons was what it had been made for — what it longed for.

The house was as much a corpse left to rot as the bodies outside. It'd been built with enough ambition and grandeur to stand the test of time, and now it was nothing but a mausoleum. Portraits of ancestors long gone lined the walls, bearing witness to its fall.

Rane tried to imagine what the house would've been like with children running through it, staff bustling this way and that and Lord Haversham at the center of it all. How had Marcus found it when he came here to work, so far removed from the life he'd known at the front? His friend would have been a fish out of water. The thought was enough to bring a smile to Rane's face for the briefest of moments, but no more than that.

Satisfied downstairs was deserted, Rane took the central staircase up. More portraits lined the way up the stairs, generation after generation of Havershams. The men seemed to change little over the years except in fashion and facial hair. They all had the same golden locks and deep-set, piercing blue eyes. Rane stopped before one particularly impressive painting, far larger than the others around it, of an imposing gentleman with long hair falling past his shoulders. He was sitting in the center of a room with three children, all close to adulthood, around him. A small plaque proclaimed the picture to be of the latest Haversham with his children, Edgar, Catherine and Rebecca, each as striking as he was. The artist had managed to give them all the air of the very rich who viewed the rest of the world as beneath them.

Haversham dominated the image, though — there was no mistaking the authority in the man. He commanded attention even as a painting. But where was he? Rane had yet to see his body.

The stairs creaked, echoing through the silence as he climbed. The feeling that he was being watched grew with each step. He searched the gloom for the source of his unease, but everywhere seemed devoid of life. Only the eyes from the portraits were on him.

The stench grew stronger with every step, if such a thing were possible. His skin crawled with it. His lungs struggled to deal with it. Still, he took his time, checking empty bedroom after empty bedroom until finally he stood before two great doors.

Somehow, Rane knew that whatever he was looking for was waiting behind them. The fire of vengeance burned in him. Ready to fight, ready for war, Rane tightened his grip on his sword and pushed the doors open with his other hand.

Flies shot towards him, angry at being disturbed, and the smell of rot hit him with almost physical force. Only the Gods knew how Rane managed to stand his ground, transfixed by the horror before him.

A four-poster bed sat in the middle of the room. Haversham's corpse lay on it, his flesh barely hanging onto his bones. A neat gap separated his head from the rest of his body.

But worse lay on the floor. Every inch of it was filled with the bodies of the dead. In some places they were piled two or three high. All had died violently, either eaten, hacked up or ripped apart. Blood, guts and brains decorated the walls.

With his hand covering his mouth, he stepped into the room. Rane had to force his feet into spaces between the bodies as he made his way through the horror. Each face he looked at broke his heart a little more. Young, old, male, female — there was no discrimination. Just lives, destroyed. He only hoped they'd been dead before they were brought to this room. To face this carnage and know that your death was imminent was a horror no one should face.

When he reached the heart of the room, Rane stopped. He stared down at a face he knew only too well.

Blood streaked his friend's face, far gaunter than Rane remembered. He could barely see any of the comrade he once knew in the corpse in front of him, but there was enough left to know it was Marcus. The sword in the scabbard beside him, identical to Rane's own, was only more confirmation.

He'd failed Kara — again. Grief struck him through the heart. He'd lost his friend. They'd lived, fought and bled together for so many years, vanquished the Rastaks together — only for Marcus to die in a slaughter pit.

What monster could have killed him? Marcus was as strong and as deadly as Rane, and yet there he lay. The demon must've taken him by surprise — it was the only explanation. Blinding rage consumed Rane. Whatever the demon was, it would die that day. It had to be hiding in the house, and Rane was going to find it.

Back in the hallway, slivers of light sneaked through gaps in the shutters, reminding Rane that the day was passing outside. *Kibon* pulsed in his hand, eager for blood. He'd find the monster even if he had to rip the house apart. There must be somewhere he hadn't seen. A basement, or an attic... Rane looked up at the ceiling. Yes, somewhere in the roof. It'd want to stay close to its food. There had to be a way up there.

A hand clamped itself over his mouth and another gripped his sword arm, holding him firm. A cold body pressed up against Rane's back.

"Leaving so soon?" a voice whispered in his ear. "Please, stay awhile."

11

The creature was strong. It yanked Rane off his feet and dragged him back towards the room of death. Rane kicked and pulled against the demon's grip, but its power was incredible. Even with Rane's magic-enhanced muscles, he couldn't break free. Warm breath tickled his neck as he felt teeth graze his skin.

But Rane wasn't going to die easily. He slammed his head back into his attacker's face with all the force he could muster. Bone crunched, and the demon released its grip. Rane spun around, swinging his sword at the creature. Let *Kibon* deal with the monster he faced.

The blade met steel as another sword stopped it in its tracks. The blades skidded off each other with a clang. Rane looked up at his assailant's face and staggered back in horror.

Marcus stood before him. Blood streaked his face. Other people's entrails hung from his body — a body all twisted and warped all out of proportion, pure muscle and sinew. Marcus' sword was in his hand, identical to Rane's — except the blade was stained jet black.

Rane couldn't tear his eyes away from his friend. "Marcus?" A stupid question, but the truth was so unbelievable. What had happened to his friend?

The voice told him that it didn't matter. Here was an opponent worth killing. *Kibon* twitched in anticipation. There was no need to hold back.

"Hello, brother," Marcus replied with a tip of his head. "It's been a long time."

"What have you become?" asked Rane. He retreated into the hallway, maintaining his distance from Marcus, looking for space to fight.

"I've become glorious." Marcus grinned. Teeth — no, *fangs* — gleamed in the darkness. He stepped towards Rane. "Let me show you all the ways."

"I see only horror." With a two-handed grip on *Kibon*, Rane slid his left foot forward and turned his hip towards Marcus. He raised his sword above his head, ready to strike.

Marcus dismissed the move with a chuckle and a wave of his own sword. "Put your sword down. It doesn't have to be this way. You should be by my side — not against me. We're the same, you and me. We're Legion."

Marcus took another step forward as if he didn't have a care in the world, but Rane saw the way his eyes moved from Rane's face to his sword and back again. He was wary of *Kibon,* with good reason. If he was scared of getting hurt, it meant he could be killed.

"I'm not like you."

"Come now, brother. Don't lie to me. You feel the urges, hear the whispers in the back of your mind, demanding blood, seeking violence. The sword requires it." Marcus came on. His voice had a singsong quality, like a child's. "The sword deserves it."

"My sword doesn't speak to me." Still Rane retreated, but already he could feel the pressure building within him to strike. Tingles spread along his fingers and hands from *Kibon*'s hilt. It wanted to attack. "I'm not a monster."

"Don't lie to me. I can see it in you." Marcus raised his own blade, black as night. "The lust. The desire. The sword sings with it."

The man was mad, demented, corrupted. Rane had to stop him. Had to kill him. He couldn't allow anyone else to die at Marcus' hands. He had to kill his best friend. "The sword is just a tool given to us. It doesn't think. It can't demand. You've committed this horror. The evil is yours, and yours alone."

"You don't believe that." Marcus closed the gap between them.

"I do," replied Rane, but the words tasted bitter on his tongue. He knew he lied. He knew the truth in Marcus' words.

Marcus' laughter rang through the house. "Poor fool," he said, and attacked.

Rane threw his own sword out in riposte. Sparks flew in the darkness as the two blades met. But whereas Rane's sword glimmered with light even in the darkness, Marcus' blade all but disappeared amongst the shadows. Rane countered, but his sword slashed through empty space as Marcus moved at speeds too quick to track. He spun, sweeping his sword around, and Rane only just got *Kibon* up in time to deflect the blow.

Again the black blade came at him; Rane threw himself to one side, rolling out of the way, desperate for some breathing room. But as he turned back, he found Marcus pressing down on him once more.

The force and the fury of Marcus' assault drove Rane down to one knee. He swept his own sword up from the side, intending to split Marcus in half, but his friend easily blocked the attack. He slid his blade up Marcus' sword, aiming for the neck as he pushed himself back onto his feet, but Marcus side-stepped out of the way, leaving him nothing to cut but air. As they passed, Marcus punched him in the side of the head, sending Rane reeling. Laughter chased him as Rane tried to keep his senses together. Marcus had always been his equal, his brother in all things, but the creature Rane faced was so much faster, so much stronger.

Sweat stung his eyes as he lashed out with *Kibon*. Marcus blocked the strike almost without looking. He turned, kicking out at Rane's legs, knocking him to the ground once more. Marcus hacked down and Rane only just managed to roll out of the way.

Gripping his sword two-handed, Rane swung at Marcus, putting all his strength and speed into the swing. Marcus barely seemed to move, and yet stopped the blow with a casual ease that frightened Rane to the core.

Ever since that night in Candra, Rane had feared no opponent. The Legion had become deadlier than anyone or anything they faced, armed with blades that could cut the Gods themselves. The Rastaks and the Jotnar had fallen in their hordes before them. But Marcus was so much more.

Marcus circled him, sword lax in his hand, and a grin spread across that warped face. "Can we stop this? It's almost time for the hunt. I'm hungry and my prey is waiting. Why don't you join me?"

Rane lunged forward, thrusting his sword. Marcus swayed out of the way and countered with a side kick, sending Rane flying into the wall. As he struggled to get back on his feet, he didn't even see the punch that drove him back to the floor, rattling his teeth. Darkness flooded into his mind. Death called.

Rane managed to roll to one side before Marcus could stamp on him, leaving the monster's foot to plunge through the floorboards. He scooted backwards as Marcus pulled his foot free. How could he defeat this monster that his friend had become?

Rane struggled to his feet, but Marcus gave him no respite, no time to catch his breath. He knew every move Rane was going to make and countered each one effortlessly. His black sword flashed down time and time again. Each blow Rane blocked shook him to his very bones. And each time it became harder to raise *Kibon* to stop the next assault.

A swipe of Marcus' foot took Rane's feet from under him, and he went down hard. His old comrade was on him in the blink of an eye, two hands lifting him up off the ground and into the air before he had a chance to recover. Rane dangled like a fish on a hook, all the air gone from his lungs. Marcus pulled him closer so that they were all but touching nose-to-nose. Soul-dead eyes examined him.

"So good to see you again, brother," whispered Marcus as if to a lover, "but it's time to say goodbye. I've dinner waiting for me in Rooktown." Marcus flicked a wrist and threw Rane through a shuttered window. Glass and wood shattered around him, and then he was falling.

12

It was dark when Rane awoke. Panic swept through him, fighting with the pain. Where was his sword? He needed *Kibon*.

He turned his head, relieved that he still could move, and saw his sword only a few feet from his hand. Not far, but far enough.

Rane tried to sit, but another wave of pain hit him with a ferocity that took away what little breath he had left. He closed his eyes, sucked in a lungful of air, and tried to move again. Prepared for the agony, he rolled over onto his stomach and dragged himself along the ground with his hands.

Rane had to stop several times as the pain became too much to bear, until finally he reached the sword. For a moment, he thought he was going to pass out with the effort, but his fingers closed on the hilt and he drew it to him. With the sword in his arms, the fear and panic retreated and the pain lost its edge. Even so, he wasn't in a rush to try and stand. He lay back down, clutching his sword to his heart, drawing on its magic while he gathered his strength.

A wave of despair struck him as he lay there. Marcus had beaten him easily. Rane had been one of the greatest soldiers in the Legion — the best of the best — and yet Marcus, with his new powers, had brushed him aside as if he were a child. All his training, all his strength and speed, had been as nothing compared to what Marcus had become. Rane was amazed he was still alive.

Suddenly, he realized that Marcus might be watching him lie there on the grass, broken and defeated. He would surely die if Marcus attacked again. Gripping his sword, Rane found some reserve of courage and forced himself to check. He spotted the gaping hole in the window he'd been thrown through, but there was no sign of Marcus.

Slowly, painfully, Rane got himself onto all fours and then on to his feet. He was covered in sweat from the effort as pain shot through his body, but he was still alive. Alive meant he still had a chance to put things right — though only the Gods knew how he was going to stop Marcus.

Sheathing his sword, he stared at the dead bodies that littered the gardens. He could so easily have been left to rot among them.

The click of a pistol hammer being pulled back broke the silence. Someone was behind him.

"Don't move." A woman's voice. A South Islander judging by the accent. Dangerous by the no-bullshit tone.

Rane did as he was told, and cursed himself for being caught off-guard a second time.

"Turn around real slow. Make a move towards any weapon and I'll shoot you in the head."

Again, Rane followed her orders. The woman stood a few feet from him, the pistol rock-steady in her hand. Rane knew there wasn't much chance of her missing if she was inclined to shoot. She'd not miss even if she were shooting from ten times the distance. She was, after all, the deadliest woman he had ever known.

"Hello, Myri." She'd not changed much in the two years since he'd last seen her. She'd grown her hair out into long dreadlocks, but that was about all. Her chocolate skin was as smooth as ever, and her eyes were big enough to drown in. Myri Anns, as deadly and as beautiful as they came. She'd another pistol holstered underneath her long leather coat, and three knives hung from her belt. Her sword, identical to his own, sat on her back. "It's good to see you."

"Hello, Nathaniel." Her voice was cold. Her eyes hard. Professional.

"Why the gun? You going to shoot me?"

Myri curled her lip. "I might just do that. Depends if you killed these people. Depends how far gone you are."

"This isn't my work. Marcus killed everyone here. He's turned into some sort of monster."

He could see the news rocked Myri, but she did her best to keep her composure. Her gun remained still in her hand. "With your left hand, unsheathe your sword enough for me to see the blade."

"What's going on?"

"Just do what I fucking told you to do."

Rane slid two inches of steel out of the sheath. The blade sparkled in the moonlight. He felt the urge to free it; to kill Myri. She had a gun on him, after all. Could he do it before she pulled the trigger? He ground his teeth as he fought the urge.

"You can put it away now." Myri's eyes never left Rane's face as she spoke, examining him for other things unsaid. He let *Kibon* slide back into its sheath but kept his hand on its hilt.

"You going to put the gun away as well?"

Myri lowered it so the pistol was aimed at Rane's gut. "When I'm sure you're not going to try and kill me."

Rane made a show of letting go of *Kibon* with his right hand as his mind catalogued the ways he could still hurt her if he had to. He was fast. Maybe fast enough to reach her in time. "Mind telling me what's going on?"

Myri ignored him and looked towards the house. "Is Marcus still in there?"

"He threw me from a window, said he was going into Rooktown to eat. He's turned into some sort of demon. I don't know why he didn't kill me."

"Shit. Too late. Always too late." She shook her head. "Another one fucking lost." She released the hammer on the pistol and placed it back in its holster. "Fuck!"

Rane grabbed her arm and swung her around to face him. "Myri!

Tell me what's going on. In the last ten days, I've found out I have a price on my head, had bounty hunters turn up at my house and kill my wife, then I discover my best friend has turned into some kind of flesh-eating monster. And now you appear, threatening to kill me if I don't show you my sword."

Some of the tension fell from Myri as her eyes filled with sadness. "There's a reason why magic is outlawed. A damn good reason why we're not supposed to mess with that shit."

"Myri — tell me what's going on. Please."

"Fucking damnation is what's going on. We're all cursed."

"Cursed?"

"We all agreed to put part of our souls into our swords in exchange for speed and strength and crazy healing powers — but we never questioned what was going to happen to our souls once they were in there, did we?"

"No." A knot formed in Rane's chest.

"We didn't stop to think what would happen every time we killed someone, or every time we plunged our soul into a demon and bathed it in their blood."

"No." Rane struggled to draw breath. Somehow *Kibon* was in his hand again and when he looked, Myri had her pistol out once more. He sheathed the weapon. "Sorry. I don't know how that happened."

Myri wasn't so quick to put her gun away this time, but eventually she did. "The steel drinks the blood of whoever we kill — that's why you never have to clean it after battle. That's how it makes us stronger. It absorbs the essence of our enemies. Trouble is, each death taints the soul in the sword."

Again, the urge to attack Myri rose up inside him like a tidal wave, as if her words were putting his very life in danger. He swallowed the feeling back down. He needed to hear what she had to say.

"The more we kill, the stronger we get. The more we kill, the more tainted we get," said Myri.

Rane closed his eyes, shook his head. "No." Not his sword. It wasn't true. The voice urged him to shut her up. Put an end to her lies.

"The more blood we feed the sword, the stronger the urge to use it grows. It takes over our minds until using the sword is impossible to resist. The deeper the taint, the worse our desires."

Rane's mind drifted back to a bounty hunter he'd killed without even noticing. The mob he slaughtered in Candra. The urges he'd had to kill anyone since the war. He shivered.

"Then one day you're gone, and all that's left is a real fucking flesh-and-blood, deadly monster. As bad as any Jotnar or Grendun or Valkryn." Myri paused. Swallowed. "I've seen Legionnaires — people you and I know well — eat human flesh, commit mass murder, do things that would turn your stomach. Things you can't even imagine." Her eyes shone with emotion. "That's why they're hanging us. That's why they're offering such a big reward for us, dead or alive. We're as dangerous as anything Mogai ever sent against us.

"The color of the sword is the only way to tell how far you're gone. It changes color as the taint takes hold. The blacker the blade, the less of the person remains — until there's only the monster left."

The voice growled a warning. Rane stepped back. He wrapped his fingers around the hilt of his sword. "In that case, show me yours."

Myri nodded, but took her time reaching for her sword. She swung the sheath off her back, jaw clenched. She looked at Rane, almost afraid. Then there was a flash of anger and she pulled two inches of her sword free. The metal was mottled; dark stains ran along its length. But not black. Not yet. She slid it back into the sheath with a grunt. "I've still got time."

"How bad have you got it?"

"You saw my sword. The color. I'm pretty far down the path. Sometimes it can take everything I've got not to draw my sword and just give in. Take the pain away and enjoy the buzz that makes me feel like a god. Seems like the easiest way out — except I know it's not. I've seen what happens at the end of that road. So every day, every hour, every minute I can ignore the voice in my head and keep my sword in its sheath is another victory for me."

Rane breathed in slowly, trying to calm his thoughts. Make sense of what Myri was saying. "And this... taint is happening to all of us?"

"There were four hundred and fifty of us at the ceremony. Born fighters, one and all. Killing's what we're good at. No one's sword got starved of blood, especially in those last years of the war." Myri paused as if the memory was too difficult to accept. "Too many of us had turned before we knew what was happening. Before we could do anything about it."

Rane's mind reeled with the information. He watched her, looking for any signs she wasn't telling the truth, anything that might betray her true intentions. He wanted her to be lying. Even seeing her blade, even having fought Marcus, he didn't want to believe her.

But her words. Her words explained so much. The urges, the voice. By the Gods, what was he becoming? "Does the Lord General know?"

Myri nodded. "He does. I was with him when the bounty went out. He tried stopping it, asked for calm from the heads of the five nations, but they wouldn't listen. After everything we've done for them, they wouldn't give him time to fix things."

"Can we be cured?" He fiddled with Kara's locket. Rane was almost too scared to know the answer. He'd rather kill himself than turn into a demon.

"We didn't think so at first, but the Lord General has found a way. He's gathering what's left of us at the old castle in Orska."

Rane felt the knot in his chest loosen just a little. There was a way out of this mess. A way to be free. "Orska? Up on the northern coast? It was a ruin the last time I saw it. The Rastaks overran it when they first crossed the border."

Myri nodded. "It's also in the middle of nowhere. Far enough away to be forgotten. Safe for us to gather without the world noticing and marching against us. He sent a few of us out to find what's left of the Legion; warn them of what was happening, and tell them to meet up at the castle. Marcus was the last name on my list," said Myri. "I was too fucking late."

"By the Gods. I can't believe it." But he could. It explained so much. His sword was poisoning his soul.

"At least I found you." Myri's face tightened with resolve. "I've got a spare horse. Let's get out of here."

"And go where?"

"Didn't you hear me? Orska. To Orska. Join up with the others and get fucking cured. Unless you want to hang around here and turn into one of the tainted."

"What about Marcus?"

"He's not our problem now. We can come back and deal with him once we're cured — and with the whole Legion behind us."

Rane shook his head. "What about the people he's going to kill before then? What about the ones he'll kill tonight? We owe it to them to try and stop him."

"You only just survived your encounter with him. Why do you think it'll be different next time?" shouted Myri. "Do you know how many Tainted I've fought?"

"No."

"I've faced three. Do you remember Johnny Rose? He was eating a priest's intestines when we came across him. He killed three of us before we stopped him. The second was near Rostland. I had four others with me. We didn't think the demon was one of ours at first. She had the sword, of course, but we thought she'd stolen it. But Anam recognized her. Sara something-or-other. They'd fought together at Gettis. Took six bullets to put her down long enough for one of us to cut her head off. She still managed to gut Oscar and Helga."

"And the other?"

"I was on my own." Myri's anger dropped as the memories took her back. "I was rounding up the people on my list, telling them to head to Orska. His name was Stannias. Lived in a little town a few days ride from here. Seemed as normal as can be when we met — but I didn't check his sword. I'll never make that mistake again."

"But you got him?"

"Shot him in the head while he was trying to rip my throat out with his teeth. Seems that still does the trick."

"By the Gods," muttered Rane. What were they all becoming?

"So we leave Marcus, get this fucking curse lifted off our heads, and then we can come back mob-handed and deal with him. All right?"

Rane couldn't argue with her logic, but he still shook his head. "It's our sworn duty to help. Remember — 'Those weaker than ourselves.' But it's more than that. If the positions were reversed, and it was Marcus hunting me down, he wouldn't stop until he'd succeeded. He wouldn't want me to suffer any more than I had. He's my friend, and he needs me. I'm not going to let him down. You can go to Orska. I won't stop you. But I'm going after Marcus. It's the right thing to do."

They stood staring at each other, the argument going on unspoken, until finally Myri looked away. "It's not that I'm scared, or that I don't care — but you saw my sword. I don't want to become one of those monsters. What if killing Marcus is what sends me over the edge?"

Rane held Myri, drawing her close. "Then don't use your sword. We have other weapons. If it comes to it, let my sword be the one to strike him down. And then we go straight to Orska and the Lord General."

Myri chewed her lip, looking like she hated Rane at that moment. He didn't blame her — but he also knew he couldn't handle Marcus on his own.

"Fine." Myri forced the word out. "Let's get this fucking done then."

And the two Legionnaires went to kill their friend.

13

Rane and Myri rode towards Rooktown with only a sliver of moon to guide them. Soon, even that was gone as the darkness of the woods swallowed them. At least the journey gave *Kibon* time to work its magic on Rane's battered body, but with each pulse of energy that took away another ache or bruise, he felt sick at the thought of what it was really doing to him. How long before he turned into a demon like Marcus? He glanced over at Myri. How long did she have?

He slumped in the saddle, exhausted from the fight with Marcus and by Myri's revelations. The fire that had fuelled him since Kara's death was all but extinguished. What revenge was there to seek when suddenly the warrants for the capture of the Legion made perfect sense? Kara had been right to fear him after he'd told her what the Legion had done. If she were still alive, he'd have no option but to leave her for her own safety. And what of their child? What effect would the taint have had on the baby? He shuddered at the thought. And now he was hunting his best friend — a mass murderer. By the Gods, what a mess.

The half-hour ride back to Rooktown seemed to take an eternity. The slightest sound or movement had both of them jumping in their saddles, hearts racing as a fear long forgotten blossomed once more in Rane's stomach. Since he'd been bonded to his sword, he had become unbeatable. There was no enemy he couldn't defeat, no injury that wouldn't heal. And, in that time, Rane had forgotten what it was like to be truly afraid; to face a better opponent and find the courage to stand and fight even though he knew he might die in the attempt. But in facing Marcus, that sense of mortality — the awareness of his own limitations — had come flooding back. Marcus was stronger, faster, more ruthless than he, and Rane had no idea if he could stop him, even with Myri's help. And now he knew the very thing that kept himself alive was killing him. The voice that wanted him to kill was his own corrupted soul.

As they left the woods once more, Rooktown appeared. No lights burned in any window, no sound carried on the breeze, no movement caught the eye on the walls or beyond. It hurt even more to see it like that, knowing that Marcus had been the one to pick it clean.

"Place looks dead already," said Myri, as if reading Rane's thoughts.

"You didn't see all of the bodies up at the manor. Marcus has been busy," replied Rane.

"Wait a minute," said Myri, stopping her horse. She reached back into her saddlebag and pulled a short sword free. She offered it to Rane. "Take this. Might keep you alive for an extra minute or two."

Rane pulled it free of its sheath. The single-edged blade caught a glimmer of moonlight. It was smaller than *Kibon*, but otherwise identical. "Is this an Edo-made sword?"

"Yes, and you know how fucking priceless they are, so don't lose it. I want it back afterwards."

"I can't take this. You use it."

"I'm okay," replied Myri. She reached back into the saddlebag. "I'm going for quantity over quality." Rane watched her produce knife after knife from the bag and fix them about her person. Finally, she produced a musket. "And something that'll make a big hole in the bastard."

"That will."

"Ready to go and get killed?"

Rane took a deep breath. "I am."

"Any chance I can persuade you to just leave with me now?"

"No."

Myri sighed, nudged her horse forward. "Let's get it over with."

The buildings loomed overhead as they weaved their way back to the town center, watching the cracks and the crevices, the ledges and the rooftops for any sign of Marcus. At least they didn't have to work out where he was going. The whole town had been reduced to what was inside the Hare and Hound. If it was lives he sought, he would only find them there.

Rane had to make a conscious effort to resist the urge to draw *Kibon.* He drew a pistol from its holster, keeping his thumb on the hammer. The voice didn't like it, grumbling and complaining every step of the way until Rane's head swam in confusion.

He scanned the buildings and the rooftops, looking for anything out of place — a shape that didn't belong, a reflection that shouldn't be there, a silhouette breaking the skyline or a sudden movement where there should be none.

"Trouble is, Marcus has been trained like us," said Myri without needing to ask what Rane was doing. "He knows what to avoid."

"Maybe before, but with any luck he's lost that discipline. I can't believe there's much of the old Marcus left in the demon I faced."

"You know what they say about luck."

"Only fools believe in it." Rane smiled. "But I bet you've still got that rabbit's foot tucked away somewhere."

"Damn right. It's the only reason I survived the war."

"That and a cursed sword." The moment Rane said it, he regretted it. The look Myri gave him confirmed it. Maybe once they were cured they could joke about it, but not now. Not when they were about to try and kill one of their own. Not when their swords were slowly killing them.

"I'm sorry. I..." said Rane, but Myri cut him off with a wave of her hand.

The town square was as deserted as when Rane had left it. They dismounted and tied their horses and Rane led them on foot over to the inn, his stomach churning with dread at what they might find, but the hum of chatter escaping into the night helped ease the fear.

"We're in time, by the looks of things," said Rane.

Myri arched an eyebrow but said nothing as Rane holstered his pistol and entered the inn.

Inside, the Hare and Hound was just as packed as before. Once more, every head turned their way as they entered, and Rane was painfully aware that he and Myri both looked like they were about to start another war. He spotted Kaitlyn by the fire with her husband and headed over.

"You made it back alive, then," said the old woman. "And found a friend."

"Only just," replied Rane, keeping his voice low. "This is Myri. She's another old... colleague of mine. She's going to help, too."

"Pleased, I'm sure," said Kaitlyn with a tilt of the head towards Myri. "And what of the creature?"

Rane glanced at Myri before replying. "We found him as well. We fought... but he got away."

"And?" said Kaitlyn, her voice a broken whisper.

"He's coming here — but you should be safe as long as you stay inside. We'll stop him from coming any closer." Rane hoped he sounded more confident than he felt.

Kaitlyn looked up, her eyes full of tears. "We're a good town, full of good people. We don't deserve this."

"No one ever does," said Myri. "Life just doesn't give a shit."

"Please save us," said Kaitlyn, gripping Rane's hands.

"We'll do our best," replied Rane.

The door opened, startling everyone. Three men came in and Rane realized things were only going to get worse.

Jahn Mathew'son, the Sheriff of Eshtery, stood next to the blond bounty hunter who had escaped from Rane's house. Lurking behind them was Jeriah Miller'son's father, Samuel, his big arms and shoulders as wide as any house from the pounding of all that corn.

They obviously weren't expecting to find Rane inside. Shock and confusion flared across their faces as recognition dawned. Jahn did a double-take and went for his gun, quickly followed by the bounty hunter drawing his sword. Even so, they weren't quicker on the draw than Rane. He had both his pistols out and aimed at them before they'd even got their weapons halfway clear. "You don't want to do that," he called out.

His words froze everyone in the inn, all transfixed on what was happening.

"Fucking murdering bastard demon," shouted Samuel, red-faced with fury. He still fumbled for his weapon, all sense gone.

"I don't want to shoot you, Samuel. Please don't make me," said Rane.

But the miller wasn't listening. "You killed my son, you piece of shit." He whipped his pistol out of its holster, but Rane fired first. After what happened to Kara, he wasn't going to take any chances. The bullet struck the barrel of Samuel's pistol, sending it spinning from his hand.

"I didn't mean for your son to die, Sam. But he came for me with murder on his mind and got my wife killed in the process. Think that makes us more than even." Rane put the used weapon back in its holster. Better to have the hand free than clutching a useless gun. "Now, all of you calm down before you get hurt."

The bounty hunter had his sword free, but Myri had her musket cocked and aimed straight at his head. He got the message and let his hand drop.

"Surprised to see you here, Jahn," said Rane.

The old man rubbed his chin. "You didn't think we were just going to give up once we didn't find a body at the bottom of that gorge, did you?"

"Actually, I kind of did."

"Everyone's wrong sometimes." Jahn glanced around the room at all the frightened faces. "What's going on here?"

"Just helping a few folks out," replied Rane.

Jahn nodded at Myri. "She one of your Legionnaires too?"

"Why don't you ask me?" snapped Myri, moving her aim from the bounty hunter to Jahn. "I can speak for myself."

"No one's looking for trouble," said Rane to both Jahn and Myri. "Why don't you boys just turn around and head home?"

"I can't do that, I'm afraid." Jahn shrugged. "Come too far to find you. Followed you to Candra, and the mess you caused there, then to here. Surprised at how easy it was."

"I've not been hiding," replied Rane. "But I'm also not going to give up just like that. Remember — no reward's worth dying for."

"I agree," said Jahn with a smile. "To be honest, I couldn't give a shit about rewards. I'll leave that to the kid here. Samuel's got revenge covered. I just care about justice, and you've left too many dead bodies behind you for me to leave you be."

"More people are going to die, if that's the case," said Rane. He could feel *Kibon* eager as anything, niggling away at the back of his mind.

"You try killing us, you piece of shit," roared Samuel. "See how you do against real men."

"This isn't about us..." replied Rane, but a woman screamed before he could say another word.

14

M arcus stood on the stairs, grinning, black sword in hand. "Am I interrupting?"

Rane drew his remaining loaded pistol and fired in one motion. Marcus was twenty yards away and impossible to miss, yet he twitched his body and the bullet struck the wall behind him. Myri fired her musket an instant later, but she might as well have been shooting at thin air.

The inn erupted into chaos as the shots galvanized everyone into action. Screams filled the air as people ran for the door, pushing Rane and Myri this way and that. Marcus laughed and leaped into the chaos. His sword flashed left and right as he carved people down, hacking limbs and chopping heads. Rane tried to force his way to the creature, but the tide of bodies surged in the other direction and he could only watch in horror as more people fell beneath Marcus' blade.

"What the fuck is that?" screamed Jahn, wide-eyed and helpless. The bounty hunter dragged Samuel towards the exit, unwilling to face the tainted man.

Bryan, armed with a meat cleaver, took a wild swing at Marcus and got backhanded for his trouble without the tainted man even looking in his direction. The barman flew into a table, smashing glass, spilling tankards and knocking burning logs from the hearth.

Rane spotted Kaitlyn, petrified, hiding with a family behind an upturned table. Next to her was another man brandishing a table leg like a club, with a little girl holding onto him, screaming for all she was worth. Another woman was trying to crawl to safety, leaving a trail of blood in her wake.

"Jahn!" shouted Rane. "Help get these people out of here. They'll die if they stay."

"What about the demon?" Jahn had his pistol drawn but looked like he had no idea what to do with it.

At the other end of the bar, Marcus's sword arced up and down, twisting from one killing stroke to another.

"Leave him to us," replied Rane, wishing there was some other way.

The sheriff, still with his eyes locked on Marcus, moved. He grabbed the people nearest him and pushed them towards the door.

Finally, the space cleared and Rane and Myri threw themselves into battle. Rane ran in with his short sword while Myri propelled herself off a table and jumped high, knives in each hand, stabbing down.

Sparks flew off as steel met steel. Marcus countered Rane's strike before twisting around to bring the black blade up to stop Myri's blows. He kicked out as he did so, catching Rane in the side of the head, sending him reeling. Rane's vision wavered, forcing him to lash out wildly just to try and keep Marcus at bay. Marcus dipped below the swing and drove an elbow up into Rane's stomach, knocking the wind from his lungs. Marcus followed up by smashing his forehead into Rane's face.

He staggered back, water filling his eyes, blood streaming from his nose. He stumbled over a stool and knocked into a table as Myri launched another assault on Marcus, her sword already in her hand.

She hammered her sword down on Marcus again and again, giving him no respite as he defended himself. Grey blade crashed against black as her face contorted in rage. She was fast and strong, but Marcus matched her every move. She kicked out; he blocked it with a knee, then stamped down on her foot in return. He brought his blade round and sliced into her ribs before Myri could even try to block. She went down with a cry. Smoke filled the room as flames crept from the hearth, making it hard for Rane to see if Myri was still alive. The smell of burning flesh added to the horror as the fire found its way to nearby corpses.

Without even knowing he'd done it, Rane drew *Kibon* from its scabbard, and with the short blade in his other hand, leaped to Myri's aid. He attacked in a flurry, striking out at every part of Marcus' body, trying to catch him off-guard. But no matter what Rane tried, Marcus' black blade was there to stop him. The man moved at impossible speeds with a look of sheer joy on his face, while Rane put everything he had into each strike. He kicked out, hoping to break Marcus's knee, but stamped down on nothing but floorboard. Marcus soared into the air, spinning into a roundhouse kick of his own. Rane was too slow — too human — to avoid it, and Marcus's boot thundered into his temple.

The room spun as Rane went down onto one knee. Only the Gods knew how much more of this punishment he could take. He gripped *Kibon*, needing its magic to keep him on his feet as Marcus loomed, sword overhead, ready to strike down and separate Rane's head from his shoulders.

Someone screamed from the left, and Marcus turned just as Myri threw herself into the fray once more. The sight of her on her feet gave Rane renewed strength. He pushed himself back to his own feet and together they cut and thrust relentlessly, desperately seeking an opening.

Marcus pulled his head back just in time as Rane's sword whistled past, nicking his cheek. A thin line of blood appeared on his white skin as he skipped back from a blow from Myri, batting it away with the edge of his own sword, his smile all of a sudden not so certain. He retreated under their attacks, stepping back towards the fire. For a moment, Rane thought they had him as he thrust with his short sword and took a chunk of flesh off his old friend.

Marcus jumped over another sword strike and kicked out with both feet at Myri, knocking her into the flames. He spun around and pressed his advantage once more with Rane, moving so fast that Rane struggled to stop him even with two swords. Slivers of pain shot through him as Marcus's sword found its way through his guard, nicking him here and there.

Smoke burned his throat and stung his eyes as Rane battled for his life. Marcus chopped down with his sword and Rane just managed to block it with both of his weapons crossed. Marcus pushed down with all his incredible strength, forcing Rane down onto his knees. The black blade inched closer as Rane's arms shook with effort.

Then Myri reappeared out of the smoke. Blood streamed from the side of her head, but that didn't stop her as she ran up behind Marcus and hacked down with her sword.

The blade sliced through Marcus from shoulder to waist. He screamed in pain, dropping his own weapon. Only the Gods knew how he was still alive, but Rane wasn't going to waste the opportunity. He stabbed his short sword through the demon's leg. Marcus staggered and fell to his knees. Rane went to strike with *Kibon* but Myri grabbed his wrist, stopping him. She twisted her blade in Marcus and the demon howled. Blood spurted everywhere as she pushed the sword down towards his heart. The demon seized her arm with both hands, trying to stop the blade's movement, but Rane could see Marcus' strength failing.

Myri pressed her weight down on her sword so her face was almost touching Marcus'. "Die, you bastard!" She pushed one final time.

But Marcus held her blade firmly in his hands. He snarled into Myri's face as he pushed back. Rane knelt, transfixed, as Myri's sword began to edge out of Marcus. How could he not be dead?

Kibon screamed at Rane to strike lest the moment be lost, but it was as if Marcus could read his mind. The tainted man's head snapped towards him and he punched Rane in the face, knocking him back. Flames nipped at his clothes as he skidded along the floor, crashing into a table. He flipped himself back onto his feet as Marcus dragged Myri's sword from his body and reached for his own sword once more.

"No!" screamed Rane as a beam fell smoking from the ceiling, blocking his way in a shower of sparks. "Myri!" The fire roared up in front of him, but Rane threw himself through without hesitation. He had to get to Myri before Marcus killed her.

Rane rolled as he hit the ground and sprung to his feet, *Kibon* ready. He spun around, looking for his enemy, but only smoke and fire filled the air. There was no sign of Marcus.

Myri lay unconscious on the floor, her sword by her side. Rane rushed over, picked her up in his arms, and noticed the bloody stump at the end of her arm. Her right hand, still clutching her sword, had been cut from her. It was a wound not even the sword's magic could heal. Already she'd lost a lot of blood.

Rane sheathed *Kibon* and dragged Myri through the flames, coughing on the black smoke. He had to get her out before it was too late.

Ten yards from the door, a hand grabbed his shoulder and Rane's heart lurched. He spun around to find Jahn behind him. "Let me help you," said the sheriff.

They carried Myri outside and clear of the inn. Everyone was gathered by the fountain in the center of the square, but they made space for Myri.

"I need something to bandage her arm," called out Rane.

Kaitlyn strode forward, all covered in soot and dirt, and ripped a length of material from her dress. "Take this."

Rane tied it around Myri's forearm, just above the wrist, to stop the flow of blood to the wound. But as he worked, more wounds were opening up across her face. Old wounds long forgotten. Wounds her sword had once healed.

By the Gods — her sword.

"Jahn, look after her," said Rane. "I have to go back inside."

The sheriff looked over his shoulder at the inn, now fully ablaze. "You won't last two minutes. Whatever you need in there is gone."

"If I'm going to save her life, I have no choice." Rane removed his coat, holsters and belt. He didn't need anything on him that could suddenly blow up — it would be bad enough in the inn without carrying gunpowder. He jumped into the fountain and soaked himself in its stagnant water; then, before he could worry about it anymore, he sprinted back to the Hare and Hound.

Rane shouldered his way through the wall of fire that blocked the door, covering his face with his arm. The heat inside knocked him back a step, but he forced himself on, ignoring the sensation of searing skin. Smoke filled his lungs and stung his eyes. It was like entering the underworld, with Heras waiting somewhere in the furnace. Every sane part of him told him to give up, but he had to find Myri's sword. She'd die without it.

Fire spat across his back and shoulders, licking his scalp, and Rane slapped the flames down before his whole body caught alight. A coughing fit doubled him over and he crouched down looking for cleaner air, only to find every mouthful scorched his throat and lungs.

He seized *Kibon*'s hilt, and another burst of magic took some of the sting away, but Jahn was right. He wasn't going to last much longer in there. All around him, the structure complained as the fire ate away at the floor and walls. A chunk of ceiling crashed down, dragging with it part of the upper wall. Fresh air raced in through the gap, urging the flames ever higher.

Rane scrambled on, coughing and spluttering, his eyes watering and his skin burning. It was hopeless. How was he supposed to find Myri's sword in all the chaos? Every second without her blade would cause another wound to open, more blood to leak from her. How much time did he have? For her, and for himself?

He reached for *Kibon* again but felt no comfort from his sword.

More ceiling came down and he only just managed to avoid getting crushed. But as he picked himself up, he spotted Myri's sword sticking out from under a fallen beam, her hand still attached. He tried to pull the sword free, but the weapon was trapped.

Rane uttered a prayer to all the Gods as he squatted down and hooked his fingers underneath the beam. His hands protested as the red-hot timber made light work of his flesh. The flames danced along the wood and kissed his face as he tried to lift the beam. Whatever moisture had been in his clothes was long gone, and they finally caught alight. Rane screamed with the pain and the effort as he strained every muscle.

Slowly, the beam moved. Rane shuffled his feet to get under it better and then rolled it from his arms. It clattered to one side and Myri's sword was free.

Rane didn't waste another second. Leaving her hand to the fire, he snatched the weapon up. The sword was red-hot, burning him more, but he didn't care. He staggered back to the doorway. Flames belched from the bar as bottles of spirits exploded, but there was no time to find another way. He knew he was on fire. But he also knew Myri was dying. He'd save her first, then worry about himself.

He all but fell through the doorway. The cold air hurt his skin as much as the fire had. Someone screamed. He couldn't blame them, but all he cared about was getting to Myri.

"Hold her," he ordered Jahn as he grabbed her wounded arm.

"What are you..." said Jahn, but Rane ignored him and pressed the hot metal of her sword against her wounded wrist. The flesh sizzled as the blade touched it. The smell of burnt meat filled the air, but Rane had no idea if it was Myri's flesh or his own that stank so much. Myri's eyes bulged open and she screamed as the heat closed the wound. She tried to pull her arm away, but Rane held it in place with his other hand. Tremors shook her body and her feet kicked against the ground, but Jahn held her firm, and Rane kept the hot metal on her arm until he was sure the wound was sealed shut. Only then did he remove the sword. Myri went limp once more as unconsciousness saved her from the pain.

Rane stood up, still clutching Myri's sword, and walked over to the fountain. He thrust it into the water and watched it sizzle as it cooled. Pain shot through his own hand and up his arm, all red and blistered, skin hanging off it like melted wax on a candle.

Once her sword was cool again, he returned to Myri and wrapped her good hand around its hilt. She trembled as the magic did it work, but it wasn't enough to wake her. Rane thanked the Gods for that small mercy.

Kaitlyn came over and Rane could see the shock and revulsion in her eyes as she took in his ravaged skin. "Are you okay?"

Rane slowly reached over his shoulder and pulled *Kibon* off his back. He cradled the sheathed sword in his arms and held tightly onto the hilt with both hands. The magic was no more than a tingle, but he knew it was starting to do its work. He breathed in, feeling the cool night air soothe his tender throat. "I will be."

"You saved us all," said Kaitlyn.

"The demon got away again," said Rane as he watched the inn burn. The survivors had formed a line, passing buckets of water from the fountain to throw over the flames to stop them spreading to other buildings.

"I don't think he'll be back," said Kaitlyn, "and that was down to you."

"I've seen some brave things in my time," said Jahn, "but nothing like what I've seen tonight. Take credit where it's due, son. You did good tonight. Kara would've been proud."

Rane smiled at the sheriff and nodded. "Thank you."

"Get out of my way," shouted a man. People parted to allow Samuel and the bounty hunter through. "There he is. He's the one we want."

"He's a demon," shouted the bounty hunter at the crowd, pointing at Rane. "Seize him."

Samuel waved a bounty poster at the smoke-smeared faces. "There's a reward. We'll share it with anyone who'll help us."

Kaitlyn stepped forward. "I think you're mistaken. We all saw the demon. This man and his friend just saved our lives — including yours. They'd hardly try and kill one of their own." She took a step closer. "And I don't remember you lifting a finger to help anyone earlier."

"He's Legion. A wanted man." Samuel tried pushing past the town leader, but others stepped up to her side, forming a barrier in front of Rane and Myri.

Kaitlyn smiled. "Now, we don't want any more trouble after what we've been through tonight, and we've still got to try and put out a fire. So why don't you take your leave before you get yourself hurt for no good reason."

Samuel wasn't having any of it. He jabbed a finger in Rane's direction. "That man murdered my son. He was only fifteen — not even fully grown, and that bastard sliced him in half like he was a lump of meat. I demand justice."

Rane shook his head. "Please believe me when I say I'm truly sorry it happened, but getting yourself killed isn't going to make things right."

"Why, you fucking—" Samuel lunged at Rane, but Jahn hauled him back.

"This isn't the time," the sheriff said. "He isn't the monster we thought he was. He's a war hero who deserves to be left alone." He glanced over at Rane and nodded, letting him know enough was enough. "You saved a lot of lives tonight, Nathaniel. I wish you the best."

"Take care, Jahn." With a nod, Rane walked to the fountain, scorched skin protesting with every step, and sat down on the steps with *Kibon* laid across his knees. The two men stared at each other, carrying on an unspoken argument. Rane winced as a sliver of pain shot through him from one of his many wounds. He wasn't worried about Samuel or the bounty hunter. If they were going to make a move, they'd have done it by now. Trying to get the locals on their side was the last throw of their dice, and it hadn't worked. Now, with Jahn calling it a day, it was a just a question of how long they'd posture before backing down.

"You'd be better off killing those two, but I know you won't."

Rane looked down and saw Myri watching him. "You're awake."

A ghost of a smile flickered across her lips. "That I am. My hand hurts like hell." Her eyes fell to the freshly bandaged stump where her hand used to be, and she rocked back in horror. "Fuck. I can still feel it. Why can I still feel it?"

"Ghost pains. Goes after a while, I'm told."

"Shit. Shit." Myri closed her eyes. Tears ran down her cheeks. "Why did I fucking listen to you?"

Rane looked down at her, lost for words.

"Tell me it was worth it. Tell me we got the bastard, at least. Tell me I didn't lose my fucking hand for nothing," said Myri.

"He got away. I don't know how. I thought you had him. A cut like that should've been enough."

"I shouldn't have stopped you when you had the chance to finish him."

"Why did you? I thought we agreed it would be my sword that killed him."

"Couldn't let you do that, Nathaniel. You're one of the good guys." Myri smiled. It was good to see she still could. "Didn't want you getting tainted on that bastard's blood. You've still got a chance. I'd like to keep it that way."

"You're still one of the good guys, too. Remember that." Rane kept his hand tight around the hilt, feeling the tingles as its magic healed his wounds. "You know what scares me the most? I didn't even think about whether to use my sword or not. It was just there in my hand. I might as well have promised myself not to breathe. How are we supposed to stop ourselves from using them if we're not even aware of what we're doing?"

Myri cocked an eyebrow. "Stay out of trouble until we get to Orska?"

Rane shook his head. His hand went to Kara's locket. He rubbed the silver between his finger and thumb, as if that would take all his troubles away as easily as it removed the soot and ash that covered it. What he'd give to be back at his cottage with Kara, away from all the madness. But she was dead, and all the wishing in the world couldn't make things the way they had been. Already her face was starting to blur in his memories. It was as if he could only see her out of the corner of his eye and not gaze at her directly. How much longer before he'd not be able to do even that?

Life. Just when you thought you couldn't feel worse, it finds a way to prove you wrong.

"I miss you so much, Kara," he whispered to the wind.

"Pardon?" said Myri.

"Nothing. Just feeling sorry for myself. Ignore me."

"You're allowed to. You look like a human candle."

"What a pair we make." Rane tried to laugh, but failed.

"I suppose we're going after him, then?"

"Once we've healed. You know we have to."

"The oath again?"

"The oath." Rane owed Marcus his life many times over. He deserved to be put to rest. Rane had no idea how they were going to do that, though. Twice now they'd faced him, and twice they'd only just escaped with their lives. "It's all I have left."

Myri didn't reply, and when Rane looked, she was asleep again.

He hugged *Kibon* closer, needing its magic, knowing it was killing him. Had Marcus known his sword was changing him as the blade turned black? Had he fought the transformation? Or was he unaware, even now, of the horror he'd become?

Overhead, streaks of purple and scarlet turned the early morning sky into a viscous bruise. How apt, thought Rane as he struggled to his feet.

PART III

15

Rane stopped his horse on top of the rise and gazed out over the road ahead. His hand drifted to the hilt of *Kibon*, hanging on his hip, but he barely noticed the buzz of magic it gave off. The sky was a wash of the purest blue with only the occasional wisps of cloud to mar it. Even the air tasted different, cold and clean, with just a hint of pine on the tongue. It soothed his skin, still red and raw three days on from Rooktown. For a moment, he was happy just to sit there and enjoy the view.

"Any sign of Marcus?" asked Myri, drawing alongside, her right arm in a sling.

"Not for a few miles," replied Rane. He shifted in his saddle, grimacing as another part of his body complained. *Kibon* had done wonders for him, but he was still far from being back to his best. If only they'd had the luxury of resting until they'd healed — they'd spent a day sleeping in one of Rooktown's many abandoned houses, but the fear of losing Marcus' trail stopped them from staying longer.

Myri leaned over the side of her horse and gazed down at the sheer drop from the narrow path. "Do you think he's doubled back?"

"I don't think so. He was more hurt than we were. I don't think he'd be able to climb either up or down to get back around us, and this is the only path through the mountains."

"At least he's heading in the direction we need to go." Myri spat over the edge and watched it drop before turning to Rane. "Once we go around the Dead Lands, it's a straight run to Orska. Personally, I still say we leave him for now, get cured, then come back and get the bastard."

Rane rubbed his hand over his face and instantly regretted it as the burnt skin protested. "He could kill a lot of people between now and then if we did that."

"Yeah, he could, but I don't see how we can do anything except end up dead ourselves. You might not have noticed, but we're not in good shape."

"You nearly cut him in half. It'll take him a long time to heal from that, and we can't give him that time. He's weaker than us for now. We've got to take advantage of that."

"Speak for yourself — you've still got both hands. He could be cut into quarters and still be better than me in a fight." Myri's voice was full of anger and frustration.

"You'll adjust, be as good as you ever were. You just need—"

"A miracle?" snapped Myri.

"I was going to say 'practice'," replied Rane. "Look, I'm not suggesting you're wrong in what you're saying — I just don't see how we have any other choice."

"Let's get on with it, then." Myri spurred her horse forward. She didn't look back to see if Rane followed.

Rane let her build a slight lead on him, giving her some space. Myri had changed since Rooktown — there was no denying that. Hardly surprising after what had happened, but even so, it worried him on top of everything else. There was a tightness to her that never seemed to disappear. An anger that was just looking for an excuse to unleash. He hoped that, as she accepted her injury, the old Myri would return.

He didn't blame her desire to get to Orska quickly, either. By the Gods, he was as keen to get there himself. He could almost feel the place calling to him, the tug of some invisible rope pulling him north. But they had to stop Marcus first. Too many people had died by his hand already. Rane's oath — and his conscience — wouldn't allow him to risk that tally mounting.

At first Marcus' trail had been easy to follow, despite the delay in going after him. The man — if he could still be called that — had lost a lot of blood from his wounds. When he'd escaped from the inn, he'd headed straight out of Rooktown, not trying to hide his path. He spent some time under a bridge, judging by the blood he'd left there, but that was the last obvious stop they'd found. As the distance grew, the trail had grown fainter and fainter until they were following broken twigs and crushed grass. No doubt Marcus' black sword was healing him just as *Kibon* was helping Rane.

Now, on the mountain path, things were even harder. There was no blood to follow, or tracks left in grass. The stony ground and rocky slopes left nothing. At least there was only the one path, with a sheer drop on one side and a mountain face on the other. All Rane and Myri could do was keep going.

As much as he didn't believe Marcus could have climbed back past them, Rane continued to look for signs that he had, or for a potential hiding place where Marcus could be taking shelter. The man was weak, wounded, and no doubt desperate, but he was still dangerous. Rane wasn't going to chance losing him.

He sucked in the cold air, enjoying the way it soothed his burnt lungs as he watched Myri disappear down the trail. A thought flashed through him — that she was the enemy, that everything she'd told him had been a lie, designed to trick him — and he found his hand was already on his sword, the blade half out of the scabbard. But no; he forced *Kibon* back down, unclenched his hand from its hilt. Thoughts like that were proof Myri was right. He tried to remember who he had been before the darkness grew within him — the boy who'd signed up to become a soldier, who found pride in helping people. A man bound by an oath. Strengthened by it. Kara had found it in him. Now Rane had to hold onto it. He had to keep the monster within him at bay. He couldn't become like Marcus.

At least the journey down was quicker than the ascent. Despite the beauty of the mountains, Rane was happy to back on level ground again, moving forward. The rocky path turned into a worn gravel road through green fields of wild grass, a welcome wash of color rolling off towards the horizon.

Myri seemed happier, too. She waited for him to catch up once more. "Sorry about earlier."

Rane waved the apology away. "Don't think about it. It's been hard on both of us. It's not like we planned for this."

"Do you mind if I ask you a question?" said Myri as they rode through the long grass. "Why'd you leave the Legion? We all thought you were a lifer, destined to take over from the Lord General when the time came. "

"Maybe once, but not towards the end. Not once I could see an end to the war, see us winning. I gave everything to the Oath, but it also took everything from me."

"We saved a lot of lives."

"I know that. But I was enjoying the fight too much. Enjoying every life I took. Every one. Loving that rush as they died. The burst of magic. And as much as I loved it, I hated it. I knew it was wrong."

"The sword was making you feel like that."

"But I didn't know at the time. In the end, I just had to get away from you all, from the Legion. Find another life. Try and find some peace." Rane laughed, but there was no humor in his voice. "I used to count the days I'd gone without killing. Felt proud every day I kept my sword in its sheath."

"But you're Legion. You're like me. This is our life. We don't do peace. We weren't meant for cottages and countrysides, fishing and nights cuddled up by the fire. Weren't you going mad with boredom?"

Rane thought of watching sunsets with Kara, eating fish caught from the brook behind their house. "No. Never. It was all I ever wanted."

"Fuck. You surprise me." Myri lifted her stump. "You know why I'm pissed off about this? Not because it hurts or any shit like that. It just means I'm not going to be as good a fighter as I was. And I was pretty fucking fantastic when it came down to it. But what am I going to do now? I can't even sweep the streets." Myri paused, looked at Rane with fire in her eyes. "You know what? Marcus chopped the wrong person's hand off. He should've got yours. By the sounds of it, you won't need it."

"I've got a few debts to call in before I hang up my sword again. Some people have got questions to answer."

Myri inclined her head. "As I said, peace isn't what we do. Fighting's as easy as breathing to us. We live by the sword, and we'll die by the sword, whether we find a cure or not."

"I remember you were always talking about heading back home after the war as well. Seemed pretty set on it, too."

This time it was Myri's turn to laugh. "Oh, I did. Went back South to my hometown in the Islands. Had dreams of picking up my life where I'd left it, maybe having a family. You know, normal stuff, like you. Turned out I wasn't the same person anymore." She raised an eyebrow. "Wasn't so good at normal stuff as I thought I would be."

"What happened?"

"Nothing happened. Maybe that was the problem. People there hadn't experienced the war — hell, most of them hadn't even left the town in the time I'd been away. They'd heard about the fighting, but it was just stories passed on by travellers or when the taxman came looking for more money. They'd not had people bleed to death in their arms while they tried to hold their guts in. Hadn't experienced that all-consuming fear of not knowing if they were going to live or die from one minute to the next."

"That's how life's supposed to be."

"I know. By the Gods, I know. But I walk into the local inn and everyone's there and it's as if the last five, six years haven't happened. Erin's behind the bar, like he'd been when I left, and he saw me, and he just said, 'Hi Myri, how are you?' Like I'd last seen him the day before. I wanted to cut his throat open from ear to ear."

Rane didn't tell her he knew that feeling only too well. It was why he'd lived in the middle of nowhere — he hadn't trusted himself not to act on the impulse. "But was that the sword making you feel like that?"

"Who the fuck knows? I just knew I didn't fit in." Myri shook her head at the memories. "I smiled at familiar faces, tried joining their conversations, pretended to be interested in their lives as they pretended to be curious of mine — but it was all too hard. Too trivial. I walked around the next few days like a ghost, a memory too stubborn to fade away. But I eventually got the message. When a caravan came through, I signed up with it, working as a hired sword. Didn't even look back or say goodbye, and I can't say if any of them even noticed I'd gone again.

"The caravan took me to back to the mainland, on to Napolin. Picked up more work there. I had to use my sword a few times — enjoyed that, so I went looking for more trouble. The more dangerous the gigs, the better. Felt like I was alive again, out there on the edge with people like me who'd survived the war, and the blood, and the mayhem. For a while, being an ex-Legionnaire got me respect and rewards. And I loved every minute of it. Loved having my sword in my hand again." Myri laughed again, but there was no humor in it, only pain. "Then I headed back to Candra, met up with Jefferson and got back into the game properly. He'd lost too many Legionnaires after the war and was happy to have me back. Being amongst soldiers again was good for me, especially Legionnaires who were just as crazy as I was. Barracks life helped drown out that voice in my head, or maybe it just gave me plenty of opportunities to indulge it with blood.

"Didn't even notice my sword turning black. I just wanted to kill every fucker I could." She looked at Rane, eyes blazing with fury. "I still do."

"I was lucky," replied Rane. "I had Kara to concentrate on. It helped suppress those feelings. When she died, they all came flooding back. Part of me was glad, if I'm being honest. I finally had an excuse to fight again. To kill again."

"You must be bloody ecstatic, then, with this current situation. Because there's no end of blood waiting to be spilled."

"Believe me, I'd rather be at home with my wife. I'd give anything for that."

"Oh, I don't doubt you. You'll just have to make do with being stuck with me."

Rane smiled. "There are worse things."

"I'm sure."

They crested a hill and found a small, single-story building, made of stone with a sod roof, nestled amongst the green fields. Just an ordinary working home, not much different to the cottage Rane had left behind. Two pens for livestock were at the rear of the house, but both appeared empty. A small pond was to the right of the building. It had to be said: it was a beautiful spot for a farm.

"Shall we call in? See if they've seen Marcus?" suggested Myri.

Rane looked at the farm again. It was too quiet. Too tranquil. A sickness crept into his gut. "Come on." He ran his hand over his weapons as they rode down, reassuring himself that his pistols were in his holsters, *Kibon* on his back. He wished he had more weapons; wished he wasn't still raw from his burns, wished all was going to be well. But every soldier could tell you what wishing was good for.

They came in at a trot and stopped outside the main building, dismounting and tying their horses to a fence railing.

The front door was smashed off its hinges. Whoever had done it had gone in hard and heavy. Rane pulled a pistol out, and Myri did likewise. *Kibon* protested painfully, promising safety and success if only Rane had his sword in his hand instead, but he knew where that desire led.

They waited outside the door, listening for any sounds from inside, but all was silent. Myri pointed at Rane, indicating that he should enter first. He nodded, mouth dry, and stepped inside.

It took a moment or two for Rane's eyes to adjust to the darkness of the interior. The main room was completely ransacked; the table overturned, pots smashed, a small chest of drawers pulled apart. And there was the smell, a mix of blood, piss and shit. Somewhere, a corpse waited to be found.

Rane stepped further into the room, *Kibon* screaming in his head, looking for the dead, and the danger.

The body was the easiest to find. In the far corner of the room, a man was tied to a chair. His head tilted to the ceiling, and a vicious cut opened his neck from one side to the other. Every part of his body was stained red, and his blood covered most of the floor in front of him.

Rane pointed to the body as Myri entered the cottage behind him, then to a trail of blood leading to a doorway just past the corpse. They moved silently towards it. Was the killer on the other side of it, unaware the Legionnaires were there? Or was he waiting to attack them the moment they opened the door?

As Rane passed the dead man, he reached out to feel his skin. It was getting cold. A good chance that the killer was gone. Even so, Rane's heart raced as he reached for the door handle. He paused, counted to three inside his head, and opened the door. Inside was a small bedroom with a bed and two children's cots to one side. And more dead. The man's wife and children lay slaughtered in their beds.

"Shit," said Rane, holstering his weapon. "Shit. Shit."

Myri peered over his shoulder. "Marcus."

"Marcus," agreed Rane, almost choking on the word. They stepped back into the main room. Rane cast his eyes over the room while Myri checked the man out.

"Tying him up is new," she said. "The mutilation's more controlled."

"Torture."

"Look at this." Myri walked around to the back of the man, careful not to step in any of the puddles of blood. She tilted the man's head to one side so that it caught the sunlight sneaking in through the front door. His ear had been hacked off. She turned the head again to show the same had been done to the other ear as well.

"Not good," said Rane.

"Hands, too." Not all, but most of the man's fingers were missing.

"Why kill him like this?" Rane moved in closer so he could get a better look at the man's face. It was about as ordinary as it could get. Dark hair, roughly cut. Weather-beaten skin, well-lined from hard living. "He's just a farmer. He didn't deserve to die like this. Nor his family."

"No one does."

Rane bent down to inspect the dead man's wounds. The cuts on the neck and hands were clean and precise. Why had Marcus bothered? There were no toothmarks, so Marcus hadn't fed on the body. Why hack away at the man like this?

Myri rubbed her face. "You're right. We have to stop him somehow. Otherwise he'll keep doing this."

"Look in on the wife and children again. Did Marcus cut them in the same way?" asked Rane as he stepped back. There was a lot of blood in front of the man, as there should be from a throat wound like his. Marcus had been standing behind the man when he cut the windpipe open and the blood would've shot out, especially as the man must have been petrified. He'd suffered a long time, after all. And yet there was almost too much blood.

"The others aren't as bad as the man here, but Marcus has given them a pretty good going over," said Myri, returning to the room. "All have multiple cuts."

"The blood trail to the room," said Rane, pointing to it. "I think Marcus made the man watch."

"Why would he do that?" asked Myri.

"Back in Rooktown, at Haversham's mansion, I remember thinking that bedroom was an awful place to die. I hoped no one living had been brought there to see the carnage before Marcus did whatever he did to them. But maybe they were. Maybe that was the point. Maybe he needs them scared."

"Needs?"

"You said the more people we kill with our swords, the more our souls get corrupted."

Myri nodded. "That's right."

"So what if Marcus is killing good people, innocent people with his sword? Would the corruption be quicker? Would the hit of magic that comes with it be more powerful? Maybe if the person is terrified, the effect is intensified."

"Marcus is hurt," continued Myri. "He needs to get better — just like us — and then he finds this cottage and the family..."

"Exactly," said Rane. "He tortures them, feeding his sword's magic with their fear and their blood."

Myri picked up a chair from the ground and sat down. "Shit. So the more scared they are, the stronger he'll get?"

"Looks that way," agreed Rane. "But unless he found a horse here, Marcus is still on foot. If we leave now, we can still catch him."

"Shit. It keeps getting worse." Myri sighed, shaking her head as she got up. "Come on. Let's find the bastard."

They stepped out into the cold morning air, grateful to leave the carnage behind. Rane breathed in deeply, trying to get the stink out of his nose. "We head north, see what tracks we can find."

They rode in silence, leaving the dead behind, Rane full of guilt for not stopping Marcus when they had the chance, and for not staying to give the farmer and his family a decent burial.

The grasslands were a series of small hills, up and down into another small valley so they could never see more than half a mile ahead, forcing them to ride frustratingly slowly as they looked for signs of Marcus' passing.

"He could be waiting for us on the other side of the next hill," said Myri as she spat into the dust. "Or miles away by now."

"Rushing isn't going to change that. We'll only miss his tracks if he turns back on us," replied Rane.

"If he's got any sense, he'll stay on the road. The dirt's too fucking hard to leave a footprint for us anyway. Put as many miles between as he can."

"Marcus was never stupid," agreed Rane. They reached the peak of the next hill to find a small convoy of wagons stalled halfway along. "Odd place to stop."

"Too early to camp." Myri leaned forward in her saddle to get a better look. "Missionaries. The big wagon in the middle is a mobile temple. It's got the sign of Odason stuck on its roof."

They nudged their horses on, moving slowly so as not to spook anyone who spotted them. Even so, the first scream rang out when they were still a good few hundred yards away.

People scrambled around, ducking for cover behind wagons while two men marched out to meet the Legionnaires. They wore missionary clothes like everyone else, but in their hands were flint-lock pistols.

When there were fifty yards between them, both parties stopped. One of the men aimed his pistol at Rane. "Come any closer and I'll blow your brains out."

16

The man's gun wavered in his hand, but Rane had no doubt he was going to use if it he had to. His friend next to him took a moment longer to get his pistol raised, but when he did his hand was steady. They might've been wearing the robes of religious men, but they weren't strangers to violence.

Rane held up his hands. "We're not looking for any trouble. Just wanted to ask you a few questions and then we'll be on our way."

"How about you just turn around and go back the way you came, and keep your questions to yourself?" suggested the second man, a Fascalian judging by his accent.

Myri nudged her horse forward. "We're not going to do that, but you're welcome to try and make us."

"Hold on! Hold on!" A burly woman, well into middle age, stepped out from behind one of the wagons. She strode past the two men, pushing their weapons down towards the ground as she did so. "We've had enough violence for one day." Her hair was tied back into a high ponytail, with the sides shaved off to show she was one of Odason's priestesses. Sunray tattoos disappeared down her neck and into her heavy woolen robes. She wasn't part of the Inquisition, though, as far as Rane could see. That was something.

"They're trouble, Mother," said the first man.

"Go and load that pistol properly, Douglas, before you hurt yourself," she replied before turning to Rane. "I'm Mother Fia. Who're you?"

"My name is Nathaniel Rane, and this is Myri," said Rane. Douglas stepped back, eyes blazing with fury at Rane. The other man remained by Fia's side, tense and alert.

Fia's eyes drifted over them, taking in their injuries but also their weapons. "Would you mind showing me your right hands?"

Myri waved her stump at the priestess with a smile while Rane held up his still-burnt hand.

"Fucking convenient injuries you got there," snapped the Fascalian.

Myri started forward. "As if I'd cut my own—"

"Please, everyone! Calm down," said Fia. "William, please mind your language. I know we've had an ordeal, but there is no need for such profanity."

The man bowed his head. "I'm sorry, Mother. I wasn't thinking."

"We've just been attacked," said Fia to Rane and Myri. "By a man, or what seemed like a man, carrying a sword like yours. A Legion sword. Two of my flock are dead, and he's driven off in one of our carriages with three children on board."

"How long ago?" asked Rane.

"Maybe two hours," replied Fia. She looked away for a moment. "The men wanted to go after them, but William and Douglas are our only guards left alive. I don't want to leave everyone else unprotected. Besides, they'll only get themselves killed if they catch up with him. The man was a demon."

Rane dismounted. "You did the right thing in not pursuing — he's a dangerous man. We barely survived our last encounter."

"Are you bounty hunters?" asked Fia. "Douglas said the man was a Legionnaire, and I hear they're offering a lot of gold for them these days."

"Something like that," said Rane. "We mean to stop him."

"We haven't got much money," said Fia, "but we'll pay you to return our family to us."

"Mother, you can't trust them," roared William. "We'll get the kids back. I promise you. We don't need these two."

Fia placed a hand on his arm. "You're lucky you're not dead, my dear, and I don't want that changing. If Odason has brought Nathaniel and Myri to us in our hour of need, I'd be foolish not to ask for their help."

"We're not for hire," spat Myri. "We've got enough to deal with."

"We do, but we can still help if we can," said Rane as he gave her a look to calm down. Myri shook her head at him, but said no more. He turned his attention back to Fia. "Did the wagon have any weapons? Provisions? Anything we should know about?"

"Some food, some water. No weapons. We keep them on the back wagon," replied the priestess. "The one he took is as ordinary as the rest of them."

"And the children... how old are they?" asked Rane.

Tears came to the corners of Fia's eyes. "Eight, five, and four. Hardly grown at all."

"Right." Rane didn't want to think of children that young in Marcus' hands; of how afraid he could make them. "We'll go after him. Hopefully, by the time you catch up, we'll have good news for you."

Fia drew the sign of Odason in the air. "Bless you, Nathaniel. I'll pray for your success."

"Thank you," said Rane. "We'll need all the help we can get."

"We'll follow on behind you as best we can," said Fia.

Rane nodded. "You do that, and the Gods willing, we'll get the children back for you."

Fia looked at him. "There is only the one God. Odason, God of Life."

"Of course," replied Rane. Mounted once more, the Legionnaires left the convoy of wagons behind and continued on their way. This time at least they knew what they were looking for. There was no need to look for scuffed earth or broken twigs. Marcus had three kids in a wagon with a two-hour head start.

They kept a good pace without pushing the horses hard, not wanting to tire them out too soon, just hoping they were going faster than Marcus.

Trees appeared along the road and dotted across the fields, but still there was no sign of the wagon.

Overhead, the sun passed the midday point and began its long, slow descent once more. The trees grew denser, and in the distance, Rane could see a forest waiting for them. He knew they'd find Marcus there, amongst the trees and the shadows. It looked the place for dark deeds. He prayed the children were still safe.

They picked up the pace. The horses pounded along the road as it twisted down a small hill. It curved off to the right, turning once more when it met a small river and ran parallel to it through to the woods. Trees curled over the path, forming a tunnel of leaves and flickering light. Rane's unease grew — so many places for Marcus to hide. So many places to torture the children, to kill them.

"We're going to have to slow down soon," shouted Myri. "We're going to kill the horses if we don't."

Rane ignored her, eager to find Marcus and only too aware of the lives at risk. He could tell his horse was struggling, but he needed it to go on a little longer. Marcus was close — he could feel it.

"Nathaniel!" Myri rode in close and grabbed his reins. "Stop."

Rane gave in then, pushed down on his stirrups and pulled the reins to slow the horse from a gallop to a canter and then to a walk. Myri matched him, all the while looking at him as if to question his sanity.

"What are you doing?" asked Myri finally.

"I'm sorry," replied Rane. He scrunched his face up as he swallowed the reality of the situation. "I'm sorry... I don't want to find three dead children. Marcus has killed enough."

"We'll find him, but killing the horses isn't going to help us. We have enough problems as it is."

Rane scanned the woodland around them, looking into the

shadows and through the trees, desperate for a sign. "He's close. I can feel it."

"Me too," said Myri, her jaw tight. "It's the sword. I've been fighting the urge to draw it ever since we rode into the forest, but it keeps niggling away at me, whispering in the back of my head."

"It's worse than any hunger I've known."

Shadows fell across Myri's face, hiding her eyes. "Believe me, you don't know the half of it yet."

"So where is he?"

They let the horses walk and catch their breath, with nothing but the trees and the occasional squirrel for company. Time passed, each minute a heavy weight pressing down on Rane. Another minute the children got closer to meeting Heras; another minute Rane drew closer to letting someone else down.

The woods grew darker around them as the sun crossed the sky. Rane was starting to question his instincts when he noticed the birds had stopped singing, and he cursed himself for a fool.

Another corner and the wagon waited for them in the middle of the road. It lay upside down, broken, shreds of awning littering the road. There was no sign of its horses, the children, or Marcus.

They stopped a few yards away, and Myri and Rane approached on foot. Claw marks were everywhere, gouged into the wood, chunks bitten away. The wagon's contents were scattered across the road and in amongst the trees. They found one horse nearby, ripped in half, blood and guts everywhere. Another trail of blood suggested the other horse had been dragged deeper into the woods.

"This doesn't look like Marcus' work," said Myri.

Rane stared at the gouges in the wood and knew full well what had caused them. "Bracke." There was no need to say any more.

Kibon was in his hand a heartbeat later, glistening, full of power, telling him not to take any chances. There was a sigh as Myri unsheathed her sword — the blade so dark, so frightening.

They both stood waiting, watching, listening. Every sense straining. Their horses skittered about, unnerved by the blood and the scent of death in the air.

"Grab the horses before they bolt," said Rane.

"Remember I've only got one fucking hand," snapped Myri, but did as he ordered anyway. They both knew he was going to be more useful in a fight.

The slaughter of the horses made the tracks hard to read. From what Rane could tell, there'd been at least two, if not three, Bracke in the attack. Three too many for Rane's liking, even with *Kibon*.

"You see anything?" called Myri.

"Nothing," replied Rane. "Maybe they went after Marcus and the children."

"Do we go after them?"

"What choice do we have?"

Rane was about to head back to his horse when he heard it, so faint it could have been a whisper on the wind. The second time, he was sure. A child's sob came from under the wagon.

He squatted down beside it, knocked on the wood. "Is someone in there?"

"You found something?" asked Myri as she brought the horses closer, but Rane put up a hand to silence her.

"I'm here to help," called out Rane, trying to make his voice sound as calm as possible. "Mother Fia sent me to get you."

The sob was louder this time, full of tears and snot.

"I'm going to lift the wagon off you, okay? Stay calm and we'll have you out of there in a minute." Rane waited for a response but got none. He looked up at Myri. "I think its one of the children."

"Thank the Gods."

Rane stood and sheathed *Kibon*. "Tell me if anything's coming," he asked Myri.

"That's going to be a bastard to shift," said Myri. "Must be at least a thousand pounds."

"Thanks for telling me," said Rane. "It's still got to be lifted." He squatted down once more, hooking his fingers under the wooden side. "Grab the kid as soon as you can."

Rane adjusted his feet once more, filled his lungs full of air, and pushed up with his legs. The weight was immense, threatening to buckle his knees and burst every muscle, but the wagon shifted a few inches off the ground. His arms and shoulders took the strain and he pushed up once more, grunting with the effort, grateful for *Kibon's* magic and the strength it gave him. His legs straightened, and the side of the wagon rose by a couple of feet. "Do you see anything?"

"It's a little girl." Myri was on her knees, reaching out with her good hand. "Come here, don't be afraid."

The wagon seemed to grow in weight in Rane's hands and little shivers of agony ran through his arms and legs. His burnt skin protested as it stretched under the pressure.

"It's okay," said Myri and Rane looked down to see her disappear under the wagon. If he dropped it now, she'd be crushed.

Seconds passed. Each one felt like an hour.

"I'm Myri. What's your name?"

Rane couldn't hear the answer to Myri's question. He couldn't move. All he could do was hold on as sweat ran down his face and stung his eyes. Every muscle in his body burned. His strength was fading fast.

"Crawl to me, Gemma," said Myri from under the wagon, but all Rane could think was that she was taking too long. Too damn long. He couldn't hold it much longer.

"Good girl. I've got you," said Myri.

Out of the corner of his eye, Rane thought he saw some movement; a darting shadow some thirty yards into the trees. "Whatever you're doing down there, be quick. We've got company."

There was a scuffling noise from beneath him and a cry from the child, and then Myri scooted back. Rane looked down, trying to ignore the pain spreading in his arms.

Myri reappeared. She crawled backwards, until only her head and shoulders were under the wagon. All he had to do was hold onto the wagon for a few seconds more. His arms and legs shook violently, but still he held on.

He closed his eyes, retreating into himself. Nothing else existed as he put all he had into holding the wagon. "Come on," he urged.

"We're clear!" shouted Myri and Rane let go, falling backwards as he did so. He hit the ground at the same time as the wagon, feeling the impact of the heavy weight slamming to the ground. Myri sat next to him, cradling a small child — a girl— in her arms. She stared wide-eyed at them both, petrified.

"This is Gemma," said Myri as she got to her feet. "She's a very brave girl."

"Pleased to meet you," said Rane, only too aware of how he must look with his burnt and puckered skin. "My name is Nathaniel. We're going to get you back to your family." He smiled, but the girl slunk further into Myri's arms.

"We should get..." Myri started, but movement from the bushes silenced her.

Rane felt the danger too and was back on his feet in an instant. He whipped *Kibon* from its sheath.

The immediate pulse of magic helped calm the shaking in his limbs, feeding some energy back into his body. He wiped sweat from his face with his other hand, flicking it to the ground as he scanned the undergrowth around them. Something was out there.

The horses stomped the ground, snorting and grumbling, eager to leave.

More movement, this time on the other flank.

Bracke. It had to be.

"Get the girl out of here. Get her back to her family." Rane didn't even look at Myri as he spoke. Didn't watch her retreat. He stood with his back to her, offering what protection he could. "Find me when she's safe. I'm going to go after Marcus, find the others." He didn't mention that he needed to kill the devil dogs first. There was no point.

He heard Myri mount her horse as a Bracke jumped on top of the wagon, and the little girl screamed.

Blood dripped from its jaws as it curled itself up, ready to pounce. The claws on its hands and feet dug into the woodwork, its eyes focused on Rane. Its tail whipped behind it.

Rane shifted *Kibon* into a two-handed grip as he listened to Myri gallop back down the road, followed by his own horse. He had to get his strike just right. He'd only have the one...

The Bracke roared and launched itself at Rane.

He swung *Kibon,* but he was too tired, too hurt, too slow. The Bracke hit him with all its force, knocking him over as it slashed down with its claws. Rane kicked out as they fell, pushing the Bracke off him before it could hook its claws into his flesh. The ground smashed into his shoulder. His momentum rolled him through bushes and undergrowth. Dirt, sky, trees — all flashed past his eyes. He bounced against a tree and cracked his head against a rock and then the world stopped moving. He reeled, punch-drunk, trying to bring his senses back under control.

The Bracke leaped once more.

17

R ane threw himself to the ground as the Bracke sprang, and felt it pass far too close over his head. He rolled back onto his feet, *Kibon* ready in his hands to strike back.

The Bracke was ten yards away. It snapped its jaws at Rane, watching him, twitching this way and that to see how Rane would react.

Rane held *Kibon* high in a two-handed grip, blade parallel to the ground as he shifted his feet, retreating to create some space between them. Fear coursed through his body, but he was still alive. He still had a chance. And he had a weapon in his hand that the beast should fear, as sharp as any tooth or claw. As long as he had that, he wouldn't die.

The Bracke snarled, baring its teeth, and reared up on its hind legs to stand almost as tall as Rane. He stepped to the left as it moved right, keeping his eyes on the creature for any sign it would attack. The rest of the world disappeared as he concentrated on the Bracke. Sweat ran down his brow. There was no room for mistakes. Rane had gotten lucky twice, but he had to do more than that if he was to stay alive.

The Bracke's tail twitched. It pressed down on its hind legs. It clenched its hands and then it sprung, two hundred and fifty pounds of pure fury intent on tearing Rane to bits.

Rane sidestepped and dropped to one knee, bringing his sword around, pouring momentum into the move. A claw flashed past his face as he felt the blade bite. A jolt of energy rushed through him as the sword struck home. He pushed up off his knee, driving all his weight behind the stroke. He turned so his shoulder crashed into the beast, pushing it away as he dragged the sword through its body. Warm blood spilled over his legs as the Bracke crumpled to the ground.

His hands shook as he took deep breaths, trying to steady himself, riding the wave of magic flowing from *Kibon*. Already the creature's blood was disappearing into the sword, leaving the blade spotless. But Rane had no time to worry about the effect the creature would have on his soul. There were other Bracke, and Marcus and the other children to find.

Rane looked back down the road and was relieved to see no sign of Myri or the girl. Unfortunately, his horse was gone with them. He was on foot from there on. He checked to the north, found the road empty as well. But Marcus was out there somewhere, as were the Bracke. He'd no choice but to follow, and meet whatever devil he found first on the road.

Slinging *Kibon* over his shoulder, Rane set off at a run, his exhaustion gone. *Kibon* had done its work well. Even his burns felt better. He sprinted faster than a normal man, aware that the Bracke could be anywhere and waiting for him to pass by before attacking.

The ground dipped down before turning to the right and leveling off once more, allowing Rane to pick up speed. The canopy overhead thickened, cutting off most of the natural light, but still he went on. A mile flew by, then a second, and still all he had were footprints in the dirt to assure him that he was on the right path.

After the third mile, doubt began to niggle away at the back of his mind. Had he missed something? Was the trail Marcus'? Had the Bracke driven them deep into the woods miles back?

He jumped over a small stream, nearly slipping as he landed on the muddy bank, and then he was off again. He swerved around a fallen tree before the ground started to climb once more. His thighs burned as he pushed on, and he could feel even his magic-enhanced stamina begin to struggle. Rane reached over his shoulder, grasped *Kibon*'s hilt, felt a boost and kept on going.

Rane reached the top of the hill and burst out of the woods into fields of green grass and blue skies. The sudden light blinded him, and he almost didn't see what waited in the middle of the road. A second Bracke stood on a corpse, feasting on its flesh, ripping it to bits with tooth and claw. Common sense told him to stop, to approach with caution, but he knew that wasn't an option. He drew both pistols and charged the Bracke.

The beast turned when he was a few yards away, lumps of human flesh in its clawed hands. Rane brought one pistol up and fired on the run. The gun boomed — a puff of gunpowder smoke, a burst of flame. The Bracke's head jerked back as the bullet struck. A spray of blood marked the bullet's impact. But it wasn't dead.

Rane raised the other pistol as the beast shrugged off the wound, its focus on Rane, snarling, roaring, ready to pounce. The space between them was non-existent. The Bracke's teeth, razor-sharp, were covered with blood and gore. And then it sprang.

Time stopped. Their momentum drew them together. Rane could see his hand disappearing into its cavernous mouth. He pulled the trigger as the creature's jaws closed. The boom, the smoke, the flame were all smothered by the Bracke's mouth, but then the bullet erupted from the back of the creature's head, throwing it off Rane. It hit the dirt, twitched once, twice, then was still.

Rane skidded to a halt, holstering his weapons and unsheathing *Kibon*. If more Bracke were nearby, he wanted his sword to hand. He turned slowly, scanning the ground all around him for any movement in the grass. At least the open ground gave the creatures fewer places to hide. His heart hammered away in his chest as he tried to work some moisture back into his mouth, but he saw no danger.

Sure he was safe, he went to check the body. It was a boy — the eight-year-old, judging by the size of him — but the Bracke hadn't left much that could be recognized. Rane muttered a prayer and cursed himself for being too slow, too late to save him.

Two of the children were accounted for. Only one remained with Marcus. Rane was tempted to wait with the body until Myri and the others arrived. Could justify it easily enough — someone had to look after the body, and he was tired and worn out, lacking even water to drink — but he knew he was only making excuses. Truth was, he was afraid of Marcus. He'd beaten Rane easily at the mansion and in Rooktown, and Rane had no reason to think the next time would go any differently — especially if Marcus had recovered from his injuries.

He sheathed *Kibon* and reloaded his pistols, pretending he wasn't doing it to buy himself some time. He could see Marcus' trail still, disappearing off into the distance. How much further was it until he reached the Dead Lands, though? Another couple of miles, maybe three? Already he could smell the smoke in the air. Once there, there'd be no hope. Not in that graveyard.

The sun was starting its descent as well, leaving only a couple of hours before dark.

With his pistols back in their holsters, loaded and primed, Rane took one last lingering look back down the road to confirm what he already knew — there was no sign of Myri, and he couldn't wait for her. With a shake of his head, he set off again, heading north. Marcus' trail was fainter in the dust, but at least there was no sign of any more Bracke after them.

Long shadows stretched across the road as the sun dropped down over his left shoulder. Two miles fell under his feet and still there was no sign of Marcus. The ground rose once more, climbing out of a vale, and Rane suddenly knew with certainty what waited on the other side. The air was tinged with soot and smoke from a thousand fires that would never stop burning. He slowed, unable to stop himself, not wanting to reach the top.

It was almost dark by the time he eventually reached the peak. How fitting. How apt. He stood looking out across the Dead Lands — the scene of the five nations' greatest victory. The scene of their greatest failure. In the early evening light, the fires glowed like little pockets of hell, sending snowflakes of ash into the wind. Two years since Babayon's magic had done its work, and still no sign of them abating.

It was an area of land once known simply as the Steppes. Mile after mile of grassland populated only by wild buffalo, a sea of green crossed by any and all travelling north or south. A good three days' travel as straight as the crow flies. Even now the well-worn road stood out, cutting its way across the ruined land. But no one went that way anymore. It was still the Crow's Road, but for different reasons now.

A second road now marked the circumference, because no sane person crossed the Dead Lands. They took an extra three or four days to go around it. They took the Long Road, as it was known. The safe road. It had been Rane and Myri's plan to take it. Most likely the pilgrims', too. Of course, Marcus' trail didn't take the sensible way. The sane way.

His trail went straight on. Down the Crow's Road. Into the Dead Lands.

But Rane wasn't going to follow. Not alone.

18

Rane waited for the pilgrims by the boy's body. He'd thrown the Bracke into the wild grass, away from the track. No parent should see what had fed on their child. Even so, he wished he had something to cover the body with. He would've spared the pilgrims that sight too if he could.

As it was, he waited as the night crept on, wishing he was home with his wife looking forward to the birth of his baby, not sitting vigil over the corpse of someone else's son. But the world was what it was: a violent place, full of broken dreams and ruined lives.

It was fitting that he had such thoughts then, just a couple of miles from the Dead Lands and all the ghosts that lurked there. A place of horror created by the same man responsible for Rane's present predicament.

Babayon. Where had he got such power? Had he known what his magic would cause? The tainting of the Legion's souls? The contamination of the land by constant hellfire? Was he waiting with Jefferson at Orska? Was he the one who would undo the damage he'd created?

Rane heard Myri's horse approach and stood to greet her. The rumble of the pilgrims' wagons followed, still a good distance away.

"You okay?" she asked.

"Yeah," replied Rane, sounding far from it.

"That one of the kids?" Myri indicated the body with her chin.

"Yeah. Found a Bracke eating him."

"Shit. Marcus?"

"Followed him as far as the Dead Lands."

"Shit." Myri dismounted. She didn't ask why he'd not followed Marcus. She knew.

The wagons rumbled into sight a few moments later, expectant faces looking down at him, waiting for good news when he had none to give. He stepped back from Myri and she passed him her waterskin without the need for him to ask. The water soothed his throat as he tried to work out what to say.

William and Douglas drove the first wagon, both looking mean and surly, trying to reclaim some of their courage. A musket sat across Douglas' lap.

Fia followed in the wagon behind, straight-backed, prepared for what was to come. Her driver was a thin man with hangdog expression. In the back, just visible through the door, a woman cried. Most probably she was one of the lost children's mothers, and Rane couldn't help but glance down at the poor boy at his feet. He'd done his best, but the thought offered him little comfort.

It was too dark to see the riders of the other carriages, for which Rane was glad.

Douglas called a halt as they drew near. Reins pulled on horses and brakes squeaked against wheels. He jumped down, but his approach faltered when he saw the body. "Is that Joseph?"

"I'm afraid so," replied Rane.

"May Odason look over us." The man drew the sign over his chest, for protection or a blessing — either way, it was too late.

Fia hurried over, close behind. "What's happening? Have you found the other children?"

"Only the boy," said Rane, glancing down. "I'm sorry, but I was too late."

"What about Sarah? What about the third child?"

"Marcus — the man who took them — must still have her. I

followed their trail as far as the Dead Lands. Once I realized where they'd gone, I came back to wait for you all here."

Fia exchanged looks with Douglas — so they too knew of the Dead Lands. The bodyguard put his arm around the priest as her shoulders sagged, whispered in her ear. Whatever he said had an effect as Fia pushed Douglas away and straightened herself. "I will not believe Odason has abandoned us. His will may be unclear to us now, but it will not always be so. Our faith is being tested, and we will be found worthy."

Douglas bowed his head. "Yes Mother. I'm sorry."

"Let Hazia know we have her son. Once she's had some time with him, get William and bury the poor thing." Douglas bowed once more and headed back to the other wagons. Fia turned back to Rane and Myri. "Thank you for what you've done so far. You've already achieved more than I hoped, but I have to ask what your intentions are now."

Rane glanced at Myri, who nodded her assent. "We'll go after them at first light."

"Into the Dead Lands?" asked Fia.

"Yes," replied Rane. "Into the Dead Lands."

Fia looked north, as if she could see what waited a few miles down the road, and shivered. "Our plan was to take the Long Road around on our way to Napolin. Is it as bad as they say?"

"I don't think you'll find anyone alive who could tell you what it's really like," said Myri. "Ever since the Lands were created, everyone takes the Long Road."

Fia drew Odason's sign over her chest. "Magic."

Rane nodded. "Bad magic."

"You're not scared?" Fia leaned in closer, looked him in the eye.

"More than you can imagine. But what choice is there?"

"But it's still a three-day journey across the Lands. You won't be able to leave."

"We won't travel when it's dark. With a fire and standing guards..." Rane left the rest unsaid. He didn't want to talk about hope any more.

Fia nodded as if it were the best plan she'd ever heard, and not suicide. "We shall go with you. You'll have Douglas and William to help. We've enough clean water and food. Sarah will want to see a familiar face when you find her."

"Don't you think you need to ask your pilgrims before you sign them up for something like that?" asked Myri.

Fia glanced over her shoulder and saw Douglas returning with a woman — the boy's mother. Fia indicated that they continue the conversation elsewhere and started walking. "I will — but I have no doubt they'll follow. It's Odason's will."

Rane and Myri fell into step behind her. "It'll be hard to protect you all," he said once they had some privacy again. The boy's mother's cries filled the space they'd left behind.

"What's in there?" asked Fia.

"If we're lucky," replied Rane, "only ghosts. But the fact no one's ever made it out of there alive suggests there are worse things lurking. Probably more Bracke, maybe Jotnar."

"You shouldn't go with us," Myri said to Fia. "We're trained. We're experienced. We're..." She stopped herself from saying 'Legionnaires' in time. "...prepared for what we'll find. You're none of those things."

"I'm not suggesting you don't lead us and do whatever needs to be done," replied Fia with a smile, as if none of what she was about to say needed saying. "But we have weapons. Douglas and William are capable. We can help in whatever way we can, and at night we can rotate the guards and give everyone a chance to rest. And we'll be with you when you find Sarah."

Rane went to speak, but Fia held up her hand to silence him. "I'm not asking. I'm telling you that we will follow, with or without your permission. This is Odason's will — bringing you to us in our hour of need, bringing us all to this spot, this crossroads. I'll do as he commands us to."

Rane could think of a thousand arguments why the pilgrims shouldn't follow them, but looking into her eyes, he could see none of them would change her mind. "Just make sure everyone knows what they are getting themselves into. And spread out whatever weapons you have — Odason isn't going to be able to help us in the Dead Lands."

Fia bowed. "Thank you. Now I'll go and help bury our dead. I'll speak with you again when we eat." She looked over at the mother crying over her dead son. "If any of us have an appetite for food after this."

The priest wandered back to her people, leaving Myri and Rane alone once more.

"I know we're not going to do it," said Myri, "but the sensible thing would be to leave all of them behind, take the Long Road and be on our way. The girl's more than likely dead. Marcus, too."

"We don't know that for sure," said Rane softly. "There's still a chance."

"Maybe now. Maybe tomorrow. But it's at least three days to cross that wasteland. They'll never reach the other side. Nor will we."

"There's still a chance," repeated Rane.

Myri shook her head in exasperation. "I'll remind you how fucking insane this is when we're dead. For the rest of eternity, I'll keep moaning on about it."

Douglas and William dug a grave by the roadside. The thunk of their spades was a steady rhythm in the night. Someone else on the far side of the wagons had got a small fire going; there was a brief flash as more wood was added to it.

"You asked me earlier why I left the Legion," said Rane eventually. "I only told you part of the reason." He gestured to the north with his chin. "This was the other part."

"The Dead Lands?"

"What we did here."

"What we did? We won the war here," said Myri.

"We committed genocide here. We used magic to commit mass murder here."

"We won the war! How is that murder?" Myri rubbed her face, eyes full of disbelief. "We chased the Rastak Army here after years of defeat, years of them murdering everyone in their path. They formed up on the Plains, ready to make a stand, ready to fight once more —

and gave us a chance to end it in one fell swoop. We took it. Be proud of what we did."

"We became as bad as the Rastaks — as monstrous. There was no honor in what we did; just Babayon sending demon fire to do our work for us. I can still hear the screams, smell the roasted flesh. And everyone was so happy about it. Drinking beer and joking while the world burned."

"Would you rather we'd all died?"

"No... but none of the choices we made have worked out for the better, have they? Our souls trapped in cursed swords while we slowly turn into demons ourselves; people starving; crops failing; towns dying. And the heart of our country looks like Heras' kingdom more than anything the Rastaks tried to do." Rane sighed. "Yes, I wanted to win the war, but not like that. That's why I left. I was ashamed of what we'd done, of what we'd become... of what I'd become. We shouldn't have done what we did."

Myri scuffed her feet in the dirt as she thought about what to say. The pilgrims were singing by the grave as the boy's body was lowered into the ground, a haunting melody full of sorrow and pain. Finally, Myri looked up. "Guess we'll find out tomorrow."

19

The pilgrims, nine adults in all, stood around Rane and Myri in a half-circle, faces grim and pale but determined. Dark circles framed their eyes from lack of sleep. Douglas had passed weapons to them all earlier but, apart from the two guards, none looked comfortable holding them. The four surviving children huddled together in Fia's wagon, watching but not understanding what was about to happen. They'd moved all the food and most of the water there as well. The mobile temple was larger and sturdier than all the other wagons, and they'd agreed it would be protected at all costs. The other wagons could be sacrificed if need be, but survival meant keeping the temple moving; keeping the food and water safe.

"The Crow's Road goes straight through the Dead Lands," said Rane. "We keep to it no matter what. If you see Marcus or Sarah, tell Myri or me. Don't get drawn off the road. Don't get off your wagons unless your life is in danger and there's no other choice."

He watched their faces, only too aware the pilgrims weren't soldiers. Fia's husband was a Fascalian called Karn, and he looked tired enough that a hundred days' sleep wouldn't make a difference. He gripped an axe that had seen plenty of action in its life, judging by the nicks in the blade's edge, though Karn's slight frame suggested it'd had a previous owner more suited to using it. The Hendersons, Olivik and Tanya, were the parents to two of the remaining children. As a carpenter, Olivik at least had the build of someone used to manual labor, with big shoulders and powerful arms. His wife had agreed to stay with the children, armed with a knife, to try and stop them seeing anything they shouldn't. Joassa Alrick would be with her too, which was only a good thing. Out of everyone there, she looked the most intimidating, and ready to use the meat cleaver in her hand. Hazia stood next to her, eyes red from a night of crying. She had no weapon — the fight was gone from her. Her husband, Regas, wasn't much better, fingers constantly twitching in and out of the trigger of his crossbow. Chances were he'd shoot one of their own before they'd got too far. And Rane had thought the soldiers he'd commanded on the wall at Candra had been inexperienced. What he'd give to have a dozen with him now. What he'd give for everything to be different.

"Has anyone got any questions?" he asked before his own thoughts got the better of him.

The pilgrims shuffled their feet as they looked at each other, wondering if anyone was going to speak. Finally, Karn found his voice. "What exactly are we going to see in there?"

"No one really knows," said Myri. "That's the truth. Two years back, we pushed the Rastak army back here. They were using the Plains to regroup. A mage set the ground on fire and killed them all. The land burned for over a year. As you'll see when we get to the borders, some of it's still burning today. Rest is ash and bones."

"Don't sound so bad," said Olivik, chewing his lip.

"The reason we don't know what else is in there," continued Rane, "is because no one's made it out of the Dead Lands alive since. People who entered the Crow's Road have never been seen again. Chances are there's every type of demon in there left over from the war. Make no mistake — we'll be lucky if one of us makes it out alive. If you want to turn back, now's the chance."

"Shit," said Regas, lifting his crossbow, and for a moment Rane thought he was going to pull the trigger. Rane stepped forward and pushed the weapon back down to point at the ground.

"Keep your finger away from the trigger until you want to use it," he told the man. "If you're scared, pass it to someone else. There's no shame in feeling that way."

The pilgrims all looked at Fia, taking their lead off her. Good credit to the woman, she acknowledged it, taking her time to choose her words carefully. "You all know how I feel. Yes, it's dangerous. Yes, we may all die, but death is the only certainty in life anyway. I believe this is Odason's will, His desire for us. We all embarked on this journey together, to build a new home for Him after the Rastaks destroyed all of His temples. It is no coincidence that our path has taken us to this place, where His enemies paid for their crimes. This is a test of our faith in Him, and one we will all pass. Because I know each and every one of you believe in Him. Believe me when I say Odason will look over us."

"Odason will look over us," chorused the others.

Fia turned to Rane. "We go."

Rane had to admire them for their spirit, even if he doubted their sanity. "Okay. Myri and I will take the lead. Douglas and William the rear. Fia's wagon goes in the middle. Let's go."

"Nathaniel, before we go, may I have a word?" asked Fia, holding up a hand.

"Certainly," he replied.

Fia waited for Myri to reach her horse and mount up before speaking. "Your burns are looking much better this morning. A night's rest seems to have done wonders for you."

"With everything going on, I hadn't noticed," replied Rane. His skin was better, a bright pink as opposed to the violent red it had been. He rolled his shoulders and was happy to feel the tightness gone from the movement.

"I have to admit," said Fia, "when I saw your injuries yesterday I was amazed you were alive, let alone on your feet. I don't think most normal men would be."

"I didn't think I was that bad," laughed Rane, knowing it was probably worse.

"Magic is a false gift." Fia's voice was soft as a mother's to her child. "It always bears a terrible price."

"I'm aware of that," replied Rane with a tightness to his jaw. *Kibon* stirred, alert.

"Odason's path for us is never easy. It tests us at every turn, searching to see if our faith in Him is real. He offers no shortcuts, nor should we look for them." Fia looked him in the eye with an intensity that showed the determination in the woman. "Pain is what makes us who we are. That's why I'm not afraid, either for myself or for my flock, of what we may face in the Dead Lands. We'll discover much about ourselves by the time we reach the other side. As Odason intends."

"Let's hope we're both around to find out what that is."

Fia nodded, went to say something else, but stopped herself. She gave a curious half-smile full of sadness, squeezed Rane's arm and wandered back to her wagon, touching the heads of her companions as she passed them. Rane watched her, aware of how much he liked the woman. He only hoped she'd keep her purity of spirit in the face of what was to come.

"We're wasting time," called out Myri from the back of her horse.

"I'm coming," replied Rane. Fia clambered into her wagon and took the driver's seat. She caught Rane's eye again and nodded. Time to go. He checked his saddle and kit, making sure everything was secure. A yew longbow hung on one side with a quiver of arrows; a gift from Fia. None of the pilgrims had the strength to use it, but Rane didn't have that problem. The arrows were beautifully weighted, with steel heads more than capable of punching through plate and shield.

The convoy rumbled on its way with Rane and Myri in the lead. No one was talking. All too nervous, too scared. It was one thing to believe Odason watched over you; another to test that faith like they were all about to do. Rane shifted in his saddle. He'd stopped believing long ago, back in the war. After what he'd seen — what he'd experienced — it was hard to believe in a higher power looking after his welfare. He had

Kibon and, cursed or not, it would keep him alive. The voice in his head assured him of that. He could feel its eagerness, its hunger for what they were about to do. It knew blood would be spilled in that cursed place.

The Dead Lands were even more shocking in the daylight. The group crested the peak of the hill where Rane had stopped the night before, already coughing on smoke-stained air. When they saw what waited for them, gasps and cries broke out among the convoy. The black grass spread as far as the eye could see to the west, north and east, the horizon interrupted only by orange pockets of fire spewing black clouds into the sky. It was as if part of Heras' kingdom had been recreated in the world above. At least the road they followed was still clear to see — a straight gash through the ebony fields.

Joassa whispered words of comfort to the children, but they could do nothing to lessen the horrors in front of them all. Rane looked back to find, to all their credit, the wagons were still following.

"Do you want to give them one last chance to take the Long Road?" asked Myri.

Rane shook his head. Fia wasn't going to be one for turning back from their course. "Let's get it over with."

They crossed the Long Road five minutes later, leaving life behind them, and took their first steps on the Crow's Road. One of the black birds, one eye missing, stood sentry on a branch of a burnt-out tree and squawked as they passed, an ill omen for the journey ahead. The ground crunched beneath the horses' hooves as they forced their mounts on. The animals protested, fighting their riders, only too aware of the dangers of where they were being asked to go.

The sun disappeared behind clouds as soot swirled around them. Rane gazed down the empty road. "Marcus has a good head start on us."

Myri wrinkled her nose. "Bastard's on foot, though, dragging a kid along with him. We should reel him in easily enough."

"As long as nothing else stands in our way." Rane shifted in his saddle, *Kibon* a gnawing pain in the back of his neck. The weapon's urgings were getting worse. It was if it could sense the danger around them and wanted to be free. Wanted to be blooded. Wanted to be strong. Or was it Rane's own fears making him think that? He doubted every thought, every feeling. What was him and what was the sword? Was there a difference anymore?

His hands shook as he gripped his reins tighter. He wasn't going to give in. Somewhere out there, a child needed him. He was doing good again. Being a true Legionnaire. He wasn't a mindless killer like Marcus. Not a blood-crazed demon. Not yet.

Myri rode next to him, taut as a bowstring. Only the Gods knew what she was feeling, but Rane could imagine well enough. If he was suffering, the pressure on her had to be immense. They'd not talked about her sword since leaving Rooktown, but Rane hadn't forgotten how black the blade was. Not ebony like Marcus', but close. They needed to get to Orska as quickly as they could, otherwise Myri would be lost as well, and Rane with her.

Time became difficult to track as they trundled along, the horizon never changing in a sea of burnt grass. Even the sun abandoned them, leaving the sky grey and grim behind clouds of smoke. Shards of black tree trunks jutted out of the ground here and there, and always the fires burned — even though there seemed nothing left to fuel them. The pilgrims muttered amongst themselves, repeating prayers over and over again, their words faster and faster, as if there was a certain quantity of faithfulness needed to bring Odason's protection over them all.

But if there was ever a place where Odason had given up on the world, they'd found it. No amount of prayers was going to make a difference in the Dead Lands.

It was a couple of hours or so before they saw their first skeletons. They were easy enough to spot — white bones sticking up out of the black earth. Babayon's magic had stripped the flesh from the Rastak army but left their bones unmarked as eternal markers to what had been done.

There were individual skeletons at first, then small clusters of two or three bodies, but each step, each roll of the wheels, brought more and more of the dead into sight until they filled the endless horizon like a field of white flowers.

Humans lay mixed up with Jotnar, Bracke, Grenduns and
Valkryn. Fingers and claws, teeth and fangs; giants and dogs, man
and beast; nothing but bone now beneath their feet. The dead lay
together, intertwined with no clear sign of where one body ended
and another began. All twisted, all tortured. Theirs had not been an
easy death.

"How many died here, do you think?" asked Myri.

Rane glanced up, furrowing his brow as he tried to answer. *Kibon*
filled his thoughts, a pounding inside his brain that made thinking
difficult. It was angry at being ignored, demanding to be unleashed.
"All of them," he replied eventually.

"At least we've nothing to fear here. Ghosts aren't going to kill us."

"There's still Marcus to worry about."

"Aye," replied Myri, and Rane couldn't help but notice her hand
was on the hilt of her sword. A sliver of black steel showed. She
clicked her heels and moved her horse ahead of him, finishing the
conversation.

Despite the lack of sun, the temperature rose steadily from the
thousands of fires that burned as they made their way down the road.
The ash got everywhere, stinging Rane's eyes, choking the back of his
throat. Sweat added to his discomfort, running down his neck and
back, soaking his clothes so they rubbed his burnt skin raw with even
the slightest motion. He took a slug of water, but it brought little
relief.

Surrounded by the dead, he wondered just what he was doing. He
wanted to scream at Fia's people to shut their mouths, stop their
blathering prayers; wanted to leave them behind to look after themselves. Marcus was gone. The child was dead. They were wasting time
with these fools. Orska was all that mattered. Everything else was a
waste of time. It was as if a hand held his heart and was trying to drag
him north.

He tried to shake the thoughts away, but the pounding in his head
refused to allow it. *Kibon* refused to allow it. This quest wasn't what
the blade wanted. It wanted to kill things. Anything.

He muttered his Legionnaire's oath under his breath to help him focus. He was doing the right thing. He had to do the right thing. He was in control, not *Kibon*.

The smoke grew thicker, choking them with every breath. Scarfs and handkerchiefs were tied around mouths to try and keep the worst out. The horses grumbled, but kept their pace. The pilgrims grumbled even more, but kept at their prayers. But there was no sign of their quarry. Occasionally Rane thought he saw movement out of the corner of his eye, but when he looked, there was nothing there. The last thing he needed was his mind playing tricks on him.

A building murder of crows followed them, circling and shrieking, amused at the convoy's folly in entering the Dead Lands, eagerly anticipating when they would become their next meal.

Myri slowed down so Rane could draw level with her. "Getting dark. Might be a good idea to stop soon while we can still see enough to set up camp."

Rane stared down the Crow's Road to its endless horizon, wishing their journey were somehow over. "You're right. Let's do it." He held up his hand, signaling the stop, and was answered by the creak of wagon brakes. "We're going to camp here for the night," he called, turning in his saddle. Worried faces watched him, their prayers silent on their lips. "William, Douglas — let's clear some of the bones away from the side of the road so we can circle the wagons and give ourselves some protection."

Douglas spat onto the road, made a show of wiping his face. "Ain't you gonna get off that horse and give us a hand? Or are you just good at tellin' others what to do?"

Rane locked eyes with the man; felt the urge to do him harm rising. "Myri and I are going to take first watch. We're a day in, and the Gods only know what's out there."

"Ain't nothing but a bunch of old wives' tales been scaring folks away from here." Douglas slapped William's arm. "Ain't that right?"

William didn't look quite so convinced. "Let's just do what the man says. I've had enough for one day." He jumped down from the front of the wagon without waiting for Douglas to reply.

In the next wagon along, Olivik stood up. "I'll help, too. Sooner we get it done, the happier I'll be."

Douglas cursed to himself, but he joined the others and the three men got to work.

"Come on, girls," called out Fia as she too clambered down from her wagon. "Let's get a fire built and some food cooking."

"Why don't we camp around one of those fires?" asked Joassa, pointing out into the Dead Lands. "Plenty to choose from without us wasting our wood supply."

"Those fires were started using blood magic, and blood magic keeps them burning still," said Rane. "I don't recommend getting to close to them if you can help it. And I wouldn't be keen to eat anything that was cooked over them, either."

Joassa drew Odason's sign over her chest and said no more.

The familiar routine of setting up camp seemed to ease everyone's jitters. Even the horses calmed down once they were tied up behind a wagon. Soon, the smell of stew bubbling away countered the burnt air.

"What are we doing here?" muttered Myri as they watched the pilgrims take their seats around the fire. "They'll be singing fucking songs next."

Rane smiled. "It's been a hard day, with harder ones to come. Let them enjoy what they can."

"Well, don't expect me to join in."

"I wouldn't dream of it."

"Get some food. It doesn't need two of us to look for trouble."

"I'll make sure they save you some."

"Can't wait," said Myri, turning her back on him.

Rane wandered over to the fire and sat down. Douglas glared at him, but the rest looked happy enough to see him. Hazia was to his right, staring into the bowl of stew in her hands but not eating. Joassa had her arm around her, but Hazia was beyond comfort. She'd lost her son, and Rane knew only too well the pain she was suffering.

Fia came over to Rane with a bowl of stew. "Here you are. It's not the best, but it's warm and filling."

"Thank you," said Rane.

"The ride seems to have done you some good," said Fia. "Your burns look almost healed."

"It didn't feel like that earlier." Rane pinched his brow in an attempt to ease his headache. The pain was getting worse. "So, what waits for you in Napolin?"

"We answer the call of Odason. His priests are few and far between since the war, and most of his temples nothing but ruins. My order has called all who wish to retake His word back out into the world, and we have answered." Fia gestured at the rest of the pilgrims. "We'll be assigned a new town, so we can build a new temple and care for a new congregation."

Rane took a bite of stew. It tasted better than anything he'd had since Kara died. "Where are you from originally?"

Joassa leaned forward so she could see around Hazia. "Donaston, down by the Balrus border. Wasn't much left of it either after the war, so moving seemed an easy choice, especially after the crops failed for the second year running. The children need to eat."

"We knew the roads were dangerous," said Olivik. "But William and Douglas have experience. They were soldiers once, but no one was prepared for..." He glanced over at Hazia. "...what happened."

"It weren't our fault," snapped Douglas. "We're trained to fight men, not demons. We're lucky he didn't kill us all."

"Be quiet," snapped Myri.

Douglas jumped from his seat, veins in his neck bulging. "Who are you to tell me what I can—"

Rane stepped in, placing a hand against Douglas' chest. "What is it, Myri?"

"There's something out there."

They all heard the sound of bones snapping out in the darkness.

"What the fuck was that?" shouted Douglas, fumbling his pistol from its holster.

Fia held out her hands, trying to reassure everyone. "Odason will protect us. Odason will protect us." Rane wasn't so sure — whatever was coming sounded big. He scanned left and right, searching for the source. The red flames of the undying fires dotted everywhere gave little help, throwing shadows here and there amongst the bones, ruining his night vision.

"Nathaniel — get your ass over here," called Myri.

"Stay by the fire. Watch the children," ordered Rane as he grabbed a burning branch from the fire. He raced over to join Myri, *Kibon* already in his other hand. His headache was gone. His aches were gone. He was ready for whatever came their way.

He raised the torch, trying to see what lurked amongst the bones, straining to hear where it moved.

Minutes passed, and nothing attacked. Still Rane and Myri stood sentry while the pilgrims huddled in fear behind them.

"See anything?" whispered Rane.

"Nothing. But that doesn't mean something's not there. There are a million places to hide amongst the bones." Myri's sword shook in her hand as she watched the shadows.

"Could it be Marcus?"

"Or something worse. We shouldn't have fucking come here."

Rane glanced back at the pilgrims. Had he led them to their deaths? "There's no going back. We stand our ground."

20

R ane sat by the fire, running his thumb over Kara's locket as the new day broke. He'd not slept, waiting for an attack that never came. The endless soot and ash of the Dead Lands only made the tiredness worse, drying out his throat and blocking his nostrils. He wasn't alone in that. After a day and a night, half the convoy had hacking coughs — no doubt the rest would join them by evening. A wind had picked up from the north-east, dragging the dirt up and throwing it around to make things even more uncomfortable.

Around the fire, the other pilgrims were shuffling to their feet, stretching, yawning, whispering words of encouragement to each other. They'd survived a day and a night, but there was still a long way to go.

Rane pressed down on the locket and tried to let thoughts of Kara fill his mind, but she was an elusive ghost, little more than a shadow. The more he concentrated, the harder she was to see. By the Gods, how he missed her. To feel her touch once more, her warmth, her love. She'd be five months pregnant if things had continued as they were, probably just starting to feel the baby kick and move around. Another dream lost.

It seemed another life, belonging to someone far luckier than Rane. What would Kara have made of what was happening now? Of her husband chasing her brother — her brother turned demon, her husband facing the same fate? Truth was, he was grateful she wasn't around to see it, to know of their fall. And who knew what effect the magic would have had on their child?

He could feel the anger growing in him; a flicker, then a flame. All the good things in his life taken away because of what he'd done. *Kibon* lay next to him. How he hated that sword now. Hated it as much as he'd once loved it. Resented it as much as he needed it. Would he have agreed to the Lord General's plan to bond his soul with the sword if he'd known the real consequences? Were the lives saved worth the cost?

Yes. He'd followed the oath. He'd done what was needed to protect the weak and save lives. Once he got to Orska and cured himself of the curse, the doubts would go with it.

"You ready to move out?"

Myri was standing next to him, her sword strapped to her back, the stump of her right hand held awkwardly against her chest. Her scarf covered half her face, but there was no hiding the black rings under her eyes.

"Sure," he lied, not feeling ready for anything. Better to be moving, though. Better to be heading north. He climbed to his feet and arched his back. "How're you?"

"Been better." Myri pressed her finger to the side of her nostril and snorted mucus out onto the ground. "But that's not to say things can't get worse."

Rane couldn't argue with that. "Let's get on with it, then."

Overhead, the crows circled, urging them all to move on. Others loitered, perched on broken ribs and shattered spines, squawking away. They hoped the convoy would provide their breakfast and weren't in the mood for any further delay.

"A word, please." Douglas marched over, musket in his hands.

"Everything okay?" asked Rane, knowing that it wasn't.

Douglas chewed on what he was going to say, as if he didn't like the taste of the words but knew he couldn't force them back. He was shaking, too, underneath all his bluster; scared, but determined to tough it out. "I know who you are. Took me a while to place you both." He tapped the side of his head for effect. "But the old mind still works sometimes."

"And?" replied Myri, managing to make the word sound like the worst kind of threat.

Douglas wagged his finger at them. "Fucking Legionnaires, the pair of you. Fought with you back in the day, in Candra. I was there when you massacred the Rastaks, pushed them back from the walls." He coughed, then spat whatever had come up at Rane's feet. "Thought you were a blessing from the Gods that day, I did. But now I know different."

His musket wasn't pointing at them, but Rane wasn't so sure it would remain that way. He glanced over at Myri, hoping she wouldn't react before there was a chance for things to end peacefully. She stared daggers at Douglas, but that was all — for now.

"We're just trying to help," said Rane, holding both hands up.

"And that's why we're talking. There's a little girl that needs saving, and as much as I hate it, the fact is you two are still her best hope." Douglas jabbed his finger towards Rane. "But that don't mean I'm going to let you put the others' lives at risk. You got Heras' magic in your blood, so maybe you can't help yourselves, but first sign of any trouble and I'll put a bullet in your heads before you can hurt Fia or any of the others. I promise you that."

Myri stepped forward. "I'd like to see you try."

Rane pulled her back, tried a smile instead. "We understand. Believe me, we just want to get the girl back. Your friends will be safe from us, at least."

"You remember that," said Douglas. "Now, let's get on our way." He headed back to his wagon under William's watchful eye in the driver's seat.

"Piece of shit," spat Myri. "Lucky we don't leave them on their own. See how long they last then." She clambered up onto her saddle as best she could, gripping the reins tightly in her one remaining hand.

"You can't blame them for being scared," replied Rane, mounting his own horse. The road stretched endlessly ahead, a grey gash through the sea of bone. "Of us. Of this place. Of this world. We swore an oath to protect people like them — the weak, the needy — and it's us who have failed them."

"I know. I know." Myri moved her horse level with Rane's. "It's just... the sword plays on my mind. I want to fight. I want to kill. Doesn't matter who, or what. Who's to say I won't turn on them when the time comes? Every day — every *minute* gets harder to hold the urge back." She held up her stump with its dirty bandage, shaking. "Ever since I lost this, I've needed the sword more and more. I need a hit of its magic just to get up. Just to take a step forward. But even that's not enough anymore."

"You need to try to do without it," said Rane, feeling the itch himself, hearing the voice whisper away. "Bad enough we have to carry them with us, but we have to resist the temptation to touch them, to use them. That's our only hope."

Myri laughed, a laugh as cold as death. "Resist using it? Have you seen where we are? Do you remember whom we chase? What are you going to do when the next demon shows its face — or we catch up with Marcus? Whisper sweet nothings, or draw your steel and fight with every ounce of strength you have?" She kicked her horse forward. "We both know the answer to that."

Rane watched her, knew the truth of her words no matter how hard he wished it wasn't so. He kissed the locket dangling from his wrist. "Kara, watch over me." The prayer brought little comfort, but it was all he had. He turned in his saddle and saw the convoy waiting for him. He gave Douglas a nod and then squeezed his horse with his thighs, moving him on. The wagons rattled into motion behind him and they were on their way once more. A crow shrieked with glee; out of the corner of his eye, he saw the black cloud above turn in response and follow.

As he rode, he turned their situation around and around in his mind. Two days to reach the other side of the Dead Lands. A week from there to Orska — and possibly a cure. Myri was already on the edge — could she last that long? Could he? He was too scared to look at *Kibon* to see if the taint was in its metal. The headache was back, as was the voice. That told him enough.

They couldn't destroy their swords, or hide them out of sight. When they found Marcus, they'd need them quickly enough, had no choice but to use them. A bullet wouldn't stop Marcus, or an ordinary blade.

But what if the Lord General didn't have a cure, couldn't reverse the mage's magic? What then? A slow, painful, inevitable transformation into one of the tainted? By the Gods, no. He'd rather die than submit to that fate. If the time came, he'd kill himself.

The ride was harder than the previous day's. The wind saw to that, adding to the discomfort caused by the heat. Sweat ran down Rane's face, dripping off his nose, soaking the scarf that covered his mouth, doing its best to get the billowing ash into his lungs. His poor horse suffered more as it labored along the Crow's Road with nothing to protect it. Rane patted its flanks and whispered words of comfort, but they had little effect.

They stopped more frequently to give the animals some rest and water. The slow going added to Rane's frustration, his life ticking away second by second with still no sign of Marcus or the girl.

On and on they went, the only sound the clop of hooves and the creak of wheels. Even the pilgrims' prayers had stopped. No doubt they were feeling far from Odason's gaze.

The wind picked up, rattling the bones of the dead and dragging even more muck into the air. As ash danced across the road, any tracks Marcus might have left were swept away with it. There was no luck to be found in the Dead Lands, no break from the misery.

The day was nearly done when Myri called out that there was something lying in the road.

Rane held up his hand to stop the wagons before riding to Myri's side. "What is it?"

She gestured with her stump. "See for yourself."

Something lay dead twenty yards away, watched over by the crows. Several perched on the corpse, digging their beaks in for a mouthful of flesh. One thing was clear, though: it wasn't Marcus or the girl. Rane would've been thankful if it wasn't for the fact he was looking down on a dead Bracke.

He jumped down from his horse. The crows scattered as he approached, furious at being disturbed.

"Do you think that's what made the noise last night?" asked Myri.

Rane shrugged. "Could be. Or it could be just one of many."

"What killed it?" asked Myri, scanning the bones.

A cut ran from its groin to its neck. "Marcus."

"How long's it been dead?"

Rane placed a hand against the Bracke. Not warm, but the flesh hadn't begun to harden. "Maybe four or five hours."

"He's still far enough ahead of us."

Rane rubbed his temples. The damned headache was getting worse. "How many hours before dark?"

Myri looked up, sniffed. "Maybe two if we're lucky."

"What's going on?" called Douglas, standing up in his seat.

Rane ignored him for a moment, trying to blink some life back into his eyes before turning back to Myri. "We push on. Maybe we find Marcus and the girl. Hopefully the Bracke hurt him enough to slow him down. If not, we try and find somewhere to camp down for the night."

"Agreed."

"I'll tell the others." Rane left Myri and headed towards the wagons. His head pounded and, without thinking, his hand drifted to *Kibon*'s hilt for a hit of magic to take the pain away. Kara's locket caught his eye and he stopped himself in time. He kissed the locket instead, and thanked Kara for watching out for him. The pain was still there, but he felt better. The voice called him a fool, but he ignored it as best he could.

Douglas and William watched him approach, giving their best tough stares to hide their fears.

"What's dead up there?" asked William when Rane got close enough.

"A Bracke. Killed by the man we're chasing," replied Rane.

"I thought they didn't exist anymore," said Douglas. "Thought we'd killed them all."

"There're still some running around," said Rane. "Probably more here than anywhere."

Douglas shot up, musket ready, scanning all around them. "Are there others?"

" Probably. Bracke never travel alone. We go on regardless. Look for somewhere we can defend if we have to."

"There's a dead Bracke ahead," shouted Douglas down the line. "Keep your eyes peeled."

Cries, curses and prayers answered him in equal measure. Even the horses were jittery. Rane hoped it was only the smell of the dead demon dog that was affecting them. He forced himself to be calm and unhook the longbow from his saddle. If the dogs were abroad, he'd rather shoot them from a distance than fight them up close. *Kibon* disagreed, eager for more blood of its own. The pain between Rane's eyes sharpened as if to emphasize the point, but Rane still wouldn't give in. He dug one end of the bow into the ground beside his foot and leaned in to bend the yew. Once he had the curve right, he slipped the bowstring in place. He'd let his arrows do the killing instead of his cursed steel.

He headed to Fia's wagon next.

"Is everything okay?" asked the priest. Her husband sat next to her, axe propped against his leg, brows knitted together in worry.

"Need Karn to get on top of the wagon," replied Rane.

Karn exchanged glances with Fia, none too happy at the news. "I'd rather stay here, look after my wife."

"Need someone to look out for all of us, and you'll have a better view up there." Rane pulled a pistol out of its holster. "You ever use one of these before?"

Karn nodded.

Rane passed the weapon to him, butt first. "Keep it to hand, but call me first if you see anything. Understand?"

"Yeah. But the smoke..." Karn's voice shook with fear as he spoke.

"Just do the best you can." That was all any of them could do.

To Karn's credit, he didn't protest. He passed the reins to his wife before he clambered from one wagon to the other, shaking and sweating. He settled uncomfortably on the roof of Fia's wagon, one arm hooked through the golden circle at its center, and nodded to let Rane know he was ready.

"Do you think we're going to be attacked?" asked Fia.

"Let's pray not," said Rane. "But I'd be happier if Hazia and Tanya joined you in your wagon, with Joassa and the children as well. Just to be safe."

"As you say," agreed Fia. "It'll be a squash, but we'll make do."

Tanya, looking lost and scared without her husband beside her, led Hazia, all red-eyed and deathly pale, by the hand to the temple wagon. Joassa stood waiting for them with the wagon door open, full of grim determination. It took a few minutes to get everyone rearranged. Rane could hear the upset children inside; there wasn't any hiding the concern on the adults' faces, but nor was there anything he could do to make it better. Keeping them alive was going to be hard enough.

Soon enough, they were ready to move on. Myri led the way and Rane rode beside her, an arrow nocked on his bowstring as he watched the bones on either side of the road for signs of more Bracke.

"Douglas had a point," said Myri. "The Bracke are meant to be dead. We burned them here. Their bones are all around us."

"Maybe they didn't all die. Maybe some have been living here in the Dead Lands. It'd explain why no one else has made it across alive. I was attacked by one the day before Kara died, at our cottage down south, but it could have come from here. Maybe they're breeding here amongst the fires."

"Fucking wonderful." Myri reached back and touched her sword hilt, twitched as the magic hit. "As if we didn't have enough troubles."

"Better than the possibility Heras has released them out into the world once more. With the Legion in hiding, we're not in a position to fight and win another war with Her forces."

Myri raised an eyebrow. "Sounds like perfect planning."

21

They moved slowly. Cautiously. Rane's heart raced as he scanned left and right for danger, arrow at the ready. Myri was no better, scowling through the gap between her hood and scarf, twitching at the wind.

The wind swirled smoke and ash around them, rattling the bones enough to spook Rane every dozen or so yards. Trouble was, there were too many places to hide. A demon could be a yard away, buried in the bones, and no one would spot it. But there was no turning back. Only forward. But Rane couldn't help feeling he was leading everyone into a trap that they'd not walk away from.

Each passing minute and each passing yard brought no respite from the fear that the demons were out there, waiting, watching. Tension built amongst them all.

Behind them, William drove the first wagon. Douglas sat next to him, the butt of his musket lodged in his shoulder, finger resting next to the trigger, seemingly unsure whether to watch the Legionnaires or watch the road. Fia's wagon trundled after, with Karn perched on its roof and the rest of the women and children locked inside. At the rear, and out of sight, were Olivik and Regas. Not much of an army if trouble found them, but all Rane had.

As the day drew closer to its end, the Crow's Road stretched on to the horizon, bones piled high on either side, fires burning in every direction, choking them with smoke and ash. Nothing had changed after two days' slog through the Dead Lands. It felt like they'd made no progress whatsoever. Only now, Bracke possibly lurked amongst the dead.

"Nathaniel." Myri's voice was a whisper as she pulled on her reins, stopping her horse.

"What?" replied Rane, halting beside her.

She stared straight ahead. "Marcus."

Rane raised his hand to let the others know they were stopping and squinted down the road. Clouds of smoke billowed across. He couldn't make anything out, but that didn't stop the fear rising in his gut. "I can't see any..." And then there he was. A hundred yards ahead.

Marcus stood facing them. Smiling. His clothes hung off him in tatters, displaying an ugly red scar where Myri had opened him up from shoulder to hip, but otherwise he looked normal. Like his old self. Not twisted. Not tainted. All the years had fallen from his face, like he was young again, without a care in the world. But there, held casually by his side, was his sword — unsheathed and as black as night — to remind Rane of who he really was. *What* he was. A body lay at his feet. The girl, not moving. "Greetings, brother. So good to see you again. And you've brought me new friends to play with."

Rane's only reply was to raise his bow and pull back his bowstring. As his right hand brushed his cheek, he took aim, locked his left arm, let out a breath and released the arrow. It shot towards Marcus as Rane reached down for another.

Marcus swatted the first shaft away with a flick of his sword as Rane released his second arrow.

"Nathaniel." Marcus took a step towards them. "You disappoint me." He twisted his hip to let the second arrow fly past without breaking stride. "Why go through this charade? You must feel the call as I do. Let us journey together, and leave these sheep behind."

"I'll show you who's a fucking sheep," said Myri, drawing her pistol.

"Don't waste your bullet," said Rane. "He's still too far away." He released another arrow, for all the good the others had done.

Marcus, eighty yards away, knocked the arrow to one side. Seventy-five yards. Seventy. "Good to see you're still with us, Myri. How's the hand?"

"What's going on?" shouted Douglas from behind them. "Can you see Sarah?"

"Stay where you are." Rane didn't dare look back. Didn't dare say the girl looked dead. They all had to stay alive through whatever happened next.

Rane slid from his saddle as Marcus closed the gap to fifty yards. Dropping to one knee, he took aim once more. Smoke drifted across the road, obscuring his view, but he shot again, hoping this time it would strike Marcus. The arrow disappeared into the murk. Rane sent two more swiftly after it.

Rane and Myri watched and waited as the smoke billowed and swirled through the bones and over the path. For a fraction of a second, Rane felt hope, but it shattered as Marcus burst through the clouds and came at them in a sprint. He swung his sword back over his shoulder, eager for blood.

The boom of Myri's gun roared above Rane's head, but it didn't stop Marcus. Rane dropped his bow and reached for *Kibon*. The time for arrows was past.

Time slowed as Marcus closed the gap, his face contorted into an insane grin. Rane had his hand on *Kibon*'s hilt; felt the first pulse of energy in his fingers. The voice roared in his head. It was time.

Marcus ran at them, feet pounding the ground, little clouds of ash trailing behind. *Kibon* sighed as it slid from its sheath, eager as always. The blade sprung free just as Marcus leaped. Rane followed through on his stroke but found only empty air as Marcus soared above it. His foot struck Myri in the mouth, knocking her from her saddle with a sickening crack, and then he was past them both, heading for the others.

Rane spun around and gave chase. He jumped over Myri, lying deathly still, and prayed to the Gods she wasn't dead.

Marcus slashed one of the wagon horses across the neck. Blood gushed as the animal collapsed, dragging the other one down with it. Douglas stumbled as the wagon tilted, throwing off his aim. His musket went off and the bullet struck the floor of the wagon. He didn't get a second chance. Marcus was up on the wagon in an instant and thrust his sword though Douglas' heart, laughing all the while. Impaled, Douglas was lifted up off his feet by the force of the blow. Marcus threw him off the wagon with a flick of his wrist. He turned on William as the man tried to draw his pistol.

Rane skirted around the dead and trapped horses, desperate to get to Marcus, afraid of what would happen when he did. The man had beaten him twice already. What hope was there that this time would be different? But he had to try.

He jumped up, swinging *Kibon*, as Marcus brought his sword down on William. The man screamed, took a step back and fell off the side of the wagon just as the black blade came down.

Marcus turned as Rane reached him, stabbing straight at Rane's heart, fast as lightning. Rane only just managed to bat his blade away.

Marcus' sword swung down, seeking to split Rane from shoulder to hip. He reacted on instinct, blocking where he thought Marcus' blade would be rather than by what he could see. Steel kissed steel again and again.

As Marcus attacked again, Rane flipped back off the wagon, desperate for some breathing room. Marcus followed, giving Rane no time to catch his breath. Marcus slashed his blade from left to right and Rane dropped *Kibon* to block it just in time. The swords skidded along each other in a shower of sparks until guard locked with guard, the two men's faces all but touching. Marcus pushed down, grinning from ear to ear, forcing Rane to his knees. The black blade moved closer to his face. Death was only an inch away.

Rane managed to get a foot under him and used that to twist himself sideways, breaking free and sending Marcus clattering to one side. He was back on his feet in an instant, pressing his attack, forcing Rane back once more. He countered Marcus's thrust, swung a boot out in response and caught the demon's elbow, but the blow had little effect. Rane retreated, fighting for his life, using every bit of skill and knowledge built up over ten years of war, drawing on every ounce of power within *Kibon*.

Marcus rushed at him, but he sidestepped the assault and struck with *Kibon*, hacking at his friend's neck. Marcus ducked down under the blow and brought his own blade up in response. Rane threw himself back, feeling the slightest of nicks as the black blade caught his neck. His hand went to it — could feel the blood, warm and wet — but it wasn't deep. He could still breathe. Thank the Gods.

"Having fun, brother?" Marcus smiled. "How I've missed you."

"The feeling's not mutual," replied Rane as he backed away, swallowing his fear. Marcus was so much faster and stronger than he was.

There was a crack of pistol fire, but only the Gods knew where the bullet went. It hurt neither man. Karn on the wagon, wasting the one shot he had. Rane would've cursed the man if he wasn't so desperately trying to stay alive.

Marcus laughed at the madness of it all and came at Rane again. Rane deflected the first lunge, parried the second, but the third strike drew blood, slicing through cloth and flesh. He jerked back, dropping his guard, and Marcus flicked his blade across Rane's face, cutting him from jaw to cheek.

Rane chopped down at Marcus' knee, hoping at least to slow him down, but Marcus swept his sword away almost before Rane had begun the move. He followed through with an elbow strike at Marcus' face, hitting nothing but air as Marcus danced away, giddy with delight, punching Rane in the face when he moved. Rane rocked with the force of the blow, but somehow managed to stay on his feet.

"Come on, Nathaniel. You can do better than this," chuckled Marcus. "I thought you were a great warrior. The best. Do you need a moment to catch your breath? Perhaps I should go and have a chat with the women and children while you work out what to do?"

Rane hacked at Marcus with all the strength he had left, but again Marcus twisted around the blow and pummeled Rane with the hilt of his sword, sending him sprawling in the ash. As Rane pushed himself up onto all fours, Marcus kicked him in the stomach, cracking ribs and flipping him onto his back. He gasped for air, trying to get his lungs to work as Marcus stood over him.

"I can taste your fear, Nathaniel," goaded Marcus. "Never took you for a coward. How could you be afraid of me?"

Rane swung his sword, but Marcus simply stepped over it like a child with a skipping rope. He picked Rane up so that they faced each other. "Don't make it too easy for me. Use your gift," he whispered. Rane spat blood and phlegm in Marcus' face in reply. Marcus smiled. "Still some fight left in you, then. Good."

Marcus threw Rane through the air. His head smashed into the side of a wagon and his sword flew from his hand. A surge of panic hit him. Everyone was going to die. He'd killed them all, leading them here. Blood dripped from the cuts across his face as he hauled himself onto his hands and knees. He had to find *Kibon.*

He spotted it underneath the wagon and crawled after it, every part of him screaming with pain. His fingers clawed lumps out of the dirt as he dragged himself closer. Someone somewhere was screaming, but Rane ignored it. *Kibon* was all that mattered.

He stretched out and his fingers brushed the hilt. Relief flooded through him as his fingers closed around *Kibon* once more. A pulse of magic deadened the pain and Rane pulled the sword closer, hugging it to his chest. Each breath brought stabbing pains from his cracked ribs, but he was still alive.

Though a half-closed eye, he spotted Myri still lying in the dirt. Was she dead? Please, not another one lost. Rane slumped down. He had no energy left. No fight. He'd failed too many times. Marcus was too strong.

It was over.

"Nathaniel!" A woman screamed his name. Fia. Desperate. Scared.

Only Rane could save her, save the others. Only Rane, beaten, broken and bloodied.

He had to try.

With one hand gripping *Kibon,* he hauled himself out from under the wagon. A wave of nausea hit him as he got to his feet, but he managed to blink away the black from his mind. He spat blood from his mouth.

Marcus was playing with those defending Fia's wagon. He could've killed them in an instant, but Marcus wanted them frightened, needed them scared. Marcus had Olivik dangling in the air with one hand while fencing with Regas with the other, cutting him here, nicking him there. Regas' body was a mass of cuts, but none were fatal, and to his credit he still fought on. Fia stood on her wagon, her body barring the door, prepared for when the men finally fell. Karn was still perched on the roof, watching helplessly.

Rane stumbled forward and took *Kibon* in a two-handed grip. If he was quick, he might stand a chance while Marcus' attention was elsewhere. He raised *Kibon* over his head.

But Marcus spotted him. He threw Olivik to one side and kicked Regas in the face, dropping him like a stone. Then he reversed his sword before thrusting into Rane's gut.

Rane almost didn't notice. So sharp, the sword simply slipped in without any pressure or resistance. A momentary burst of pain and then a cold sensation as it passed through Rane's stomach and out of his back.

Rane looked down in disbelief, but even the sight of the black blade piercing his body didn't seem to register. He coughed, spilling more blood down his chin and onto the floor. *Kibon* fell from his hand.

Marcus had killed him.

His old friend turned to face Rane, drawing as close as a lover, his eyes wide with delight. And then Marcus twisted the blade.

Rane screamed. The world disintegrated around him. He pulled his head back, trying to focus on Marcus' face. How could it have come to this? All for nothing.

Blood seeped down his back, his life leaking away.

No. Not like this. His hand fumbled for the pistol on his hip as he screamed once more. The darkness filled his vision. If he could just...

"I'm sorry, Nathaniel," Marcus whispered. "But your death will make me mightier still."

He pressed the pistol against Marcus' heart and pulled the trigger. He rocked with the blast as Marcus flew back, spraying him with blood.

Rane fell to his knees, Marcus' sword jutting from his back.

22

The world lost all meaning as Rane knelt in the dirt and ash. *Kibon* lay next to him. He knew he should pick it up, but his fingers didn't work. Nothing did. He watched Marcus twitch on the ground a few yards away. The man wasn't dead; not yet. But Rane soon would be.

Someone grabbed him — Karn — and dragged him backwards. His heels dug a groove in the dirt as he was pulled away from Marcus, away from *Kibon*. "My sword," he croaked. "Need... sword."

"Just rest," said Karn, propping Rane up against a wagon wheel.

Fia leaned over from the driver's seat. "Is he dead?"

Rane didn't know if she meant him or Marcus, but it didn't matter. Soon nothing would matter. He coughed blood down his chin. "Get my sword." The pain had gone from his gut, but he could feel ice spreading through him from the wound.

Karn nodded, mouth open, wide-eyed with fear. "Don't move."

Rane would have laughed if he'd been able. He wasn't going anywhere — except, maybe, into the ground. Karn sprinted back to where Rane had dropped *Kibon* and scooped it up in his hands. "I got it," he said, holding it up for Rane to see.

Next to him, Marcus lay still.

"Bring it here," asked Rane. He tried to beckon Karn over, but even lifting his arm was too much.

The man took forever to return. Rane's vision shifted in and out of focus as he waited, aware of the blood leaking away, the cold getting worse. Kara filled his mind: a bright star in the dark, love to fight the fear. At least if he died he'd be with her once more. Would she forgive him for his failings? For her unavenged death?

Then a jolt as Karn pressed *Kibon* into his hands. Rane gripped the hilt of his sword, but the magic was faint. He'd drawn too much from it already.

Regas staggered over to join them, bone jutting out from his left arm. "Did you see Sarah? Did you see my daughter?"

Rane nodded. "Was lying in the road."

The man didn't need telling twice. With Fia supporting him, they headed off to find the girl.

"I'm going to see if the others are okay," said Karn, leaning in.

Rane gripped his arm as best he could. "He's still alive. You've got to kill him."

"Who?" replied Karn. He looked around, saw Marcus, and realized what Rane was asking him to do. "But you shot him. He's already dead."

"No, he's not," he grunted. A bullet to the torso wouldn't kill him in the same way Marcus' sword hadn't killed Rane. Yet. "Get your axe and chop his head off. Then he'll be dead."

"What? No." Sweat broke out on Karn's forehead and he began to shake. "I can't do that. I'll get one of the others. William... Olivik..." He glanced around at the bodies of his friends. There was no telling if they were alive or not. He looked at Rane, pleading with his eyes, but found no reprieve from the task. "Shit."

"I'm sorry."

"My axe. It's in the wagon." With one last shake of his head, Karn left Rane and clambered back onto the driver's seat. Rane heard the scrape of metal on wood and then Karn was back, the weapon in his hand.

"You can do it," said Rane. "Be quick."

Karn took a deep breath and then blew it out again. "Okay. I can do it."

Rane watched him walk over and stop by Marcus' head. Karn adjusted his grip on the axe, juggling it around in his hands, shaking all the more. He lifted the axe up, then lowered it again. He looked over at Rane. "I can't do this."

"Fuck." Rane somehow managed to get to his knees. The world around him faded in and out as the darkness tried to claim him once and for all. Every breath was labored as he pressed *Kibon* to his chest, but the sword had nothing to give.

With his other hand, he fumbled for the hilt of Marcus' sword, closed his fingers around it.

Its magic hit him like a hammer blow. Burning through him, shredding his veins, exploding in his heart. Power. Strength. He dropped *Kibon*. It was no longer needed, useless compared to the fury within Marcus' sword. Rane got to his feet, no longer weak, no longer dying. The darkness was gone. He saw the world in its true light, and he was its master. Fire burned in him, brighter than the sun. He was a god. The god of death. Of war. Of misery.

Karn watched, open-mouthed, scared. Nothing but a weak fool. Blood to feed the sword. Meat to kill. A life to snuff.

Rane pulled the sword from his gut, feeling no pain. Inch by inch, it slid free. Inch by inch, he could feel the black blade moving through him, and he didn't care. He watched the steel exit his stomach and then saw the wound close. Barely a mark to show it had ever been.

He screamed at the Heavens. The Gods themselves should fear him. If any were foolish enough to cross his path, he would murder them, too. He was the immortal, not them.

"Rane... What are you... Are you... I..." Karn spluttered the words as the axe fell from his hands. He retreated as Rane advanced, aware that death approached. Joy swelled within Rane at the sight of the other man's fear. He could feel the excitement in Marcus' sword at the thought of more blood to feed on, and it promised him more power in return. A new voice screamed in ecstasy. He knew this was only the beginning, knew he was going to become so much more.

"Come. There is nowhere to hide." Rane raised the sword. How could anyone think such a glorious weapon was evil? Only his enemies. Rane would hunt them all down. Watch them bleed. Listen to them beg. Slaughter them all.

Power surged through him. Strength to destroy the world.

"Nathaniel." The voice came from behind. Rane spun around as the hammer smashed into his face. Once, twice, three times. It struck his wrist, knocking Marcus' sword from his grasp. He staggered back, the fire within him suddenly doused.

Myri stood before him, an ironsmith's hammer in her hand, ready to strike again.

"Myri," said Rane, out of breath, and as weak as a newborn. He wiped his face as a wave of emotions came over him — guilt, desire, anger, pity, hunger. He had to stop himself from lunging for the sword again. "The sword. Don't touch it. It nearly had me."

"We could all see that." Myri still stood poised, ready to attack Rane if need be. "Are you good? Or do I have to beat the shit out of you until you see sense?"

Rane held up both hands. "I'm good. I'm good."

Myri grunted and marched over to where Marcus lay. The man's fingers twitched as she loomed over him. "Die, you bastard." She brought the hammer down hard, smashing into his skull. *Crack. Crack. Crack.* Marcus' body jerked with each blow until his head broke open. Down and down went the hammer, splattering blood and brains, until there was nothing left. Only then did Myri stop.

Myri stood up and spat on Marcus' ruined face. "That's for taking my hand." She dropped the hammer at her feet just as Fia returned with Regas, holding his daughter in his one good arm, tears in his eyes. Karn rushed over and hugged his wife.

"Is she alive?" asked Rane.

"Yes, thank Odason," replied Fia. "She's alive." She glanced down at Marcus' body.

"Don't worry about him," said Myri, before Fia could ask. "He's definitely dead."

"Thank you," said Regas. "Thank you for saving my daughter. I owe you more than I can ever repay."

"The bastard nearly killed me," shouted Karn. "He's as dangerous as the other one."

Fia stepped back, her eyes darting from her husband to Rane and back again.

Flushed with new-found anger, Karn jabbed a finger towards Rane. "He picked up the other bastard's sword and went mad. If Myri hadn't hit him with a fucking hammer, I'd be dead right now. He'd probably have killed all of you."

"By Odason." She fixed her eyes on Rane and Myri, but spoke to the others. "Karn, check on Olivik and William. Get Tanya and Joassa to help you. I want everyone back on their feet and ready to leave here as soon as we can. Put the dead on one of the wagons. I'm not going to leave anyone in this cursed land."

Karn shuffled off. He clambered up on Fia's wagon and banged on the door while Rane, Myri and Fia all stood around watching each other. Rane's heart still raced with residual magic from Marcus' sword. He knew he had the strength to rip the wagons apart with his bare hands if he had to. By the Gods — no wonder his friends were falling to the taint. *Kibon*'s hold on him was powerful, but it was nothing compared to what it could be — what it wanted to be.

"Are you two going to start being honest with me?" asked Fia once they were alone.

"We're Legionnaires. Me, Myri, the dead man on the ground," replied Rane. "He was my best friend once."

Fia curled her lip in disgust as she looked down on Marcus' corpse. "The demon?"

"We were given magical powers during the war so that we could beat the Rastaks," continued Rane. "That magic is turning us slowly into what he — Marcus — became. The more tainted we become, the blacker our swords." He pointed at Marcus' sword on the ground.

"When I picked up his sword, its evil overcame me, and I attacked Karn. My mind wasn't my own."

Karn and the two women had both William and Olivik back on their feet. Neither man seemed to have any permanent damage.

Fia smiled at them as they passed, then returned her attention to Rane and Myri once more. "And your own blades?"

Rane picked *Kibon* up off the ground and showed the priest the blade. Even in the dusk, the steel still carried a shine. Fia nodded and then raised an eyebrow in expectation at Myri.

With a grunt, Myri used her thumb to push an inch or two of her sword from its sheath.

"It's black." Fia's voice was cold, matter-of-fact.

"Not completely. Not yet. But bad enough," snapped Myri. "Don't worry. I'm not going to hurt any of your precious flock. I just want to get out of this hellhole as quickly as possible and leave you to be on your way."

"And then what?" asked Fia.

"We're heading north, to Orska. Our old commander is waiting for us there with other Legionnaires. He's found a cure for us all," said Rane softly, as if the truth of the words were too fragile to be spoken.

"More magic?" Fia drew a circle over her chest and shivered as Rane nodded, looking very much alone and far from her God's gaze. "How far till we reach the end of the Dead Lands?"

"Probably a day's travel."

Karn unhitched the dead horse from William and Douglas' wagon while Olivik tried to calm its companion. Joassa and Tanya helped William sit down against one of the wagon wheels. A nasty gash ran down the side of his face. He was lucky to be alive. They all were.

Fia watched her companions work. "And if we leave now? Travel through the night?"

"We could be out by first light," said Myri.

Rane glanced over at her. "But it won't be safe. Better to rest up somewhere. Travel when we can see what lies ahead."

"There are enough fucking fires burning to see by, Nathaniel," retorted Myri. "And Marcus is dead. I don't think his corpse is going to trouble us none."

"I agree," said Fia. "We move soon as we are able. Travel through the night. And I think it'll be safer if we then go our separate ways in the morning."

Rane sighed. He wasn't going to be able to sleep anyway, not with all the magic still in him. "Okay. It's your call. We can hitch my horse up to William's wagon and I'll ride with him for now. But first sign of any trouble, we stop. I don't want anyone else dying just because we're all in a hurry."

"Let's get to it, then," said Fia. "We'll need to haul the dead horse out of the road first. Can you help Karn?"

"No need. I can do it on my own," replied Rane. He marched over to the animal, glad for something to do, glad to not be talking anymore. They'd saved two of the children Marcus had taken. They should be glad of that, Rane himself in particular. He should be happy that he'd fulfilled his oath — served and protected those weaker than himself. The curse, the taint, was nothing new. It had been there before Marcus' sword possessed him. It was still there now, waiting in his own sword. Instead, he just felt sick to his gut. Couldn't help but feel he should just put a gun to his head and call it a day. Better that than end up like Marcus.

Karn stepped back as Rane approached, still scared of the Legionnaire. Probably a long time before he'd get over what happened, and Rane couldn't blame him. He bent down, wrapped his arms around the horse's neck and, with a grunt, hauled the corpse to the side of the road. It weighed near enough two thousand pounds, but it might as well have been a feather. Was it only a day before that he'd struggled with lifting a wagon? He tossed the horse in amongst the bones. It deserved better than to rot amongst the Rastaks, but that was the world. Rane doubted his own resting place would be much better. He fingered Kara's locket, glad that she wasn't around to see what he was becoming, what her brother had become.

He turned back, but stopped dead in his tracks when he saw Myri. She was watching him, Marcus' sword in her hand.

"What are you doing?" asked Rane.

"Don't worry. I've got a glove on. I'm still me." She held her hand up to prove the point. "We can't just leave this lying here in the road."

Before he could say a word, Myri drew back her arm and then threw the cursed sword into the night.

Rane watched it arc through the air and disappear into the smoke and the bones. "We should've destroyed it."

"It's safe enough there. No one will find it," replied Myri without looking at him. "Come on. Let's get out of this shithole."

Karn had returned to his place by Fia's side on the temple wagon. Rane couldn't help but notice he had Douglas' musket cradled in his arms.

William himself lay in the back of Rane's wagon, a bloody bandage wrapped around his head. He raised his eyes as Rane climbed into the driver's seat, but the effort proved too much for him and he lapsed back into unconsciousness.

Myri passed Rane his bow and quiver before mounting her own horse. After securing the weapons beside him, he stood up and looked back over the convoy. "Everyone ready?"

Scared faces looked back, nodded. Time to go.

23

"Thank you."

Rane almost missed the words, not much more than a whisper, coming from the back of the wagon. All his attention was on the road ahead, looking for any danger, hoping for some sign that they were about to reach the end of the Dead Lands.

"Thank you." A cough followed on this time. Rane looked over his shoulder and found William staring back at him, eyes wide and bright, blood staining the bandage wrapped around his head. His skin was white as death, but for now, the man was alive.

"You're awake." Rane passed a waterskin back to William, but his eyes were already back on the road. The convoy was making good progress, but only the Gods knew how much further there was to go. Myri rode some thirty or forty yards ahead. They'd not spoken in the hours since they left Marcus' corpse behind.

Rane heard William drink with another cough and splutter. Then, with a groan and a grunt, William climbed up front and sat alongside him. "I mean it."

"Mean what?"

"Thank you. For saving my life back there. Saving the kids.

Weren't for you, they'd be dead. Most probably the rest of us would be, too. Where I come from, that deserves a bit of gratitude."

Rane shifted in his seat, uncomfortable with William's words. He could still feel the magic in his veins, and the disgust at what he'd nearly done pulsed away just as strong. Nearly murdering those he was protecting didn't seem the actions of someone who deserved any sort of gratitude. Kara's locket jangled on his wrist. At least she'd not seen the two men she loved become murdering animals. "There's nothing to be said. Hopefully you'll be able to get back on the road to Napolin soon enough. Put all this behind you."

"Ain't that the dream?" William laughed. "Seems all we ever do is leave shit behind us and try and head somewhere new, pretending the same shit won't just be waiting for us when we get wherever it is we're going. And then we act all surprised when it shows its ugly head again."

Images of a lost wife and home flashed through Rane's mind, his sword a weight on his back. "Seems cynical for a believer of Odason."

"I'm not sure I do believe in Odason, or any other God, not after what I've seen. But I believe in Mother Fia, and that's good enough for now."

"How did you come to join her?"

"I thought I was one of the lucky ones. I made it out of the war alive; returned home to discover my wife and family were some of the ones who didn't. Not so lucky after all. Fia found me when I was lost in despair getting up to some bad things, asked me to join her. I used to be a carpenter before I was a soldier. She thought both skills would come in handy." William took another slug of water and wiped his mouth with the back of his sleeve. "I've not done much building yet."

"Fia seems a good person. Determined. A good person to have faith in."

"Without her..." William shook his head. "I'd be... we'd all be... Let's just say she makes it easier to believe we can find somewhere worth starting anew."

Rane looked back at Fia and Karn, driving the next wagon behind. Neither looked happy, scowling at the world around them, and Rane couldn't blame them for that. "Sounds like someone worth having in your life." He ran his finger over Kara's locket. He knew what that was like. And what it was like to lose them.

"So you're a Legionnaire," said William.

Rane looked at him. Couldn't see any point in denying it. Enough of the convoy knew already. "Yes."

"Shit. Explains a lot. Douglas knew, didn't he?"

"He fought with us in the war."

"I came across a few back then, but never saw any fight. Just heard the stories."

"Most were exaggerated."

"No. You guys were real-life heroes to us grunts in the trenches and on the walls."

"We're not so popular now."

William chuckled, then coughed some more, then groaned. "Fuck, that hurts. Shouldn't laugh, but I would've thought being worth ten thousand gold pieces would make you very popular indeed."

"With the wrong sort of people, perhaps."

"Well, as I said before, you got my thanks. How old were you when you joined up?"

More memories came back, of times long forgotten. Innocent days. "Sixteen. A couple of years before the war started. Life was taking me the wrong way, and the Legion gave me a chance to correct that," replied Rane. "Seems like another lifetime."

"The war can do that. I think about being with my wife, my kids, and it's like it's someone else's life that I've been told stories about. Not stuff that happened to me. Only the pain makes it still feel real. That never seems to fade."

Rane could relate to that. "Where did you fight?"

"I joined up near Haverstock. Fought under Lord Rayner's banner, which really meant we retreated a lot. My friends died around me. Somehow I didn't. Not because I was better than they were. I just missed Heras' hand when She came calling. May it long remain that way." William drew the sign of Odason over his chest. "What about you?"

Rane swallowed. He didn't talk about the war. Hated what had happened. What he'd done. What he'd become. But his secret was out now — the magic, the curse. He now knew why he'd loved fighting so much. Why he'd taken such pleasure in killing his enemies. But that knowledge didn't make the memories any easier to deal with. Even now, he could feel *Kibon* niggling away inside his mind, hungry for more, needing more.

Emotions drifted through his mind. Anger mixed with excitement, the feeling of invincibility only the young possess at the start. Without even realizing it, the memories began to spill from his mouth.

"First battle I fought was at Ypressia. The war hadn't properly started. The Rastaks were raiding farms this side of the Naijin Desert. When we heard about it, we thought it'd just be a tribe out looking for trouble. Didn't think they'd found a king to unite under.

"We headed up there ready to teach them a lesson. Give them a hiding they'd never forget. Send them back over the border with their tails between their legs." Rane shook his head. "How much more wrong could we have been?"

"No one knew any better."

"It was a hard lesson to learn," replied Rane. His eyes drifted off to the horizon. "Three hundred of us rode out from our castle in Orska to face them, laughing and joking the whole way. We were the mighty Legion of Swords, after all. I think only forty of us made it back.

"We knew where the Rastaks were camped; a valley basin two days' ride away. The scouts counted the bivouacs. Told us we were facing a small raiding party. Easy for us to ride down, wipe them out and blood our blades. What they didn't know then was the bivouacs simply covered holes in the ground, and their main force was underground. Including Jotnar. That was the first time we encountered them, too."

Myri had stopped her horse a hundred yards away and was waiting for them with a look on her face that said she was unhappy about something. The carriage trundled towards her, with Rane in no hurry to hear more bad news.

"How many were waiting for you?" asked William.

"Only the Gods know. They swarmed out like ants, smothering the horses, pulling riders down, swallowing them up. I was near the back with the other new recruits — they called us the newborns and didn't trust us with much else than holding up the rear — and the moment the captain leading us realized what was happening, he sent us back to warn the others at the castle. Even then we barely made it. I remember just hacking my sword down, left and right. I didn't have to aim at anything. There were so many of them, grabbing at me, tugging my legs, my clothes. Every time I swung my arm, I hit one of them. They didn't seem to care about their own lives. At some point my horse went down, throwing me."

Myri was fifty yards away, staring at something ahead. A jolt went through Rane as the carriage bounced over a small rock.

"The captain hauled me onto the back of his horse before a demon could drag me away. I just hung on for dear life as he whipped the horse to run as fast as it could."

"Shit."

Rane smiled at the heartache of the memories. "A hard lesson. Sometimes I think I was only truly born that day. I am who I am because of that day."

Myri had the hammer she'd hit Rane with hanging from her saddle, and judging by the look on her face, she was more than ready to use it again. Seemed like William was the only one grateful with the current situation.

"Everything okay?" asked Rane as they drew level.

"This is as good a place as any to rest the horses for a while," replied Myri. "Get some food. Still half a night to go." She ran her eyes over William, apparently surprised he was alive, but said nothing.

Rane nodded and stood up to signal to the other wagons to stop. "See to your horses and yourselves. Be ready to move on in half an hour."

"Do we have to?" asked Fia. "I'd rather we keep moving." Karn fidgeted next to her, his finger not far from the musket's trigger.

Rane jumped down from his wagon and wandered over to the priestess. "The horses need the rest. We can't afford to lose another if we want to be out of the Dead Lands by first light."

"Fine. Half an hour it is." Fia knocked on the side of her wagon. The sound of shuffling came from inside and then Joassa opened the door. "Bring the children out one by one to attend to their toilet and get something to eat from Olivik's wagon. Only some dried meat and bread, but better than nothing."

"Thank you, Mother," replied Joassa with a slight bow of her head before ducking back inside.

"I'll feed the horses," said Karn, his eyes fixed on Rane and full of hate.

A shiver ran through Rane as *Kibon* reacted to the perceived danger. A reminder that his own sword would betray Rane soon enough, just as Marcus had fallen to his.

As Karn climbed down, Joassa re-emerged with a little girl in her arms. Rane recognized her as the first girl they'd saved, Gemma. He smiled, and the girl smiled back. Immediately he felt calmer, a little brighter. He'd sworn an oath as a Legionnaire to protect the Gemmas of the world. He'd given away half his soul to save them.

Fia followed his gaze. "She's young. With Odason's grace, she'll recover quick enough."

"I hope so." Rane smiled.

"Thank you, Nathaniel. Be proud of what you've done for us — despite what happened at the end. Two children have futures now because of you."

"I'm glad I could help."

"Unfortunately, I find myself in a bit of a quandary. On one hand, I owe you and Myri a great deal. On the other, I am sworn to report all uses of magic to my church. And they have very firm opinions of the Legion."

Rane remembered his comrades swinging in the gallows in

Candra and the priest who led their execution. He knew what the Inquisition demanded. "I know."

"I can't ignore my vows — no matter how much I'd like to — but I don't wish you to come to any harm either. You say a cure awaits in Orska?"

"So I've been told. So I hope."

"More magic." Fia sighed. She suddenly looked very tired. "I can only pray Odason will guide me."

"Do what you have to do," replied Rane. "I understand."

"Now, if you'll excuse me." Fia disappeared inside the wagon. Rane remained where he was for a moment. In a different world, he and Fia could have been great friends.

The convoy wasted no time in seeing to the children and the horses, passing what food and water they had left out amongst themselves. Even William regained some color to his cheeks with some bread inside him. There was little chatter; the reality of where they were — and whom they had with them — pressed down heavily on them all. They all avoided the Legionnaires.

"What a merry bunch we make," said Myri. "Now they have their children back, they can't wait to get rid of us."

"We've given them enough cause to be wary," replied Rane. "More than enough."

"We saved their lives!"

"If not for Marcus, they wouldn't have needed saving."

Myri stared at him for a moment, a thousand things boiling away inside, then turned and mounted her horse. "Let's go. We've wasted enough time."

She kicked her horse into motion and rode off down the Crow's Road, not waiting for anyone else. Rane watched her disappear into the darkness, feeling helpless. So much depended on reaching Orska and what waited for them there.

"Let's get moving," he called out and everyone scurried to their wagons. William held out a hand to help Rane climb up onto their wagon.

"Is your friend okay?"

"Maybe one day. Not now." Rane flicked the reins and the wheels groaned into motion. He and Myri had to get to Orska. Get this curse off their back. Before they were lost for good.

Resuming the endless journey, the wagons rolled off into the night. The only sound was the crunch of gravel under the wooden wheels and the steady clop of the horses' hooves. Time crawled as they trundled along under the black sky. William slept in his seat next to Rane, occasionally jolting awake as the wagon hit a bump in the road, and Rane was happy to leave him be. He was in no mood for any more conversation.

As the hours passed, even Rane started to feel the strain of the night's travel. His eyes stung, not helped by the swathes of smoke lingering around them. As he tried to rub some life back into them, he glanced to the east and was rewarded with the first glimmer of the sun dragging itself up into the sky. A golden smudge on the horizon. They'd made it through the long night. The end of the Dead Lands had to be close. Soon they could say goodbye to the bones and be on their way to fresh starts.

Then he heard the yapping behind him and his blood ran cold.

Bracke. And lots of them.

24

"Bracke!" Rane stood up and screamed the warning to the rest of the convoy. "Go as fast as you can, and don't stop for anything."

"What's going on?" William shook himself awake. "What's happening?"

"You hear that yapping? That's Bracke. Lots of them. Closing in." Rane thrust the reins into William's hands. "You drive."

William looked at the reins as if they were poisoned. There was no hiding the fear in his eyes. "What about you?"

Rane shrugged his coat off and snatched up the bow and quiver. "I'm going to the last wagon. See if I can stop the bastard creatures before they cut us all down."

Up ahead, Myri had wheeled her horse around and was racing back to join the convoy. Whatever darkness was at war within her soul, for now the good still prevailed. Thank the Gods for small mercies.

Rane scanned the darkness for the devil dogs, but for now there was no sign. With all the bones scattered around, though, they'd be able to get too close to the convoy without being seen.

"How close do you think they are?" asked Myri as she brought her horse alongside.

"Only the Gods know. But you know how fast they are. We've not got much time." Fear bubbled away inside Rane as his body itched with the need to draw *Kibon*. "Keep everyone moving. I'm going to the Hendersons' wagon. Hopefully I can shoot the bastards from there."

"I'm fucking useless with one hand, Nathaniel."

"It doesn't matter. Just keep everyone alive."

"You stay alive, too."

Rane nodded. There was nothing else to be said. Plenty to do. He jumped from the moving wagon and ran to the rear of the convoy. "Keep your weapons handy," he called out as he passed the other wagons. "Keep the children inside, and don't panic. We're nearly out of the Dead Lands. One more push and we'll be safe and clear." The lies tasted bitter on his tongue as the yapping grew louder. What chance did they have?

The wagons were picking up speed as Rane hooked his arm onto the Hendersons' wagon, swinging himself up and on board.

"What the fuck is happening?" shouted Olivik, knuckles white as he gripped the reins for dear life.

Rane placed a hand on his shoulder. "Just concentrate on the road. I'll deal with the Bracke."

"But my wife... my children..."

"They're inside Fia's wagon. It's the safest place for them."

"But..."

"Just drive." Rane clambered into the back of the wagon. Dust swirled up from the wheels, mingling with the smoke and the darkness as the yapping echoed from everywhere. So loud. So many. By the Gods, how many of the creatures were there? Rane knelt at the rear of the wagon, conscious that the only cover he had was a thin piece of wood not more than one-and-a-half-feet high. He placed the bow and arrows beside him and then checked his guns. At least both were still loaded.

"You see anything?" called out Olivik.

"Nothing yet. The road's empty," replied Rane. "They must be moving through the bones, using them for cover."

The wagon picked up its pace, rattling and jolting along the road as the landscape blurred on either side. All the while the howls of the Bracke grew louder and louder. They had to be close — but where?

Rane picked an arrow from the quiver and nocked it on the bowstring, holding it in place between his fingers. Anticipation gnawed in his stomach, fuelling the adrenalin in his blood, while *Kibon* whispered in his ear with promises of power and survival.

"Where are they?" Olivik's voice cracked with fear. "The horses won't be able to keep up this pace for much longer. They're not used to this."

"Who is?" replied Rane.

Minutes passed. More yards flew by. And still there was no sign of the creatures.

"Come on, come on," muttered Rane to himself. "Where are you?"

And then, if answering his call, something burst from the bones, out on to the Crow's Road, and raced towards them. The Bracke was a beast, as big as any Rane had ever faced before. It bounded along, closing the gap with every step it took.

Rane raised his bow and drew the bowstring back, locking his left arm as he aimed. He aimed the head of the arrow at the Bracke's head and tried to compensate for the roll and lurch of the wagon.

Archery was meant to be done on the ground, calmly and slowly, not charging along at speed, being shaken this way and that. When he'd joined the Legion, they never stopped practicing shooting arrows in every type of situation. Some of the recruits had complained, wondering who would want to use a bow when there were pistols to hand. But once they'd stood facing the Rastaks or had Jotnar rush at them, and experienced how slow it was to load a pistol or a rifle, they never complained again. A seasoned soldier could load and fire a rifle three times in a minute. An archer who knew what he was doing could shoot six arrows in that time with greater accuracy over a longer distance. Rane could only hope that experience would still serve him well.

With a final breath, Rane released the arrow. It shot towards the demon dog as he reached down for another.

The arrow missed the Bracke's head but struck its neck, burying itself deep within the creature's flesh. The Bracke stumbled and for a moment Rane thought the creature was going to go down, that his arrow had been enough, but the demon dog roared, fangs glinting in the firelight, and it resumed its race towards him, hurtling itself along on all fours.

With another arrow nocked, he pulled back the bowstring, felt the tension mount in his arm as he held the arrow and aimed for the Bracke once more. But the wagon was going too fast, throwing his aim all over the place with each rattle and roll. Rane gritted his teeth and prayed for just one moment of smooth road so he could kill the demon dog. But no moment came and the Bracke drew closer and closer, all teeth and claws and fury.

The Bracke roared. It was almost on Rane, close enough for him to see its eyes gleaming with its eagerness to kill. Close enough for Rane not to miss.

He released the arrow.

The Bracke flew backwards off its feet as the arrow struck home. Dead instantly. It lay still, the shaft visible from inside its throat.

But there was no time to rejoice. The howling of the others filled the air, growing in intensity as if acknowledging the death of their brother.

"Talk to me, Nathaniel," pleaded Olivik. "What's happening? What the fuck is happening?"

"I got one," replied Rane, but before he could say any more, another Bracke burst from cover, followed quickly by another. And another. Filling the road. Too many of them to count. Too many for Rane to deal with. He looked over his shoulder, found Olivik staring back, eyes wide with fear. "Just keep going. Don't stop," said Rane.

He turned back to the road, to the Bracke, and what he had to do. He pulled out another arrow, but resisted the urge just to shoot blindly into the pursuing pack. Instead he selected a target before releasing the bowstring. He didn't wait to see if it hit home, just took another arrow, aimed at another Bracke, and released. Again and again he acted almost without thinking, barely acknowledging when Bracke fell. His arrows flew into the beasts, hurting some, killing others. But still they came on, so many, so fast, so deadly.

One by one, he emptied the quiver until only one arrow remained. He held it in his hand as he stared at the Bracke. How many were left? Fifteen? Twenty? One arrow wasn't enough. Added to that, Rane could tell the horses were struggling dragging the wagon along at full speed, and nowhere near quick enough. They'd never outrun the dogs.

He scuttled back to the front of the wagon to rejoin Olivik. "Climb out onto one of the horses. I'm going to cut them loose from the wagon."

Olivik looked at him as if he were mad. "What?"

"We're going too slowly. They'll be on us if we don't do something."

"I don't want to die."

"Nor do I. That's why we're getting on the horses."

"Shit." Olivik's eyes followed the route he'd have to take, over the front of the wagon and then down onto the center tongue, and from that onto one of the racing horses. What Rane was asking him to do wasn't easy. But then he looked past Rane, at the pack of Bracke behind them, and he knew staying wasn't any safer. "Shit."

He passed the reins to Rane, shook his head at the insanity of it all, and clambered over the front of the wagon. He stepped onto the tongue and froze. "I can't do this. I fucking can't do this."

"You can. Think about your wife and kids in the other wagon. They need you alive. Think of them, and move."

"Fuck. Fuck. Fuck." Olivik crawled along the center pole, wrapping his arms around it as he held on for dear life, inch by inch, until he could reach out and get his arm on one of the horses.

From behind Rane came the crunch of claw on wood. He spun around, raising the bow as he did so, pulling back the string. A Bracke had leapt onto the back of the wagon. It reared up, claws extended, ready to fall on Rane, and got the last arrow through its heart. The Bracke tumbled backwards off the wagon, knocking another devil dog down as it fell.

Rane threw the bow away and followed Olivik. He moved quicker, almost running along the center of the wagon beam to straddle the other horse. "Take this." He passed Olivik one of his knives. "Cut the harness."

Olivik set to work and Rane drew *Kibon*. Power surged through him and his confidence flooded back. By the Gods, he could take on the world with this sword in his hand.

Olivik cut through the harness and his horse sprang free. Rane didn't wait. He slashed down, slicing the straps that held his own horse. *Kibon* made easy work of the leather, and with a lurch, the wagon fell away.

Rane glanced back as his horse sped away. The wagon dipped down and flipped with a crunch of wood on stone. It twisted as it turned, blocking the Crow's Road. And then the Bracke hit it. The wood shattered against their fury. It barely slowed them for a second. Rane had been a fool to think it could do more.

The remaining two wagons rumbled on ahead. Karn sat on the tail of Fia's with his musket ready, but what would one shot do against so many? Myri rode alongside with another pistol, another sword. She looked back, but Rane waved her on. They had to keep the children safe. That was all that mattered. And with *Kibon* in his hand, he knew what he had to do. The only thing he could do.

He slipped off the horse and turned to face the oncoming Bracke.

25

R ane watched the Bracke race towards him. *Kibon* roared in his hands, setting fire to his blood. He knew it was working its magic on him, but this time he didn't fight it. He embraced it. He needed it.

By the Gods, he was almost excited to fight the devil dogs. Time for them to see real power, face real fury. Their claws were nothing against *Kibon*'s steel. He counted them, no longer afraid to know their number.

Sixteen of them.

Sixteen Bracke, eager to die. Stupid little dogs.

"Come on, you bastards," shouted Rane as he gave in to the rage building inside.

He shifted his stance, dropped *Kibon* lower. The leading Bracke was ten feet away, nine, eight, six. The Bracke leaped, claws outstretched. Rane moved fast and furiously, sidestepping the Bracke as he swung *Kibon*. Energy flowed through the steel as the blade cleaved the beast's flesh.

He turned as another Bracke attacked. The claws cut his chest, but they were nothing more than rain in fire. He separated the Bracke's head from its shoulders and moved on to the next, gutting it from left to right.

But still the Bracke came on. He hacked another down and stabbed the next. Claws and fangs left their mark on him, but the Bracke paid for each wound with their lives. Their attacks stopped only when the bodies piled up around him.

Eight Bracke remained, wary of his sword. They had learned their lesson. They circled him as a pack, looking for strength in numbers where sheer ferocity had failed. Rane almost laughed at the futility of it all. He was death incarnate. What were eight dumb animals compared to the multitude he had sent back to Heras' embrace?

The Bracke snapped and snarled as they tested their boundaries. *Kibon* flicked this way and that as it looked for more blood to drink. Seconds passed, vital moments for the convoy to escape. Not that it mattered. None of the Bracke would survive to threaten them again.

A part of Rane, deep within, reminded him that he should be afraid, but he dismissed the foolishness of the thought. He smiled. He would never be afraid again. He glanced up the road. Dust and ash swirled in the distance. Good. The others were safe and on their way. Time for him to go back to work.

He danced left, took a dog across the jugular as it reared up, then stepped left, removing the arm of another foolish enough to try to strike him. He reversed *Kibon* and stabbed the creature through the head as it fell.

A weight hit him from behind. Claws hooked into his back and teeth pierced his neck. He barely felt the pain as another came at him, thinking him weak. *Kibon* taught it the folly of its ways. The demon on his back bit down. Blood, warm and wet, ran down his neck. No matter. He thrust *Kibon* behind him, impaling the creature, and pulled the blade up, finding its heart, its lungs. The Bracke went limp, dead, but it did not fall. Its claws were too deeply embedded in Rane. It could wait, though. Five Bracke remained. He dared not take his hands off *Kibon* to pull the claws out of his side.

He feinted towards the one to his left. It retreated as he took a step closer, while the one to his right took the opportunity to attack. Rane was ready for it; he dropped to one knee and cut its legs away. Blood spurted across the white ash as it screamed.

The others came at him as one. Claws slashed his stomach, opening him up. Teeth closed on his right hand, digging deep, grinding against bone. He was pulled from behind and his footing went from under him. The dead Bracke on his back protected him, but he still went down hard. He tried to lash out with *Kibon,* but the other demon dog held his hand in its jaws.

The creatures pressed down on him, slashing and gouging and biting, slowing him, weakening him. But Rane would not die. He was the killer, not them. He got his free hand on a pistol, drew it, and fired into a Bracke at point-blank range. There was a yelp as the Bracke died and fell away. Rane dropped the gun, useless now its job was done, and went for a knife. The fire roared within him, burning away any pain, any weakness. He punched the knife into the Bracke that had his hand, again and again, cutting holes with all the strength he had. Blood flew everywhere — his, theirs, it didn't matter. *Kibon* had to be free. But still the creature held on.

Another weight landed on his sword arm, pinning it down. Another Bracke. They knew the danger was *Kibon.*

Rane twisted around, brought the knife up. Hacked at the demon dog. The Bracke lashed back with a swipe of its claws. It climbed over its dead companion and snapped at Rane. He jerked his head back as the teeth missed his face by an inch and then buried the knife in the Bracke's eye.

One remained.

Rane squirmed, trapped between dead demon dogs. He reached down, pulled the claws out of his side to free the one attached to his back. The last Bracke snarled as Rane worked free each claw. He ignored the wounds; could feel the magic racing through his veins from *Kibon,* healing him.

He shrugged off the Bracke on his back and hauled the other off his chest. There was only the one still clamped to his sword arm to deal with. But the last living Bracke wasn't prepared to wait. It came at Rane, mouth roaring, all claw and fang. Rane drew his last pistol as it leapt. Claws pierced his flesh once more as he pulled the trigger.

The creature's body muffled the boom of Rane's gun as it fell on him. He seized the Bracke by the neck, straining every muscle to keep its snapping jaws away from his face. Blood dripped from its fangs as Rane dodged his head from side to side. He could feel warm blood leaking all over his chest as the Bracke's claws slashed away at him. He jerked his legs away as the devil dog stomped down with its powerful hind legs, trying to pin him to the ground.

But slowly, ever so slowly, the fight faded from the creature. Its jaws snapped sporadically without power and its slashing claws grew more feeble. Finally, the hatred in its eyes — its terrifying eyes — dimmed. The last Bracke was dead.

Rane heaved the corpse off and then lay back, sucking air into his lungs. He'd done it. The convoy was safe. A smile spread across his face as he gazed up at the stars. He'd bloody well done it.

It took some time to force open the jaw of the Bracke clamped to his wrist. The teeth had gone almost completely through. He winced as they slowly slid out of his flesh, leaving his wrist in shreds.

Rane staggered to his feet, only too aware that without the magic of *Kibon* he'd be dead. His clothes hung off him in strips, soaked in blood, a lot of it his. Too much of it his. But the fire raged inside him, fuelled by each life *Kibon* had taken, and so the magic did its work. Flesh and muscle grew on his wrist, knitting together before his eyes, leaving the faintest of scars as the only reminder. The magic spread, repairing holes and sealing cuts. The bloodlust faded with his injuries, and he could feel his old self returning, his sanity restored.

The sun rose in the east, spreading like blood across the horizon. Rane examined *Kibon* in the new light, looking for the darkness he knew was coming. The sign that said his soul was lost. The little black dots that speckled the blade were easy to find as the blood-red light danced across the steel. He still had time.

Kibon went back into its sheath without a fight — another sign Rane was still in control.

"Rane!"

He looked up. Myri rode towards him, leading another horse. For once, the tightness has gone from her face. Relief had taken its place. She looked five years younger for it.

For the second time that night, Rane smiled. "Good to see you." And it was. She was his family. He may have lost Kara, lost their child, but he wasn't alone. Not while he had her. Had the Legion.

Myri stopped her horse and dismounted. She pulled Rane's leather coat off the back of her saddle and tossed it to him. "You look like you need this."

Rane smiled as he put it on over his ripped-up clothes. "Good to see you, Myri."

Myri threw her arms around him. "By Odason's balls, it's good to see you too. I thought I'd find your corpse."

"Wasn't my time to die."

"Let's hope it never is." Myri squeezed him one last time before letting go. She stepped back, looked over the mound of dead Bracke, then back at him. "But let's not push the odds like this again, either."

Rane raised an eyebrow but said nothing, suddenly aware of the tang of blood on his tongue and how dry his mouth was. He took a water skin off the spare horse and gulped some down. It was the sweetest thing he'd ever tasted. "Thanks for coming back."

Myri held up her stump. "I may not be much use in a fight, but I'm sure not going to leave a fellow Legionnaire behind if I can help it." She looked again at the dead Bracke. "Of course, there was a part of me that just wanted to get killing again, one hand or not. Not sure if I'm happy or pissed off that you did it all before I got here."

"Be happy, Myri," replied Rane. "We did good today. We acted like real Legionnaires again — we lived up to our oath. Saved good people."

Myri sniffed, glancing back the way she'd come, and a little of the sternness returned to her face. "Fuckers. I wouldn't mind if it wasn't for all their whining. Some of them could do with being put out of their misery."

Rane waited for the grin that said she was joking, but none came.

"They've been through a lot — shit they're not used to like we are. You can't blame them for being scared."

The storm in Myri's eyes told Rane she could.

"We'll go our separate ways now the children are safe. We'll ride on to Orska," continued Rane. "Everything will be better."

"You keep telling me everything will be all right once we get to Orska. Well, I'm not so fucking sure." Myri waved her bandaged stump in front of him again. "Can't see how this will be all right once the fucking magic's gone. I won't even be ordinary. How many one-armed soldiers do you know? Maybe I can get work as a town drunk somewhere once we're fucking cured? Who's going to hire me? What the fuck am I going to be good for?"

"You won't be a monster."

"No. I'll just be a fucking freak."

Rane reached out to comfort her, but Myri turned her back and marched over to her horse. He watched her, helpless. There were no words to make her feel better. None that he could think of, anyway. Myri was halfway down the road before Rane could force himself to follow.

They rode in silence, Myri leading the way. The sun climbed higher, brightening the world while the bones and fires began to thin on either side of the road. The end was near. A wind joined them as they rode, dragging ash from the ground to reveal patches of grass amongst the scorched earth, and blue sky previously hidden by smoke. Rane could see another belt of green waiting for them not that far ahead, where the bones ended and nature resumed.

"Fuckers," spat Myri as she slowed her horse.

"What is it?" asked Rane.

"Those fucking God-mutterers. I left them just up ahead. Told them to wait while I went back for you."

The grassland stretched out for a couple of miles before dropping down over the horizon, but there was no sign of Fia and her followers. "Maybe they went on ahead in case it was Bracke coming out of the Dead Lands after them and not us."

Myri laughed at that. A sharp, unpleasant noise. "Maybe they didn't care either way. Just glad to see the back of us."

"Can't blame them either way," replied Rane. "Half the world's scared of us at the moment." A memory of Kara backing away from him, horrified at what he'd done, flashed through his mind. A part of him was glad she wasn't around to see the path he and the rest of the Legion were on. He hated himself for feeling that way.

"Yeah. And the other half wants to collect the rewards on our heads." Myri nudged her horse on. "And you feel good about honoring vows to people like that? People who can't even be bothered to wait to see if you were alive or dead? To say thank you for saving their miserable lives? I thought you were cleverer than that."

A cold shiver ran through Rane as Myri rode on. She was losing her battle with the darkness, drifting further away from him, and as much as he wanted to hold on to her, keep her safe, he didn't know what to do to stop it from happening.

They had to get to Orska before it was too late for all of them.

26

They found the pilgrims a day later. Rane spotted them first, their two battered wagons rattling along the road ahead. Fia's temple and William's cart, all overflowing with people. Karn was sitting on the back of Fia's wagon, musket on his lap, feet dangling off the kickboard. When he saw Rane and Myri approaching, he hollered a warning to the others. Familiar faces turned towards the Legionnaires.

At least Fia had the good grace to call a halt.

Joassa and Hazia watched from the temple wagon's rear window, their children peeking up over the window lip as well. The Hendersons and their kids rode with William in his wagon upfront. Fia herself stood up in the driver's seat, hands on hips, ready to take on the world.

"You're both alive," she said as they drew near. She smiled. "I don't believe it."

"We are," replied Rane, aware of a shimmer of anger coming to life inside.

"Good of you to fucking wait to be sure," snapped Myri, but Rane held out a hand to silence her. Shouting wasn't going to do any of them any good.

Fia raised an eyebrow and continued as if nothing had been said. "I thought it best to keep moving and put some distance between us and the Dead Lands. I'm sorry, but I didn't think we'd see either of you again."

"I don't blame you. I didn't think I was going to make it either." Rane looked at the faces around them. Fia may have been welcoming, but there was open hatred on Karn's, and the rest look petrified. Only William had the decency to look guilty at the way they were all behaving.

Kibon niggled at the back of his mind. It knew what to do with them. It beat at the darkness and the anger within him, urging it to life, telling him they were ungrateful. Blood would be a good price to pay for what Rane had done. A fair price.

He rubbed his face, reminded himself who he truly was. Not the killer. Not a monster. A good man. "I understand."

"Like fuck you do," said Myri. "You ungrateful fuckers—"

"Watch your mouth, freak," warned Karn, raising his musket. "Don't think we don't know what you are."

Fia fixed her a husband with a glare. "Enough."

"You know what I am, do you?" Myri nudged her horse towards Karn as if she didn't have a care in the world, stopping only when she was a few inches away from the end of his musket. Her hand rested on the pommel of her sword. "Well, let me tell you who I am — just so we're both clear. I'm someone who earns her way, little man. I'm someone who doesn't bleat like a five-month-old babe desperate for his mother's tit every two minutes. I'm someone who's killed more fucking demons than the days you've been on this earth. Does any of that sound like who you thought me to be?"

"I know you're a killer," spat Karn, his hands shaking and his eyes wide. "I know you're a harbinger of death and we've been cursed since we met you."

"Everyone calm down *now*," ordered Rane, his eyes locked on Myri. He was painfully aware either Myri or Karn would spill blood if things continued. The whole convoy waited, the pressure of violence pressing down on them while they watched Karn and Myri stare at each other.

"Another time, little man." Ever so slowly, a smile spread across Myri's face — the most frightening grin Rane had ever seen, especially when she turned to face him. "You ruin all my fun."

"Wait up the road for me," said Rane.

"My pleasure," sneered Myri. She kicked her horse forward without another word.

"I'm sorry," said Rane to Fia once Myri was gone. "I wish we'd met under different circumstances."

"Magic has its price," said Fia. She sighed. "Before we part, let me give you some clothes and food to help you on your way. Odason knows you could do with both." She looked over to William, who nodded and started filling a sack.

"Thank you," said Rane.

"You might not be so thankful for what I'm about to tell you." For a moment, the steel in her was overcome with sadness. "I believe you are a decent man struggling with whatever was done to you. But what you did — messing with magic, tainting your Gods-given soul — is still blasphemy. And the orders of my faith are very clear on the subject. When I get to Napolin, I have to tell my order about you, about Myri, and about the rest of the Legion at Orska. I have no choice."

"They'll send an army after us," replied Rane. "And every bounty hunter for a hundred miles will be tagging along, hoping to get rich. A lot of people will die."

"Magic has its price," repeated Fia.

"You know, we did it to save you all. The Rastaks would have either killed or enslaved everyone. They liked to torture priests like you before burning them." His hand twitched, eager to feel *Kibon*'s hilt once more. The sword knew how to prevent a new army from marching against the Legion.

"Heras finds ways to tempt weaker souls into Her machinations. No man thinks his actions are evil." Fia paused while William handed

Rane a small sack with food, a couple of waterskins, a shirt, and an old, battered waistcoat.

"Thank you," said Rane. He changed his clothes, aware of the shaking in his hands as he did up the buttons on the shirt. Thoughts of cutting them all down, removing whatever threat they possessed, flashed through his mind. *Kibon* could deal with the problem with ease. But Fia and her pilgrims were innocents. Just ordinary people looking for a better life. People he'd sworn to serve and protect. He slipped his coat back on. "I wish you good luck on your journey, and all I ask is for you to reconsider your plans. Hopefully by the time you get to Napolin, this curse, this magic, will be lifted from not just myself and Myri, but all the Legion."

"I'll certainly pray for you," replied Fia. "I'll pray for all of you."

Rane nodded and nudged his horse on after Myri. He could feel *Kibon*'s frustration pressing down on his back, warning him that he was being foolish. Why risk the Legion's safety for people he barely knew? But *Kibon* wasn't going to be his master. Fear wasn't going to control him. He had to be better than that.

Myri's mood hadn't improved by the time he caught up with her. She'd moved her sword from her back to her hip and looked keen to use it.

"How many days to Orska?" asked Rane.

"About five," replied Myri.

"And to Napolin?"

Myri glanced back the way they'd come, back to where Fia and her pilgrims were. "Seven or eight. Why?"

Rane hesitated, unsure if he should tell Myri what had happened, but they had to have trust between them, especially if their lives depended upon it. "Fia's reporting us to the head of her order when she gets to Napolin, telling them about Orska."

"The church of Odason hangs Legionnaires. We'll have the Inquisition after us."

"I know."

"I hope you put them all in the ground."

"You know I didn't."

"Fool." Myri went to turn her horse and head back, but Rane put his own mount in her way.

"We stick with the plan. Go to Orska. Get cured," said Rane. "Once we've done that, we can get this death sentence lifted off us. With the magic gone, there's no need to hang anyone. The Lord General can talk some sense into them."

Myri shook her head. "Nothing's that easy."

"Gathering a force against us won't happen overnight. We could have two or three weeks before any sort of army or militia would be ready to march."

"It's still safer to remove the risk altogether. The dead don't talk."

"We're Legionnaires, not monsters. Not yet. Fia and the others are just scared. We need to show them we're better than that."

"Not monsters?" grunted Myri. "We're monsters all right. Have been for a long time. It's just that we're not as bad yet as some of the others out there. But give it time."

Rane was lost for an answer. Too many dead flashed before his eyes, and the joy he'd felt in killing them. He held onto Kara's locket, the last part of the life he'd wanted.

Myri saw him and sneered. "Sometime soon you'll realize that's just a sliver of metal and it won't stop you becoming whatever you're going to become."

"Then why are we going to Orska? Why are we fighting this curse? We might as well kill ourselves right here, right now."

"Aye, we could." Myri smiled that dead grin of hers. "I'll tell you what: you go first. I promise I'll cut my own throat right after." She stared at him for a moment, then arched her eyebrow as she waited for his answer. Finally, she chuckled. "Thought not. Let's move on. It's a long ride."

For two hours they rode in silence. At least they were moving forward again now, with nothing to stop them getting to Orska. Marcus was gone, the children safe, and the Dead Lands left further and further behind them. Whatever pressure Myri was under, and regardless of the danger both their lives were in, worrying about any of it wasn't going to change anything. Rane just had to concentrate on the road before them. Their path — for now — was set.

At least there was pleasure to be found in the countryside around them after the scorched earth, bones, and constant fire and smoke of the Dead Lands. The colors of the grass and trees around them looked more vivid than any Rane could remember seeing for a long time. Even the autumn hues starting to creep in amongst the green had a beauty that almost brought a tear to his eye. And the easterly wind carried fresh air to clear out the muck that had accumulated over the previous days. Rane almost felt human again.

But the weight of *Kibon* on his back reminded him otherwise.

They stopped next to a small brook to rest the horses, and to eat. The pilgrims had given them two loaves of bread, some rice and some dried meat. Enough to keep them going most of the way if they were careful. Myri sat with her back against a tree, facing back down the road, squinting into the distance.

"No one's following," said Rane.

His voice seemed to startle her, as if she'd forgotten he was there. "What did you say?"

"No one's following."

"I know," replied Myri and went back to eating her heel of bread. But every now and then, her eyes would look up to confirm the road was empty all the same.

Later that afternoon, they passed a village consisting of not much more than an inn and a couple of farmhouses, but the Legionnaires stuck to the woodland and kept out of sight.

As day turned into night, they reached a crossroads; to the north west was the road to Napolin, to the north east was the way to the coast, and Orska. It was the point where they should have been saying their goodbyes to Fia and the others, but they weren't living in the days of fond farewells.

Rane caught Myri looking back again, and this time he too turned to gaze down the road they'd just travelled. It stretched long and empty, back into the woods and out of sight. The pilgrims were probably a half-day behind them at the speed they moved. Despite how they'd parted, Rane wished them a safe journey on.

They found a hollow off the main road, a nice dip in the ground with a fallen tree to one side, offering some decent shelter for the night as well as cover from anyone on the road. Myri and Rane tied up their horses and began setting up camp.

Rane soon had a fire going and a pot of rice cooking. "I can't tell you how much I'm looking forward to this. When was the last time we had hot food?"

"Probably the last time you bathed," replied Myri, and this time her smile was genuine, as warm as the fire they sat around.

"We must stink," chuckled Rane.

"Something else to sort out when we get to Orska."

The rice, when it was cooked, provided enough for a small bowl each, but it was more than enough for Rane. He savored every grain, enjoying the taste of something warm again, of food untainted by demon fire. The two Legionnaires may only have had a dry patch of ground to sit on, but Rane had a full stomach, and was warm and comfortable for the first time in an age.

"Why don't you get some rest?" said Myri after she'd finished eating. "I'll take first watch."

"Are you sure?"

"Sure." Her voice was soft and gentle. "You've been through enough these past few days. Get some sleep."

"Thanks. Wake me in a few hours and I'll take over," replied Rane. He lay down on the ground, the dirt feeling softer than any bed. How long had he been awake? Two, three days? He was so very tired. He closed his eyes.

27

R ane woke to an empty campsite. Myri was nowhere to be seen. Her horse was gone.

Where was she?

It was still early, the sun no more than a promise in the sky, the wind sharp enough to quickly clear the fog from his thoughts. Had she left him, headed off to Orska on her own? The road ahead was empty — how long had it been since she'd left? He glanced back the way they'd come, back towards the crossroads, back to where Fia and the others would be travelling. Unease grew in his mind. Her threats churned his gut.

No.

She wouldn't have gone back to kill them — not after all they'd been through to save them. But even as the thought flashed through his mind, he knew only too well that she could.

Had he lost her to the sword?

He stared down the road, full of dread and fear, praying to the Gods that he was wrong.

"You're awake," said Myri from behind him. He'd not heard her approach.

"Where were you?" asked Rane without turning. *Kibon* burning in his mind, warning him that Myri could be tainted. Lost forever. Better to kill her now. Before it was too late.

"I heard noises. Went to investigate." There was a thud on the ground. Something heavy.

Rane looked over his shoulder. A Bracke head lay in the dirt.

"Thought I'd bring you a souvenir just in case you didn't believe me," said Myri, her sword sheathed and on her hip. She walked out of sight again and returned with her horse.

Rane took deep breaths to try and get his fears under control, aware that he was grinding his teeth and his body was racked with tremors. Was it *Kibon* making him that way?

She unsaddled her horse, seemingly unconcerned that he was watching her. When she was finished, she walked past him, squatted down and threw more wood onto the fire.

NO screamed *Kibon*. Myri was a threat. Best be quick, attack before it was too late. The voice pounded away in his brain. His hand twitched, eager to feel *Kibon* once more. But Rane fought back. The sword's weight pressed down on him a thousandfold, but the sword wouldn't be his master. His arms shook with the effort but he ignored its warnings.

"Gets harder each time, doesn't it," said Myri. She raised an eyebrow as if she knew everything he was thinking. "You should try doing when it's as black as night and you've only got one fucking hand." She stood up, walked towards him. "Trouble is, you and I are both charged up with all this magic and power and got nothing but each other to take it out on."

Rane shifted his posture, unsure of what was about to happen. But her sword was still sheathed.

"Do you ever think about us?" she asked. The firelight danced across her skin.

"Us?"

She smiled. "In *that* way."

"Oh."

"We used to have fun together back in the Legion." She took another step closer. Inches separated them.

"To be honest, I didn't think you remembered. It was a long time ago."

Myri placed her hand against his chest. "You haven't forgotten either."

"I haven't, but..."

"Come on. We've got this curse hanging over us. I lost my arm, for Gods' sake. People are eager to do us harm. So I've been thinking. How I'd like to feel something good. Feel something that can make me forget this blackness that's growing inside me — even if it's only for an hour or two. Don't you, Nathaniel? Imagine what it would be like with all this power screaming inside us right now." She pressed herself against him, her cheek next to his.

"Myri, I..." He cupped her face in his hand, only too aware of the primal rush he was feeling inside. "I wish I could, but I can't."

"You can't?" Myri took a step back, pulled her face free. "There's no threat to us nearby. We're safe."

"I lost my wife only a short time ago. She may be gone, but I still feel her here," Rane patted his heart, "and I still feel married to her. I can't be with anyone else. Not now. Not for a long time. I'm sorry."

"Un-fucking-believable." Myri laughed, shook her head. "I under-stand — or rather, I don't — but whatever. Look, forget we had this conversation. I need some fucking sleep."

"I'm sorry." He reached out for her again, but she shrugged off his hand.

"Don't be. And don't worry — it won't happen again." She spoke with her back to him, a shadow. "Wake me in a couple of hours."

"Shit." Rane ran his hand through his hair, rubbed his face. "I'm going to go for a walk. I won't be far. I just need... I'll be back soon."

Myri didn't reply; just curled up on the floor with her back to the fire and dragged her blanket over herself.

Rane stood for a moment, watching her, wondering if he'd made another mistake in more ways than one. But it was what it was. He picked up the severed head and walked until he came to a sharp drop. The forest continued a couple of hundred feet below.

He threw the head over the side and watched it drop out of sight, glad to see it go. But deep down, he knew there would be more on the way. What were they even doing back in the world? Jotnar, Bracke, Valkryn, Grenduns — the Legion was supposed to have killed them all. He'd given up his fucking soul to rid the world of them, allowed half of Ascalonia to go up in magic fire to destroy them. Was it all for nothing?

Rane dropped to his knees, letting out a loud sob as tears formed in the corner of his eyes. "Damn you. Damn you all," he said and punched the ground. Again and again. Right, then left. He pounded the ground until his hands bled and the bones broke. Tears ran down his face, and still he hammered away at the ground.

Finally, his fury died. He looked at his hands as *Kibon's* magic set about healing them. Before his eyes, the bones fused and the wounds closed as if nothing had happened.

He staggered back to camp, holding on to Kara's locket as if it alone had the power to save him from becoming a monster. Myri hadn't moved. She might've been sleeping or just pretending to be; either way, Rane was grateful not to have to speak to her again that night.

Her horse snorted at him as he passed, so Rane stopped to give the animal a pat. When he touched the horse, he was surprised to find the animal damp from sweat. Myri had ridden the horse hard somewhere while Rane had been asleep. He picked up some grass and began to rub the horse down. The last thing they needed was for the horse to go lame with so far still to go.

As he worked, thoughts of where Myri had been played through his mind. She'd dealt with a Bracke, but that must have been nearby for her to have heard it. So where had she gone to get the horse so worked up?

The dread came back as only one answer made sense. Fia and the other pilgrims. Had Myri gone to find them? And there was only one reason why she'd do that.

Myri had said they were safe, that there were no threats to the Legionnaires out there. He looked down at her sleeping body. Had she murdered Fia and the others?

PART IV

28

"Nathaniel, wake up," whispered Myri.

Rane was up in an instant, hand reaching for *Kibon*. It was still dark. How long had he been asleep? Not long enough, that was for sure. "What is it?"

"Bracke." Myri crouched, her own sword already unsheathed and ready. As she spoke, the horses picked up the scent of the demon and strained against their tethers, stomping the ground in fear.

"How many?"

"Just the one. Heard it coming up the slope."

Rane sighed with relief. He was almost tempted to lie back down and leave the devil dog to Myri, but better safe than sorry, no matter how tired he was. "We could've had a fire after all."

"Least we know now." In the week since they'd left Dead Lands, the two of them had been plagued by Bracke. Even some Valkryn had attacked them, swooping down from the night skies on their heavy wings.

Rane and Myri had tried everything to shake the creatures off their tail, but it hadn't done any good. That night they'd camped with no fire, hoping that would help hide them. But it had obviously not made any difference. The demons were drawn to them no matter what they did.

"Let's get it done so I can go back to sleep." Rane pulled *Kibon* free from its scabbard. Immediately, a thrill ran through him, pushing the weariness from his bones. He moved to Myri's right, watching the peak for the Bracke to appear. "How many have we killed now?"

"Too many. Not enough." Myri was her usual talkative self.

They'd barely spoken since that night; the night she'd gone off only the Gods knew where. A week of silence that grew heavier by the day. If it weren't for the demons coming after them, Rane doubted Myri would've said a word. But the demons kept appearing, and Rane and Myri kept killing them. So much for hoping they'd left them back with the bones in the Dead Lands.

"Where are they coming from?" said Rane.

"Fuck knows," replied Myri. "But I'm happy to slaughter them all." She grinned, her black sword bouncing in her hand. With Orska so close, any restraint in using her blade had all but gone. She was going to be cured tomorrow, so why should she worry about today? Even so, the sight of her so close to the edge terrified Rane. Every life she took, he worried that it would be the one that turned her into a demon like Marcus.

He'd tried to deal with as many of the monsters as he could to spare Myri from adding to her blade's taint, but there had been too many, too often. Neither of them were getting much rest, their nerves frayed, kept busy by the demons, fuelled by their swords' magic and dragged on by the pull of Orska. Even *Kibon* was showing more signs of the taint. But what could they do but follow the path they were on? At least a cure waited for them.

The Bracke took its time approaching, claws scratching on rock as it made its way up towards them. It crept over the lip of the hill, pausing when it saw the two Legionnaires. It pulled back with a roar, baring its teeth and putting all its weight on its hind legs, ready to pounce.

"Let me..." said Rane, stepping forward, but Myri was already moving to attack, no longer worried about fighting with her left hand after all the practice she'd had.

The Bracke launched itself at her with a roar, claws extended and jaws wide. Myri's sword cut it down in mid-air, the black blade barely visible in the night. She shuddered with the blow as the magic hit her.

More blood fed to her sword.

"Are you okay?" asked Rane once they'd sheathed their swords.

"I'm fine," she replied, thin-lipped and taut.

"Orska's close." Judging by the sea air and from what Rane could remember, they would be at the castle later that day — and not a moment too soon. Hopefully not a moment too late.

Myri glared at him. Her eyes were flint. She sucked in air through her nose as she chewed on something to say. "I'm fine."

"You can talk about it. It's hard."

"I'm fine," she repeated. Her body shook with the faintest of tremors, as if it was taking all her effort to control her temper. Rane had no doubt that violence would follow if he dared asked one more time.

"Okay. Sorry." There was another twist in his gut. Sadness seeped through him, tinged with fear. He remembered what Marcus had become; what Myri was close to becoming. How many more kills would put her over the edge? Or was she already gone? Had she killed the pilgrims? He'd not asked her. Not that night, the morning after, or any of the days since. It was just one more nagging fear that he tried not to think about.

Perhaps his face betrayed what he was thinking, as Myri softened for a moment. "I really am fine. You don't have to worry about me." Her voice was a whisper, the anger gone.

Rane nodded, not reassured. He hoped Fia and the others were alive, even if it meant the pilgrims would eventually send an army to Orska after them. Better to hope that than to believe his friend was lost.

"There's no way I'm going to sleep now," said Myri, "so you might as well get some more rest. We'll move at first light."

"Can't see myself sleeping either," replied Rane. "Dawn's not far off. Let's make a start now. We could make Orska in a few hours."

Myri headed over to the horses, untied them and then threw the reins of Rane's horse to him. They both mounted, and with only a click of the tongue from Myri, they were on their way again.

It was strange being back in the border regions. So much of his life had been spent there, yet while he'd been with Kara the war years had seemed like a dream best forgotten. Now he was back, the feeling was reversed. It was as if his time with Kara in Ascalonia had never existed, as if his days of love and happiness were some half-remembered dream. It was too easy to exist in a world of blood and death. It was all too natural.

A clear, cold, star-filled sky gave them light enough to see by, but they didn't push the horses, allowing them to find their own way down the slope. There was no point injuring the horses on an unseen hole when they were so close to the journey's end. The path led down into a small valley before climbing up the side of another mountain. Small pockets of thistle dotted the slopes here and there, but otherwise it was just as barren as Rane remembered it from the early days of the war.

After the Rastaks had torn through Naijin and Fascaly, they'd laid siege to the city of Napolin at the crossroads of the five nations. No one believed that Napolin would hold them for long, or that the Rastaks would be satisfied with the lands already conquered. When it came time for the Rastaks to head south, Orska lay directly in their path.

The Legion had headed to Orska in force, dragging with them every soldier and militia they could find along the way, armed with as much cannon as they could muster. It was the largest fighting force that had been gathered in over a hundred years, determined to stop the Rastaks war machine in its tracks.

The first sign Napolin had fallen was the refugees crossing the border. They'd started coming in small groups, the luckier ones on horseback, but a trickle soon became a flood. Most only had the clothes on their backs, and only a few had much to eat. Even so, they'd not wanted to stop at Orska. They knew what was following.

The Legion marched out to meet the Rastaks three days later at Hasloken. But when the two forces met, it wasn't a battle. It was a massacre. The Legion held their own against the Rastaks, but once the demons joined the attack, the tide turned quickly. The battle only lasted a day but Rane could still vividly remember the mounds of dead left in the field.

As the Legion retreated back to Candra, they could hear the Rastaks singing their victory songs, and the screams of their prisoners as they were sacrificed to Heras.

And there Rane was, years later, riding out to Orska once more.

By the time Rane and Myri reached the valley floor, the sun had started to climb the other side of the mountain. Streaks of red and purple heralded its arrival, but it would be hours yet before the two Legionnaires would feel its warmth. At least they could see that no other demons lay in wait for them along the path ahead. Hopefully it would remain that way until they reached Orska.

Orska, where Jefferson was waiting with a cure for them both. Just thinking that gave him a new burst of energy. Soon, all their problems would be over.

It was well into the afternoon by the time they reached the top of the last mountain, and the sight that waited for them made the whole journey worthwhile.

Orska.

The castle hadn't changed. It straddled the road north with its big walls and its back to the Pacini Sea, sparkling blue behind it. Two watchtowers stood guard either side of the main gate and Rane followed the battlements along with his eye, past the round mural tower, the main keep looming behind, across the upper bailey to the square siege tower and arsenal tower at the other end. It was his whole life, once, where he could easily have died. Now it held all his hopes for the future.

The fortress seemed smaller than he remembered, a fragile place to have withstood so much. Time had weathered the stone walls to match the surrounding hillsides, shrinking it further. It was hundreds of years old, built for the skirmish wars with Fascaly before the five nations became allies, back when everyone seemed happy to go to war over a careless remark or a wandering flock.

Behind it, the harbor was a bed of grey calm topped by small wisps of waves. A perfect spot to launch ships out into the world and cut off any seeking Ascalonia's shores.

However, the walls of the castle seemed deserted. Rane couldn't see any guards or sentries, despite the fact a garrison should still be posted there. No flags flew on the walls; no light burned in the windows. The only sign of life was another murder of crows circling overhead. He could hear their squawks, telling the world of their arrival. Evil creatures. Rane hated them as much as any Bracke.

The wind drifted past, plucking at his clothes and hair. For the first time, Rane could feel the seeds of doubt begin to break though the surface of his hope. What would he do if Jefferson wasn't there? If no cure waited for them? What if his whole quest had been nothing but a fool's errand? Fear filled his mind as he imagined the worst.

If Myri felt the same, she didn't show it. Just kicked her heels and got her horse on its way. Rane followed, wondering if she was lost already.

Orska grew more imposing as they drew near. But just when Rane was convinced the post was abandoned, he saw movement on the battlements. Then a voice called out, warning that two riders approached, and Rane found himself grinning like an idiot. Thoughts of everything that had happened since Kara died raced through his mind — what he'd endured, what he'd survived — and he thanked the Gods it was over. The Legion was there, waiting for him. Soon, he would be back amongst his brothers and sisters. Soon, the curse would be gone, and they could set about repairing the Legion's reputation. He gazed up at the walls, wondering who might be there with Jefferson, which old friends he'd find.

The southern side of the castle hadn't taken the beating from the Rastaks that the other side had, but time had taken a toll of its own on the building. Wind and dust had worn the stone smooth in places, and turned walls into jagged edges in others.

They stopped before the main gates and dismounted. The portcullis was already raised, but the large oak doors were closed. Rane glanced over at Myri and found she had a grin of her own. She was standing straighter, as if a weight had been lifted from her shoulders, and a fire burned once more in her eyes.

"We made it. We fucking made it," she said, shaking her head in disbelief.

"That we did," replied Rane.

Myri pushed the gates, but they were locked. Instead, she rapped on the wood with her sword's hilt. The sound echoed into the castle.

As they waited, Rane felt *Kibon* whisper in the back of his mind, urging to be freed. What if danger waited for him on the other side of the gates? Better to face whatever was coming with naked steel. Better to have his sword in his hand, ready. He watched Myri out of the corner of his eye, but she didn't seem to be experiencing the same feelings. If anything, she looked happier than she had in a long time. So why was *Kibon* so restless? Perhaps it could sense its end was near.

Approaching footsteps shook him from his thoughts and doubts. His heart quickened as bolts were slid free and a cross-beam moved. The gates groaned as they opened, straining on rusted hinges, and a streak of sunlight forced its way out. Two men with shaved heads and in full Legion uniform stood before him. Rane didn't recognize their faces, but they had the look of soldiers used to living on the front line. Hard men, ready for violence at a moment's notice. Their swords were sheathed on their backs, but both had muskets aimed at Myri and Rane. Other soldiers, also in full uniform, waited in the lower bailey on the other side of the gatehouse, weapons drawn. No one was taking any chances.

"Greetings, brothers," Rane said with his right hand raised, happy to show the scar. "No one's looking to cause any trouble."

The Legionnaires' gaze drifted over Rane and Myri. "Let's see your swords before you come any closer," said the Legionnaire on the left.

"Move slowly while you do it. We'll be just as happy to shoot you if we have to."

"As I said, we're not here to cause trouble," replied Rane. "The Lord General sent for us."

"The swords. Now," replied the sentry and raised the musket to his shoulder, aiming it squarely at Rane.

Rane slipped his sword off his shoulder. A thrill ran through him as he touched the sword's hilt, *Kibon* excited to be free, but he controlled the emotions, taking his time to slowly unsheathe the sword. Dotted along the blade, Rane could see the stains marking the otherwise perfect steel.

"Put it away," said the sentry before turning to Myri. "Now yours."

Myri placed the sheath of her sword under her right arm and drew the blade out with her left hand. It was all but black.

At the sight of the sight of the sword, Rane was forgotten.

"Don't fucking move!" screamed the first sentry, finger wrapped around the trigger of his weapon. "Don't even fucking blink." The sentry next to him had his own musket up and aimed at Myri a half-second later. Others from the rear guard rushed to join them, adding spears and pikes to the weapons massed against Myri.

"Take it easy," said Rane. "She's not turned."

"I'll be the fucking judge of that," snapped the sentry. He jabbed his musket towards Myri. "You! Put your sword on the ground and walk backwards. Don't fucking stop till I tell you."

"Just get Lord Jefferson..." said Rane, but the sentry shouted over him.

"Do as I say. Put your sword on the ground and walk backwards. Do it, or I'll fucking kill you here and fucking now."

Rane looked over at Myri and was petrified by the glint in her eye. Her fingers tightened on the hilt of her sword.

29

"Put the sword down. Put the sword down." All the guards were shouting at Myri and it wasn't going to take much for someone to start shooting. That's if Myri didn't draw her sword first.

"Myri, do as they say. We've come too far," Rane urged. "Don't get killed now when there's a cure on the other side of this door."

Myri smiled again beneath cold eyes. For one dreadful moment, Rane thought she was going to attack. His mind raced for ways to stop it — stop her — but all he could see was a bloodbath. But then Myri bent down, and gently placed her sword on the ground as if it were a baby being put down to sleep. She lay the sheath next to it. Only then did she step backwards, her eyes locked on the first sentry, smile fixed to her face. When she was twelve feet away, Rane could see old wounds start to open. Little red lines sprang up over her skin, growing wider with each step. She staggered, clutched her stomach, and swayed on her feet. Two more steps and she went down, a red flower blossoming on her chest. Myri tried to stand, to push herself up with her good hand, but her strength was gone. She fell backwards, all her energy and fight gone.

"What the—" Rane started towards her, but a musket in the chest stopped him.

"Leave her," said the sentry. "George, get the fucking sword. Simon, Reynard, get the girl. If she so much as opens her eyes, cut her fucking head off."

The men moved as one. George, a huge Ascalonian, stepped forward, pulling on gloves. Even so, he took care picking up Myri's sword, sheathing it and then placing it in a bag. The other two men picked up Myri and then moved as a group back into the castle, always maintaining the same distance between themselves and Myri's sword.

"She'll die if you keep her from her sword," protested Rane.

"Not yet she won't," said the sentry. They watched Myri disappear inside the mural tower. Once she was out of sight, the tension disappeared. Weapons were lowered. "I'm sorry about that, but we can't take any risks. Believe me, she'll be well taken care of. She's one of us, after all."

Rane hesitated, a sense of unease growing in him while *Kibon* whispered away. It wanted to fight. It warned him of enemies, and of danger. He pinched his brow. By Odason and Heras, how he wanted the voice silenced.

The sentry slung his musket over his shoulder. "You've come a long way. Come in. I know that wasn't the welcome you expected, but we lost two men to a Tainted a few days ago. As you said: no one wants to die this close to a cure. My name's Isaiah. This is Gregor. I recognize you from back in the day, but I can't recall your name."

"My name's Nathaniel. Nathaniel Rane. I was garrisoned here during the war."

Isaiah held out his hand. "Good to meet you, Nathaniel."

Rane took the offered hand as he tried to place the name and face, full of unease. "And you, Isaiah."

"Let's get you settled." Isaiah guided Rane through the main doors and into the barbican while Gregor slipped into position behind them. "I'll get some of the boys to stable your horses while we find you a room and some hot food. We'll let you know when the Lord General can see you."

They passed under the second portcullis and entered the lower bailey.

"What about Myri?" asked Rane.

"Is that the Tainted's name?" Isaiah looked over to the mural tower.

"She's not Tainted." *I hope.* He prayed.

"Whatever you say. Until we're sure, however, we'll put her in the cells with the others. Can't risk having her loose, I'm afraid. Hopefully it won't be for long."

Rane nodded. "I understand. Her name's Myri Anns." He looked around the old castle. "How many others are here? I was hoping she could — I could — be cured as soon as possible."

"There's about forty of us here, including five tainted in the cells. Not enough; not nearly enough. Most of us have been cured already." Isaiah shared a glance with Gregor. Both looked happy at that. "Jefferson's waiting now to see who else turns up before he breaks the curse again. It takes too much of a toll on him to do it often."

"I understand," said Rane, though he couldn't help but disappointed at the news. He was in Orska with the people who could cure him, and he was going to have to wait.

"We're using rooms in the main keep at the moment. It's this way." Isaiah pointed towards the other side of the bailey and the second gatehouse.

"I remember," said Rane, forcing a smile. It was like walking through memories. Each step brought the past back in greater focus. None of it felt good.

"Of course," replied Isaiah. "I actually fought with you, back in the day. I was part of a group you led to help Marcus Shaw and some others to safety in Candra."

"That all happened in a bit of a blur," replied Rane. There was something vaguely familiar about Isaiah, but Rane still couldn't place him. The man was battered and scarred as any veteran, with a chunk missing from an ear, but he looked too young to have been in the war for long. Perhaps he'd been one of the new recruits back towards the end. Still, it was odd that he hadn't recognized any of the Legionnaires he'd seen so far. "Is Babayon here as well?"

Isaiah hesitated for a moment. "No. He's not been seen since the war. At least, not by me he hasn't."

"Has anyone seen him, or spoken about him?" They passed through the second gatehouse into the middle bailey. Sentries walked the battlements, watching them as they crossed the courtyard.

Isaiah scowled at Rane. "I've already told you I haven't seen him. Maybe Jefferson has, but he's not going to tell me. I'm hardly the Lord General's confidant."

"I'm sorry," said Rane. "I meant no offence. I just wonder if Babayon knew what he was doing to us — what he was really doing to us — when he transferred our souls to our swords."

"By the Gods. Enough with the questions." There was a bite to Isaiah's words and his cheeks colored, as though he struggled to control his temper. He glanced over Rane's shoulder at Gregor and unspoken words passed between them. *Kibon* sensed something wrong and stirred once more. Kill them, it whispered.

"I'm sorry. I didn't mean to upset you. I'm just tired. I'm looking forward to getting a good night's sleep," said Rane, changing the subject. "It's been a long road here. Bracke seem to be everywhere."

That took the fight out of Isaiah. "I can imagine. It couldn't have been easy, especially with your friend."

"I'm just glad we got here in time."

Isaiah pushed open the door to the main keep and they headed for the eastern stairs. "Hopefully others will, too."

Rane let the Legionnaire lead the way. They walked up the spiral staircase to the upper levels. He'd forgotten how claustrophobic the confined space made him feel, especially after all his time travelling outdoors. Even the air felt trapped. He twisted his body to allow more room for his shoulders. At least the stairs negated the need for more awkward conversation with his companion.

"Rooms are this way," said Isaiah as they reached the third floor. "Soon get you settled in."

They never made it to the rooms. As they walked down the corridor, a flurry of footsteps approached from the other direction, followed by voices. A second later, there in front of him, surrounded by a small personal guard of Legionnaires, was the Lord General himself: Sir Henry Jefferson.

"By Odason, Nathaniel, it is you. How I prayed for this moment." Jefferson held his arms out wide and the two men embraced like a father and son reunited. "It's so good to see you. So good to see you alive." The old man stepped back, still holding Rane's arms, to get a better look at him, smiling like all their troubles were already over.

"It's good to see you too, sir," replied Rane. Truth was, he was shocked to see the man before him. He remembered what Jefferson had looked like when they all thought Candra was going to fall: frail, a man with far too many years bearing him down into the grave. He'd changed slightly over the following years as they pushed the Rastaks back to the Steppes — his back had straightened, and color had come back to his skin so that it was no longer wax-thin and white. His body had filled out with the regular meals that came from the country's abundance of wildlife. Jefferson had been energized by the Legion's victories, or so Rane had thought. But the man before him had changed even more. The years had fallen off, taking their wrinkles with them. Jefferson had grown broad of shoulder, and looked like a fighter once more, not a thinker. He resembled Rane's older brother, not his grandfather.

Jefferson chuckled, seeing Rane's confusion. "I know. I don't look quite the same." He waved his hand, his scar bright in the torchlight. "The magic had side effects that weren't quite so bad for me. Even I don't recognize myself these days if I dare look in a mirror."

Rane forced a smile, the fake one he'd worn when he thought death waited with the next sunrise. "I'm just happy to be here. It's been a long road." The words were starting to feel more like lies every time he said them.

Jefferson slipped his arm around Rane's shoulder, turned him back towards the stairs. "Come, let's get some hot food inside you and we can talk. There's lots I need to tell you. Lots that we've learned. The world's falling into darkness and trying to drag us down with it."

With Isaiah, Gregor, and the Lord General's Legionnaires following, the two men headed back down towards the Great Hall, Rane's opportunity for some rest disappearing with each step they took.

Jefferson led the procession back down the stairs to the great hall. Soldiers were scattered around various tables, eating and drinking. All fell silent as the men entered the room, and quickly stood to attention when they spotted Jefferson. The old man waved them back down without a word and guided Rane to a corner table. The others sat elsewhere, leaving the two men to talk with some privacy.

"You look tired, Nathaniel. I'm sorry I couldn't let you get some rest first, but I was too excited to see you when I'd heard you'd finally arrived." Jefferson paused while some bread was placed on a table. He gestured to the food. "Please eat. I can prattle on regardless. There'll be more food coming soon enough."

"Thank you, sir. It's a been a long journey." Rane tore off a chunk of warm bread.

"Please don't 'sir' me. You're not in the ranks anymore. It's Henry now."

Rane nearly choked on his bread. "I'm not sure I can do that, sir. You'll always be my commanding officer."

"Ah, well. At least try, eh?"

"Yes, sir."

Jefferson chuckled, but let it pass. "I hear you brought Myri with you. How is she? I haven't looked in on her yet."

"Her sword's pretty black but she's not turned yet. She's holding on. I think."

"You don't sound so sure."

"I don't know. I hope so. We met some pilgrims on the road. We were pursuing Marcus Shaw — he'd turned, killed a lot of people, and kidnapped three of the pilgrims' children."

"Oh, Marcus." Jefferson's gaze drifted away for a moment. "The transformation is a horrible thing. We've lost too many because of it."

"We followed him into the Dead Lands. Got two of the kids back and killed him, but afterwards... The priest was from the church of Odason."

"Ah. And this priest knew you were Legionnaires?"

"Fia. Her name was... is Fia. She knew we were heading here and said she was going to report us to the church at Napolin. She could be only a couple of days from reaching there as we speak."

"Could be?"

"The first night after we left them, Myri was supposed to be on watch, but she disappeared. Took her horse. I fear she went back to silence Fia and the others."

"Ah. But you don't know?"

"She's been so close to the edge that I couldn't ask. I didn't want to destroy what was left if I was wrong. I don't want to believe she did, but I still have doubts."

"Well, she's here and we can look after her now. And if the Inquisition turns up with an army at our doors, we'll know your fears were for nothing." He smiled as if it was of no importance.

"I wish I'd come with better news for you, sir."

"These are the days we find ourselves in, Nathaniel." Jefferson sighed. "My heart bleeds with the news of every life lost. I'd hoped for so many more to heed the call and return, but only a tenth of our numbers have made it."

"It's not easy getting here. Apart from the arrest warrants, we've encountered Bracke and Valkryn on the road. They seem to be coming from everywhere."

Jefferson leaned back in his chair. "I'm afraid the war's starting again. Heras has sent her creatures out to seek us specifically. She knows we're her biggest threat to victory."

"But how?"

"The demons are drawn to our swords — to the magic in them — and I fear they won't stop until we're all dead. They even come to the walls, trying to get into the castle. You'll hear our men shooting them from the walls, or occasionally we go out and kill them by hand."

Jefferson paused and looked around at the room at the other

Legionnaires before returning his attention to Rane, who asked, "Do you know where they're coming from?"

"I have men out searching, but we're making slow progress. The arrest warrants make our movements difficult. And we're not the only ones working abroad."

Rane leaned closer. "Who else?"

"The Rastaks are back. From what we've discovered, Mogai didn't die on the Plains. He made it back to Rastak and has been rebuilding his army. A few of my spies have made it over the mountains to see what he's up to, but few have returned, so our information is patchy."

"Is he going to reinvade?"

"No doubt. No doubt. But he's learned his lessons from the last time. He has agents of his own out in the five nations: poisoning crops, contaminating drinking wells, causing unrest — forcing people to move from their homes and generally causing chaos. Weakening us."

Rane remembered the shantytowns around Candra, the pilgrims and their tales of their devastated crops. Suddenly, a lot of things started to make sense. "Surely we're not letting them get away with it?"

"We are for now. We've got enough problems, with the Legionnaires undergoing the transformation and the bloody arrest warrants. Things will be different when everyone is settled once more."

Rane shook his head. "I've not heard anything of this."

Jefferson shrugged. "Why should you? It's hardly information for the general public to know. If the truth got out, there'd be mass hysteria. It's bad enough the world is hunting our brothers-in-arms."

"How long before Mogai attacks with his army?" asked Rane.

"I wish I knew. By the Gods, I wish I knew. All we can do is be ready for when that moment comes."

"Why aren't the five nations doing something about this?"

"They don't believe it. I tried telling them, but they wouldn't listen. Just because we won the last war, they think the threat is gone. They saw me as some raving madman. And when the transformations started — well, it was all the excuse they needed to dismiss my warnings." Jefferson waved a hand. "The fault's ours — we should have invaded Rastak and finished the job. Put the whole country to the sword instead of being satisfied with killing their army."

"But isn't that what the Rastaks want to do to us?" replied Rane, shocked at the severity of the Lord General's words.

"What other option is there? Build a wall to keep them out? Or wait till they are strong enough to attack us openly once more?"

"But a whole nation—"

"Should be accountable for the actions of its leaders. For what is done to serve their religion." Jefferson fixed his eye on Rane, as daring him to contradict.

"Sir, when can you remove the curse from Myri and me?" asked Rane, changing the subject.

"We try not to call it a 'curse' here."

Rane was confused. "Why wouldn't you call it a curse?"

A plate of roast chicken appeared on the table. "Ah, perfect. Just what I needed." Jefferson smiled at the servant, a young girl from Nortlund going by her shock of near-white hair. Once she returned to the kitchens, he turned his attention to Rane. "And you? How are you? Have you felt any changes?"

"I get urges. The sword needs blood. Makes me want to kill." Rane pulled *Kibon* off his back and placed it on the table. "I've tried not to use it, but the demon attacks left me with no choice."

"Do you mind if I see the blade?" Jefferson's voice was quiet, almost impossible to hear over the noise in the great hall.

The question threw Rane for a moment. But Jefferson was his commanding officer, and he had come to Orska for the old man's help. He pushed his discomfort to one side. "Certainly." He slipped *Kibon* free from its sheath.

Jefferson leaned forward, as if drawn to the sword by some invisible power. His hand went to touch it, but Jefferson stopped himself. "Such a beautiful weapon. The steel has hardly colored at all. Just some specks here and there. I would have expected more. You were one of our best."

"I was living with my wife in an isolated part of Ascalonia. I never had any reason to draw my weapon."

The Lord General looked up, eyes wide and bright. "Your wife? Is she..."

"She's dead, sir. Killed when bounty hunters came looking for me to claim the reward."

Jefferson reached out and clasped Rane's hand. "I'm so sorry, my boy. Really, I am. War is a ghastly thing. It claims so many innocents."

"I thought we'd won the war, sir."

Jefferson squeezed Rane's hand once, twice. "Not yet, but we will."

Someone approached from behind Rane, attracting Jefferson's attention. Rane didn't look to see who it was; if it were a friend, no doubt they'd greet him of their own accord. Jefferson acknowledged their unspoken message and stood up. Rane followed suit.

"I'm afraid something else demands my attention, but we'll speak more in the morning. Now eat and sleep — there's still lots left to do, and I need you fighting fit." Jefferson shook Rane's hand once more. "I'm so happy you're here."

"Thank you, sir. It means a lot to me."

"I'll see you in the morning."

Rane watched Jefferson leave and then sat back down at the table. He picked at the chicken, but he'd lost his appetite. *Kibon* lay on the table, unsheathed once more. For some reason he was almost scared to put it back in its scabbard. He had to force himself to do it. *Kibon* fought him every inch until it was covered once more. Thank the Gods he was at Orska. Resisting *Kibon* was getting harder and harder by the day.

He yawned, his tiredness weighing him down, desperate for bed. He looked for Isaiah, hoping he could show him where his bed was. The sentry was sitting with Gregor at another table. Both were studying Rane, and for a heartbeat he felt like a prisoner under scrutiny.

Rane rubbed his face, trying to wake himself up. The lack of sleep was making him paranoid. He was back with the Legion. He was safe.

30

The next morning, Rane stood on the wall, looking out over the north-eastern hills in the direction of Napolin. Fia and the pilgrims would reach the city soon — if they were still alive.

Two sentries stood watch further along the battlements. With their immaculate Legion uniforms, swords on their backs, and shaved heads, they didn't have the look of retired veterans but of troops used to living on the front line. In his worn, borrowed clothes, Rane looked out of place, but he hadn't come back to join a new war. Or had he?

He wanted justice for Kara, for himself. He wanted to be cured. But if the Rastaks were on the verge of returning, where did that leave him? Would he stay and fight with Jefferson and the others? He'd no other place to go, after all.

Kibon knew the answer. The thought of war, of a multitude of enemies to fight, was what it was made for. It sang with joy at the thought. But now Rane was back at Orska, the weight of the sword had lifted slightly. That pull in his chest dragging him north was gone. Instead, he could feel the promise of violence around him, taste the excitement on the sea breeze. He was a killer, the voice at the back of his head reminded him, and killers need war. And he'd found one.

"How are you feeling today?"

Rane jumped at the sound of the voice, and turned to see Isaiah walking towards him.

"Fine. Still a bit out of sorts," replied Rane. "It was a hard journey here."

"There are no easy miles anywhere." The Legionnaire stopped beside Rane, snorted up phlegm from the back of his throat and then spat over the battlements.

"How's Myri?"

"She's all right. Safe."

"I'll go look in on her soon."

Isaiah shook his head. "Nah. Don't think that's a good idea. She's not the only one down there. Best you leave her alone for now. She's got people who know what they're doing looking after her. All you'll do is complicate things."

"I'm not some wet-nose who doesn't know his ass from his elbow," replied Rane, feeling the first flush of anger. "Myri's been through a lot with me. I want to make sure she's well."

"You will. In time." Isaiah stared at Rane, daring him to continue to argue.

"We've got company," called out one of the nearby sentries, a Souskan, pointing out to the hills. "Couple of Bracke."

"Fucking demons," said Isaiah, but didn't bother to look over his shoulder at what was approaching. He kept his eyes on Rane.

Rane followed the sentry's directions and spotted a pair of Bracke, as big as any he'd encountered on his journey, making their way towards the castle, slinking down between the rocks and scrubs.

The second sentry was a tall Ascalonian woman with blonde stubble covering her scalp. It took Rane a moment or two to place her face as he watched her bring her rifle to bear on the approaching demons.

"Is that Simone?" asked Rane. Finally, a familiar face. Finally, another Legionnaire at Orska he could call a friend.

This time, Isaiah looked. "Yeah. She's been here about a month."

Simone aimed her rifle at the Bracke, waiting for them to come closer to the castle. Five hundred feet was too far for her weapon to hit anything without sheer luck guiding the bullet.

The Bracke took their time, sniffing the ground, sniffing the air, and using the rocks for cover. Four hundred feet; still too far. Simone settled the rifle butt into her shoulder as they came within three hundred and fifty feet, her index finger resting to the side of the trigger. Her form was perfect. Rane didn't need to be close to tell her breathing was under control — deep and steady.

Her finger slipped around the trigger when the Bracke closed the gap to three hundred feet. Ambitious for a rifle, but not impossible.

Overhead, the crows swooped and soared on the wind, eager for their next meal.

The demon dogs crept towards the castle, unaware death had its eye on them.

Simone pulled the trigger.

The hammer hit the primer, igniting the gunpowder. There was a *crack* as the bullet flew from the barrel, exiting with a puff of blue-grey smoke.

A second later, one of the Bracke jerked its head as the bullet struck its eyeball and it collapsed to the ground. The other Bracke ran, back towards the hills, but there was no escape. Arrows chased it, shot by the Legionnaire beside Simone, and by others on the wall. It covered a mere twenty yards before it fell, peppered with arrows.

The crows shrieked their approval as they flew down to dine.

Isaiah yawned. "Looks like the excitement's over for the morning. Let's get something to eat."

"I'm just going to say hello to Simone," replied Rane, but Isaiah put his hand up to stop him.

"Best leave that till later," said the Legionnaire. "She's on duty still."

"I'm not going to interfere with her doing her job."

"The Lord General's requested any civilians restrict their movements to their rooms, the mess hall and the main courtyard."

"A civilian? By the Gods, I've done enough for the Legion not to be called that."

Isaiah looked him up and down. "Wearing that sword doesn't make you one of us again. When you're wearing the uniform, then we can talk."

"Now listen—"

"No. Unless you want to be in a cell next to your friend, you listen." Isaiah stepped closer. "This isn't some sort of holiday camp. This is a military base, and we run it properly. That means you go where we say you can go and you don't go where we tell you not to. And if you see any old 'comrades' and want to have a chat with them, you wait till they're off fucking duty. Do I make myself understood?"

Rane stared back, boiling inside, the urge to fight bitter in his mouth. *Kibon* itched on his back, pressing down on him, demanding to be drawn. It smelled blood — wanted blood. Isaiah deserved to be cut down — as did anyone else foolish enough to stand in Rane's way. His breathing sped up as blood rushed through, readying him to fight. His hand flexed, eager for *Kibon*'s hilt.

He glanced over the man's shoulder, saw Simone and the Souskan watching, their weapons ready. The hackles on his neck told him others were behind him, waiting to see what he did next. Just like the Bracke, they saw Rane as the enemy.

No. No. This wasn't what he wanted. It wasn't right.

Rane forced a smile onto his face. "Sure thing. You've made yourself perfectly clear."

Isaiah's mouth twitched, as if disappointed the matter hadn't come to violence.

"I'll leave you to your duties," added Rane. He nodded past Isaiah towards the exit from the battlements. "May I?"

Isaiah stepped to one side to allow Rane to pass. Simone and the Souskan tracked him as he made his way to the door, and Rane knew he had no ally in his old friend. With each step, there was a part of Rane that expected an arrow or a bullet in the back. He was almost surprised when he stepped through the door into the darkness of the tower without being shot. His heart hammered as he tried to calm himself, tried to make sense of what had happened. *Kibon* howled in frustration. There were enemies to fight. Why had Rane run away? He had the power. It was the others that should fear him.

He slumped against the wall, shaking. Logic and emotion warred inside. It was the sword making him feel this way. It had to be. Isaiah was Legion. Just following orders. By the Gods, he needed the curse lifted. Before he went mad. Before the taint took hold.

He forced himself down the stairs, legs weak, holding on to the wall for dear life. He sucked in air, but none seemed to reach his lungs. Sweat broke out on his forehead as the stairwell closed in on him.

Rane staggered out onto his floor, found his room, fell through the door. He pulled *Kibon* off his back and threw it across the room. He dropped to the floor, grateful for the cold stone against his burning skin.

Kibon. How could he call it that? How could he have been so foolish? There was no hope in that blade. Only damnation.

31

A scream woke Rane. Eyes wide open in an instant, he fumbled around, caught up in unfamiliar sheets, confused by where he was. A room, ten feet by eight, with a small arched window drawing the early morning light into the room. By the time he got himself free of his sheets and on his feet, he remembered he was at the castle in Orska.

He stood in the center of the room, the stone floor cold against his feet, *Kibon* naked in his hand. The only sound he could hear was his racing heart. Outside, dawn threatened a bruised sky over the far mountains. He saw two Legionnaires patrolling the battlements, unalarmed; clearly, they hadn't heard any screaming.

Rane opened the door and looked out into the corridor. Twelve rooms lined either side of the passageway, illuminated by a single torch burning halfway down, but no other door was open. No one else was investigating any sounds. No one else stirred. He loitered, listening to the silence, waiting for another cry, another clue as to what was going on. Again, he checked the window and saw nothing to alarm himself with.

Aware that he couldn't do too much naked, Rane shut the door and sat back down on his bed, wondering if he'd imagined the scream, looking for an excuse to draw *Kibon* once more. He slipped the blade back into its sheath, feeling better about himself once it was done.

With the blade secured, he leaned back on the bed and gazed out the window, aware that something wasn't right. Three days he'd been back in Orska. Three days, and he was still jumpy as hell. He might as well have been out on the road for how rested he felt. Three days since he'd seen Myri or the Lord General.

Three days, and still no mention of a cure.

Maybe it was him. Maybe he'd been away too long, or his mind was playing tricks on him. Maybe it was just all the shit that happened on the road. But he felt like he was falling apart, and it was only getting worse with every day he was there.

The Legionnaires he'd encountered were strangers to him and treated him as such. There was no camaraderie, no connection. Only the sense of threat, of danger. Nor had he seen Simone since the incident on the walls, despite looking everywhere for her — or rather, everywhere he was allowed to go.

Even the conversation with Jefferson when he first arrived hadn't helped. He seemed so relaxed about everything. Since then, there'd been no sign of the old man, despite Rane badgering everyone he met to see him.

No one seemed to care that Rane was still waiting for a cure. No one seemed to care that his sword was tearing his mind apart.

By the Gods, if Fia was still alive she'd be in Napolin by now. How long before she reported to the church that the Legion was gathering in Orska? How long before an army would be ready to march on the Legion? Even that news had been shrugged off. Why didn't Jefferson or any of the others care that there could be an army on their way to fight them? Nothing made sense.

He played with Kara's locket between finger and thumb, trying to shake his unease. He closed his eyes and tried to remember the good that had been in his life, all the little things that used to make him happy: the smell of Kara's hair as they lay curled up in bed; the warmth of her body as she pressed up against him in the night; her laugh; her sigh. But each memory carried with it a renewed sense of hurt. It was as if the last three years had never happened; as if the war had never ended, as if Kara had never married him and their life together was a figment of his imagination.

Rane couldn't go on like this.

He dressed and armed himself. He strapped his holsters on and made sure each pistol was loaded. *Kibon* took its usual place on his back.

Rane hated the sword. Hated the weight of it. Hated his dependency on it. Once the curse was gone, he was going smash the weapon into a thousand pieces. The love he'd had for it was long gone; now, it was just the work of dark magic on his mind.

He wandered down the corridor to the main stairwell and descended. It was better once he got outside. The fresh sea air stung his nostrils, clearing his mind and blowing away any lingering tiredness. The sun was reclaiming the sky, bringing with it some welcome warmth. A sentry watched him from the battlements and Rane waved, only for the woman to turn her back on him. Two others stood guard at the gatehouse on the other side of the inner bailey, but they paid him no heed.

"You're up, then?"

The voice startled Rane and he turned to find Isaiah standing behind him as if he'd never left Rane's side. "I heard a scream. A woman cried out. Did you hear it?" Rane asked him.

"The Lord General was wondering if you'd join him for breakfast," replied Isaiah, ignoring Rane's question. He pointed back inside the main keep. "It's this way."

"Sure," said Rane, trying to ignore his dislike for the man. He followed him back into the darkness of the keep, happy to see Jefferson.

They met in the great hall. Jefferson sat at a table facing the door, a cup of tea in his hand. He smiled when he saw Rane. "Ah, good to see you're an early riser like me. Take a seat and have some tea. The food will be along shortly."

Rane sat opposite Jefferson. Being with the Lord General again eased the tension that had been building. "Not through choice. I had a dream that woke me up. I thought I heard screaming."

"After everything you've been through, I think you're allowed the odd nightmare." Jefferson poured tea into a cup and passed it to Rane.

"It didn't feel like a dream."

"Remember — you've been through a lot. It must be strange being back after all this time."

"It's taking me time to settle. I must admit I've felt almost like a prisoner at times. Isaiah seems to be always at my side, stopping me from speaking to anyone or wandering past the main keep."

"He's a good man, but he can be overzealous in his duties sometimes. I assure you we certainly don't want you to feel unwelcome. Quite the opposite, in fact. A few more days here and you'll be feeling better."

"It certainly seems to be doing you the world of good."

"Orska has that effect on me. After the war, I spent far too much time being feted by politicians and monarchs in the various capitals, all of them trying to rub off the glory the Legion had earned. Dinners, galas, balls — you wouldn't believe the nonsense I had to put up with." Jefferson sipped his tea. "I shook so many hands and had my ass kissed by so many others, it made me ill. I couldn't wait to get back on my horse and ride here. When the troubles started, I had the perfect excuse to stay."

Rane leaned forward in his seat, frowning. "So you were here already? Before Legionnaires started falling to the taint?"

"By a month or so. I was so shocked when I heard the news. Heartbreaking. Believe me, it wasn't meant to happen like that."

"Was it meant to happen at all?"

"By the Gods, no. They were desperate times, but not that desperate. Remember, we were losing the war. The Rastaks would've overrun Candra within twenty-four hours, and then the doorway to the rest of the world would have been open to them. We were all that stood in the way."

"I remember."

"We needed an army that was stronger than the Rastaks, faster, indestructible. As we move into this next phase of the war, that's still the case."

"But surely when you undo Babayon's magic, we'll lose our powers? We'll just be ordinary soldiers again."

"There will never be anything ordinary about the Legion of Swords, Nathaniel. As Mogai and the Rastaks will find out."

"But if they come at us en masse again, reinforced with demons... we're not prepared. As you said; the heads of the five nations don't even believe there is a threat."

"For now. But that will change. The world needs bold leadership from people with vision."

"At least once the curse is undone, the governments can remove the bounties from our heads and we can start working together to stop the Rastaks."

"Quite." Jefferson sipped his tea, avoiding Rane's gaze.

"How is the magic undone? Is Babayon here?"

"No, he's not — but that doesn't mean we don't know what we're doing." Jefferson smiled for the briefest of moments. "I was so sorry to hear about your wife the other night. How long were you together?"

Rane suppressed his annoyance at the change in conversation. "I met her just after the war. I went to stay with Marcus at his family home. Kara was his sister. We married a few months later." For some reason, he didn't want to mention the fact Kara was pregnant when she died. He needed to keep that information to himself.

"Does their family know what's happened to them both?"

"Not yet. Once I'm cured, I'll visit them and let them know."

"And then?" Jefferson put down his teacup, giving Rane his undivided attention. His eyes seemed to pull Rane closer.

"I don't know. I haven't thought that far, to be honest. Since Kara died, since I learned the truth about the taint, all I've cared about is getting Myri and me here alive. I need to work out who I am after the curse is gone — find out how much of the darkness in me is the result of the sword and its magic, and how much is really me."

"Nonsense. You're one of our best. That's all you need to know. You just need purpose again. A cause."

"Become a Legionnaire again?"

"Why not? This is where you belong. Stop denying it. It's time you rejoined the Legion. Rejoined the fight. We need men like you — leaders, warriors. Find your place with us by your side, our swords. You have the power to change the world, Nathaniel."

"That's what you told me when you first asked me to join you."

Jefferson smiled. "We did it once, we can do it again. This time we can learn from our mistakes, do things properly."

"We're hardly an army anymore, sir. How many of us are here? Forty odd? I don't even recognize many of them. Most must have been kids when I left. I'm not sure how we can change the world with so few of us, especially once our powers are gone."

"You'll be amazed at what we can do." Jefferson glanced towards the door. "Now, I'm sorry, but I must go." He leaned forward, squeezed Rane's hand. "Think about what I said. There's a war coming, and you are one of my finest. Join me. Save the world."

"I'll think on it," said Rane.

"Excellent, excellent," replied Jefferson. He stood up. "We'll speak again soon."

"But the cure—"

Jefferson waved the comment away. "In good time."

Rane watched him leave, feeling more uncertain than before. He glanced around the room, lost amongst strangers. Isaiah and Gregor sat watching him as always. He *was* a prisoner, and he didn't like it.

He stood up. Time to push back. See what would happen.

It was time to see Myri.

32

"Hold on a minute," called Isaiah as Rane crossed the bailey. "Where are you going?"

Rane waved away the question without breaking stride. "Don't worry. I know my way around. I'm sure you've got other things to be doing." He didn't look back, just kept his eyes on the mural tower.

The Legionnaire on guard duty at the tower put up a hand, as if that would magically prevent him from passing.

"Don't even think about it," snapped Rane as he shouldered past.

Isaiah caught up with him and grabbed Rane's arm. "Stop there. Stop."

"Why?" Rane shrugged the hand off and kept going, forcing the man to walk backwards so he could stay in front of Rane.

"You're not allowed in this part of the castle," said Gregor, hand hovering over the grip of his pistol. "If you don't stop, I'll fucking shoot you."

"Draw, and I'll shove that pistol up your ass before I pull the trigger," warned Rane. He meant it, too.

Isaiah moved his hand to Rane's chest, pushing him back. "Turn back, soldier."

Rane took the hand, twisting it. Isaiah buckled as the pressure forced him to his knees. "I'm not a soldier anymore — as you quite rightly pointed out."

Gregor drew his pistol. "I'm warning you — I will fire. Now let him go."

Rane looked from Isaiah at his feet to Gregor and the gun. Things had escalated quickly. Far quicker than he thought. Blood was going to be spilled because he wanted to see Myri.

Footsteps pounded towards them. Rane glanced over his shoulders as the bailey filled with more Legionnaires, all armed with spears and pikes.

"Put your weapons down and step back *now*," ordered Gregor as the new troops surrounded Rane.

Rane released Isaiah. The man stood up, cradling his arm. No one spoke. The threat of violence was a physical presence in the bailey, ready to tip someone over the edge. *Kibon* screamed in Rane's mind. *Fight. Fight. Kill. Kill.* It wanted blood, and the men all deserved to die. His hand twitched. Rane didn't know if he could fight the urge; wasn't sure he wanted to.

"What is going on?" Jefferson's voice roared out from an upper window, shattering the tension. His was a voice that was used to being obeyed. Rane looked up and saw the Lord General glaring down, red-faced with fury. "No one move until I get there."

"Shit," said Rane as Jefferson disappeared from view.

"I'm going to enjoy putting you in the cells," laughed Gregor. "Jumped-up asshole full of your own self-importance."

Rane cracked his neck to one side and swiveled back to the Legionnaire. "What did you say?"

"I said—"

Gregor didn't get another word out as Rane slammed his forehead into the man's nose, flattening it. The man dropped instantly unconscious at his feet, blood pouring out over the stone.

"I thought I told you not to move?" barked the Lord General as he crossed the bailey. "By the Gods, what's going on?"

Rane shrugged. "I was just trying to see Myri."

"I remember expressly telling you a mere hour ago to leave her be." Jefferson looked at Rane, daring him to say differently.

"I thought it was only a suggestion, not an order, sir," said Rane.

"Well, I'm giving you a fucking order now." Jefferson stopped, closed his eyes and inhaled deeply. Then he opened them again, calm once more. "There are things going on here that I haven't told you about. Things that will only help us in the long run. Things I don't want you blundering into, no matter how well intentioned you are. Please keep to your quarters, the great hall and, if you wish to exercise, the outer bailey. Everywhere else — and just to be clear, I mean *everywhere* else — is out of bounds for the moment. Do I make myself understood?"

"Yes, sir," said Rane.

"Now, if it's all right with you, may I return to do some actual work?"

"Yes, sir."

"Thank you." Jefferson turned to the rest of the Legionnaires. "The rest of you, get back to your posts. You've all got jobs to do as well. And someone take the fool on the floor to the infirmary."

Rane watched Jefferson storm back to the keep.

Isaiah gestured to the main tower and Rane nodded. He started walking without another word. He'd nothing to say to the man.

Back in his room, he looked out the window at the mountains. It was all wrong. Seriously wrong. What was going on? What was Jefferson up to? Why bring everyone to Orska if there was no cure?

Rane went back over everything that had happened since he'd returned to Orska, the conversations he'd had, trying to unpick what was bothering him.

All he could do was play their game for now. Stick to his room, eat and be friendly, and wait for them to drop their guard. Jefferson didn't have that many people— Rane could no longer think of them as Legionnaires — at the castle, so they couldn't be on duty for twenty-fours a day.

Someone knocked on the door. Rane opened it.

Isaiah stood there with Gregor behind him. Other Legionnaires loitered further along the corridor. "The Lord General would like to speak to you. To apologize about earlier."

Rane turned to get his sword. While his back was turned, a man stepped into his room. Rane recognized another face he knew — Jerome Rikard, a beast of a man from North Belarus, as wide as he was tall. They'd fought together many a time over the years, saved each other's lives countless times. Yet there was no warmth in his friend's eyes. No welcome. Just plenty of weapons within easy reach.

"What's going on?" asked Rane. Rikard punched him in the face. As he staggered back, the others piled into the room and fell on him in a flurry of fists and boots and clubs.

Rane went for *Kibon,* but his arm was seized, his weapon taken. He tried to fight but the soldiers holding him were stronger, faster. There was no escape from their grip. Blows fell, striking him across the back of the head, in his face, across his body, knocking the air from his lungs. He was kicked in the back of the knee, forcing him down. His head hit the stone floor, battered what little sense was left. Blood filled his mouth as a boot cracked into his jaw. He curled up, trying to protect himself as best he could, but there was no escape from the beating. A foot came down on his leg, snapping the bone with a crack of white-hot pain. Rane screamed, spitting blood. But the Legionnaires didn't stop. They kicked and stamped and hit and clubbed until the darkness took him away.

33

I t was the fear more than the pain that woke Rane. The rush of panic dragged him from the last dregs of blackness. The stone floor was cold against his face, sticky with his blood, but it meant nothing to him. The white-hot shards of fire running up from his leg were just flickers within a much greater inferno tearing him apart.

Kibon was gone.

He opened his one good eye, desperate to be proven wrong.

He was in his room. They'd left the bed, but nothing else. *Kibon* was nowhere to be seen, taken by the Legionnaires who'd beaten him. His comrades. His friends. He'd been betrayed.

But his old wounds hadn't reopened, so the sword was close. Close enough to still be keeping him alive — but not in his room, within reach. He stared at the wall opposite, the wall that separated his room from the corridor outside. *Kibon* had to be on the other side, probably with whoever was guarding him. He tried to picture it in his mind, draw some comfort from its proximity, but it did nothing to satisfy the hunger in him, nor quell the overwhelming need to hold *Kibon* once more.

Rane pushed himself up, groaning with the effort, and sat up against the wall. Sweat broke out across his face as a wave of pain hit him. He sucked in air, determined not to pass out again. Bone jutted from his leg. His left wrist was broken, too, along with some ribs and his nose. One eye was swollen shut. His nose was blocked with blood. What was left was battered and bruised, his skin purple and black.

The Legionnaires had beaten him well, holding nothing back. But why? Because he had tried to see Myri? It made no sense.

At least *Kibon* was close. That told him the Legion wanted him alive for now. Alive, but not healed.

He looked at the wall opposite once more. No more than six feet away, then another foot of stone. *Kibon* was perhaps only seven feet from his hand.

With a deep breath, Rane began to crawl across the room. He held his broken wrist against his chest, ignored the stabbing pains that came with every intake of air. He tried to turn his leg, but the bone grated with every movement and caught on each slab of stone. Tears ran down his face and he cried out, not caring who might hear. He had no shame — only the need to get closer to *Kibon*.

Every nerve strained for the slightest hint of the sword's magic as he dragged himself closer. Somewhere on the edges of his mind, he knew he could hear *Kibon* calling him.

Halfway across the room, he coughed, spitting blood over the floor, but he didn't stop. The voice urged him on. His need forced him on, inch by painful inch, on one hand and one leg. Smearing his blood across the stone on the way.

By the time he reached the wall, dizzy with the pain, he was sure he could feel a slight tingle of magic. He pressed his face and hand against the stone, desperate to get closer. It was there, on the other side. So close. So far.

By the Gods, he was almost tempted to try and smash the wall down. Use his fists, his feet, his head — anything to break down the barrier separating him from his sword. But no; he knew that was madness. He wasn't that desperate. Yet.

He ran his fingers over the wall, tracing the joins, looking for weak spots, finding none. The metal door was just as unmoving but still he tried, tugging away at the door handle, crying all the while.

He retreated to his bed, somehow managing to haul himself up onto it. He pulled his boot off his broken leg and ripped the trouser leg open so he could see the bone. It had pierced his skin at an angle, and blood seeped steadily from the wound.

Rane screamed and cursed as he tried to push the bone back in, spitting threats to the bastards who'd done this to him, taken *Kibon* from him. Slowly, it slid back inside, but with only one good hand, it was not enough. The bone popped back out, spilling more blood, and unconsciousness took him once more.

It was dark when he came to. Cold. Rane pulled his blanket over himself but found little comfort. He shivered as he tried to make sense of what had happened. Why had they beaten him? Why had the Legion turned against him? It couldn't have been because he'd tried to see Myri? Surely not.

His mind raced, doubt and suspicion darting back and forth. Nothing made sense. Did the Lord General know what had happened? Was it on his orders? What had happened to Myri? Had she been beaten? Was she a prisoner, too?

But one thought overwhelmed all others, breaking his concentration, preventing him from coming to any conclusions.

Why had they taken *Kibon*?

Kibon. His sword. He had to get his sword back.

He ran his finger over Kara's locket, tried to picture her, draw up some happy memories to fill the hole inside him. By the Gods, how he hated that sword; hated its hold on him, hated the curse that ate away at his very being. Where was the fucking cure he'd been promised? The cure he'd crossed half of Ascalonia to find?

What was Jefferson playing at? Why had he allowed Rane to be beaten and locked up? Did he even know? Perhaps the Legionnaires had imprisoned the Lord General, too. Was he lying in another cell, beaten and broken? Was this a coup? A way of claiming the rewards?

His mind reeled with it all. If only Rane could hold his sword, use its magic, he could understand what was going on. Do something. He just needed *Kibon*.

Rane drifted in and out of consciousness, battered by pain from his wounds, hurting for his sword, lost in the madness of it all. At one point, gunshots rang out from the battlements, startling him, but the world soon fell back into silence. The occasional voice carried with the wind, but otherwise he heard nothing else. No footsteps in the corridor, no voices, no visitors.

Morning came, bringing with it a little warmth. Rane sat, staring at his leg, the blood black and congealed around the discolored bone. How long did he have before gangrene set in? He'd seen plenty die from rotting flesh during the war, and watched friends have their limbs cut off while trying not to be sick from the stench. Was that the Legionnaires' intention? To just let him rot away, *Kibon* just close enough to make him suffer for only the Gods knew how long?

He wet his parched mouth with small mouthfuls of water from the jug that was in his room, aware of how little he had. His stomach complained at having nothing to eat, but compared to his other pains it was but a minor inconvenience.

The castle came to life outside his window. He tried to picture what was happening: guards walking the walls, Legionnaires crossing the courtyard to the great hall to eat, others training, swords clashing — just regular army life. Just another day. With Rane as their prisoner.

A crow dipped and dived past his window over and over again, cutting across the clear, blue sky until it eventually got bored and disappeared elsewhere. He watched a cloud drift past, inching its way from right to left with the breeze. He counted the seconds and marked the minutes and the hours in his head, trying to fill his mind with anything other than his longing for *Kibon*.

The pain in his leg changed. The wound radiated heat. Infection had set in. The rot had begun.

It might have been midday when Rane found the courage to try to go to the toilet. With the only container in the room still holding his drinking water, Rane's only option was to go in the furthest corner of the room away from his bed. He swung his legs off the bed, gritting his teeth as broken bones knocked against each other. Tears filled his eyes and it took all he had not to cry out. He placed his good foot on the ground and stood up. Using the wall for support, he hopped across the room. Each step sent shards of pain shooting up his leg. Halfway across, he slipped and fell, landing on his broken limb.

He woke up once more to find night had fallen and he was lying in his own piss. He had no idea how long it was before he found the strength to remove his wet clothes and retreat to his bed. Once there, he covered himself with his blanket, shivering either from the cold night air or from the fever that was taking over his body.

He'd been imprisoned for two days and he had no idea if he'd survive a third.

If only he had *Kibon*.

34

Rane used his thumbnail to scratch another mark on the wall. A small line, joining four others. Five.

Five days. He'd been locked up for five days. Five days without food. Five days without visitors. Five days of pain. Five days without *Kibon*. Five.

He would've screamed if he could, but his parched throat was incapable of making sounds to escape his dry, cracked lips.

He was a pathetic sight. He knew that. Naked, filthy, stinking of gangrene. His leg was black with it, good only for cutting off. But even that was an option long gone. Gone. Like his mind. Thoughts flew back and forth, sliced apart by his need for *Kibon*. Love, loss, betrayal, friendships, failures, murder, revenge, escape, despair, death, forgiveness, hatred, *Kibon*. Always *Kibon*. He wept at the thought of his sword; cried for it, begged for it, cursed it, loved it, and needed it.

Kibon. Kibon. Kibon. Kibon.

Outside his cell, outside his window, life went on. He could hear the Legion going about their day, talking, laughing. The sounds of gunfire had become more frequent, and somewhere in the back of his mind he registered that more demons were approaching the castle.

But he didn't care. None of it mattered. Let him have his sword, and then he'd spare a thought for other things.

"Nathaniel." He looked up. Myri stood a foot from his bed with a look of disgust on her face. Her hair was shorn back to a Legionnaire's standard crew cut, and she wore an immaculate black Legion uniform. Her sword was slung on her back, and a cloak covered her right arm.

Somewhere at the back of Rane's mind, he knew he should be feeling some shame at what he'd become, but he was just so glad to see someone again. Then doubt hit him. How could it be Myri? The Legionnaires had her locked away. She was just his imagination. He knew that. He'd not heard the door being unlocked, or seen it open. Hadn't noticed Myri as she entered. It was his mind. Playing tricks. Lost. Mad.

He closed his eyes, tried to gather his thoughts. When he opened them again, Myri was still there. Was she real?

He tried to say her name, but couldn't even manage a croak.

"I brought you something to eat and drink," she said with that beautiful, lilting accent of hers. A tray with a bowl of food and a cup of water was in her left hand. Rane barely gave her time to place it on the end of the bed before he fell on it. He attacked it, scooping food into his mouth with one hand while throwing water down his throat with the other. His broken wrist screamed in protest but Rane ignored it. The plea from his stomach was louder, more desperate.

"Go slowly," warned Myri. "You're going to be sick."

The warning came too late. Hot acid rushed back up his throat and Rane vomited the food and water over himself. There was no denying the shame now. He looked up at Myri with tears in his eyes and so many questions behind them.

She shook her head. "I'll come back tomorrow."

Rane watched her leave, tears running freely down his cheeks. Myri didn't look back. The door closed. This time, he heard the lock slam shut, like a gunshot to his heart.

He lay back on the bed, never more lost and alone.

Myri returned the next day looking younger, better than he'd seen her in a long time. The trauma of the road to Orska was gone, the weight of the curse lifted. With the cloak covering her missing hand, she looked like the perfect Legionnaire once more, as if she'd stepped right out of his memories of when they first met.

Another Legionnaire was with her — Rikard. Rane flinched when he saw him, but the man simply waited by the door, carrying the tray of food and drink, eyes fixed on the window. Rane wasn't worth his gaze.

This time, she gave him the water first and held the jug while he drank, forcing Rane to take his time.

The water soothed his throat enough to allow him to find his voice. "Thank you."

"You're a mess," replied Myri.

Rane pulled his vomit-stained blanket tighter over his shoulders. "My sword..."

"It's near," said Myri.

Rane's eyes flicked past her to the door, blocked by Rikard. For a moment, he thought of trying to force his way to *Kibon,* but he had no chance. Naked, weak, ravaged by rot and fever, sitting upright was too much for him.

"You're cured?"

"I'm better."

Myri took the bowl of food from the tray and placed it on the bed. A stew of some kind, still warm enough to give off steam. She took a spoonful, blew on it to cool it down and then fed it to Rane like a mother to a child. "Eat. Then we'll clean you up. Fix that leg."

Rane was too busy eating to reply. The sensation of food in his mouth was almost too much to bear. Anyway, there was no point telling Myri the leg was lost. Anyone could see the black, dead flesh had nearly reached his groin. Even if she hadn't noticed, the stink of it filled the room, polluting the air.

Myri patiently fed him until the bowl was empty. She returned it to Rikard, who left the room.

"What's going on?" asked Rane. "Why am I being kept here? You've got to get me out. Get my sword back."

Myri stood up, gave Rane one last pitying look, then followed Rikard out of the room, locking the door behind her. Leaving him alone with his tears. His pain.

Rane screamed, filling the emptiness of the room with a desperate howl. From the hallway, he heard a man laugh. Was this all just a joke to them? Making him suffer just for their amusement? Why was Myri with them? Why had she not saved him?

His stomach grumbled, unused to having food inside it. Cramps hit, doubling him up. He fell off the bed, knocking his broken leg, jarring his broken wrist. Fresh agony reminded him he wasn't dead yet.

Enough of him left still to kill.

35

They came for him on day eight.

Led by Rikard, nine Legionnaires entered his cell. They held him down while one seized his broken leg and pulled. Rane screamed as the bone slipped back through the rotten flesh. The Legionnaire continued to tug until the leg was straight. The others moved quickly, placed strips of wood on either side and bound the limb in position. They stepped back, leaving Rane panting with exertion.

"What's going on?" asked Rane. They ignored him. Rikard gave a nod and the others seized Rane by the arms, lifting him from the bed. They dragged him from his room, naked, half-dead from rot and fever. Down the stone stairs, not caring what part of him was hit, bumped or knocked along the way. For his part, Rane kept quiet. What was pain now except the only friend that had never deserted him?

Cold air hit his skin. His eyes burned in the bright sunlight. It all seemed so alien after so long confined to his room. He struggled again, not really wanting to escape anywhere, just trying to be free, to get anywhere other than where they were taking him.

"No. No. Take me back. Back to my room," he pleaded. At least he knew his room; knew the pain that lived there, knew how his life would end there.

But the Legionnaires marched him on, across the bailey and over to the mural tower.

Inside.

Back into darkness. A torch burned in a bracket on a wall, but its light had little effect. Rikard led them on without saying a word, taking the stairs down.

Rane could hear *Kibon* whispering once more in his mind. His hand twitched as the need to draw the blade grew inside him. Someone had it nearby. He glanced back, desperate to look at his sword. See who had it. One of them did. It was close. Close enough. He squirmed in their grip, but still he couldn't break free.

He was dragged down more steps, past more torches burning stale air, deeper than Rane thought the castle went. Through a metal door and down more stairs. Silent but for the stomp of the Legionnaires' feet. Along a corridor, twisting, turning. Past doors that housed the Gods only knew what. On they went, dragging Rane. On and on. Until they came to a door of their own. A door for Rane. Made of old iron, all beaten and worn, a small spyhole in its center and a set of iron bolts to lock it shut when the time came.

Fear hit him hard. He didn't want to know what waited behind that door. Not after what he'd been through. Only misery waited for him in there. He wriggled and thrashed in the Legionnaires' grip, desperate to break free, but the Legionnaires held him firm. Blows struck him around the back of the head, encouraging him to be still.

Rikard cranked it open, hauling its heavy weight back. As thick as the castle wall, it moved slowly, revealing a large open space within. Another cell. A bigger cell. Torches lined the walls, just enough to lift the gloom. Enough to show the shadows of the people inside. People waiting for Rane.

"No. No. Take me back," he pleaded. Even his words had no strength.

They hauled him into the room, stopping before Jefferson in the center. His back was straight, proud. Myri was next to him, beautiful, dangerous.

"Sit him on a chair," commanded the Lord General.

A stool appeared and was placed in front of Jefferson. His escorts dropped Rane onto it. He nearly toppled to the ground as the Legionnaires released their grip on his arms, but Rikard grabbed hold of his head to keep him upright. The others stood at attention near the door.

Rane's heart hammered, eager to keep him alive. Fresh sweat broke out over his naked body as his eyes took in the room. He wasn't the only prisoner. Three others in civilian dress were chained to the wall in front of him. Samuel Miller and the blond-haired bounty hunter looked on him with beaten faces. The third was a stranger, but shared their injuries. At first, Rane thought it was a boy with short black hair, but a second glance told him it was a girl. Her sex hadn't saved her from the Legionnaires' attention. Her chest heaved with silent sobs. They were all just as broken as Rane.

But suddenly, Rane didn't care why they were there. He was no longer afraid.

Isaiah had walked over to the Lord General with *Kibon* in his hands.

The sight of his sword sparked some life back into Rane. He lunged for the weapon, throwing his weight forward, hand outstretched. But his broken leg betrayed him, and he fell to the ground. Hands picked him up. Dragged him back. He fought, trying to break free, trying to get to *Kibon*. But they were too strong and he too weak. They placed him back on his stool and held him there.

The Lord General looked on him with a pitying eye. Whatever friendship between them was gone.

"Please," begged Rane. "What's going on? Why are you doing this to me?"

Jefferson held out his hand and Isaiah placed *Kibon* in it. Rane twitched. The blade was so close. He could feel its power, feel its pull. He licked his lips, eyes wide, pain gone. *Kibon*.

"I gave you this sword when you first took your Legionnaire's oath.

Years later, I placed power in it for you. Now I'll set you free with it —
if you wish."

"Please," croaked Rane, his eyes fixed on his sword. Nothing else
existed in the cell other than *Kibon*. It was so near, so close. It would
take all his pain away, make him whole once more. All he had to do
was touch it.

But Jefferson stepped back, taking *Kibon* with him. "Do you recognize the prisoners behind me?"

"What?" Rane shook his head, pulling his thoughts back, seeing
the rest of the world again. The two men from another time in his
life, so long ago. "Yes."

"People come to Orska for many reasons. For hope. For a cause.
You came for a cure." Jefferson pointed *Kibon* at the prisoners. "They
came for revenge, for murder, for profit."

"I don't understand," replied Rane, but his attention was locked on
his sword once more. Nothing else mattered.

Jefferson lifted up Samuel's chin. "Tell him."

"We were in Napolin," whispered Samuel through swollen lips.
"When a priest came into town, causing a commotion."

Jefferson smiled at Rane. "Go on."

"Said she'd run into Legionnaires, described Rane and the
woman. Said she knew where you all were." Blood dribbled from
Samuel's mouth as he spoke.

"Sound like anyone we know?" said Myri.

Rane nodded. "Fia." Myri hadn't murdered her, thank the Gods.

"The authorities started mustering an army to come here,"
continued Samuel. "But we thought we'd get here first."

"Why?" Jefferson asked the prisoner as if he didn't know the answer.

Samuel looked up, looked at Rane, and some fire returned to his
eyes. "To kill him. Kill Rane. He murdered—"

"Enough," interrupted Jefferson, holding up a hand. He walked
over to Rane, bringing *Kibon* nearer. "It would seem you're right about
the army coming here, Nathaniel. It would seem our war is starting
sooner than I planned."

"War? But you can tell them everyone is cured. That we don't pose a threat to anyone," said Rane. "There's no need to fight."

"Oh, my boy." The Lord General rubbed Rane's scalp. "There's every need." He smiled. "You see, no one is cured. And we certainly pose a threat."

The words hit Rane. "No cure?" He slowly looked at all the Legionnaires in the room; from Jefferson to Myri to Rikard to Isaiah, working his way around the others. They all had the same look, the same air. "You're all tainted."

Jefferson wagged a finger at him. "There's that word again. It's almost like you're trying to be offensive. We're not tainted — we're transformed. Mightier than you could ever think possible."

"But why? Why bring us here if there is no cure?"

"Because I want all my soldiers together once more. Because the transformation process is painful and dangerous. Best to be some-where safe, where friends can help while you undergo it."

"Is that why I was beaten? Starved? Held prisoner?"

The corners of Jefferson's mouth twitched. "Some need their minds opening first. You more so than others." He pulled *Kibon* from its sheath. "Are you ready?"

Kibon gleamed in the torchlight; beautiful, deadly. "I don't want to become a monster."

Jefferson shook his head. "Do I look like a monster? Do any of these men? Does Myri?"

Rane glanced from one face to another — committed, deter-mined, perfect. He couldn't see any of Marcus' twisted dementia in any of them. There was nothing to fear in what they'd become. "What would you have me do?"

"Kill those who would kill you." Jefferson stepped to one side so Rane had an unimpaired view of the three prisoners. There was no hiding the fear on their faces. Only Samuel tried to glare back. Jefferson held out *Kibon*. "Kill your enemies. Be whole once more."

Rane looked at the sword, ready for it. Desperate for it. Only faint specks of darkness stained the blade.

Kibon whispered in his ear. Three deaths. A small price to pay to be well again. To be strong again. To have *Kibon* again.

He looked at the prisoners. Hard to see them as enemies when they were already so beaten and broken. Like himself. It was just as easy to imagine himself in those chains, with his life at stake.

Jefferson stepped closer. Brought *Kibon* closer. Its voice was no longer a whisper but a roar, demanding Rane's attention, promising cures for his pain, a fire to purge the rot. All he had to do was take it. Take what he wanted. What he needed.

All he had to do was seize it.

And kill three people. The sword wanted blood.

The bounty hunter had yet to look at him. He hung from his shackles, no strength left in his legs to even stand. If anyone deserved death, he did. He'd come with the men to his house, been part of the group that had killed Kara — and hadn't Rane sworn revenge on those responsible? He'd sought Rane again in Rooktown, tried to capture him then. And now — a third time — he'd followed Rane to Orska, eager to claim the reward for his head. If ever there was someone Rane could call an enemy, it was him.

Samuel was no better. His son had brought the bounty hunters to Rane's home, and the man had sworn a blood oath to kill Rane. His failure at Rooktown hadn't been enough to dissuade him. By the hate in his eyes, if their positions were reversed, Rane would already be dead.

But the third woman was a stranger, guilty only by association with the others. She didn't look like a warrior or a bounty hunter. Not older than Samuel's son, not any braver. She cried in her chains. It was hard to see her as a threat, an enemy to be feared.

He wanted *Kibon,* but at what price? Could he kill her? "I don't want to become like Marcus."

"There's nothing to fear," said Myri. "Look at me." She swept her cloak over her shoulder, revealing her right arm — her right *hand,* regrown but red raw as if it still missed flesh. It looked almost too big for her arm as she waved it in front of his face. "I'm whole again."

"How is that possible?" he asked. How many people had died to give her that gift?

"Find out," said Jefferson. "Take your sword, feed it the blood of your enemies. And feel its power burn away the rot that's destroying you. Become better than you ever were."

Rane's hand moved of its own volition. He couldn't have stopped himself even if he wanted to. His fingers wrapped themselves around *Kibon*'s hilt. Grasped it. He screamed as the surge of magic flooded into his body, bringing with it strength he'd thought long gone. He could feel it begin to purge the rot. Bones began to knit. Bruises faded. Life returned. The sword was his once more.

"So, Nathaniel," said Jefferson. "Will you join us? Become our brother once more?"

Rane stood, a man reborn. With three prisoners to kill.

36

F ive feet separated Rane from his victims. With each step he took towards them, he could feel his strength returning. The rot faded. *Kibon* burned in his hand. His blood sang with life. He could feel their fear, sweetening the moment.

He stopped in front of the bounty hunter. "Three times this man has tried to kill me. No more." *Kibon* flashed in the torchlight. Took the man's head from his shoulders. Blood shot from his neck, staining the walls, the floors. Covering Samuel. Magic roared from *Kibon* into Rane, setting his blood on fire. All his injuries disappeared. His skin turned from black and dead to pink and alive. Starved for so long of its touch, *Kibon's* power almost overwhelmed him. Still he walked on, his rage burning bright.

"By the Gods, no. Please, no. I'll walk away," pleaded the miller. "You'll never see me again. I'll tell everyone the castle was deserted. Please, no."

"This man swore to see me dead," said Rane. "His son led killers to my door. Helped murder my wife. His life will settle the debt."

"Nooooo," screamed the miller, but *Kibon* shot forward, eager, hungry, without mercy. It plunged into Samuel's heart, drinking his fear, stealing his life. The man's eyes bulged, and he coughed his last breath. Again, the magic flooded into Rane, filling him with ecstasy. He growled with pleasure, forced his lungs to breathe in and out and rode the rush. Lightning shot through his brain, heightening his senses. His nose flared with the scent of blood. His mouth watered at its metallic tang.

When Samuel had no more to give, he pulled *Kibon* free.

He wondered how anyone had managed to keep him prisoner for a second, let alone eight days. Let Rikard try and restrain him now. Let Isaiah try and take *Kibon* from him again. With the power in him, Rane could tear the world asunder.

He strode over to the last prisoner, stood before her naked but for the sword in his hand and Kara's bracelet dangling from his wrist. His heart roared. His muscles bulged. By the Gods, he didn't need *Kibon* to kill this fool. Rane could rip her throat open with his teeth, pull her heart out with his bare hand.

The girl wept. Squeezed her eyes shut as if that could stay death's hand. Stupid child. Her fear only made Rane stronger. He now understood why Marcus had killed so many in the way that he had.

"Go on," urged Jefferson. "Be done with her and rejoin your broth- ers. The Legion needs you."

"This woman," said Rane, "came with others to kill me. Se... she..." Rane shook his head. No. No. The girl was no one. A child. Someone's daughter.

By the Gods, Rane wanted to kill her, hungered for it, but was she his enemy? Was this how Marcus fell? Did one kill become another then another until he slept in a bed of corpses? There was no beauty in that transformation — only horror, only despair.

"Kill her," whispered Myri. Kill her, urged *Kibon*.

"This woman... this girl... has done nothing to me," said Rane. *Kibon* screamed in anger, trembled with frustration. It demanded Rane strike, urging him on, a tsunami of emotion threatening to drown him if he stood in its way. It would be so easy to let it wash over him. Give in. He wanted to. By the Gods, how he wanted to. Stop his suffering. Lose himself in the magic. Not care.

But that wasn't who he wanted to be. His oath meant something to him. His love of Kara meant something. He came to Orska to free his soul, not destroy it forever. He closed his eyes, breathed in, stood his ground against *Kibon*'s power.

"She is not my enemy."

Kibon howled in frustration.

"She is if I tell you she is," snapped Jefferson. "There's a war coming. You don't have the luxury to question who is and who isn't your enemy. That's why we have a chain of command. Why we have orders. Now kill her and be done with it."

"No." Rane turned to face the old man, the others. Let them try and force him. Let them try to stop him. Let them try to take him back to his cell. There was still blood enough for *Kibon* to spill.

Eleven swords slipped from sheaths in response. Black blades one and all. Rikard, Isaiah, the other Legionnaires — even Myri — eyes bright and ready for anything Rane tried. Only Jefferson kept his sword in its scabbard. He waved them to stand down. "I'm not willing to give up on Nathaniel just yet."

"I'm not going to kill the girl," replied Rane.

Isaiah stepped forward, more than happy with Rane's refusal, but again Jefferson stopped him with a glance. "Leave us alone."

As one, the other Legionnaires turned and marched from the room.

Myri was the last to leave. She paused before Rane. "Don't fight it. You'll become glorious."

"That's what Marcus said to me," replied Rane, looking to the floor. "And there was nothing glorious about what he was."

Myri shook her head. "He didn't have guidance through the transformation. The Lord General will look after you. Trust him." She placed her hand against his chest. "I'll look after you."

Rane tightened his grip on *Kibon*. "Go before I kill you instead."

"Oh Nathaniel," sighed Myri. "You always were a fool."

Jefferson turned his attention to Rane once she'd left the room. "There are monsters out in the world, Nathaniel, and the only way we can defeat them is to become deadlier than they are. Become so powerful that they shake with fear at the very mention of our names. Run when they see our swords. Die at our touch.

"Heras knows this. That is why she sends her demons against us once more, why they hunt us down. Did you think it some coincidence that her infernal creatures dogged your every step here? They can smell the power hidden in you. She wants you dead before you can become what you are destined to be."

"But this girl is not a Jotnar, Bracke, Grenduns or Valkryn. She's human," replied Rane.

"So were the men that killed your wife," said Jefferson. "So were the other two men in this cell. That doesn't mean they weren't Heras' agents. The army that marches to us is made up of humans but they come because of Heras' lies. When the battle comes, how will you judge who's worthy of your sword and who is not? You were willing to kill the Rastaks when they were her agents, were you not?"

Rane rubbed his face. It was so hard to think in that small room, with his body on fire with *Kibon*'s magic. Jefferson's words made sense — or did they? The sword wanted blood and didn't care where he got it. "What about all the innocents who have died because of us? The horrors that Legionnaires have done while undergoing this transformation?"

Jefferson shrugged. "Unfortunate but necessary. All done for the greater good."

"But we swore an oath to protect those weaker than ourselves," said Rane. "We did all this for them."

"Of course," replied Jefferson. "And we still do. But sometimes a few must make a sacrifice for the greater good."

"Including my wife?"

"I'm sorry for your loss. I truly am. But the Rastaks will return and we must be ready. Stronger and more powerful than ever before."

"Ready? You have forty men here. Hardly an army."

"Forty men?" replied Jefferson. "Whoever gave you that idea? I have one hundred and fifty transformed Legionnaires in this castle alone. More are out in the world doing my bidding. Believe me when I say I have an army."

Rane stared at the Lord General, suddenly seeing everything in a new light. It was all so hard to believe. "Did you know our souls would be tainted when you first asked us to bond them with our swords? That we'd be transformed?"

"Of course."

"And you didn't tell us?"

"I am your commanding officer. It was for me to make the decisions. Would you have me put the matter up for debate? Ask for a show of hands? We're the chosen ones, Nathaniel. Accept that."

"But at what price? Our souls? Destroying what makes us human?" shouted Rane.

Jefferson scoffed at Rane's words. "I wanted to make you so much more. I wanted to make you a god. Only a fool would turn that opportunity down."

"I hear voices telling me to kill. I was scared of hurting my own wife! By the Gods, I've murdered people that didn't deserve to die. How can that be right? How could anyone want that?"

"We're the architects of a new age that will rise from the ashes of the old world. We must be above such concerns."

"You're mad."

"I have the vision to see what needs to be done. History will judge me right."

Rane lunged at Jefferson, with all the fury, all the pain, with all the magic at his disposal. *Kibon* no more than a blur as it cut through the air, going for the old man's throat.

But Jefferson was faster. He didn't even draw his sword. There was no need. He drove the palm of his hand into Rane's sternum. Rane flew back, crashed into the wall with such force that the very stone cracked and crumbled around him. He fell to the floor hard, lungs paralyzed. He spat blood as he tried to rise, drawing on *Kibon*'s magic.

Jefferson looked down on him with disgust. "Don't disappoint me, Nathaniel. Ideally I want every one of my Legionnaires but that doesn't mean I won't kill you if I have to. Kill the girl and join me. Let her live and you can both die together. The choice is yours."

He left the room without looking back. The door clanged shut and the locks were rammed into place.

And once more Rane was a prisoner.

He stood staring at the locked door, feeling utter hatred for the man he once thought of as a second father. How could Jefferson have done this to him? To all the others? And to have control of an army of soldiers with all of Marcus's speed, strength and ferocity without any of the madness? No one would be able to stand before it.

He trembled with *Kibon*'s magic. Now his need for it was sated, he hated himself for giving in to its demands. While it had a hold on him, he would be forever at its mercy. He'd managed to resist it but what about next time? Could he still be strong as the taint consumed his sword?

The two dead bodies hung from the wall as a testimony to his weakness. Did they really deserve to die? How much of his anger towards them was because of *Kibon*'s hold on him? His need for its magic? Was Samuel's desire for revenge for his son's death any different from Rane's after Kara died?

He'd got *Kibon* back, got his hit of magic, but for what? His wounds may have healed but he was still a prisoner.

He cut the splint from leg. Even seeing the perfect skin once more didn't make him feel any better. Perhaps it would've been better if he'd died.

Dead and his misery would be over.

Kibon pulsed in his hand. And Rane saw a way out. He'd give the sword one last life to take and his suffering would be done. He wouldn't be in *Kibon*'s thrall any more. He could be reunited with Kara. At peace. Let the old man fight his war. Rane needn't be around to see it.

He flipped *Kibon* around so the tip pressed against the base of his chin. One push and it would go straight through his brain. No magic would heal that. It would be all over. Thanks the Gods.

Fuck Jefferson and fuck his curse.

It was time to die.

37

"What are you doing?" The girl's voice startled Rane. Cracked. Raw. "You can't leave me here." She'd stopped crying but her eyes still glistened through swollen lids. The Legionnaires had given her a pounding that would take a long time to recover from. "You have to get me out of here."

"There's no way out," replied Rane, sword digging into his chin. "Not alive."

"Then why didn't you kill me when they asked? Why save me if you're going to let me die anyway?"

"I won't be what they want me to be. I'm not a monster."

"Then free me. Let's get out of here. Don't give up. Please. Please don't." The girl brought her arms around as much as she could, offering the shackles to Rane. Her thin arms shook with the effort.

Rane had no idea where she found the courage. Maybe that was all she had left. It was more than he had. "I'm sorry. It's too much. Better this way."

"Please. I'm only fifteen. I've not even lived yet. I don't want to die. Not here. Not like this."

Rane lowered *Kibon*. "What were you doing with those two men?"

"I was their property. They bought me in Napolin. Dragged me here. I don't think they ever planned to bring me to the castle but the soldiers found our camp..."

"You were their slave?"

"Theirs and others."

"I thought slaves were outlawed in the five nations."

"There'll always be slaves when some men have money and others don't. I was a child when my first owners found me. I was eight years old, alone and starving."

"What about your family?"

"Dead long before that."

It wasn't hard to imagine the horrors she'd been through when she should've been protected and cared for. The Legion of Swords existed to look after people like her — why they'd sworn their oaths. It wasn't to wage war on the world. The Lord General had forgotten that long ago and now was so twisted and tainted, he'd have his men — have Rane — murder instead.

No more. If Jefferson wanted Rane to become a Legionnaire once more, he would — but a true one. Devoted to the oath, sacrificing everything to protecting the weak. Starting there and then. He'd protect the weak, serve the innocent.

He placed *Kibon* on the floor. Hesitated only for a moment at the thought of leaving it, long enough to feel more disgust at its hold over him.

"What's your name?" asked Rane as he gripped one of the chains.

"Zee."

"I'm Nathaniel." Rane grunted as he pulled. Each link was an inch thick. Old steel but well made. It resisted as it was meant to, but Rane's muscles were pumped full of blood magic. The chains groaned and creaked as he pulled with all his might. He grunted with the effort, felt his veins bulge as the pressure built.

Just as he thought the iron was too strong, a crack pierced the silence. The chain snapped apart. One arm was free.

"Thank you," gasped Zee.

Rane said nothing. There was still one left to break.

He moved to the other side, took hold of the chain and tugged once more. This time the chain fought harder, lasted longer, but it was still no match for Rane. The last chain fell to the floor with a clatter.

The girl fell into Rane's arms, sobbing with relief. He let her cry, as he held on to her, angry at what had happened to her, angry with himself for almost giving up. For forgetting who he was.

Once Zee had brought her tears under control, Rane led her over to the stool and sat her down. "Wait here for a moment, then we'll work out how to get out of here."

Zee nodded, sniffing, arms wrapped around her knees.

Rane returned to the dead prisoners. He stripped Samuel of his trousers and boots and put them on. The trousers were too big but the man had a good belt to hold them up. The boots were a good fit. The man's shirt was soaked in blood so he left that where it was.

Rane picked up *Kibon* from the floor, its weight heavy in his hand, uncomfortable.

"You look at it like you hate that sword," said Zee.

"I loved it once," replied Rane. "Loved using it. Loved the way it made me feel. Then one day I met someone who showed me all it was good for was killing and reminded me that I was more than just a killer." He shook his head. "Life seems to have other ideas though."

"Life or the man with the beard?"

"The Lord General? I thought of him as a second father once. Trusted him so much I gave him my soul. A mistake I hope I can rectify." Rane smiled. "First though, we have to get out of here."

"How are we going to do that?"

"I'm going to kill you."

Zee screamed.

38

"**O**pen up!" Rane pounded on the cell door. It was hard to tell how long he'd been locked up — maybe ten or twelve hours — but he'd waited long enough. Most of the castle would be asleep. He knew though someone would be on the other side of the door, guarding him, waiting to see if he succumbed to Jefferson's wishes. "Come on!"

The cover over the spy hole slid open and a pair of eyes peered through. "What do you want?"

"To get out of this shit hole," replied Rane. He stepped back so the guard could get a good look inside the cell. And see Zee's body.

The eyes went straight to her, lying amongst the other dead, covered in blood and gore. "Shit. You did it." The man chuckled. "You fucking did it."

Rane's face twitched and he clicked his jaw from side to side. "I did. Now let me out of here before I rip the door off its hinges."

The guard's attention drifted back to the bodies. Again he laughed. "Settle down for a minute. My orders are to get Jefferson, tell him before I let you out."

Rane leaned into the spy hole, eyeballing the guard. "Do I know you? Voice sounds familiar."

"Yeah, we fought together plenty of times. Pet'r Sears."

"I remember." A pockmarked nasty brute of Fascalian popped up in Rane's memory. Sears had been a vicious brute before the taint, and he would only have gotten worse.

"Damn. I had money you wouldn't join us."

"Sorry to disappoint you."

"Nah, it's all good. Always good to have a tough bastard like you back on the team," replied Sears. "I'll tell you this much — you're going to love what you're going to become. Fucking love it."

Rane smiled. "Then open this door and we can go tell the Lord General together. Let's not waste anymore time."

Sears stepped back from the spy hole. Silence followed. For a moment, Rane didn't think he was going to do it but then he heard the sound of bolts slipping free. Thunk, thunk, thunk.

The door groaned as it opened. Fresher air slipped into the cell first. Rane clenched his teeth, sucked it in through his nose. He was ready for this.

"You really did it," said Sears as he entered, sword sheathed and on his back, two pistols holstered on the strap across his chest. No one else followed. Rane took a step forward and checked the corridor outside the cell. Empty.

Sears walked past, headed to the bodies. He bent over Zee. "She was a cute one. Almost didn't want to beat the shit out of here when the old man asked me. Could think of better things to do to her to get her to talk." He looked up and winked at Rane, grin plastered all over his face. "You know what I mean?"

"Yes," said Rane, stepping closer.

Sears turned Zee's face to him. "Bet it was a rush when you killed her. Fuck; I love that. And it only gets better. Get them screaming and it's the best feeling in the world. Better than sex."

"I know."

Sears ran his finger through the blood on Zee's neck and then raised it to his mouth. "I still love the fucking taste." With eyes closed, he sucked the blood off the finger.

Rane said nothing.

"Hey." Sears looked up at Rane. "The blood's stone cold."

"I know," replied Rane and hacked through Sears' neck with *Kibon*. Another burst of magic hit Rane as the body toppled forward, a fine red mist spraying everywhere. His body shook with the intensity of the rush, almost bringing him to his knees. The room swayed as he tried to control it.

"Are you okay?" asked Zee, standing up.

"Stay back," he shouted, waving her off with his hand. He didn't trust himself, didn't trust *Kibon*. There was never enough blood to satisfy the sword. Satisfy him. Not when it promised such power. Who was she anyway? Nothing. A slave. A fool who should already be dead.

"What's happening to you?" Her voice cracked with fear. Even Zee could sense a change in Rane. See the fire in him.

No. No. He wouldn't give in. He swallowed, forced the fire in him down. Breathed in, breathed out. Like he'd been taught. Found his center and held onto it for all he was worth. He couldn't kill the girl. Shouldn't. Mustn't. Protect. Save. Oath.

By the Gods, Rane felt like he was going insane.

The girl backed away, looking for some dark shadow to cower in.

A man. A man. Rane was a man, a human being. Not a monster. No. "I'm okay. I'm okay." He picked up *Kibon*'s sheath. Slipped the blade inside it. He was in control. Not the sword. Never the sword. "Let's get out of here."

"What happened to you when you killed him?" asked Zee, pressed into the corner.

"The sword makes me stronger and faster than a normal man. But it needs blood to feed that magic. The more lives it takes, the less human I become. Jefferson — the old man — and the others have already been transformed."

"Into what?"

"We're about to find out." Rane stripped Spears of his shirt and his guns. He found a knife tucked in the man's boot and passed that to Zee. It wouldn't be much use against the Legionnaires, but something was better than nothing. "If you have to use it on a Legionnaire, stab them in the head. Only place you'll stand a chance of killing them."

"In the head," repeated Zee, staring at the blade as if it was the first time she'd ever seen a knife.

"Stick close to me. Move slowly. We don't know what's waiting for us. If we meet any Legionnaires, I'll deal with them — all you have to do is stay out of my way."

Zee nodded, gripping her knife two-handed in front of her, and followed Rane out into the corridor.

Despite the darkness of the tunnel, Rane could see as clear as day thanks to the magic stolen from Spears. His hearing was enhanced too. He could tell Zee's heart was hammering away despite her best efforts to appear brave, but the only other sounds he could pick up were from the flickering torchlights.

They came to the last door that led into the stair well and up and out. Even through the thick iron door, Rane could hear the rumple of thunder above and he smiled. A storm would help them escape, keep the Legionnaires inside and out of Rane and Zee's way.

The door wasn't locked — another good sign. They moved quicker now, with no cells to worry about, and the thunder obliterating any sound they could make. It grew fiercer with each step they took up, each rumble all but rolling into the next. As they moved up, Rane could pick up the sound of voices, shouting and hollering amid the commotion. People were outside.

The tang of gunpowder drifted down the stairwell as they continued up. It wasn't a storm of nature that waited for them outside. It was a war.

It was the thunder of cannons they could hear.

Rane stopped as he caught sight of the entrance to the Mural Tower. Two Legionnaires on were on sentry, but they were watching the chaos in the courtyard, not the stairwell. The cannon fire was coming from outside the castle walls and Jefferson was mustering his troops to respond. In all the confusion, Rane would have the element of surprise. *Kibon* twitched in anticipation. It sighed as he slipped it from its sheath.

Zee gripped his arm, scared.

"Just stay out of my way," whispered Rane in reply.

He took the remaining stairs two at a time. He was fast. Fast as death. He swung *Kibon* at the nearest guard, aiming for the man's neck. Sensing something, the guard turned at the last minute and *Kibon* entered his shoulder. Rane forced the blade down, driving it towards the man's heart, riding the current of magic flowing from the man.

The second guard was faster, drew his own sword, a streak of black, and Rane yanked *Kibon* free to counter the new threat. Steel met steel, clashing in the doorway.

The guard pivoted, swung his sword around at shoulder height, but Rane dropped down, under the blow. He thrust *Kibon* up, skewering the man through his heart. The guard's eyes bulged and spat blood over Rane as he died. But Rane didn't care as more power roared in to him.

"Nathaniel!" shouted Zee from behind him.

Rane turned just as a knife sunk into his gut. The first guard was back on his feet despite his arm and shoulder all but separated from his body and was intent on killing Rane. The knife worked fast, biting into him again and again as the guard snarled in Rane's face. Little jabs of ice in the fire that consumed him.

No matter. *Kibon* darted forwarded, and took the man's head from what was left of his shoulders. Magic flowed, healing the wounds, powering Rane in a glorious, insane rush. He staggered with the strength of it, so much more than he'd ever experienced before, aware that each death tainted his soul — just as Jefferson wanted.

Rane roared in frustration. Even by fighting back, he lost. By the Gods, he'd make them all pay.

He slipped *Kibon* back into its sheath without protest. It knew more blood would follow and for once, was happy to wait. Hands free, Rane grabbed the man's body and threw it down the stairs, kicked his head after it. The bastard deserved no better.

"Take the shirt off the other guard," said Rane to Zee. "It won't fool anyone who gets too close, but from a distance it'll help."

"Your wound..." said Zee, wide-eyed.

"... is already healed."

Zee stripped the corpse quickly and put on the shirt. She took the guard's holster and strapped his pistol to her leg.

"Do you know how to use that?" asked Rane.

"Well enough." She smiled, despite her injuries and their predicament. She bent down to pick up the dead man's sword.

"Leave that," said Rane, grabbing her arm.

"I'm better with a sword."

"Not that sword. You'll only ever be worse. Leave it."

Zee looked at him with a thousand unspoken questions but Rane left them unanswered. He crept to the main doorway and peered into the courtyard. One look was enough to send him back into the shadows, heart racing. Jefferson was there, with what could only have been the whole of the Legion. He inched back to the door, looked again.

Jefferson wasn't lying when he said he had one hundred and fifty Legionnaires in Orska. Nearly all that number was in the courtyard, in light armor with steel helmets covering heads and faces. Black swords drawn. Unconcerned at the battering the walls were taking from the enemy cannons.

"By the Gods," gasped Zee as she joined him. "How're we going to get past them?"

"We're not." Rane pointed to the battlements. "Jefferson's left the walls unmanned as far as I can see. We'll go up there, work our way around to the main keep. Work out our next move from there."

"Why isn't there anyone on the walls?"

"The Lord General's going out to fight," said Rane. "No point leaving men and women on the walls to get killed by a stray cannon ball."

"Why would he do that? He must be outnumbered."

"He doesn't think so. Come on." Rane led the way up the stairs. He could feel the castle shake every time a cannon ball struck. It wouldn't be long before they blew a breach in the walls.

Rane and Zee reached the parapets unhindered. Below them the gathered Legionnaires looked even more impressive. Tight, disciplined, ready.

On the other side of the wall however, the enemy stretched far into the distance — over three thousand soldiers by the looks of it. The sight took him back to the war and the Rastaks laying siege to Candra. But the army before him flew the banners of the five nations and the sign of Odason. They should be friends, not enemies.

He counted twelve guns by the belch of flames as each one fired. They were all lined up in front of the castle, manned by highly trained gun crews judging by their rate of fire. To the east, a trail of torchlight led up the mountainside. Three more guns being hauled up onto higher ground. Once there, they'd be able to fire directly into Orska, making victory a formality. Considering how quickly the force had been mustered, it was a formidable sight. No wonder they'd hadn't waited for morning to launch their assault.

"He's going to attack that?" gasped Zee. "He's going to get slaughtered."

Rane had nothing to say. Logic said she was right and yet Jefferson was going to send the Legion out. He could see him down in the courtyard, speaking to his troops. Rane didn't need to hear what the old man was saying — he knew well enough the Lord General's way with words, his ability to motivate the Legionnaires to happily sacrifice everything they had for his cause. After all, he'd persuaded them all to give up their souls already. To go and kill or die for him was nothing after that.

Even over the cacophony of war, he could hear the chains groaning as the portcullis was raised. The Legionnaires moved forward as one, their every move well drilled. Not so long ago, Rane would have been among them, ready to do his part. But not now. Now he was their enemy just as much as the men gathered outside.

The gates swung open.

And the Legion rushed out.

39

One hundred and fifty men and women of the Legion of Swords steamed out of Orska. The enemy was amassed some four hundred yards away. Far enough to make it a long run to engage under enemy fire. Far enough for the gun crews to reposition their aim from the castle walls to the oncoming Legionnaires. Even with the cover of night, logic said it was a suicide run.

And yet, the Legion didn't hesitate. They sprinted, with armor, helmets, shields and swords. Faster than Rane thought possible. Black streaks of death disappearing into the distance.

Only one cannon managed to get a shot off at them but it might as well have been aimed at the air itself for all the good it did.

One hundred and fifty Legionnaires against three thousand soldiers but all Rane felt was fear for the soldiers.

"Are some of them flying?" asked Zee as a group of Legionnaires moved ahead of the main pack.

Rane shook his head, squinting. The dark made it hard to see. "No. Not flying. Leaping. They're covering yards with each jump." Thirty or so were in the lead, heading straight for the heart of the enemy line.

"Why don't they shoot them?"

"No time," replied Rane. And there wasn't. The first Legionnaires hit the coalition forces like a hammer on glass. Even from his viewpoint, Rane could see the shock waves as the two forces met. The coalition troops buckled but, by some miracle, didn't break. There was no mistaking the sound of the dying though, as swords hacked and chopped, stabbed and sliced.

Then the rest of the Legion smashed into the lines. It was going to be a massacre. As Rane had learned so well during the war, humans stood no chance against demons.

Down in the courtyard, Jefferson headed into the main keep. No doubt to watch the slaughter from his office.

"Come on," said Rane. "Let's get out of this place before they come back."

"But what about those soldiers?" asked Zee.

"They're already dead. We'll need all the luck we can get to save ourselves."

"Shit," said Zee, her strength crumbling in the face of the onslaught of the Legion.

Rane took her elbow, helped keep her steady. "We can do this. There's only Jefferson and a few guards left. We stay out of their way and we'll be fine."

Zee took deep breaths. "Okay. Let's go."

They sprinted along the battlements. There was nothing to slow them down now the cannons had stopped firing. Still, it was hard not to look at what was happening out on the field but there was nothing to be gained by standing witness to a slaughter.

It was quieter inside the keep, away from the sounds of battle and the screams of the dying. To their left, stairs ran up and down and a corridor waited straight ahead.

"Which way do we go?" asked Zee.

"We go down."

Down the stairs they went, Rane all twitchy and eager to fight, still high on magic, and Zee, quiet, following on his heels. When they reached the next floor, Rane put out a hand to stop Zee. A guard

watched the war outside from the window at the far end of the corridor, his back to them.

Rane broke into a run. *Kibon* came free in his hand. The guard
never knew what hit him. Death was instantaneous. As he stood over
the body, he looked out the window. The view caught the breath in
his throat.

The moon shone down on the battlefield. No more than thirty
minutes could have passed since the gates of Orska were opened and
the Legionnaires had sprinted out to meet the assembled armed
forces sent from Napolin and yet the devastation they had wrought
was incredible. The Legion had hit the army at its center and was
now spreading out in a growing half-circle of death. Even from a
distance, the piles of corpses were clearly visible.

"By the Gods," whispered Rane.

Zee put her hand on Rane's shoulder. "What's going to happen
when they're unleashed them on the rest of the world?"

"A friend of mine murdered nearly a whole town on his own,"
replied Rane. "An army of tainted warriors could burn the world to
ashes. I've got to stop them. I can't walk away from this."

"Yes, we can," interrupted Zee. "Right now. While they're out there.
We get as far away from them as possible. Save ourselves."

Rane watched the battle — saw the weak die at the hands of the
Legion, feeding their swords, tainting them further. He could so
easily be one of them, his oath forgotten, his humanity lost. The
anger burned within him. How dare Jefferson have damned the
Legion like this? "The old man's in the tower. Probably watching this
from his study."

"Who cares?" Zee grabbed Rane's arm, tried dragging him towards
the stairs going down. "It's not our problem. Let's get out of here."

Rane took Zee's hand, squeezed it. "Do you remember the way
Samuel brought you?"

"Yes, but..."

"Go. Down the stairs and out of this castle. Head into the hills
away from the battle, then find your way back." Rane let go of her

hand, kissed her forehead. "I need to stop the Legion, stop Jefferson some how — or the deaths will never stop."

Tears ran down Zee's cheeks. "I can't. Not alone."

Rane wiped a tear away with his thumb. "You can."

"What about you?" she asked.

"Our lives are on different paths. You're free of your master. I still have to be rid of mine." Rane smiled. "Now go."

Zee's eyes popped open. "Behind you!"

Rane spun around, *Kibon* flying from it's scabbard instantly, as two Legionnaires came at them hard and fast from the stairs.

The Legionnaires were on them in a flash. Even with his enhanced reflexes, Rane only just managed to dodge an overhead swing that would have split him from side to side. He wasn't fast enough to avoid the Legionnaire's shield as it followed through, battering him to the floor. Rolling with the blow, he came up swinging, aiming *Kibon* at his opponent's knee, only to be blocked by the man's black sword.

Rane danced back, letting the Legionnaire hack at thin air. A iron helm covered the man's face, his eyes visible through a slit in the metal.

The other Legionnaire joined in, pressing the attack. Steel kissed steel as Rane frantically defended himself. Sparks flew in the darkness as they hammered each other, the sound echoing through the corridor.

Zee rushed to Rane's aid. She fired her pistol at his opponent's back from a foot away. The boom of the gun was deafening in the confined space. The Legionnaire screamed as the bullet struck home but it didn't kill him. The man clubbed Zee across the face and she dropped like a stone.

But Rane didn't waste the opportunity. He plunged his sword through the Legionnaire's visor and into his brain. Now it was his turn to roar, as the magic surged through him.

The other Legionnaire came at him again, but this time Rane was ready for him. With gritted teeth, he let the Legionnaire get close and offered his neck as a target. As the Legionnaire's sword swung towards it, he ducked under the blow.

Kibon slashed out and the Legionnaire went down, blood spraying, as Rane opened up his guts to the world.

Rane staggered over to Zee. She was unconscious but he found a steady pulse. "Lucky girl."

He picked the girl up and placed her on a bed in one of the rooms and closed the door. Hopefully she'd be safe there until he could return for her. He set off, took the stairs at a run, eager for the fight ahead. Two steps at a time, heart racing, mouth dry. Up one flight, then the next and the next. To Jefferson's quarters.

He slowed only when the top floor was in sight and stopped just before the last step. Rane peered around the corner. Two guards.

Kibon twitched in Rane's mind, eager for what was to come. It knew there would be no holding back. No time to worry about damnation and taints. It knew it would be fed.

Rane took a deep breath, aware of the madness buzzing in his mind. Wished there was another way but knew there wasn't. He sprinted up the last few steps, and headed straight to the guards.

The first guard managed to get to his feet and his sword half-drawn but Rane dropped down and slid the last few yards towards him. *Kibon* sliced through the guard's knee. He collapsed, spraying blood but Rane already had his hand over the man's mouth to stifle his screams before plunging *Kibon* through the man's throat and into his skull, twisting it for maximum damage. The magic hit him as the man died but the rush was calmer, more controllable. Rane didn't want to think about what that meant.

The other guard came at him but he was nothing compared to the power within Rane. He was fire. He was fury. He was death. *Kibon* took the man's head from his shoulders with a whisper.

Rane kicked the door open to Jefferson's office. The door flew off its hinges and he rushed into the room, sword ready. Moonlight flooded the room through the windows, painting the empty room silver.

There was a door in the far corner and Rane headed to it. He paused by it, listening. All was still silent. Doubt raced through Rane's mind. Would that room be empty too? If so, where was Jefferson?

He turned the door handle, releasing the lock and slowly pushed the door open. The room was half the size of his office but just as well furnished, dominated by a four-poster bed with the curtains drawn. Myri sat in a chair by the bed. Her black sword sat across her lap

"Hello Nathaniel," she purred. "Don't be shy. Come on in."

Rane stepped forward, filled with horror at what his friend had become. He had no fear though. Not now, now when he had such power at his disposal. "Myri."

"I told them you'd not join us, Nathaniel. They laughed; said everyone turned, but I know you." Myri stood up, letting her sword point to the floor. "But the Lord General was happy for me to wait here in case I was right. I suggested he stay with me, make use of the bed. Perhaps we will another time."

"Where is he?" asked Rane, holding his fury in check.

"Somewhere. Watching men die." She pursed her lips and shook her head. "You really should've just gone with the plan. Become one of us."

"I'd rather be dead," replied Rane.

"My pleasure," said Gregor, pulling back the curtains on the bed. He had a pistol in his hand. The Legionnaire grinned as he pulled the trigger.

Pain exploded in Rane's head.

40

Rane lay on a cold stone floor, dimly aware of the sounds of fighting far away. Something warm and sticky covered his eyes. Blood. He was so tired it was hard to work out what was happening, remember where he was. Someone cried out in pain. He didn't know who. It could've been him. Why was it so hard to think?

He moved his hand. Dragged it more like. Managed to wipe the blood from his eyes and get them open. It took awhile to focus, move past the swirling spots and dark shapes. All he could see was the stone floor, cold, grey, polished. And the blood. Was that his blood?

Sleep tugged at the edges of his mind, telling him to stop, give up, rest for a minute, an hour, a lifetime. Where was *Kibon*? He could hear it calling him. Promising to make the pain go away, save him, warning him not to give up.

He lifted his head, saw it only inches from his hand. So close.

A wave of nausea slammed into him and he only just managed to stop himself from puking. He blinked more blood from his eye. It was coming from somewhere, leaking out of him. He wondered how much had already been lost. How close he was to dying.

He reached out and dragged *Kibon* to him, felt that beautiful pulse of magic countering the pain. Not nearly fast enough. By the Gods, no.

A battle raged somewhere. He could hear it. He turned his head and was rewarded with more pain for doing so. He might have passed out, he didn't really know but then he saw her. Myri. He had to stop her, tried to move, couldn't, and slumped back on the ground, face down in his own blood.

Myri was the enemy. Myri was the one he had to stop.

He caught his reflection in the blade, all mad-eyed and covered in blood, a nasty black mark on his forehead. Had he been shot?

He pulled *Kibon* tighter to him, both hands wrapped around its hilt. Pulled the magic from it as if he was breathing air into his lungs. Energy rippled through his body, pushing back the fog, softening the pain.

Myri watched. "I told you it'd not kill him."

Gregor sat on the bed, reloading his pistol. He looked over at Rane and laughed. "But it was fun."

Rane managed to push himself up and get his legs back under him. He swayed for a moment as he sat up, but *Kibon* sang with power, demanding revenge, filling Rane with all the magic it had, fixing him. He staggered to his feet.

Gregor raised the pistol once more. "I like hurting him." He pulled the trigger and the gun spat its bullet towards Rane. But Rane wasn't going to get shot a second time. He swerved and came at them, closing the gap between them in a couple of strides. He was fast, faster than any normal man could hope to be. He brought Kibon down in an arc and all Gregor could do was watch it descend. Rane put all his strength into the blow. *Kibon's* razor sharp edge did the rest. He barely felt any resistance as it entered Gregor's shoulder, none as it carved a path through the Legionnaire's body before slipping out just above the hip, with a splash of blood, so red against the stone. More energy kicked through Rane as *Kibon* fed. The last of his pain disappeared and everything clicked back into place.

Myri hissed as she lunged at his heart, and he only just managed to stop her riposte.

There was no time for words. He went low, aiming for Myri's leg, but her black blade knocked *Kibon* from its path. She countered with impossible speed, driving her sword up, hoping to split Rane in two, forcing him to flip out of the way. Rane struck back, swinging *Kibon* at her neck. This time it was Myri who skipped back, trying to gain some space. Holding her sword horizontally across her chest, she retreated into center of the room, and Rane followed.

He moved to the left, hoping to get behind her guard. Myri countered by twisting her body so she faced him side-on. Rane feinted a strike at her head, drawing her attention, then switched, aiming for her stomach. She dropped her sword down over her shoulder, taking the sting out of his blow but not doing enough to stop him drawing blood. Even though it was just a scratch, the sight of it made Rane smile.

Myri came at him, launching a series of overhead strikes, fuelled by rage and hatred. He blocked them, feeling the force of each one vibrate through *Kibon* and into his arms. She came again but Rane stepped out the way of her and she flew past. Rane was far too an experienced soldier to let such a target pass. She screamed as he struck, arching her back as his sword bit deep into it.

Rane pressed the advantage but Myri's leg shot out, slamming into his chest and sending him flying. *Kibon* had him too fuelled with magic and he bounced back off the ground onto his feet. However the magic worked both ways and, as he raced back to join the fray, he could see Myri's powers already healing the bloody red streak across her back.

Her movements were getting faster and faster until it seemed like they were fighting a blur. Her sword was everywhere, blocking, striking, slashing. She was tireless and it was taking all Rane had to keep up with her.

Myri caught Rane on the forearm, opening him up and then sliced a gash across his chest. She slammed her elbow into Rane's jaw and he only just blocked the sword strike that followed. Her sword skittered along *Kibon*'s edge, sparks flying as the two blades kissed, drawing the nemeses together. Rane powered his head into hers, crunching her nose. As she staggered back, Rane drove his sword into her gut.

Her scream came straight from the underworld. She punched Rane, sending him sprawling. He was back on his feet in an instant, only too aware his sword was in her gut and not in his hand. She swung her sword towards him, stopping him from attacking. With her other hand, she reached for *Kibon* blade and dragged it out of her. Blood gushed from her stomach as she threw the sword to the floor. Myri wavered on her feet but she never once took her eyes off Rane, knowing if she did, it would be the death of her.

"This isn't the end of it," she spat. For a moment Rane thought she was going to attack again, but she raced towards the window and, before he had a chance to react, threw herself through it. Glass shattered in a thousand directions. There was still a sprinkle of glass falling down like rain when Rane reached the window, but no sign of Myri in the darkness below.

She must be dead. A fall like that would kill anyone — even a Legionnaire. Somehow though, Rane didn't believe it. He'd look for her body later if he could — for now, he had to move on. He still had Jefferson to kill.

Pausing only to strip Gregor of his pistol and more ammunition, he headed for the door. Rane glanced out the window one more time. The battle looked all but over. Fia's army had been routed. Those not already dead were running for their lives. The Legion pursued but they'd be back all too soon. Rane had to hurry.

Outside, no guards walked the battlements, or manned the cannon. Their powers were making them slack. They were all too confident of their victory. Even so, Jefferson had to watching somewhere. If he wasn't in his study, he'd still want to savor his moment of victory.

Rane stopped in his tracks. He knew where Jefferson would be. The siege tower. But if he was there, Rane had no hope of getting to him. There was only one way in and they weren't going to open the door to him.

He'd just have to knock bloody hard.

Rane raced along the battlements, along the curtain wall, through the square mural tower and then back out on to the battlements above the upper bailey, excitement building. It was time to make Jefferson pay for all that he'd taken from him — his soul, his wife, his life.

He reached the arsenal tower next, where all the Legion's weapons were stored. The door leading from the battlements was locked but a good kick stopped that from being a problem.

Two guards waited for him inside. There was a flash of silver as *Kibon* swept forward, clashing with a black blade once more, but Rane's limbs surged with magic. His fear of the tainted and trans-formed was gone because he knew he had the strength to defeat them. He attacked with speed and aggression, forcing the men back. His sword slipped past one man's guard and bit deep into his chest. Blood spurted from the wound as more magic hit Rane. There was no stopping him now. Not even Odason or Heras had the might. He thrust his sword into the remaining guard. And roared at the rush that followed.

The main arsenal was stored one floor below, rammed with every kind of weapon and barrels of gunpowder.

He sheathed *Kibon* on his back and began searching amongst the boxes. He found what he was looking for in the third box he opened; small iron balls lay carefully amongst straw, with short fuses sticking out of each one.

Grenades. He filled a pouch with a dozen and slung it over his shoulder. It was time to see the Lord General.

Back on the wall, Rane peered into the distance. Already the gloom of the night was lifting as another day approached. The cursed crows circled the battlefield, picking their next meal. The Legion-naires still fought, slaughtering stragglers but it wouldn't be long before they returned to Orska, high on blood.

"Rane!" He looked up at the sound of his name. Four Legion-naires were on the battlements. Rane recognized two of them — a Naijin called Dewei and a woman called Amjad from the Balrussian borders. Old friends from the war, good people to have on your side in a fight, Amjad had saved his life once — but they both had the look of the tainted and Rane had no doubt about their intentions. They sprinted towards him with frightening speed, hungering to kill.

Rane drew his pistol, aimed and fired. The oncoming Legionnaires disappeared behind the gun smoke for a heartbeat but when it cleared, they were almost upon him. He dropped the pistol and drew the second one just as Dewei leaped at him. The Naijin's sword swept down as he pulled the trigger. From such close range, the bullet punched a hole through the Legionnaire's chest, throwing him backwards and over the edge. Amjad's sword was at his throat a moment later and Rane blocked frantically with *Kibon*.

Amjad attacked again and Rane pivoted around her sword until he was almost back-to-back with the Legionnaire. He thrust his sword behind him, through the woman's chest, felt the smack as *Kibon*'s hilt hit bone. Just as quickly, he pulled the blade free, bringing a spray of blood and guts with it. Magic flowed through him, feeding him. As she fell to her knees, he swung around once more and took her head from her shoulders. Let her powers heal that wound.

Rane rushed at the other two, eager to kill. There was no stopping hm. *Kibon* was beauty in motion. He hacked at the nearest Legionnaire. She swerved so that *Kibon* only nipped her skin and then caught Rane with a backhanded blow that sent him flying along the battlements. The impact knocked the wind from him. As he tried to force air back down inside his lungs, she came at him. Her black blade scythed down. Rane rolled out of its way somehow and sparks flew as her sword struck stone. He hacked at her feet with his own sword but she skipped over it like a child with a rope.

She kicked out, catching him under the chin, cracking his teeth and rattling his brain. He spat blood as he dived out the way of her sword again, feeling it hiss past his neck. He spun, just in time to block the return swipe, stopping her blade on *Kibon*'s guard. The Legionnaire pressed down on him, forcing Rane to the ground. He stamped down on her knee with all his might and it gave with a crack. As the Legionnaire lost her balance, Rane drove *Kibon* into her side. A rush of energy flowed into him as he thrust the sword deeper.

He wanted to scream in delight, as the power built inside him, as she screamed in death.

Kibon burned in his hand, promising to make Rane stronger still, more powerful than Jefferson's mob. With this strength he could stop anyone, slay all the monsters. Mankind would be safe. He would be transformed.

One remained. An ant before a God. Rane roared forward, *Kibon* lightening in his hand. The Legionnaire raised his own sword in defense but he might as well have tried to stop the world turning. *Kibon* smashed through the steel, into his face and down into his heart. Nothing could stop death when it came.

41

Rane pulled his sword free from the Legionnaire's corpse. Power surged through him, making it hard to think. *Kibon* cried out for more blood, more death, more strength. Rane's body shook with desire for all the sword promised. He'd smite his enemies from this world and the next, destroy them all, pound them into dust.

Revenge would be his. Justice for Kara would be his. Jefferson would regret the day he betrayed the Legion. The man's only legacy would be a rotting corpse in Orska.

From the other side of the wall, he could hear the screams and the cries of the Fia's army. He smiled. They deserved all the pain. He knew the Legion would be back soon but he didn't care. Let them come. *Kibon* waited for any foolish enough to try and strike him down.

First he had to deal with Jefferson.

The siege tower stood in the corner of Orska, a tall, square building overlooking the rest of the castle. The walls were too high to scale on either side with plenty of murder holes peppered around it. The only way in or out was through a door leading to the upper bailey, and Rane had that covered.

The first grenade punched a chunk out of the wall. The second hit the same spot, tearing more stone loose. The third opened up the interior to the early morning sky. Rane kept an eye on the murder holes but couldn't see anyone manning the positions.

Again and again he threw grenades, tearing chunks out of the walls. His ears rang with the fury of it all and his eyes stung with the smoke but still he went on.

Then the door opened. Smoke billowed out, thick and black, and then four Legionnaires came out in front of the Lord General. Rane recognized Rikard and Simone among them.

Jefferson himself walked out with a straight back as if everything was going according to his plans. As if he didn't care about all the misery he had caused. The others formed a barrier around him as he made for the bailey.

They stopped at its center. Jefferson peered up at the battlements. "Nathaniel, is that you up there causing all this trouble?"

Rane stepped forward and gazed down on the man who'd destroyed his life and the lives of so many people he cared about. He held a grenade in his hand. "I told you I'd have my revenge."

Jefferson held his hands out. "Go ahead. Throw your bombs. Fire your cannon. I'm not dead yet. See how you fare against me."

"Let's just finish this," hissed Rane.

"Why not come down here, Nathaniel? Let's talk about this like civilized people," Jefferson called out. "Like the friends we used to be. I know where Babayon is. I can tell you where to find him."

Rane ground his teeth together as he watched the man he once thought of as a surrogate father. He knew he was lying. It was all a trick. His eyes met Jefferson's. He would have his revenge the right way. Up close. Personal.

Rane filled his lungs with air and pushed all doubt from his mind. The enemy waited, and he would vanquish them. *Kibon* whispered reassurances in his mind. The grenade was heavy in his hand.

"Come on, Nathaniel," called Jefferson from the courtyard. "Let's talk."

Rane jumped from the battlements. Thirty feet down. He threw the grenade as he dropped, its fuse no more than a snip.

It arced towards Rikard and one of the other Legionnaires. Both their eyes followed it as it looped towards them, neither reacting as they should have done.

Rane hit the ground and rolled when it exploded. He felt shrapnel bite into his leg, but ignored it. The magic would heal him.

He got back onto his feet at a run, drawing two of his pistols. Rikard and the Legionnaire had taken the brunt of the blast, but everyone had felt its power. Jefferson lay on the ground. The other unknown Legionnaire was on his feet, swaying like a punch-drunk fighter when Rane shot him. He took a bullet in the chest and another in the head, putting him down. Rane dropped both pistols and reached for the third, but Simone wasn't going to give him the luxury of shooting her. She threw a knife as her comrade fell. Rane twisted, turning away from the point, but still it struck his shoulder, sinking deep. He cried out in pain, cursing himself for not being quick enough. Still, three down in under a minute. The odds were looking better.

He reached over his shoulder, felt the familiar grip of *Kibon* in his hand, felt that kick of energy he always felt. It sang through the air as it slipped free of its scabbard and came down, aiming for Simone's skull. Her blade stopped it mid-flight and she shrugged off the assault. The two Legionnaires danced the dance of blades, and attack met with attack, riposte, parry, lunge. In many ways, it was like fighting himself. Both he and Simone were experts of the sword, trained by the same teachers to be the best, both enhanced with dark magic.

Simone swung at his neck, forcing Rane backwards. He stopped himself from falling over with his left hand as her sword whistled by. He managed to get *Kibon* up in time to stop the reverse cut. He kicked out, catching Simone under the chin. She staggered back just enough to allow Rane to straighten up before launching into an attack of his own. But for all his speed and strength, Simone was faster. Fully

transformed, it soon became clear she had the upper hand. Sweat ran
down Rane's brow, stinging his eyes, as he used every ounce of experience just to stay in the fight.

Weapons blurred as Simone spun into another attack, twisting
away before Rane could do more than parry her sword. She lunged,
aiming for his heart, but then hacked down at the last second, slicing
into Rane's thigh before he could move out of the way. The pain hit
him immediately as blood gushed from the wound. It took all his
concentration to stay on his feet, but Simone leaped, snapping her
leg out to kick Rane in the nose. He went down with that, head spinning, tears filling his eyes as blood poured down his face.

Simone hacked down, only to hit stone as Rane rolled away. She
gave chase, sparks flying as she struck the ground, but it gave Rane no
chance to recover. He slashed out in reply, but she skipped over his
blade, laughing, and then cut him across the back as he tried to avoid
her full-on assault. He screamed through clenched teeth, the searing
pain telling him the wound was deep.

Rane pushed up, got slashed across his abdomen as he got to his
feet, but managed to get his chin out the way before the blow sliced
his face open. He retreated, trying to find some space to allow the
magic to heal his wounds. He gripped *Kibon*, trying to draw more
strength from the blade. Simone was unmarked, looking as fresh as
when the fight had begun. Rane reached for his last pistol, but he
might as well have been moving in slow motion. With a flick of her
sword, Simone sent the gun flying from his hand, drawing more
blood in the process. His arm, already weak from the knife in his
shoulder, hung limp at his side.

He gulped in air through his mouth; his nose was too blocked
with blood. He had no idea what to do next, how he could turn this
fight around and win. Simone was better than him in every way. As
desperate as he grew, he could see the enjoyment on her face. As his
defense became more wild, her attacks were relentless. She had no
mercy to give.

Her blade sliced his ribs. He parried her next blow, their blades
skidding along each other, bringing Simone in closer. Fast as light-

ning, she reached out and snatched her knife from his shoulder, dragging flesh with it. He cried out. She slammed him in the mouth with the hilt of her sword and Rane collapsed for the third time, his leg bent under him. *Kibon* spun across the ground, far from his hand.

Simone dropped on top of him, pinning him to the ground with her knees. She held her sword under his chin, forcing him to stretch his neck to avoid a fatal cut, and brought the knife around so he could see the point an inch from his eye. She looked down on him, barely out of breath, with a look of utter disdain on her face.

"Such a disappointment," she said.

"Fuck you," said Rane, and stuck the knife from his boot between Simone's ribs. She arched her back as it went in, yelping like a dog. She staggered to her feet, blood pouring from her side, and the moment her weight was off Rane, he was up too, snatching the stiletto from his wrist. He punched her with it as fast as he could, over and over again, not caring where he struck, only that he did as much harm as he could. She tried to get away, but it was his turn to give no respite.

Simone dropped to her knees and Rane slammed the stiletto into her temple. Her eyes rolled to the back of her head before she toppled to the ground.

Panting, spitting blood, Rane stood over her to make sure she was really dead. He kicked her sword far away from her, cutting her off from its magic. Let her suffer. They'd done far worse to him. Satisfied, he shuffled over to pick up *Kibon*. Immediately he felt better, reconnected to the sword's magic. He snorted more blood from his nose as his wounds began to heal. How many times had *Kibon* saved his life? The irony was not lost on him that it was saving him only for a far worse fate. Still, he was standing while so many of Jefferson's soldiers lay dead.

Jefferson.

Only the Lord General remained. It was time for Rane to have his revenge on all that the man had done and planned to do.

Rane turned and staggered over to where Jefferson had fallen. Except he wasn't there.

Only dust and rubble remained, stained with scarlet.

"Looking for me?"

Rane spun around at Jefferson's voice, sword raised, eager.

The old man stood, back straight, still proud, his sword still slung at his side. "You've wreaked so much havoc, Nathaniel. Not what I wanted for you."

Rane took a step towards him. "I'm glad to disappoint you."

"I wonder, though — was it worth it?" Jefferson waved a hand at the chaos around him. "Does all this make you feel better? Does it deaden the pain you feel inside?"

"It certainly helps."

"But what have you achieved, really? We had to leave this castle anyway. It makes no difference if it's intact or a pile of rubble."

"It'll make a difference when you're dead."

Jefferson chortled. "I think not." He thrust his hand out. The air rippled and something smashed Rane halfway across the courtyard.

"Wha—?" Rane spat blood over the stone as he tried to rise. A thousand shards sliced into his lungs with every breath he took. But then Jefferson's magic had him in its grip. He squirmed as the very air around him held him, crushed him, twisted him.

"See what you could have become," said Jefferson. He raised his hand and Rane was lifted off the ground. Three, four, five feet. "See what you've lost."

Unable to breathe, Rane's bones splintered under the pressure. *Kibon* fell from his hand. It clattered against the stone, sounding his death knell.

Jefferson took a step and seemed to float across the courtyard, grinning like a madman. He settled down next to Rane, then waved his hand and lifted Rane higher still. Six, seven, eight feet. The pressure around Rane intensified. Darkness clawed away at the edge of his vision. Pain filled every inch of his body.

Marcus had nearly killed Rane with his power. Myri and Simone, too. All had been faster, stronger, more ferocious than Rane. But they had been but children compared to the power Jefferson possessed.

"Don't think ill of me, Nathaniel. I gave you every chance to join us," said Jefferson. "What I do, I do for the good of everyone. We will be fair rulers of this world, intolerant of any that would do it harm. We will purge it of weakness and forge a better future with an iron spine. Die knowing this." Jefferson squeezed his hand and the life was crushed from Rane.

42

The world exploded.

Then Rane was falling.

He hit the ground hard, bashed his head against the stone and cracked his shoulder, too. But suddenly, there was air in his lungs. Sweet air. Jefferson's grip on him was gone. Rane blinked the blood from his eyes, amazed he was still alive, and saw Zee standing where he'd been on the battlements.

The Lord General faced her, both arms outstretched. A grenade hovered in mid-air, three feet from his face, caught in the same magic that had just held Rane. Jefferson grimaced with the pressure, slowly pulled back his hands. The grenade moved with them, quivering in the air. Then Jefferson thrust them forward and the bomb shot back from whence it came.

This time, there was no magic to stop it. It slammed into the battlements with all its fury. Rock and rubble flew in every direction before disappearing in a plume of dirt and dust.

"Zee!" cried Rane. Not another life snuffed out at Jefferson's hands?

"The fool." Jefferson snorted in derision. He looked down at Rane. "She was even dumber than you."

Rane scrambled in the dirt. *Kibon* was five feet away. Without it, he was dead. Even with it, he was probably dead.

"Where are you going?" asked Jefferson. "It's time you died."

A girl's scream cut him off.

Zee reappeared, two pistols in her hands. She fired, the crack of the pistols amplified in the confines of the courtyard. Jefferson waved a hand and the bullets ricocheted off an invisible barrier. Another flick of his fingers sent Zee tumbling away.

Rane had his hand on *Kibon*'s hilt. He squeezed it tight, felt the jolt as he reconnected with its magic. He pushed himself to his feet and ran at Jefferson, *Kibon* in hand and eager for blood. Everything slowed. To close the ten feet between them took an age. Every step seemed slower than the next.

Jefferson turned as Rane approached, his hands — his deadly hands — already conjuring up more black magic. The air rippled around him, crackling with death.

At the last moment, Rane dropped and slid the last few feet. Jefferson's blast pulsed over his head as he brought *Kibon* up into the Lord General's thigh. The steel bit into flesh. Blood splashed from the wound as Rane put all his might behind the blow. Jefferson's magic pulsed through the blade in an angry roar, hitting Rane like lightning. Somehow, he held on as *Kibon* cut through meat and bone, slicing through the leg.

Jefferson collapsed, screaming, blood pumping out over the stone. He thrust a hand at Rane, but the magic lacked focus. The blast knocked Rane back a yard or two, but he stayed on his feet, *Kibon* fused to his hand. The magic he'd leeched raged though him, healing him, strengthening him. He could feel its madness, its taint. By the Gods, it felt good. So good.

Jefferson clutched his severed leg, still screaming, but already the wound had closed. Rane didn't know how long it would take him to regrow the severed part, but he had no doubt Jefferson would recover. All the bastard was feeling was a bit of momentary pain.

It wouldn't do. Not after the pain he'd inflicted on Rane and so many others. There was a price to pay for what he'd done.

Rane kicked the Lord General in his mouth. Blood and teeth flew as his neck snapped back. The man's eyes rolled back into his head as he lost consciousness.

Rane stood over Jefferson's body, *Kibon* pulsing in his hand. The blade was eager for him to finish the job, to kill the man and steal his magic. With just a simple flick of the blade, the world would be Rane's.

The same old sweet words. The same temptation. Power had turned Jefferson into a monster, far worse than any Rane had fought in the war. Power had destroyed the men and women Rane had once been so proud to stand beside.

He ran his finger over Kara's locket, felt strength come from that — a different kind of magic. Jefferson was damned, but Rane wasn't. Not yet. Not if he could help it. He slipped *Kibon* back in its sheath, ignoring its howling protest. He may be bound to it, but it would not be his master. Not any more.

Protecting his hand with a ripped piece of cloth, he picked up Jefferson's sword. Twelve feet was enough to remove the effects of its power on any normal Legionnaire, but Rane wasn't going to take any chances with Jefferson. It was closer to twenty before he stopped and dropped the sword. Let Jefferson deal with that.

He checked on Zee next and found her alive. Just.

"You ok?"

"As much as I can be," she replied, looking half-dead.

Rane smiled. "Thanks for saving me."

"I almost wish I hadn't." Zee spat blood on the floor. "That hurt."

"Rest. I'm going to have a chat with the Lord General."

Zee grasped Rane's arm. "The others will be back soon."

Rane nodded. "I know. Watch for them. Warn me if they return."

Jefferson's eyes opened as Rane approached. Old wounds criss-crossed the old man's flesh and fresh blood stained his clothes. Even his leg wound was reopening. His eyes found Rane. "Come to gloat, Nathaniel?"

Rane knelt beside him. "I remember when I first met you. I was just out of training camp, and they brought me to see you. I'd never been in awe of anyone before I met you. You exuded confidence and charisma, and I thought, 'This is a man to follow.' And for ten years, I believed that. So, no, it doesn't make me happy to see you like this. To realize I was wrong for all that time, that I sacrificed so much for someone who wasn't worth anything."

"I remember you then — fresh-faced and full of self-righteousness. Not much has changed." Jefferson coughed, specks of blood staining his beard. "I'm still a man to follow if you'd just open your fucking eyes."

"I don't think so, sir. It's too late for that. It ends here. Today."

"Nothing ends here," snarled Jefferson. "Nothing. So you kill me. So what? My plans go on. You can't stop what's been put in motion."

"Why? Why did you do it?"

"Why? You foolish boy. Why? We were going to die. Isn't that a good enough reason? The Rastaks were going to storm those walls and massacre every last one of us. Babayon offered me a way to stop that, and become more besides. Not an old man in his final years, but young again, strong, immortal and with more power than I'd ever dreamed of. And by doing so, I got to save all of you as well. I didn't have to agonize over that. It was the easiest decision I've ever made."

"But you gave us no choice. You cursed us all without so much as a by your leave."

"You are soldiers!" shouted Jefferson, but a fit of coughing stole his voice away. More blood flecked his chin and beard. When he spoke again, there was no hiding the pain in his voice. "Soldiers don't get a say in what their commanding officers decide. You gave up that right when you put your mark on the dotted line. You gave up that right when you promised to follow me to the gates of hell." He paused to catch his breath and glared at Rane. "Oh, yes, I remember you saying that, Nathaniel. Well, we were at the gates of hell, and I led you out of there. I gave you the opportunity to become something far greater than you could ever have imagined. I will not feel guilty for that. I will not."

"Can it be undone?"

"Why would you want it undone? Look at what you've accomplished with only half the power at your disposal and for once in your life try and see the bigger picture. Embrace the transformation and fulfill your potential. You could be the greatest of us all."

"Can it be undone?"

"Ask Babayon. I never asked him. I didn't care. Why would a god want to become a human once more?"

"We are very different people, you and me. Where is Babayon? Where will I find him?"

Jefferson laughed. "In the wind. Enjoying the madness of it all. It's what he lives for."

"I'll find him. I'll kill him just as I've killed you."

"Then get on with it. Pull out that sword of yours and kill me." Anger flared in Jefferson's eyes. "Be a man for once in your fucking life."

Rane could feel *Kibon*'s excitement at the Lord General's words. He stood up. "I think not."

"Then run, you coward. Run as far away from here as you can, but I promise you this: I will track you down, and I'll be the one who'll put an end to your miserable failure of a life. Then you can join that whore of a wife of yours in the afterlife."

"You mistake me. I'm not going to let you live. A price must be paid for what you've done."

"Then get your sword out and do it. See what taint my soul will bring you. No matter what you do, you're damned."

Rane shook his head. "No. You're wrong. Wrong about so many things."

He fetched Jefferson's sword. The old man's eyes bulged at the sight of it and immediately Rane could see its magic work. Wounds began to heal, and color came back to Jefferson's cheeks. The old man snatched out, tried to seize the blade, but Rane kept it out of reach.

"Give it to me," demanded Jefferson, spit and blood flying from his mouth.

Rane shook his head. "I want you to know that I'm going to hunt down every one of your tainted Legionnaires and kill them. I will hunt Babayon down and find a cure for those Legionnaires yet to turn, and I will not stop until your plans for this world are as dead as you."

With the cloth wrapped around the hilt, Rane unsheathed the blade. The steel was pure ebony.

"Killing me with my own sword won't save you," sneered Jefferson. "It'll turn you into me a heartbeat later."

"On my way here, I stopped in Candra. They were hanging Legionnaires outside our old barracks. The crowds watched our brothers and sisters dance on the end of ropes, but that didn't kill them. They died only when the priest came out, took their swords and smashed their blades." Rane leaned Jefferson's sword against a large piece of rubble.

Panic flared across Jefferson's face. "No. No. No. Don't. Think about what you're doing, Nathaniel," he begged. "Think about it. This won't save you. It won't bring anyone back. Stop it."

Rane picked up an anvil-sized chunk of stone. "After this, I'm going to break every sword I find so that your twisted Legionnaires can't hurt anyone else."

"Please, Nathaniel. There's a cure. I promise—"

Rane brought the stone down onto Jefferson's sword with all his strength. It shattered on impact. Jefferson didn't even have time to scream. Whatever fire burned inside him was snuffed out in an instant. For a man who thought he was a god, Jefferson looked as human as the next man in death.

"They say Heras treats everyone the same in the end. In your case, I hope she makes an exception. May you suffer in the underworld for all eternity," said Rane to the corpse at his feet.

"Done?" asked Zee as Rane straightened up.

"Not yet. We've still got to kill the others."

43

W hile Zee kept watch, Rane fetched barrel after barrel of gunpowder from the armory and set them up around the courtyard and lower bailey. He hid them behind rubble and covered them with cloth — anything that would keep them hidden long enough for Jefferson's army to enter the castle without detecting them. It was long, hard work, made possible only by his magic-fuelled muscles. The sun climbed back into the sky. The sounds of battle faded, and the cannons had long since fallen silent. Even the cries of the wounded were beginning to die.

Zee stood by the portcullis, watching the battlefield. Rane wished there was some way to spare her the horror she had to witness, but there was no other choice. He couldn't leave over one hundred tainted Legionnaires loose in the world.

"They're coming back," cried Zee. "Whatever you're doing, hurry!"

Rane ran to her side. He could see them gathered together, confident, invincible. "They'll pay for what they've done."

He took Zee and led her back into the courtyard. They hid behind a half-fallen wall. Rane had a fuse and a taper in his hand as he watched the main gate. Time slowed. *Kibon* niggled at his mind. Why use explosives when his sword was all he needed? Why lose the power that could be his? Its voice was still so seductive, despite all he knew and had witnessed. He shook his head. He would deal with *Kibon* soon enough.

Zee grabbed his arm. Voices. They both heard voices. Laughter. Banter. The bastards were in a good mood after slaughtering thousands, high on blood and souls. The first Legionnaire walked under the portcullis, smiling, strutting. Then came the second, the third, the fourth. Blood stained their clothes, but not their swords — all black. More followed. Rane could see the shock on their faces when they saw the devastation in the courtyard, the destruction of the siege tower, the bodies of the dead. Jefferson injured and down.

They rushed to his side, checked to see if he was alive. More Legionnaires entered the courtyard. There were fifty or sixty of them at least now. He heard his name mentioned. They knew it was his work. Zee shivered with fear next to him, urging him to light the fuse, eyes wide and bright and full of tears. He wanted to — the Gods knew he did — but he had to wait. He needed more of them gathered. They only had one chance to wipe the Legionnaires off the face of the world.

More flooded in, battle-stained but triumphant, expecting congratulations for murder and finding chaos. They milled about, unsure of what to do, their only leader dead at their feet. There were a hundred Legionnaires; a hundred and ten. Rane's comrades, once. His friends. More came. Were they all there?

There was no time left to wait. Rane thought of the dead on the Plains, of Marcus, and the corpses Marcus had left in Rooktown. Of the people Rane himself had killed, wrapped up in his bloodlust under *Kibon's* spell. He thought of Kara and her gentle kiss, of the plans they'd had and lost, of the child they'd never have.

Time for them all to be avenged. He lit the fuse.

The fuse burned quickly and Rane and Zee ducked down, covering their ears.

The barrels exploded in rapid succession, their blasts aimed towards the center of the courtyard, trapped by its walls.

Even protected, Rane was battered by the fury of it all as the shock waves bounced across the castle. Smoke filled the air. His ears rang with the monstrousness of it all. Then he heard the screams and the cries and the wails. Not innocents this time. No. The Legionnaires had discovered pain and death.

He stood up, blinking the dirt and dust away from his eyes. Bodies lay in a tangled mess across the courtyard. Some were missing limbs, others torsos and heads. But a great many, ripped apart by powder and rock and shrapnel, were still alive, healing, their swords already at work. He could feel the glee in *Kibon*. It knew there was work to be done. Blood to be had. But Rane would feed it no more.

He worked methodically, moving from one Legionnaire to the next, breaking swords. As the blades shattered, they died, and there was no coming back. No healing. He tried not to look at the faces. Didn't want to remember who'd they been before, didn't want to remember the heroes he'd fought beside, the men and women who'd saved a continent. They were just monsters now, and they had to be destroyed.

Once the weapons were destroyed, Rane dragged the bodies together, building a funeral pyre with Jefferson at its heart. Crows came to watch, protesting at good food going to waste, but there was no way Rane was going to leave any trace of his beloved Legion's shame.

"Are you going to say a few words?" asked Zee, handing him a torch.

"What's there to say? Let Heras deal with them. They were the best of mankind once, but they became monsters just as evil as any we've fought," replied Rane.

He tossed his torch onto the pyre. The flames danced across the corpses. A heartbeat later, Zee's torch followed. One hundred and fifty bodies didn't take long to catch fire.

They didn't stay to watch. What was the point? The fire would do its job. They retreated into the main hall, where Zee scavenged food from the kitchens.

Rane tore into the food. By the Gods, how long had it been since he'd had a proper meal?

"Did you mean what you said to the old man?" asked Zee.

"I did," said Rane. "Four hundred and fifty of us got transformed that night. What we've done here is nothing compared to the number that are still out there. I have a duty to protect the world from those that remain."

"Do you have a plan?"

"The mage, Babayon, is the key to everything. I'll look for him first, see if he can break the curse. And I'll deal with any Legionnaires I meet on the way."

"What about me?" replied Zee. "I have nowhere to go."

"This isn't your fight," replied Rane. "I'll take you to a town. Get you settled somewhere safe."

"No," Zee shouted. "How will anywhere be safe? I'm better off with you."

"You're not safe with me. If the taint gets a hold of me, there's a good chance you'll get killed by my hand."

"That won't happen," she replied, but her voice had lost its edge. Doubt ebbed away at her conviction.

"You know it can," said Rane. "It nearly happened earlier. When the sword has me in its grip, it's hard to see sense. I can't tell friend from foe. It just wants blood, and it's all but impossible to deny it. And it'll only get worse."

Zee's chin sunk to her chest. "Then don't use it. Don't feed it."

"Easier said than done," said Rane. "There've been times when I've not even known I've drawn my sword."

"I still want to come with you," said Zee.

Rane looked at the girl, saw her determination. She had the same spark that Kara had, once. "Only until I can make sure you're safe. Only till then."

Zee nodded and said no more.

Rane sat back as his thoughts took him to all those he'd lost. Kara. Myri. Marcus. Jefferson himself. Simone. People he'd loved as much as any family.

He stood up. "I'm going to get some air."

He could feel Zee's eyes on him as he left, but he didn't look back. He climbed the stairs until he reached the battlements. The pyre still burned in the courtyard; even from up on the wall, he could feel its heat. Still see some of the bodies lying amongst the flames. By the Gods, what a world he found himself in.

He rubbed Kara's locket and thought of a cottage in the woods where a beautiful woman sat on the porch, holding her baby. It would have been a good life. "I love you Kara," he whispered to the wind.

But he knew a different path waited for him now. He'd hunt Babayon down, along with any of his brothers and sisters from the Legion that remained.

He had monsters still to fight. And a war to finish.

The End

AFTERWORD

I hope you enjoyed the first adventures of Nathaniel Rane. If you did, please leave a review on Amazon or on Goodreads. Reviews really help every author and make a massive difference.

Visit my website www.mikemorrisauthor.com to find out more about Nathaniel Rane and all my other books. If you sign up for my mailing list, you'll be the first to get my next release.

Plus you can follow me on twitter or Facebook — look for @scifimikemorris.

I'd like to dedicate this book to the memory of my grandmother, who encouraged me to read and was more than happy to spend hours discussing Star Wars with an excited seven year old boy.

Keep reading for an excerpt from CRY HAVOC, available now on Amazon.

1

IN THE YEAR 702 POST NOSTROS

"I'm going to murder you when I catch you!"

Jack Frey ran as if all the demons in the world chased after him. His bare feet pounded the cobbled stone as he tried to keep up with his brother Brendan, two years older and that much quicker, but a gap soon opened between them.

Behind him, the shouts grew closer.

"Stop! Thief! Thief!"

The wide avenue was full of traders and shoppers. Everyone turned to see what the commotion was about as the two boys raced past. A man half-heartedly reached out a hand to grab Jack's collar but he dipped down, leaving the man grasping air. A horse reared up as Brendan zigzagged past, its red-faced rider shouting abuse as he struggled to keep the animal under control. A coal cart made its way across the pathway, blocking the brothers' escape. Brendan jumped onto it and leaped to the ground on the other side while Jack scrambled beneath. He stole a cheeky backward glance and saw their pursuers clatter into the cart. The fat man, whose house they robbed, looked even unhappier behind his silly black moustache. Desperation filled his voice for one last plea. "Someone stop them! Please stop them!"

Fat chance fat man. Rich folks don't get involved. Too much trouble, too many chances of getting their hands dirty. In Jack's neck of
the woods, it was a different story. Someone would have a go. It
wouldn't be out of good will though. They'd want a reward, or nick
whatever they'd stolen for themselves. They'd do anything for a
penny in Brixteth. Because no one had anything, everything was up
for grabs. That's why he and his brother went over the river to
Grayston. If you are going on the rob, you needed to be where the
money was. There was no point stealing from the poor after all.

Up ahead, Brendan swung around a corner into an alley. Jack
followed, plunging into the shadows between two stone houses and
slipped as he turned. The sack in his hand clanged against the
ground as he rolled across the cobbles. Jack hoped nothing was
dented — his brother would beat him if it were. He scrambled back
to his feet and chased after Brendan, eager to get away.

A wooden fence blocked off the far end of the alley. Brendan
didn't hesitate. He jumped, caught the top of the fence and pulled
himself up. He straddled it, throwing a hand out towards Jack.
"Throw me the sack. Be quick."

Jack hurled the sack at his brother with all his might but he
missed Brendan's fingers by inches. The bag fell to the ground. His
brother didn't say anything. The glare was more than enough. Jack
had let him down again. He could feel the burn on his cheeks as he
picked up the sack. He swung again, harder. This time Brendan
caught the sack.

"See you at home," said Brendan. He winked at his brother before
dropping to the ground on the other side of the fence.

"Brendan!" Jack stood there, ready for his brother to reappear and
hoist him up. He knew Brendan was just teasing him, that he'd come
back. He stared at the top of the fence, willing his brother to return,
hoping it wasn't another one of his lessons in growing up.

"There he is!"

Jack spun around. His pursuers bundled into the alley, trapping
him.

"We got you now, son. It's the hangman for you," panted the fat man, waddling into the alleyway. Sweat covered his face as he fought for breath, his beady eyes locked on Jack. His lackeys stood behind him, all laughing at Jack's plight.

There wasn't any waiting for Brendan anymore. Jack leaped. He snatched at the top of the fence but his fingers caught only splinters. He felt very small as he fell back down.

The fat man cracked his knuckles as he walked towards Jack, his lackeys on his heels. Jack's stomach lurched. He blinked away the forming tears. No way was he going to show that he was scared.

"Nowhere to run now," said the fat man. "You aren't going anywhere except the magistrates — after I've beaten you to hell and back. Not even a Nostros would want to eat you when I'm done."

Jack looked around for some way to escape, a weapon to use but the alley was empty. If this was Jack's neighborhood, they'd be broken crates and piles of garbage to help him climb over the fence. Or half the fence would be missing, taken for firewood. But, in Grayston, there wasn't a crate to step on or even a stick to use as a club. Bloody rich people. Couldn't count on them for anything. He tried jumping once more but the fence hadn't shrunk.

The fat man grabbed him before he could try a third time and yanked him off his feet. The man's breath stunk of roasted onions as he pulled Jack closer, grinning all the while behind his silly moustache.

"Now where's my silver, you little runt." The man's face burned with self-righteous fury.

"I ain't got your stuff," said Jack, wriggling in the man's grasp. "I didn't do nothing."

"He's the one who stole it, sir," said one of the other men, a doorman by the looks of him; with his stiff collar and tail coat. He whacked a truncheon into the palm of his hand. "I saw him coming out of the window, sure as day follows night." The other two nodded in agreement.

"He's a liar!" shouted Jack. He struggled but there was no way to break the fat man's grip.

The doorman jabbed the truncheon at him. "You're the liar. And a thief. His lordship will see you hung."

The servant next to him looked only a few years older than Jack, but there was no help there. The third one, with mottled veins all over his beak nose, smirked at Jack dangling in his boss' grasp.

Jack didn't want to be hung. He knew that for certain.

He grabbed the man's moustache, yanking hard. The fat man screamed as tufts of hair came away in Jack's hand and he released the boy. The doorman and the young man both lunged for Jack but he skipped past, sprinting back towards the main street.

The crowds consumed Jack. He ran, darting through people standing around talking about nothing important, pushing his way past servants trailing their masters. He cut left, then right, then left again.

Horse drawn carriages filled the avenue in both directions but Jack didn't pause as he sprinted across the road and into the crowd on the opposite side. He lost himself amongst the press of bodies until he was sure he wasn't being chased anymore.

When he didn't recognize any faces around him or hear any cries of pursuit, he stopped. He stepped to one side, out of the crush, and felt his heart begin to slow down. He was free.

Leaning against a tree, Jack looked around. It was different in Grayston, the northern quarter of Arbour, in so many ways. People were happy, well-fed, smiling, with their stone walled houses and clean streets and big trees. They didn't have a care in the world as they strolled past stalls filled with too much food to choose from. Jealousy flared inside Jack. None of them would last a day in his neighborhood. Maybe not even an hour. He'd like to see them cope with the dirt and the lice and the rats, see them try and get by with no food in their bellies.

As if on cue, Jack's stomach rumbled. He'd not eaten since early the day before. Hopefully, Brendan would get the silver plates to Mr Giles in time. They could pay the rent owed and have some left over for dinner with any luck.

Brendan. He still couldn't believe his brother had left him. He looked across the sea of faces, half-expecting to see Brendan waiting for him, laughing at Jack's close call with the fat man. His brother had a cruel sense of humor sometimes.

"'Ere." A hand clipped him around the ear. A shop owner stood over him. "I'm not having your sort hanging around my shop, wanting to steal something and driving off my good customers. Sling your 'ook back to Brixteth, before I sling it for you."

Jack glared back but wasn't going to argue with the man. He flicked two fingers at the man instead and spat at his feet, then Jack was off at a run. He might be defiant but he wasn't bloody stupid. He'd pushed his luck enough for one day. There was no need for the police to get involved. One look at Jack in his tattered, filthy clothes and they'd lock him up, even without a crime to pin on him.

A man walked past with a frilly, ruffled collar sticking out of a gold embroidered doublet and Jack tried not to laugh. The man had more money than sense. Why anyone would want to waste cash on looking stupid? Better to keep it or spend it on food.

Jack trudged on towards the river and home. It was a long walk back to the southern quarter of Arbour, a long walk empty-handed on an empty stomach.

It took Jack a good hour to get to the river and there everything changed. The sun knew it as well, ducking behind a cloud. The world lost all color. Once over the bridge, it was a different world from Grayston with its space and big homes with hardly anyone in them. In Brixteth, people made use of every square inch they had. They didn't even waste the riverfront. Houses of every size perched on stilts over the water. Washing lines dangled between them and fishing lines dropped into the sludge-covered surface. Little boats nipped between and under the buildings, ferrying people home or selling scrap.

Once over the bridge, the air even lost its freshness. The stink of sweat was on everyone as they hustled past. It always seemed worse than it was at first but that was because Jack had been over to Grayston, breathing the rich man's air.

Where Grayston had wide, tree-lined avenues, Brixteth was a

rabbit warren of buildings crushed together. Some streets were no more than two people wide. Buildings climbed up into the only space left — the sky, stopping the sun from ever reaching the pavements.

There was an equal hustle and bustle on the streets in Brixteth but faces there had a determined set to them. People were going to work, coming home from work or looking for work. It might not be lawful work but everyone was on the graft of some sort. Brixteth didn't put up with any passengers. It would chew you up before you knew it.

Still, Jack loved it there. They were his cramped streets, his dirty people, and his stinking air. He'd lived there all his life with his mum and Brendan. He belonged there.

Arbour was the capital of Abios and home to every type of person. The rich had Grayston, the Royals the West and Hampford and the traders had the Docklands in the East but Brixteth was his.

Old Mrs Waters waved as he passed, asked him to pass on her love to his old mum. A chicken squawked in her other hand, soon to be in her famous pot. Maybe if Brendan got enough money, they'd be able to buy a bowl of stew from her later. The thought got his mouth watering something bad. He loved her stews. He nodded at Big John who was arguing the odds with Hamish from the house next door. Those two were always at each other over something. Probably the same row had been going on for their entire lives. Hamish's two daughters were running rings around his legs as he shouted over from one stoop to the other. The girls were younger than Jack, all wild blonde hair and non-stop mischief. Their dog lay on the doorstep, looking down on them all with disapproval. Heather, the youngest, claimed it was part wolf but it always wagged its tail at everyone.

He passed the church with the usual crowd gathered outside, listening to the preacher. Father Heath stood on a wooden box with his staff, topped with a silver circle, in one hand, and his battered holy book in the other. Behind him, two of the church ladies stood behind huge urns of soup on a trestle table. After Father Heath finished his sermon, they would dish up a free meal to anyone who'd listened. Jack had tried sneaking in line many a time but the women knew who had been there for the service and who hadn't. Most times all he got was a cuff around the ear.

After a while, Jack stopped trying and walked on by. His mother told him often enough the church was a waste of time and God was just a way for the rich to get more money off the poor. Maybe that was the case up in Grayston but Father Heath never looked well off. His gaunt face had two or three days stubble and his robes were as ragged as any of his parishioners.

"Across the sea lurk the Nostros. Demons, ready to eat your souls. Only by God's good will do we still stand free here in Abios. Be grateful for the gift of life He has given us. Be worthy of His love so He does not forsake us." Father Heath's voice was full of emotion. Mutterings of "amen" fluttered through the crowd. He held his staff aloft, drawing all eyes to the circle. "The Circle is the Holy symbol of His Church. It represents the journey of life we all undergo, from birth to death to rebirth in the Heavens above. It represents His eye under which we strive. It represents His shield that protects us from the evil of the Nostros and the shelter His sun gives us." Father Heath's face reddened. "I ask you now to bow down before it and join me in prayer lest we ever forget. Join me in thanking God for all he has done and continues to do for His flock here in Abios."

Jack watched the crowd drop to their knees. Father Heath caught his eye and smiled, gesturing for Jack to join them. For a moment he nearly did. He liked the preacher — the man had a way of talking that made you listen. But then he remembered his mother's words and the ribbing Brendan would give him if he found out.

Jack nodded to the preacher and ran off. Five minutes later, he turned into Elgin Street. He lived in one of the old houses, blackened from fire and half fallen down. The old timers said dragons had burned it but that was just a tale they told the kids to keep them from misbehaving. Jack had never seen a dragon nor had anyone he knew. It didn't stop him from checking the skies though. It would be stupid to get eaten just because he hadn't seen something with his own eyes.

Jack jumped over some rubble scattered across the street. Most of the buildings in the road had collapsed in some way but there was no money to fix them; people just blocked off what they could or moved somewhere else. He passed the Butcher's son squatting in a pile of rubble, doing his business. Jack's mother made him go down by the water for that but a lot of people just couldn't be bothered. What was another pile of muck in Brixteth?

The stairs to Jack's home were just as broken as the rest of it. The third step threatened to collapse if you put any weight on it and only a fool would trust the left railing. Inside was dark as always. Mold added to the damp in the air.

Jack and his family lived in a single room at the top, on the third floor. Mr Giles rented it to them for two coppers a week. For that, they got four walls and a roof that didn't leak. The floor and walls were warped and half rotten, but at least they still did what they were supposed to do. The door didn't lock but they'd only had to fight off squatters once. Mr Giles' reputation managed to keep most trouble-makers away. Still, they kept a few good bricks hidden to deal with anyone trying their luck.

Inside, his mother slept in the single cot in the room. It was a few hours before she started work at Jerry's bar so Jack crept in. She didn't like being woken early. At least he could only see only the one empty bottle at the foot of the bed.

Jack hated her drinking. It didn't make her happy like it did other people. She'd either get angry or sad or start screaming and shouting. She'd hit one of her boys, depending upon who was nearest — but more often than not it'd be Brendan. His brother said it was because she didn't love him like she loved Jack but he couldn't see that. She didn't appear to love either of them that much when she drank. She'd been like that ever since his father died.

Jack climbed up on to his father's old oak chest opposite the bed. He ran his fingers over it, feeling all the different places his father had been to in the chipped and scratched surface. Perched there, he felt close to his father once more and safe in the world.

He liked watching his mother sleep. It was when she seemed

most at peace. Her tightly furrowed brow disappeared and there was the faint hint of a smile on her lips. Perhaps she dreamed of father again, like Jack often did, and happier days.

The sudden click of the door opening shook him from his vigil. Brendan's face popped round the door, a big smile on his face. He beckoned Jack to come with him as if everything was all right. The cheek of him. Jack felt his anger churn in his gut. He bet Brendan wouldn't even say sorry — the git.

Jack slipped off the chest, ready to give his brother a piece of his mind but, as he passed his mother, he knocked the empty bottle with his foot. It rattled along the floorboards before stopping at the far wall with a clunk. Jack froze.

"Who's that?" she asked. She tried pushing herself upright but her left arm didn't want to cooperate. "Is that you Jack?"

"Shush Mum, go back to sleep. I'm sorry I woke you."

"You're a good boy, Jack. I knew that from the moment you were born." She rolled on to her back, her eyelids fluttering. "My little baby."

"My little baby," mimicked Brendan from the doorway. Jack gave his brother the finger.

"Sleep tight, Mum. I'll see you later." He bent down and kissed her forehead. Her skin was hot despite the mildness of the evening.

"Don't stay out late and keep out of trouble," his mother mumbled as he left the room.

"How's my little baby?" said Brendan, puckering his lips and making wet kissing noises.

Jack swung a punch at his brother. "Bugger off! Where'd you go anyway? I nearly got pinched today!"

Brendan laughed as he blocked his brother's blows, pissing Jack off even more. "I didn't leave you. I just knew we'd do better on our own and someone had to get that stuff to the fence to be sold. No one's fast enough for my kid brother." He tried to ruffle Jack's hair but Jack wasn't about to let him off the hook that easily.

"They said they were going to hang me. There were four of them."

"And did they hang you? I don't see a rope around your neck."

"No," mumbled Jack .

Brendan scrunched down so he was face to face with Jack. "Sorry, I didn't hear that. Did they hang you?"

"No," said Jack, louder. "No, they didn't."

"And you're not in front of the magistrates tomorrow are you?"

"No thanks to you."

"Well, I don't think you've got anything to moan about then," said Brendan, pulling a purse out of his pocket. He held it in front of Jack. "Instead of complaining, and since you've still got your neck, how about we go get a pie or two to eat?"

The thought of food won over his anger. His brother was the way he was after all. "I saw Mrs Waters putting a fresh chicken in her pot."

"Well, chicken stew it is then," said his brother, slipping an arm over his shoulder. The two brothers walked down the stairs. "Now, when you say you 'saw Mrs Waters put a chicken in her pot', you did see it go in, didn't you? She couldn't have swapped it for a rat while you weren't looking?"

Mrs Waters' place was two streets away. It was no more than a big room with some broken down tables and chairs with a small kitchen at the back. If you needed something hot and quick without spending too much money, it was the place to go. Mrs Waters seemed to be able to get hold of real meat and vegetables when no one else could. She spread them out in her stews and pies with some great chunks of bread on the side. A big lady, always laughing, she could just as easily batter someone over the head for upsetting the other customers as hug them to death in her meaty arms. She'd a soft spot for Jack and Brendan. She often gave them scraps or leftovers at the end of the day, even if they had no coin, so it felt good to walk in through the front door, knowing they could pay for a real meal.

The small bell above the door chimed as they entered and a sea of faces looked up at them. The ovens and the mass of bodies inside created an aroma of spiced sweat and stew. For some reason, all the customers were men. His mother said it was because men were too lazy to cook for themselves but Jack knew she was just jealous of Mrs Waters' cooking. Jack loved it all. His father used to bring him here for a meal before he went off to sea, sitting Jack on his lap while they shared a bowl of stew.

"All right lads," said Mrs Waters, ambling over, her face flush. "You are way too early if you're after leftovers. Come back in a few hours when this lot has cleared off and see me round the back. I'll let you know what I can do then, eh."

"We want to eat now, please," said Brendan, squaring his shoulders. "Can we have a table?"

"We've got money," piped up Jack.

"Have you now?" replied Mrs Waters, one eyebrow raised. "And where'd you get that then? I'm not going to find my family jewels missing am I?"

"No. We earned it," answered Jack.

"We've been working over the river," added his brother.

"Well, then young sirs, you may have my finest table." Mrs Waters bowed and swept her arm towards a rickety table tucked into the far corner, two chairs on either side. "And perhaps you would like a menu of my fine fare?"

Jack didn't know what a menu was but it didn't sound as good as chicken stew. Mrs Waters laughed when he told her so and pinched his cheek.

"You sit there, young man and I'll bring you a bowl of my best." Mrs Waters placed two spoons on the table. Jack watched her waddle back to the kitchen as he sat down. His feet barely touched the floor.

"I spoke to Mr Giles," said Brendan. "He's got another job for us."

"But we've just done one."

"Well, he's got another. Another house up Grayston. His sister's cleaning there. Said it's full of stuff and dead easy to get into. She's even going to leave a window open for us. It's a walk in the park."

"You said that last time and I nearly got pinched. And the time before that."

"This time's different. We've never had a window left open for us before, have we? So tomorrow, early, before it gets too light, we'll head over and we'll be in and out before anyone's awake. It will be..."

Brendan's voice drifted off as he stared at something over Jack's shoulder.

"What is it?"

"Don't look now but some bloke's been watching us."

"Is it the law?" asked Jack, beginning to turn.

"I said don't look! He's not the law. He's something different. Definitely not from around here. And I think he's only got one bloody eye."

The urge to look was irresistible. Jack knocked his spoon off the table. As he bent down to pick it up, he glanced through the crook of his arm. Brendan was right. The man was different. He was dressed all in black, one with the shadows by the wall. A glint of light caught on a holy man's circle around his neck but the stranger looked too dangerous to be a priest. A vicious scar ran down the left side of his face and through where his eye used to be. Only an empty socket remained but Jack could feel it looking deep within him. He shivered with fear, and it took all he had not to run from Mrs Waters right there, right then, to forget about his dinner and get away from the man with one eye.

Mrs Waters plunked two bowls of stew on the table, startling Jack even more. "What are you two gawking at?" she asked.

"Who's that man over there?" whispered Brendan.

Mrs Waters didn't even try to hide the fact she stared. "What? Him over there?" she said with a wave of her hand. "Don't you mind him. He's a Black Dog. He won't do you no harm."

"What's a Black Dog?" asked Jack.

Mrs Waters pulled a chair alongside them and sat down. "They're soldiers of God, my boy. Priests in the Order of Stephen, the First Knight. They fight the Nostros and other vile creatures. They keep us safe in our beds at night. That man over there has done things that would make your hair stand on end, seen things that would make your jaw drop and stood his ground when you'd be running as if your trousers were on fire. And more besides."

"He scares me," said Jack.

Mrs Waters tutted. "Don't you worry none. He's on our side, thank the Maker. Without him and his brothers, we'd all be food for the Nostros. The Black Dogs are the only ones keeping the demons away."

"Mum says there's no such things as demons."

"Well, lad, it's not for me to say she's right nor wrong. Maybe she's never seen a dragon overhead, burning everything beneath it. Maybe she don't realize that the Nostros rule everything on the other side of the ocean and treat humans as naught more than a decent bit of meat to eat." Mrs Waters leaned in close to Jack. "But I know. I've run for cover when all around me burned. I've hid in a cupboard when rumors of a Nostros here in Brixteth have gone round the houses. I've seen the bodies drained of blood, lined up on the street, waiting to be burned."

"Why's he keep looking at us?" asked Jack.

"They do that, I'm afraid. Always looking for people are the Black Dogs. Always looking for young healthy lads for their sodding army." She looked at the man square on and raised her voice so all could hear. "But he won't find any in my place. All anyone should be thinking of is how nice my bloody food is."

The dining room fell silent as they waited for the man to react. Mrs Waters stood with her hands on her hips until the man raised his spoon in acknowledgement. The chatter in the dining room restarted almost instantly.

"Listen, Jack," said Mrs Waters as she stood. She pushed her chair back. The smile was gone from her face and her eyes were cold. "Be scared if we don't have him. Be scared if we don't have the Black Dogs." Jack was holding his breath, hanging on Mrs Waters' every word. She leaned in closer, examining Jack from head to toe. "But you know what's scarier?"

"What?" asked Jack but he didn't want to know the answer.

A grin spread across her face. "Me — if you waste my food. Now eat your stew before it gets cold."

The boys ate their meal but Jack didn't taste a thing. His head was too full of monsters and dragons swooping from the sky. He couldn't imagine anyone being brave enough to try and fight demons like that. He turned to look at the one-eyed man once more but there was only an empty stool. The man was gone.

2

702 PN

"Come on. Wake up," said Brendan, shaking Jack.

It was early in the morning and his mother wasn't back from work. Jack rubbed the sleep from his eyes. "Do we have to go?" His head was still full of Mrs Waters' nonsense. He didn't want to go out while it was still dark and monsters could be lurking.

"Stop asking. You know we do. We turn down a job from Mr Giles and he won't give us another one. What would we do for food then?" Brendan threw a shirt at Jack before pulling on his own.

"Mum's working now. She's earning." It sounded silly the moment Jack said it. He glanced over to her empty bed. Better to go before she got back. She'd have spent any money she'd earned on drink and they both knew what happened then. Brendan just shook his head and carried on getting dressed.

Jack knew he'd end up doing as Brendan wanted. Things always seemed to work out that way. He pulled on the shirt, found his battered trousers and dressed.

"It better be an easy job," he muttered as he followed his brother out the door, taking the heel of hard bread that Brendan offered for breakfast.

They met their mother in the hallway.

She staggered towards them, ducking her head so her hair hid her face.

"Drunk again," said Brendan.

"I'm not," she replied, her voice thick with booze.

"Are you okay, Mum?" asked Jack, trying to get a look at her face. Something wasn't right with her.

"Don't worry about me, Jack," she replied wrapping her arms around him. He could smell the gin but, as he squirmed in her embrace, he saw something else. The right side of her face was one massive bruise. Her eye was swollen shut and dried blood clung to the corner of her mouth.

"What happened?" he asked.

His mother let go of Jack and covered her face with her hand. "It's nothing."

"Who hit you, Mum?"

Brendan watched them from the door, his face impassive.

"It was just a customer. Wasn't happy with me. Got a bit nasty. I'll be alright. Just need a lie down." She touched Jack's face. "Where are you off to so early then?"

Jack looked at Brendan, who shook his head in response.

"We're just going out. Nowhere special," said Jack.

That got a tut from their mother. "Your brother not got you stealing again, has he?"

"Someone's got to put food on the table," said Brendan, the door half-open in his hand. "We look after ourselves. No one else does."

"Oh, is that so?" His mother tried to straighten up as she turned on Brendan. "Do you think I like living like this? Do you think I enjoy working all night? Having some idiot beat me up just because he's had a bad day? It's not my fault your father died, leaving us with nothing. He's the one who didn't look after us. All that time at sea, leaving us alone. Then he goes and dies. He got to escape this shit hole didn't he? We don't." Tears welled up in her eyes. But it wasn't enough to stop Brendan.

"If you didn't drink everything you earned, then maybe we could do better."

"I'm just trying to do the best I can," she cried. "It ain't easy for me."

Jack looked behind him. The neighbors wouldn't like being woken up again by another screaming match. "Mum, it's okay. Go up to bed and we'll see you later," he said, trying to usher her up the stairs.

"The only thing you do best is drinking," said Brendan, not letting it go.

Jack sighed. He didn't understand why they had to provoke each other like this all the time.

"Why you ungrateful whelp..." Their mother lunged at Brendan but Jack caught her arm. He hung on for dear life as she tried shaking him free.

"You're a pair of good-for-nothings. Your father knew what he was doing. He killed himself because of you two!" she cried, spit flying from her mouth.

"That's a lie," shouted Brendan as he tried hauling Jack free. "He died in an accident at sea."

"He killed himself because he hated you! Ashamed of you, he was!" their mother screamed back.

"You're a liar as well as a drunk," said Brendan. They battled in a tangle of limbs until Brendan pulled Jack free. "Buy yourself some more to drink and leave us alone." He stormed from the house, dragging his brother after him.

"Why do we always have to fight? Why can't things be like they used to?" cried Jack.

Brendan was already five paces ahead of his brother. "Because Dad died and Mum won't stop drinking. That's life. It's shit. All we can count on is you and me. Now come on, we've got a job to do." He didn't even look over his shoulder as he stormed up the street.

The sun was still an hour from rising and the streets were deserted. The few lamps burning did little to dispel the darkness of the tight pathways. Jack couldn't help looking around to see if anything lingered in the shadows or flew overhead. He told himself he was being stupid, that Mrs Waters had just been trying to scare him the previous day, but he drew a circle around his chest all the same, like he'd seen grown ups do, just to be extra careful.

At least the grey slash of sky between the buildings was empty of any winged creatures. It was only when Jack gazed around the buildings he knew so well, he noticed something off. He was being watched.

His heart raced as his mind told him it was a monster, a Nostros — or worse. Jack called out to Brendan to stop but his brother wasn't listening, still fuming about what had happened back at home. Jack craned his neck from side to side, checking everything from ground floor doorways to third floor windows. Then he spotted something. A quick movement where there shouldn't have been. A face lurking in the shadows by the side of the Eastons' house.

The face of the one-eyed man.

"Brendan!" This time the fear in Jack's voice stopped his brother. He rushed back.

"What's wrong?"

"I saw him! Watching us!" shouted Jack, pointing back at the Easton's house.

"Saw who?"

"The man from yesterday. The man with one eye. The Black Dog."

"Where'd you see him?"

"I want to go home. I don't want to do this anymore." Tears ran down Jack's face as he shook with fear.

"Listen to me," said Brendan, gripping Jack. "Where did you see him?"

Jack pointed to the Eastons' house but the man had disappeared.

"There's no one there," said Brendan with a chuckle. "Maybe you just imagined it, eh?" He pulled his brother in close.

"I don't think so." Jack looked back to the Eastons. Had he imagined it? He had been looking for dragons and Nostros after all. He wiped his nose with the cuff of his shirt, tried a smile for his brother. "Maybe I did."

"I'm not surprised you're jumping at shadows. I am too. I'm just trying to be brave and not show it."

"Honest?" Brendan looked like he meant it but Jack could never be sure.

"Would I lie to you? Come on — let's get this job over with and we can have more chicken stew when we get back."

The boys retraced their steps from the previous day and found themselves back in Grayston just as it was waking up. Market workers maneuvered their stalls into position, stacking them with the day's wares. More than one told the boys to stay away, some less politely than others. Jack couldn't blame them. Only the dirt was preventing their clothes from falling apart and their bare feet stood out in Grayston as much as a pair of shoes would in Brixteth. And they were in Grayson on the rob after all — just not from the stalls.

Jack didn't like stealing. He hoped that one day his family would have another way of surviving, a safer way. His dad used to say there were no old thieves in life, just forgotten bones. How many close calls could they have with the law before the rope got them?

Brendan removed a small piece of paper from the waistband of his trousers. A map was scrawled on it. After a quick turn or two, he matched it to the main street. He led Jack on. They took a sharp left between a bakers and a laundry into a quieter street, full of houses. What little bustle in Grayston's main street was non-existent there. Even the air was thick with sleep. The two boys carried on walking, crossing more streets, and the houses got bigger and more spaced out. Patches of grass separated the road from the buildings and the occasional fence started to appear.

Jack gaped at the houses. "Hundreds of people could live in homes this big."

"Most of 'em only have a small family inside — four or five people and maybe the same again in servants," replied his brother. There was no hiding the distaste on his face.

"What do they do with houses that big then?" asked Jack.

"Who knows? Rich people aren't like us. They want to big houses just because they can. Show off how wealthy they are. Good job too otherwise we'd have nothing to steal." Brendan winked then stopped suddenly. He gazed back down the street, counting the buildings. In front of them was a small stone wall, behind which stood the largest house of all. To Jack, it looked like a castle. It had three floors, with so many windows that Jack couldn't count them all.

"We're here," Brendan said as he hopped over the wall. "Come on. She's left the window open around the side." He scurried across the grass, keeping low.

Jack swallowed his reservations and followed his brother. There was no turning back now. The two boys slipped down a small gap between the left-hand side of the house and a large over-grown hedge. Leaves tickled Jack's face as they squeezed past it. Brendan stopped in front of an open window and Jack clattered into him, earning a stared rebuke.

"This is it," said Brendan. "Once you're inside, go to the room to the left. That's where all the silver is. Fill up the sack and be quick about it. You with me?"

Jack nodded. "Room on the left. Silver. Got it." His gut churned with a mixture of fear and excitement, and he fought the urge to throw up.

"Ok. Let's do it." Brendan put his back to the wall and linked his hands in front of him. Jack placed his left foot into his brother's hands, stepped up as Brendan lifted and caught the windowsill with both hands. He pulled himself up, pausing on the ledge for a moment to allow his eyes to adjust to the gloomy interior before he dropped to the floor.

Jack found himself in a walk-in cupboard, thick with the stink of dust and stale air. No one had used the room for a long time. The owners had probably forgotten about it with so many others to choose from. Rich people were strange.

"An easy job," whispered Jack as he turned the door handle. He caught his breath for a moment as the hinge creaked open but nothing stirred. He stepped into a narrow corridor, filled with a thick darkness as curtained windows prevented the early morning light from sneaking into the house with him.

Again Jack had to wait for his eyes to adjust. It was five long paces to the door he was looking for. He walked on tiptoe, aware of the silence in the house. A squeaky floorboard would be all it'd take to bring the whole house down on him. He hoped he didn't have that kind of luck.

The next door didn't make a noise as he opened it. Jack breathed a sigh of relief. The room was even darker than the hallway but there was the odd glint of silver from the far wall to lure Jack in. "Easy job," he said once more and stepped inside.

"I wouldn't say that," said a man's voice from behind him as a match was struck.

Jack spun around as a lamp bathed the room in a soft light. The one-eyed man sat in a chair tucked in the corner.

Jack sprang for the door.

But the Black Dog wasn't some overweight rich man or an uninterested stallholder. He had Jack by the collar before he'd made one step.

"Who's been a naughty boy?" said the Black Dog. A patch covered his eye.

"Let me go," shouted Jack. "I haven't done anything."

The man laughed. "I think you have. Breaking into someone's home with the intent to steal. Definitely something you've done there. Something for the law."

"Let me go!" Jack kicked out with his right foot but the man stepped safely away.

An elderly couple entered the room. The man hobbled up to them, walking stick in hand, while the lady kept to the safety of the doorway. "Is this one of the young lads?" asked the old man.

The Black Dog nodded. "One of them, sir. The other is being apprehended as we speak."

"No. I'm alone," protested Jack. "It's just me."

"Be quiet boy," ordered the Black Dog. "Here comes your brother now."

Scuffling came down the hallway as two burly men dragged

Brendan along with them. His brother's right eye was closed and bleeding.

"I don't believe it," said the woman, a hand over her mouth. "Is nothing sacred? These boys were going to rob us? In our own home?"

"And probably slit your throat while you slept, ma'am," said one of the men holding Brendan.

"Now then, Mr Jones. Let's not exaggerate," said the Black Dog. "The boys are in enough trouble as it is without making it worse. They're simply thieves, not murderers. If you would be so kind as to tie the young gentlemen up whilst Mr Smyth fetches the law for us."

The men didn't need asking twice. The rope bit deeply into Jack's wrists but he wasn't going to give anyone the satisfaction of crying out. Especially the one-eyed man who now sat smiling at the boys like a cat who'd cornered its dinner. Somehow, Jack knew the law was going to be the least of his problems.

3

702 PN

It took four days to track down Jack's mother and another half day before she made it to the Grayston jail. Four and a half days of Jack hoping there was some way to slip through the rusted iron bars. Four and a half days of being stuck in a small cell in the basement of the jail, with nothing but rancid straw for a bed, a bucket for a toilet and his brother for company.

Jack had been petrified at first. Then fear turned into anger at being caught, anger at being tricked by the Black Dog. Acceptance followed. They were in jail and, at best, that's where they were going to stay. At worst, it was a short stop before the rope. Finally, all Jack felt was boredom. The cell was dark and dank, the food awful and there was nothing to do except sit and stare at the walls. Brendan was no help either. He'd shut down the moment the key turned in the lock. He sat slumped in the corner, ignoring any attempt to talk. There were no other prisoners.

The single guard, a stick thin man, with wild reddish hair, brought the two boys food each day. Jack tried everything to get a response as the man slid the slop-filled wooden bowls through a gap in the bars. From saying hello to asking what day it was to pleading for help before finally pretending to be ill. The guard didn't even look at him. He just sat at a small table a few strides away from the cell, waited for the boys to finish eating and then took the empty bowls away with him.

Jack was relieved when his mother walked down the steps to the cells. He rushed to the bars and thrust his arms out towards her. She sobbed as she returned the embrace, holding Jack tightly despite the iron bars between them.

"Oh thank God," she said. "I didn't know where you were. I've been worried for days, looking everywhere for you. I thought you'd run off or were lying dead in a ditch somewhere." The bruising on her face was not as vivid as it once was but her recent beating was plain to see.

"I'm sorry, mum." It was hard for Jack to keep the tears from his own eyes. "Are you going to get us out of here?"

"I don't know, son. If it wasn't for this kind man, I wouldn't even know you were here."

"What man?" A cold feeling in his gut told Jack he already knew who it was.

His mother stepped back from the bars. "This man."

The Black Dog looked down from the top of the stairs. He smiled.

"I'm sorry it took so long to find you, Mrs Frey," said the Black Dog as he walked towards them. "My colleagues had a dreadful time trying to track you down."

"Please call me Mary," she replied. "I appreciate the trouble, honest I do, but I have to work nights so I'm not often around or I'm sleeping during the day."

"My name's Aidan. Brother Aidan." The Black Dog shook her hand and then motioned for her to take a seat. They had a clear view of the two boys behind bars. "Now, let's see if we can help each other."

"Thank you. God bless you." She smiled at Jack before joining Aidan.

Jack slumped back down inside his cell as his mother took the offered seat. Aidan sat opposite. He reached down and produced a small wine bottle and two cups. He filled both before offering one to Mary. She smiled awkwardly as she took it, hesitating before taking a sip.

Jack's heart sunk as she drank. Jack hoped his mother hadn't been drinking before, or at least not too much so she'd still have her wits about her. She'd need to be on her toes if she was to get her sons out of the mess they were in.

Aidan swirled the wine in his cup but Jack noticed he didn't drink from it. "Your boys are in a lot of trouble."

"I'm sure it's a misunderstanding. They're good lads. They wouldn't do anything wrong." His mother took another sip of wine.

"I'm afraid it's no misunderstanding. I caught them myself, breaking into the home of a renowned citizen, a friend of the Queen's no less."

A little wine spilled from the cup as her hand shook. She glanced at the boys and Jack dropped his eyes in shame. "Is that what they were doing?" she said. "I thought they were doing odd jobs to help people out, earn a bit of pocket money. Their father and I raised them better than that, or so I thought."

"Their father's not around anymore?"

"He died. God bless his soul. Used to be a seaman. Just one trip too many I suppose. It's just me trying to bring them up now." Her eyes opened wide. "I do my best. It's just not easy. I can't be watching them all day and night, not if I'm to keep a roof over their heads and food in their bellies too. Does that make me a bad mother?"

Aidan looked at her for a long moment. He sighed as he rubbed the eye patch and sat back. The chair creaked as the frame adjusted to the shift in weight. "The way I see it, Mary, is that if we don't do something to help these boys now, today, one or both of them will end up losing a hand or hanging. No one likes thieves and we both know the road they are on only leads to the gallows."

A tear made it's lonely way down her cheek. More threatened to follow. She took a gulp of wine, the mask of restraint fallen. "I said I'm doing my best. Everyone knows it. Knows they're good boys too."

"I'm not saying they aren't. Its just hunger makes one do silly things, doesn't it? Makes one think laws aren't important when the opportunity to eat is at hand. Sometimes life just gets the better of you." Aidan lay his hand over hers, squeezing it. "Sometimes your best isn't good enough. But that's no fault of your own."

"What else am I going to do? I'm alone. I can't work any harder. Can't lock them up. They're just boys. It's a tough world out there." More tears rolled down her cheek. It broke Jack's heart to see her like this. He still remembered the woman that sang him to sleep every night cuddled in her arms. Unlike Brendan, he never doubted she loved them.

Aidan refilled her cup. His voice was soft when he spoke. "Do you know what I am?"

"Yes." Jack could hear the emotion in her voice. He wished there was something he could do to make her feel better, wished he hadn't caused her this pain. There was something else too — fear.

"What am I, Mary?"

"A Black Dog."

"I'm a Knight of the Order of Saint Stephen. We fight the eternal battle against the Nostros," said Aidan.

"Demons," said Mary in a whisper.

"Yes. Demons. Witches. Devil Worshippers. Any creature that threatens our world. The things we pretend only exist in our worst nightmares." Aide leaned towards her. "For three hundred years, we've kept Abios safe. For three hundred years, we've bled and died keeping the Nostros away from our shores. Keeping you and your children safe. But we need more people to join us, more souls to commit to the war. We need boys like your two."

"My boys? You don't mean..."

"I want them to join the Order. Become novices. They will be well fed, given warm beds, taught to read and write, raised in all the ways of God and our Order."

"To fight monsters?"

"Perhaps. All are trained but not all answer the call. Only the best are ordained as warriors. It is a hard road but one with hope. The alternative..." Aidan gestured at their surroundings.

Jack didn't understand all of what was said. Aidan wanted Brendan and him to fight monsters? He didn't want to do that even if he got three meals a day.

His mother didn't seem too happy either. She gulped her wine, emptying the cup as her tears turned into bone-shaking sobs. "I can't do that. What you ask. Give up my boys."

"You're not giving them up," replied Aidan. "You're setting them free from this path to the gallows. You're giving them to God." Aidan poured more wine before reaching into a pouch on his belt. He rummaged for a moment before placing his hand back on the table next to his mother's wine cup. There was no mistaking the clink of coin. Her eyes darted to the sound. She raised her cup to drink with an unsteady hand.

"You'll be compensated." He removed his hand, revealing two silver coins on the battered tabletop.

"Two silvers for my boys?"

Aidan smiled. "Not for your boys. For your sacrifice."

Don't do it, thought Jack as he watched his mother's hand fight its battle against the temptation of the silver. They were her children. If she loved them, for once she would do the right thing, not the easy thing.

"It's too much, what you ask," Mary said but her hand didn't move from the table.

"Too much to ask that they serve the greater good? To protect not just yourself but your neighbors, your countrymen? To ask you to think of others and not just yourself? How can that be too much?" replied Aidan. He passed Mary a small white cloth to dab her tears with. "I simply ask you to be strong and do what's best for your boys."

"What sort of mother would I be to put them in harm's way?"

Aidan smiled. "I could argue that you're taking them from harm's way. Of course, we can leave them here and hopefully the judge will find mercy on the morrow when they are brought before him." He reached for the coins but his mother's hand was there before him.

"I want to do the right thing. I want to give them a chance in life."

Aiden smiled. He'd won. "You are. They'll have the opportunity to do great things. They won't have the life you've been forced into. Now, shall I leave you alone for a few minutes to say goodbye to your sons?"

Mary looked over at the cells but Jack turned away from her gaze. He couldn't bear to look at her or let her see the tears running down his own cheeks. Their mother was giving them away. Jack couldn't believe it. At least she was letting her boys down for the last time.

"No," was all she said "No goodbyes." She stood up and slipped the coins out of sight.

Jack's bravery crumbled. He looked up beseechingly but it was his mother's turn to avoid his gaze. "Mom!"

The word had no effect.

She walked to the stairs without a backward glance. His head dropped with every step. His heart broke as he listened to her feet take her out of the jail. Only when there was silence did he look up again. Aidan stood by the bars.

"You may think me cruel but, one day, you'll thank me. You'll remember this day as the day your life changed."

"You tricked us," said Jack. "I'll never thank you. I hate you!"

"You're not the first to say that but know this — there were no tricks. I didn't make you do something you didn't want to do. I simply stopped you from succeeding. And now I offer you both an opportunity for ever-lasting glory. I'll take you both to fight a holy war. That is a gift very few are offered."

"I'll never fight for you! I'd rather be hung first!"

Again Aidan smiled and kissed the circle hanging from his neck. "We shall see, boy. We shall see what is God's will. Now get some sleep. We leave at dawn and have a long journey ahead of us."

He left the boys alone.

Jack turned on his brother. "This is all your fault. I told you we shouldn't do that job. Told you it was wrong. I hate you as much as I hate Mum and that man. I hate you all!"

For the first time, Brendan looked up. There was no mistaking the tears on his pale face. "I'm sorry. I'm sorry. I've let you down. What're we going to do? What're we going to do?"

The look on Brendan's face calmed Jack down. He couldn't be angry with his brother. Not now. He was all he had left. He sat down next to Brendan and hugged him. "We'll find a way out of this. We always do."

"Do you really hate me?" asked Brendan.

"How can I hate you? You're an idiot but you're my brother."

Brendan looked confused for a moment before he burst out in laughter. Jack joined in. It felt good after so much misery. They laughed long and hard, until their sides hurt, laughed their worries and concerns away. Let the Black Dog take them. They'd find a way to escape.

The next morning, the red haired guard led them from their cells, heavy chains securing their wrists. Up the stairs and through the door, clanking with every step, past a small room that housed the guards and the policemen. Then one last door and they were in the street.

It was strange being outside again after five days in jail. The air had a freshness to it that was sweeter than anything Jack had known before. Even the chill was welcome. The sharp morning light hurt his eyes, causing him to squint. He blinked away the water from them lest anyone thought he cried from fear. His stomach squirmed and he fought the rising bile in his throat.

He wouldn't show any weakness. He wouldn't give them that satisfaction.

The Black Dog sat on top of a large grey horse. It moved with precision at the merest flick of the reins or stirrup and bulged with muscle. It was an animal bred for war.

Aidan wore a heavy black cloak that draped across the beast's haunches and a long sword hung in a scabbard at his waist. A pistol was holstered across his chest. For the first time, Jack could see the warrior in the man.

The horse and Aidan were made for each other.

The priest was accompanied by the two men who had helped capture the boys, Mr Jones and Mr Smythe. They drove a cart pulled by a pair of horses that could not have been more different from the Black Dog's mount. They looked like the working horses that Jack was used to seeing around Arbour.

It was the cart that was different. The cart was a cage on wheels. A moving jail. Behind the bars, three boys watched Jack and Brendan. Watched the guard lead them up to the rear of the cart whilst Mr Smythe unlocked the door.

"Now, before I take these chains off you little puppies, I just want to get one thing clear," said Mr Smythe, waggling the key in front of them. "It's a lot easier riding in the back there without them but, as sure as I'm standing here, I'll have them back on you if there's any nonsense. It's a long ride to Whitehaven. Keep your mouth shut. It'll be quicker for all of us. Any trouble and you'll get the whip.

"We'll be stopping for water breaks and food but no other time. If you need to go, tough shit. Hold it. Don't hold it. It's no difference to me. You'll be the one cleaning it up and I'm sure your new friends won't like it if you piss on them. Understand?"

Jack glared at him. He wasn't threatening like the Black Dog. Smythe was bulky but not in a fighting way. He'd seen plenty of men down Jerry's that had similar builds from drinking too much. Given the chance, Jack knew he'd be able to outrun him easily. He'd be huffing and puffing but the boys would be long gone. If he kept the chains off, they'd be a chance to run.

"Yes, we understand," replied Jack.

It was Aidan on that fierce horse that they needed to watch out for. But every man must sleep some time.

"What about you?" said Smythe to Brendan. "You going to be trouble?"

"No sir," replied Brendan.

"Sir? Who you calling 'Sir'?" cackled Smythe as he unchained them. "Get inside." He slapped them hard both of them across the head as they climbed inside the cage. Their freedom from being behind bars had lasted all of ten minutes. As the lock slammed shut, Jack held on to the hope inside him — he and his brother would escape. It was just a matter of when.

CRY HAVOC IS AVAILABLE ON AMAZON.COM

<<<<>>>>

Printed in Great Britain
by Amazon